Advance Praise for *Riverton Noir*

"In *Riverton Noir*, Perry Glasser browbeats high and low brow art into a work of sublime halftone pulp picture printing, shading stuttered shadows with the darker side of your so-called comic book. His pointillistic prose pops like Pop Art, but it's as pleasing as all get out in all that it knows and shows."

　　—Michael Martone, author of *Four for a Quarter*

"It is one thing to write a crackling yarn; the literary woods are full of gripping stories. But it is quite another thing to deliver that story as Perry Glasser has done in *Riverton Noir*: it's a riveting tale, all right, but its prose is a crackler in its own right. When I consider the style of this first-rate novelist, I start conjuring one of America's truly great writers, Raymond Chandler. Glasser is in the same league when it comes to dialogue, description, humor and character development. *Riverton Noir* will leave you breathless as narrative, awed as pure writing."

　　—Sydney Lea, Vermont Poet Laureate

"High school is eternal, someone has said, and Riverton High is high school on steroids, the horniest high school in the history of American fiction. Perry Glasser brings the nitty and the gritty to this novel of exaggeration and ribaldry. Big, vibrant, laugh-out-loud funny, it is also fearless about sex and violence, which in Riverton can seem like the same thing. Don't worry—the novel's structure and theme are carefully controlled by 'the Dreamer,' not to mention the laws of modern physics, and Glasser's sentences, among such seeming chaos, are marvels of clarity. This should be the author's break-out book."

　　—Kelly Cherry, author of *We Can Still Be Friends*, Poet Laureate of Virginia

"No graphic novel ever carved such shapely, scary, sexy shadows as *Riverton Noir*! No magic realism ever assembled such a Land o'Goshen, with scuzzballs and cutie-pies, *Happy Days* and *Mean Streets*, zombies (sort of) and deep thinkers. Perry Glasser has stolen the cogitations of David Foster Wallace, the worrying over self-consciousness and what's actually out there, and grafted them to tough-guy eroticism of Marvel comics. The energy's sky-high, the verbal pleasure's unending, and the American crime novel has notched a new benchmark."

　　—John Domini, judge for the 2011 Gival Press Novel Award and author of *A Tomb on the Periphery*

Also by Perry Glasser

Suspicious Origins

Singing on the Titanic

Dangerous Places

Riverton Noir

By Perry Glasser

Winner of the Gival Press Novel Award

Arlington, Virginia

Copyright © 2012 by Perry Glasser.

Published by Gival Press, an imprint of Gival Press, LLC.

For information please write:

Gival Press, LLC

P. O. Box 3812

Arlington, VA 22203

www.givalpress.com

First edition

ISBN: 978-1-928589-75-4

Library of Congress Control Number: 2012942440

Photo of Perry Glasser by Laura L. Cuevas.

Design by Ken Schellenberg.

Artwork © Hanna Ramanouskaya | *Dreamstime.com*.

for

BooBear, Pinhead, the Gelflet, and most of all Jessica—

You are a wondrous crew.

"The shadow prowling amongst the graves of butterflies laughed boisterously."
—Joseph Conrad, *Lord Jim*

PART I

MICKEY BLACK CUT THE HONDA'S ENGINE AND DREW A DEEP BREATH. THE dark windows of Cabin #3 of the No-Tel Motel held him like the eyes of blind men, empty and unseeing. His neck rested against the sticky vinyl headrest of his bucket seat. From the corner of his eye, he ogled Madge as she unfolded herself from the car. Then he cracked his own door open to emerge into the night's damp grip.

Come summer, clouds of moths like souls at the Rapture would flutter up the cone of light cast by the spot mounted over the motel office, but on this November night, the glow only bleached their skin to a sickly pallor, a non-color aggravated by the buzzing green neon Vacancy sign. Their shadows darted before them to vanish with the gravel path in the deeper darkness among the pines.

Madge's nose wrinkled. The stink of the Merrimack River was on her like the cold hands of the dead. Tendrils of mist eddied over the river. The Riverton Shadow was already plucking at her memory, excising bits and pieces of the day from her mind like a mother might snatch bits of white thread from her daughter's black dress.

She'd been near raped and her tits squeezed purple, but as soon as Mickey's Honda passed the Kiwanis and Lions signs that welcomed everyone to Riverton, Madge had to fight feeling wholesome. The Riverton Shadow was no contagious civic can-do attitude; the Shadow robbed her of her heart and mind. She detested that reflexive sense of well-being. It was false, false, false, while the Shadow itself was terribly real. Maybe the Shadow lived in the water or maybe the air or maybe it rose from the ground or maybe it was a curse lurking in Riverton's DNA. Wherever the Shadow might lurk, everyone in Riverton felt it; a few even whispered about it. A very few, like Madge, resisted its insistent touch.

Madge was neither psychotic nor delusional; Madge was fucked up, was what she was, fucked up and twisted. Riverton people made pretzels look like plumb lines; compared to Riverton, a ball of yarn was a straight and true path.

Back in Haverhill, while they were dosing Bughouse, just before Madge had her tits near ripped off, Aunt Sosha had told her about Chuang-Tzu, the Chinese holy man who dreamed he was a butterfly but awaked to discover he was a man. Chuang-Tzu did not know if he were a butterfly dreaming it was a man, or a man dreaming he was a butterfly.

Fuck that Chinaman. Madge's problems were far worse. A goat in Riverton might dream it was a man, only to awaken to learn it had become a butterfly with no memory of ever having been a caterpillar, and it might suffer a vague premonition of transforming to a bear.

Butterfly, man, goat, dog, caterpillar. Who gave a fuck about dreams? Bughouse was Aunt Sosha's hostage. Someone better fucking wake up, and soon. Bughouse's bony ass was in a sling, and though he needed rescuing, the poor bastard would be dog-meat before his great good friend Mickey lifted a finger.

Never mind occupying Cabin #3 a second time, Madge was thinking she would not even kiss Mickey goodnight. No fucking way. She was thinking maybe instead she would kick her lover in the balls, go home, swan dive into a hot bath, and just this once give in to the Shadow or whatever the fuck it was, let it drain away this terrible, terrible day. Why not allow herself wake up clean, new, healed, to take her place as a happy pig, happy as every other happy pig in Riverton?

Rank mist floated around her waist and between her legs. Madge shivered to think of slimy, pale, colorless things that grew beneath rocks; she hunched her shoulders and pushed her hands deeper into her flannel-lined coat pockets.

Silent, gravel crunching beneath their feet, Mickey and Madge walked side by side toward the dark trees that cloaked her Subaru safe from view.

Not safe enough.

Bellowing, dropped like an egg by the moon, Big Juice, exploded from nowhere. His knees uncoiled and he sprang into the air, a baseball bat high over his head. He came down on Mickey and Madge, horrible, unstoppable, as inescapable as God's wrath.

The same thighs that could carry the All-State fullback into the end zone with three defenders pathetically clinging to his back churned like diesel pistons. His doughy face twisted with rage. His mouth was a jagged black pit. His eyes rolled, unmoored.

"You stole my girl!"

Back-pedaling, Mickey's feet slipped on damp leaves. His ass hit unyielding rocks when he fell, but the painful fall saved him; Juice's bat whiffed, missing Mickey's skull by inches. Mickey scuttled like a crab swimming backstroke on dirt. His heels and palms ground into the soil and sodden leaves.

Madge launched herself at Juice, but no 126-pound girl was about to accomplish what

700 pounds of defensive linemen could not. She hit hard as a dandelion puff, clinging to his big arm as the bat drew back for a second savage try, shouting in his ear, "Juice! Juice! It's not what you think!" which of course, it was.

The big idiot lacked all imagination, but he was not blind.

When Juice whirled, Madge's legs snapped out like wet sheets on a line in high wind. He brushed her off, spun, and raised the bat high over his head for what would have been a fatal blow except that Madge had slowed Juice just enough for Mickey to find the revolver in his pocket.

He fired up from the ground right through his jacket's cloth. Danny had said to squeeze and aim. Well, no, Danny, no slow deliberation just now. Squeeze, nothing. Juice loomed two feet above him. With five rounds in the revolver, even Mickey could not miss.

The first shot went wildly high over Juice's shoulder into the darkness. Mickey managed to pull the revolver free of his clothes. The second shot caught Juice's upper left arm. Juice's eyes flashed red with the reflected muzzle flash. Mickey's ears rang, and his nose filled with the acrid smell of gunpowder. Danny had warned that the gun had little stopping power, and though Mickey was unfamiliar with firearms, right then he'd have welcomed the stopping power of an elephant gun. Winging Juice made him spin, and while he spun, he was close enough to touch, a stationary target. Mickey's third and fourth shots went off quick as firecrackers, just like that, pop, pop, and tore into Juice just below the numbers on his jersey, 00. Juice's momentum still would have carried Juice forward, but the fifth and final round from the .38 found Juice's lower jaw. It splintered bone and teeth and ripped out most of Juice's chin and throat. His face exploded.

The bat slipped soundlessly from his grasp, he clapped both his hands to his neck, and he toppled backward.

"Oh shit oh fuck oh shit oh fuck."

Madge was babbling. Mickey rolled to his hip to hurl himself across the leaves and dirt onto her. He pushed his weapon into his deep pants pocket where the hot short barrel burned his thigh through his pocket's cloth. He willed his rigid, shaking fingers to uncoil so he could grab Madge.

Madge squirmed like a snake impaled on an electrified fence. His left hand clapped over her mouth. Her soft body writhed beneath him.

Could the sound of trucks from the highway have drowned out the sound of gunfire? Danny said the Smith and Wesson .38 Special was a woman's gun, but it made the loudest damned noise Mickey Black ever heard. Maybe it was a woman's gun because the action was more slick than Madge's thighs. The effect, however, was far more deadly.

No one ran toward them. They were busy with what people in motels do. Mickey held his breath. His heart danced a rumba with his liver. He held Madge tight.

Maybe this one time, just this once, Mickey had caught a break. Next year, he'd throw a party—the first anniversary of the only day in history Mickey Black ever caught a break. There would be streamers and balloons at the parade. Popcorn and young mothers, floats with waving dancing girls.

Madge's breath was hot on his face. She was trying to bite his hand over her mouth. Madge's green eyes rolled. Her lips, teeth, and jaws worked against his palm. Her breath whistled through her nostrils. She screamed mutely into his hand, kicking to get up. Mickey's legs scissored around her hips and across her stomach.

A foot away, Juice wheezed and gurgled wetly through the mushy space where his throat had been. Locked in an embrace, Madge and Mickey waited for Juice to die.

It took forever. Twice, Juice's back bowed with the struggle for yet one more breath. Juice sucked wind through what was left of his throat as his lungs filled with his own blood. Then his bubbling breath rattled one last time, he sighed, and the damp velvet night was again filled only by the murmur of the river.

Shadow or no, someone was dead in Riverton.

THE NIGHT BEFORE BIG JUICE DROWNED ON HIS OWN BLOOD, HOURS AFTER the fixed Haverhill-Riverton basketball game made Mickey Black feel rich, only minutes after Bughouse Smith fell from the maple tree outside Mary Swenson's bedroom window, but well before Danny Donnelly gave Mickey a .38 and grabbed Madge's tits so hard they'd bruised, Madge Klink had been contemplating The Nature of Being.

Gautama Buddha said that to live was to suffer, but Madge Klink had come to believe that the converse proposition was equally true—to suffer was to live.

If she were right, no one in Riverton had ever been alive. Not she, not Mary, not Victoria, not Juice, not Mickey, not Cherry, not Delbart, not Chukker, not Janee, not Arnie. No one. None of their parents. None of their teachers. No person in Riverton suffered. Not ever. No one.

Would the Buddha think they had broken the Chain of Being? Or was Riverton something even the Godhead could not have imagined?

Madge Klink longed to suffer.

She pivoted on her hip and swung her legs off the edge of the bed as Mickey's semen slowly seeped from her. The coarse blanket slid from her shoulder. When chilled air puckered her areolas, she pulled the poplin bedspread around her as a shawl. Madge was short; though she sat on the mattress' edge, her toes barely met the curled green linoleum floor of Cabin #3 of the No-Tel Motel. She snatched her purse from the nightstand and fumbled for her cigarettes, lighting one with her yellow Bic.

Heart hammering, Madge had awakened from uneasy sleep. She never dreamed, but some nights a phantom sense of whatever was missing from life in Riverton shimmered just beyond her consciousness. She been on the edge of profound understanding, but as her awakening mind encircled the gaping void at the center of her being, the half-felt knowledge evaporated quicker than spit off a hot rock.

Madge adored phrases like that. *Spit. Rocks.* Words could be tough and hard, which was what she longed to be. She said *fuck* a lot, and when she did, the word dropped from her ripe mouth like a pearl.

Madge shared her need to suffer with no one. How could she mention to Mary or Victoria or God-forbid a teacher that she harbored a secret desire to know pain and deprivation? If they did not take her for a sexual deviant, a kind of masochist, they would dismiss her as some no-account adolescent whose inchoate yearning for triumph after an ordeal was a hormonal flash that time would extinguish. The gossip would be withering. *Did you hear? Madge wants to suffer? She must be quee-ah.*

Nor was Madge about to reveal to anyone her secret sessions with a serrated steak knife or her Exacto. Eyes wide open, she'd draw it across the soft flesh of her inner arm, applying more pressure with each slow stroke until tiny beads of blood welled through her flesh, pooled, and formed rivulets that snaked down her arm to her elbow. Her breath grew shallow, and she could make herself believe the exquisite pain was someone else's until her head grew light and she slumped against the cooler blue tile of the shower wall.

It was reassuring to verify that red blood ran in her veins. She was alive. Mostly. And her wounds healed overnight, leaving her unscarred.

Other girls cheered on playing fields; Madge researched the greater world from the library. Computers sent her to books; books sent her to computers. Madge swam through information like fish swim through clear water—unaware.

Online, Madge came across the centrality of suffering in Buddhism. She read *Siddhartha,* the only book even close to the topic in the Riverton High library. In four days she read the book twice while she accessed web sites that explained Eastern belief systems, how the world of senses was an illusion and how the end of suffering came with the end of desire for all that was illusory.

A theory had begun to take shape: Was Riverton trapped outside the Chain of Being? Nothing was real. Time was an illusion. Might the Riverton Shadow be karma by another name?

Hesse delivered her to *Steppenwolf,* which delivered her to Freud, and the astonishing notion that the mind forgot what it needed to. That healing mechanism was called *suppression.* She was thrilled to realize she recalled nothing of her childhood. What dark traumas and shame had douched her mind clear? What sins had her father perpetrated? She looked at him with new respect that approached affection. If he had corrupted her, she loved him all the more, the stupid shit.

Briefly, Madge thought Bughouse was her partner in seeking electronic enlightenment. She'd come around his library carrel to see what captured his attention, but one click of his mouse and the screen imploded to the brown and gold Riverton High School homepage.

Bughouse's eyes dropped to his feet. "Surfing," he said, and left. When Madge took his seat, backtracking Bughouse through cyberspace was child's play.

Madge studied the pictures. Women as meat. Bondage, gangbangs and clusterfucks, naked women on hands and knees fellating squads of men, three, four, and in one case, servicing five at a time. She viewed a three minute video.

Group sex looked like work. Where was the excitement?

But at least one other person in Riverton sought sin, however pallid. Depravity shared was twice as satisfying as depravity alone.

Taking pleasure in its weight and unequivocal solidity, Madge lifted a round glass ashtray from the motel's night table. Though she was perpetually seventeen in her body, she harbored the soul of an ageing poet, possibly Anna Akhmatova. She had no time for simple heartbreak; as other women needed air, food, and love, what Madge Klink required was debilitating, soul-gouging suffering. She longed for the anguish that plagued the protagonists of Russian novels and drove them mad. Was anything more tragically gorgeous than Anna Karenina? Madge was prepared to accept the martyrdom of the streetwalker in *Crime and Punishment*, what was her name? Sonia. That was it. Sonia, a name that meant *wisdom*.

Madge fucked Mickey because she liked to fuck, an attitude so simple it was near elegant. She was not trying to rope Mickey into a life with her. Cripes, the idea of sleeping between clean sheets, spreading her legs a few times each week, eyes squeezed shut, lying flat on her back holding her knees in a bed in a house surrounded by a white picket fence, made her want to vomit. Give her a life with an adorable dog dropping adorable turds in the adorable yard while an adorable baby filled an adorable diaper with adorable shit, and sooner or later Madge would hang herself by her adorable neck from an adorable beam in an adorable attic.

Maybe she could join a convent. Did you have to be Catholic to be accepted into a nunnery? Was it like college? If you sent the Pope some teacher recommendations, your SATs, and you did an interview, maybe they gave you a cell and a cot and three meals a day, as long as you prayed at regular intervals in the specified manner. Madge was certain she could do *pious*. She could crawl on her knees on broken glass. She'd wear a hair shirt that buttoned to her chin and meditate on the sins of the common people, pray for the world's salvation, forgive those who transgressed against her, and only incidentally become a saint after excoriating her own flesh with an official, convent-approved, serrated steak knife.

Madge was willing to trade sainthood for a life of tragic dedication. The more hopeless the cause, the better. She saw herself a furtive figure scuttling through dark squalor rescuing the orphans of Rio de Janeiro; armed with no more than righteousness, she'd face down corrupt officials who countenanced child prostitution in Cambodia; she'd once briefly considered taking up Dian Fossey's work, her hair matted with mud, squatting among the great apes on the slopes of Kilimanjaro, though once she doubted the apes' ability to show gratitude, she abandoned that plan. Only the apes would know her, and what good was that?

Drooling onto a pillowcase, face down on the bed behind her, her lover, Mickey, lay uncovered. His muscular, pale ass was perfect, but it was Mickey's hair that kept her coming back, slick, black, shining, and oh-so-exactly parted. She loved to muss Mickey Black's black hair.

Fucking Mickey, her thighs gripping that perfect ass, Madge kept her eyes open until Mickey's hair grew damp with perspiration and tumbled loose. She'd lose all control, her fingers would entwine in the dark corona flaring wildly out about his face, her eyes would squeeze closed, and she would draw great gulps of air laden with the perfume of his sweated scalp.

Big Juice, her official boyfriend, however, had all the sexual magnetism of a goldfish. She could not recall how they'd met or why she was with him. They were inexplicably paired, and would be forever. It was a curse.

She'd once unzipped Juice's pants in the front seat of his father's car to deliver a hand job that should have made him beg for release, but all that happened was that he clenched his eyes, his head leaned against the seat, his breathing grew ragged, and he expelled one great sigh as he came weakly into her inverted cupped palm.

He never once tried to touch her, not once, and when it was done, he cried a little.

It was goddam humiliating. She'd needed to be touched.

Intimacy brought her no closer to Juice. How was it possible that she could be naked and wild with Mickey, but nevertheless feel they had never been intimate?

She'd come stupidly close to sharing the paradox with Mary and Victoria. Mary and Victoria, with empty heads and perfect noses, were the double star at Riverton's white-hot center, while Madge was at best the satellite of a planet out beyond Neptune, a bare, cold rock, slowly tumbling unnoticed through the silent void.

At a pajama party at the Cabot place, the three of them had worn translucent teddies. Mary was in pink, Victoria in black, and Madge in pale blue. They sat Indian-style on 'Toria Cabot's goose down ivory comforter amid a litter of tattered fashion magazines, mascara, eyelash brushes, a half dozen lipsticks, rouge, blush, green, blue and black eyeliner—everything the contemporary woman required. The bedspread became streaked and stained, but in 'Toria's opulent life anything could be replaced.

Mary lined her lips with pure crimson and then pressed them to a square of tissue. She asked, "Too red?" and Victoria tossed her a tube of something called Purple Crepe. "Try this. It's daring, but maybe not you," Victoria commented. "Madge could get away with it, though. That is, if Juice gave her permission."

Madge had not missed the light note of challenge. Vicky slapped a magazine down on the bedspread, faced her and said, "Why Juice? God, Madge, you are so pretty and could have anyone. Why Big Juice?"

"And Juice gets so jealous," Mary added, leaning toward her. "How can you flirt? How can you practice? What happens when…?"

"Exactly," Victoria said to Mary. "That's it exactly." Her powder brush spun like a propeller, obliterating the last girlish shine from her pert nose. She leaned toward Madge, her knee crinkling the cover of a magazine that screamed in yellow print, *12 New Secret Ways to Please Your Man!!* Victoria said, "What would I do if I could not flirt?"

You'd have to fuck, Madge thought, but all she said was, "Big Juice makes me feel safe."

Her two friends sighed. That, at least, they understood.

Madge, however, knew how false it was.

Safe? Juice's jealousy was a solar flare, sudden, far-reaching, incinerating all it touched. A strong, stupid man who worshipped her had definite, if limited, value, but suppose he turned on her? What if he learned his suspicions of Mickey were in fact far beyond anything he had the capacity to imagine?

Safe? No, life with Big Juice made life decidedly dangerous.

That suited Madge down to her socks.

Madge smoked and touched Mickey's damp neck. He was a forceful if not terribly skilled lover, but what brought Madge back to the No-Tel Motel again and again was risk.

The thrill began with skulking shoeless down the stairs of her house, excitement mounting as she drove through the night, peaking when she opened the door to Cabin #3. Mickey always waited for her in darkness. The screen door squealed on its hinges, the spring snapped it closed loud as a gunshot behind her, and her knees turned to jelly when Mickey emerged from nowhere to scoop her into his arms and cover her face and eyes with kisses. She'd bite his lip to taste his blood, and he'd pinch, knead, and slap at her flesh, building to an explosive first fuck that might occur on the floor, bed, bureau, chair, or, once, the sink. Their lovemaking was always hurried, hopeless, doomed, terribly dangerous, and wholly satisfying.

And there was a bonus. As long as Mickey knew a word from her could bring Big Juice down on him, she was in total control.

She sat bare-assed in a wet spot. Fuck that. She used no birth control; she doubted that Mickey could guess at the use of condoms. No matter. No need. She would not get pregnant. Teenage girls in Riverton never became pregnant.

It defied logic. No married woman in Riverton ever became pregnant, either. Riverton was free of children with birth defects because there were no births. No pregnancy, no disease, no abortion. Either no one fucked, or fucking carried no consequence. After every encounter with Mickey, her only partner, even her hymen grew back.

In the green neon light that passed through the wooden slats of the blinds, Mickey's flesh seemed striped a sickly fish-belly white. Madge's fingertip wiped drool from his lip. Like every boy in Riverton, he seemed never to need to shave. She moved a strand of hair from over his eyes. His face was unlined. Her palm came to rest on the gentle curl of Mickey's bare hip where his skin was palest, where her nails had left red welts. The motel's rough blanket was bunched between his thighs. His hairless back and chest suited her.

They must have looked very pretty together, she thought.

When Mickey rolled to his hip to smile up at her, the motel bed springs squealed complaint.

"Mick," she said, "Do you know anyone who fought in a war?"

Mickey seized a second pillow. "Always good to wake up beside you, Madge. I live for special moments like this one."

She curled her fingers around his ear. "I'm serious, lover. Talk to me about something serious."

"Why do you smoke those things?"

"Who has cancer in Riverton? Name one person."

"Let's go back to the war thing, instead. Mass death is so much more pleasant than individual disease." Mickey rolled to his back and ticked off his fingers as he spoke. "There was the Civil War, the Spanish-American War, World War I, World War II, Korea and Vietnam, right? Isn't that what Grimley taught us?"

Excited, she turned to him and kneeled on the bed. The bedspread shawl slipped from her shoulders. When Mickey reached for her thigh, she patted his hand away. "Yes, and then there was Iraq and Iraq again. And Afghanistan. Don't forget Afghanistan."

"You left some out. Wasn't there a Mexican War?"

She'd also omitted various American excursions into Africa, the conquest of the West, the Caribbean, and the Philippines, but she was not about to lose this moment to a point of technical completeness. "Do you know anyone who fought? Ever?"

"In the Mexican War?"

"God, Mick, do you have to be a total douche bag?"

"Well, there are a couple of Civil War monuments around town. Guys on horses with swords. Riverton did its part, I guess."

"But no one in modern wars?"

Mickey held eye contact and without breaking his gaze said, "How about some head? After that, we can fight any war you want."

She slapped at his hand clutching at her nipple, but not hard enough to discourage him. He continued to caress her.

When Madge had pondered the Navy as a way of moving on, she'd looked for someone, anyone, who'd experienced military life. She'd asked Daddy Kane whether he'd ever been in the service, and Daddy said, "I don't like to talk about it," and when she pressed him, simply to reveal where he'd been and when, he said, "This is Riverton! Why worry?"

Mickey's index finger gently traced the slim line of darker hair that ran from below her navel to the hair at her crotch. He propped himself up on an elbow. The room's digital clock glowed 4:32.

Madge so liked to be touched.

Mickey gently rolled her face down onto the bed, straddled her waist, and deep-rubbed her shoulders. He had good, strong hands. She gave herself up to his hands, gurgling like a happy cat.

"Too much pressure?"

She sighed, which was what Mickey needed to hear. He knew he could work her shoulders and back for hours, but she'd never relax. Eventually, she would roll over beneath him, rise to kneel between his legs, and reach up to his chest. She'd tell him to close his eyes, and then pleased Mickey in ways that made him groan and groan again.

What might Mickey think if he knew Madge took hints from Bughouse's favorite Internet sites?

The light through the slats of the blinds blushed pink as the sun rose. Madge sipped water from a plastic cup in the chilly bathroom, wiped her mouth with the back of her wrist, and scooted back to the bed across the cold linoleum. As she slid beneath the blanket, Mickey's steady breathing told her he already slept.

A truck rumbled on the highway. Madge's eyes closed. There was at least an hour before they needed to leave. Drifting into a light sleep, she wondered if the delivery of an effective blowjob was instinct, talent, or learned behavior. What might Freud say?

Fuck Freud. What Madge believed was what so many Hindus believed: orgasm was nothing less than the portal through which we glimpsed the face of God.

MAYBE SIX HOURS BEFORE MADGE WENT DOWN ON MICKEY, WELL BEFORE Bughouse met Ari, the Mossad interrogator fond of chess, knives, and gefilte fish, but very soon after Mickey won a fortune on a basketball game, as Bughouse Smith lost his footing on the damp limb of a maple tree in Mary Swenson's backyard, he lunged at a branch. The reflex near dislocated his shoulder.

It hurt like a son-of-a-bitch, but at least he did not fall and see those little whirly stars. The stars could be as annoying as the little blue birdies. His shoulder pained him, but at least there were no blue birdies.

November drizzle allowed his sneakers no purchase, but his stupid eagerness was what had made him clumsy, not rainwater. What kind of imbecile strains to stand on tiptoes in a wet tree? He'd craned his neck to see a sliver more into Mary's unlighted window. "This is really stupid," he thought just before his sneakered foot started to slide on what felt like ball bearings.

It was worse than stupid. It was *dangerous*.

Mary was not even home. Anticipation had Bughouse taking risks. Her room was dark except for the glow of a nightlight. The light itself was out of his line of vision; all Bughouse could see were motionless shadows cast by furniture.

Stiff with cold, Bughouse's fingers curled around the wet branch over his head. He owned no gloves. The kind without fingers would be best, black leather with no fingers. If the night became any colder, this rain might become snow. Snow was not out of the question in November; he liked the kind that stuck only on lawns and windshields and sparkled in the dawn's first sunlight. Snow could be pretty.

Though he had the heart of an artist, Bughouse could find clarity only when the haze of hormones that kept him in torment did not elevate an alternative body organ to supremacy. Did Tintoretto, Picasso, and Manet spend their nights staring into girls' windows? Of course not. Real artists *hired* girls to take off their clothes to study them, naked. They did not climb trees in rainstorms. Artists were preoccupied by higher things.

Bughouse despaired. He had the restraint of a chimpanzee. Defective and doomed, he was all dick and no brains.

Two or three times every day, he yielded. Bughouse exhausted packs and packs of tissues. How many cold showers might a boy endure? He did push-ups. He ran stairs. Focus on school? That was a laugh: half the people in the halls of Riverton High had vaginas. Half! They laughed; they smiled, fully aware of the gift between their legs, the gift they withheld from him. School meant hour after hour of torment. Reaching the final chapter of any text-book was a challenge. No matter where he was or what he was doing, any line he read might touch off visions of perfectly wholesome girls in the grip of irresistible lust, lips parted wetly, performing despicable sex acts, all at his bidding. His body polluted what little was left of his mind, and though he swore to stop, bargaining with himself and God, thinking, "Just once more. Once more, and never again," within hours, he was abusing himself.

What clown had decided that anything that felt that good could be called *abuse?*

Unfit for society, instead of hanging himself, here he was yet again up a maple tree with his sodden gray sweatshirt hood over his head, looking like a gang-banger from New York or Boston or Los Angeles, the kinds of places he'd never get to. Never mind *artist*, he'd be lucky not to be packed off to some triple-X adult freak show circus sideshow to be featured as Dick-boy, The Jag-Off King, the Eleven-Inch Wonder.

Hung like a donkey, with all the restraint of a barnyard animal, Bughouse was doomed.

On his tree limb, Mary could never see him unless she really stared into the darkness, and why would she do that? Bughouse withdrew his hand from his pants, made the shape of a gun, and squeezed off one round at the faint illumination emanating from Mary's window.

Bang.

He blew imaginary smoke from his fingertip.

Earlier that evening, as he pedaled up the hill to Riverton High and the Haverhill game, Arnie and Mary had whipped past him in Arnie's car. They went by as if Bughouse were in-visible. He *was* invisible. Bughouse owned no car. Come rain, wind, snow, or fog, he pedaled through town on a bicycle several sizes too small. His elbows and knees protruded like the edges of an unsolvable Geometry problem. The bike had a humiliating banana seat. It once sported a raccoon tail, but Bughouse had torn that off, used it to masturbate several times, and only then burned it.

But the moment he saw Arnie and Mary together, Bughouse knew he would not see the Haverhill game's second half. Riverton would have to lose without him. Riverton life was nothing if not predictable, and Bughouse read his friends' lives like a railroad schedule. Arnie would return Mary home by 10:00 because it was Thursday, a school night, and Mary's fa-ther, Mr. Swenson, had his rules. He'd have said to Arnie, "Mary is a good girl, Mary has a future, Mary is blah, blah, and blah. Be sure to return my daughter in the same condition as she is now." Did her father know Mary had the finest rack at Riverton High? Not the biggest, but the finest. She had an ass. She had legs. She had red lips. She had flesh the color of French vanilla ice cream. Did Mr. Swenson appreciate all that? Give Bughouse fifteen minutes with

Mary and he would leave her bowlegged for life. How would that be for respecting her condition? She might be Mr. Swenson's daughter, but she was made of *parts,* for crying out loud!

Win or lose, Arnie, the basketball team captain, would first shower then show up at The Riverton All-American Burger Shoppe. Riverton's favorite couple would share a strawberry ice-cream soda before they left at 9:50.

It was 9:57.

Bughouse shifted his grip again. A twinge of pain teased his shoulder. Could a boy his age get arthritis? The rain fell harder, pattering softly on the leaves.

Like every other kid in Riverton, Bughouse had watched the first half of the basketball game. He stood at a side door, guaranteeing an easy escape to his bicycle. At halftime, Bughouse beat it. He was supposed to meet Mickey at Daddy Kane's, but that was just too bad for Mickey. Mary would be disrobing shortly after ten, and as much as he liked Mickey, Bughouse's penis and priorities were equally straight. The only way to be at his perch on time was to pedal across town in rain to climb a tree and wait. Look, this was Mary, and there was no question about the show starting promptly at 10:00.

Goodbye Mickey; hello maple tree.

The first night Bughouse had noticed Mary's lighted window he'd been in the neighborhood on July Fourth. He needed to get out of the house after his father had bloodied his nose. They'd watched the fireworks at the Riverton riverfront stadium, and his father had had a few beers.

More than a few.

Home, his father saw no reason to end the patriotic celebration. At the refrigerator, he cracked open one more, chugged it, and then opened another. Bughouse knew the signs of a long, bad weekend to come. He said, "Dad, do you really need all that brew?" which was when his father casually backhanded him so hard and so fast that Bughouse's head smacked the wall. Blood flowed from his nose to his shirt. There had been no blue birdies; there was nothing funny about this kind of pain.

Bughouse fled, not so much from fear but to get out of the way. Until his father passed out, furniture would be splintered and crockery shattered. It was like waiting for a summer storm to pass. Bughouse ignored the pain in his thighs from straining at the too small bike, pedaling as fast as he could, forcing the cooler July night air to flow over his flushed face where it almost carried away his shame and anger.

Dad missed Mom. So did Bughouse. But when and where she had gone were details lost to him. There were photos on the living room wall. His mother had been a homely woman who wore a horrible blue hat. He had no memory of her, though when he looked at the picture he felt sorrow and loss swell in his throat.

That July night, the moon had set, and Bughouse lay on the lawn in Swenson's vast backyard watching for shooting stars. Meteors were better than fireworks because they reminded him of the size of the cosmos, how small he was, and how his troubles, despite feeling perpetual and unchanging, would someday have to pass. He gingerly touched his sore chin to remind himself that life could not be so cruel as to forever be the same.

He'd not come to Swenson's yard by design. For the kids in Riverton, every place in town was as open as every other. Except for the Cabot Estate and the other side of DuBois Hill, there were no fences in Riverton.

The Swenson home stood just yards from where he lay on the grass. The night was inky. Then, *Pow!* like an old-fashioned flashbulb, Mary's window ignited with light.

The window held Mary, framed.

Her yellow hair tumbled over her face to her shoulders as she leaned forward to brace her elbows on the sill. She tugged twice at her t-shirt to pull it away from her, cooling herself, and then she crossed her hands, gripped the shirt at her waist, and with a simple fluid movement pulled it over her head. Then she leaned forward again. The night air ran freely over her bare chest.

Bughouse rose to his knees and forgot to breathe.

Bare-breasted Mary framed in her window achieved spiritual transcendence; nevertheless, there was nothing spiritual about the record-breaking wood that popped down Bughouse's pants leg.

He returned to the Swenson yard again and again in hopes of reproducing the intensity of that first vision, but he never did. He would forever grow hard by recalling the moment she drew off her t-shirt. Her ignorance of his presence, the heat of the night, and his sense of violating her with his eyes excited him more than anything else ever had. Internet pictures were one thing; Mary's flawless alabaster flesh was another.

That summer night vision of Mary left a mess in his pants. He'd not needed his hands. There was the final proof he was a perv: who'd ever conflate Art and sex?

The rain grew heavier. Mist thickened. His sweatshirt felt like the soggy touch of Death between his shoulder blades. Chill spread from his feet, up his torso and then down his arms into his chest where it gripped his pitiful heart.

Ah-oooo-gah!

Arnie's car horn wafted three times through the darkness. Sharp as ammonia, the noise snapped Bughouse from reveries of Mary.

Bughouse prayed for the day Arnie would plow his crap Ford Mustang through a crosswalk filled with parochial school girls; the last thing twenty fourth-graders and their nun would hear would be Arnie's god-awful horn. Not that Bughouse wished nuns and parochial school girls ill-will, but the greater glory of civilization demanded that Arnie's horn be si-lenced. The death of innocents would guarantee that. Sacrifices had to be made.

Bughouse sidled closer to the tree trunk. One wrenched shoulder was plenty, thanks. He kept the tree trunk between him and Mary's window. Out front, a door slammed, and then the car radio dopplered away.

The dope had not even taken the time to kiss Mary goodnight.

Breath whistled through Bughouse's nostrils. In the dark window a shadow passed among other shadows, and Bughouse hardly breathed at all. The little porcelain vanity table lamp suddenly flared light. It had a frilly pink shade and a switch that looked like a brass key.

Mary came into view. She wore her short, white vinyl jacket, her palest blue jeans, her hair knotted back in a red kerchief. It was nothing fancy, but what she wore was perfection. She moved to his left and then to his right before passing from his sight. *Come on, come on, he muttered. Do it for me, Mary. Do it. Show us a little, sweetheart. Just a little, Mary, sweet Mary, please.*

His blood pounded.

Mary was as pure as a field of fresh snow. He wanted to take off his shoes and run all over her, feel her flesh come up between his toes like grass. Fuck his mixed metaphor—snow, grass, who cared?—he wanted to know Mary every way a woman could be known. Physi-cally, spiritually, emotionally, intellectually. He would use her, abuse her, comfort her, hold her. He wanted to climb into her skin and become her. He would wrap himself in Mary-ness. How else could Bughouse hope to transcend his worthless soul?

From out of his sight, Mary's shining white jacket flew into view, flung across the room. That was followed by her pink sequined t-shirt. Both missed the vacant chair's back, prob-ably falling to the floor, a heap of fabric holding the warm smell of Mary.

Bughouse's hand forced its way under the tight waistband of his pants.

Then she was before him again, her back to him, wearing a simple white bra, her skin luminous as a Sergeant portrait. Her two hands reached up to unclip the stays. She hunched forward. Bughouse began to sweat. The bra slid down her delicate arms just as she disap-peared yet again from his view.

The pulse at his throat choked him. He promised God he would never, never be here again if just this once, just tonight, he could be vouchsafed the total vision he required, all of Mary, beautiful, sweet, pure Mary, head to toe, uninhibited and unclothed. His.

What if they had been in the same room? What if she was drugged, or crazy, or hypno-tized, or something? She'd never be with Bughouse of her own free will, but what if?

His hand plunged deeper into his pants. *Oh sweet Mary just once more come to the window.* Indistinct silhouettes played on the visible wall. *Sweet Mary, sweet Mary, oh yes, oh yes. One more time, sweet Mary, for me. For me.*

Then, the miracle.

Her back to him again, yes, but there was not a stitch on the girl. The pale flesh at the top of her soft ass, her narrow, bare back tapering into the flare of her hips, she perched on her vanity chair, a blue metal thing made of twisted wire. She reached up to the rubber band holding her ponytail and shook loose her silken gold hair. It cascaded to her bare shoulders.

Bughouse near wept at the beauty.

He leaned dangerously to his right, but no angle showed him her chest in her mirror. Why, Lord, couldn't this tree have been planted just two yards to the right? Would the galaxy have wheeled into chaos if this tree limb had grown two inches higher off the ground?

Mary leaned forward, back, forward again. She scooped skin cream from a jar, worked it into her hands, lifted a leg, and when she bent forward Bughouse imagined how it spread thickly and smoothly on her knee and glistening calf.

Still seated, still with her back to the window, she lifted a hairbrush from the vanity top. The line of her back and arms as she pulled the brush up through her hair was poetry. *Turn, Mary. Oh please turn for me. Just once. Just once.* The fine filaments of her hair wafted onto her pancake-butter shoulders.

His eye fixed on a crescent of paler flesh just beyond her elbow. Was that the curve of her breast? Did he truly see that? Or had he imagined it? He might be struck blind, and he'd see that curve of pale flesh to the end of days.

Bughouse's chest and leg pressed against the tree trunk. He could get no closer. He strained for a better angle, craning his neck for more height. The insistent rain beat a tattoo on the tree's spare leaves. Bughouse shook with cold and desire. *Turn to me, sweet Mary, turn.*

Then, without standing or turning, Mary languidly extended her arm to the tiny lamp's brass key.

Darkness.

Bughouse teetered. His back relaxed and he lowered himself off his toes. It was careless. Next thing he knew, he lay flat on his back on the soft, wet earth beside his rusting crap bicycle. Yellow stars and tiny blue birdies circled his head.

Mary called, "G'nite Buggy. *Tee-hee.*"

THE DAY BEFORE BIG JUICE CHOKED ON HIS OWN BLOOD ON A BANK OF THE
Merrimack River, roughly the hour Bughouse Smith hoisted himself into the maple tree outside Mary Swenson's bedroom window, a full day before Madge Klink had her tits squeezed
blue by a Haverhill leg-breaker, Mickey Black sprawled comfortably in his usual booth at
the back of the Riverton All-American Burger Shoppe. He closed his eyes and languished in
gorgeous, complex, far-reaching and intricate dreams, a realm so perfect that mere language
failed to give them form.

His scalp tingled. Like summer lightning on his spine, pure pleasure crackled from his
brain to his testicles and back again. His nipples stiffened; he touched himself.

Had any drug been this good, Mickey Black would have taken it.

No, wait, check that; he'd sell it.

Mickey's leg stretched the length of the bench seat. He rubbed his aching quadriceps.
The burger shop crowd swelled. They should have been gloomy, the dopes, but no, this was
Riverton. Despite an ass-kicking by Haverhill in the annual basketball game, losing by a
dismal 63-47, the Riverton Faithful surfed on a self-congratulatory surge of admiration for
fine effort in the face of long odds.

In Riverton, spirit was what the town had instead of victories. Mickey winced to ac-
knowledge he was from Riverton. Spirit, as he saw it, proved that losers loved losing.

That fact would make Mickey Black wealthy. His future, a tapestry woven of gold
thread and the green money of Victoria Cabot's trust funds, unfolded before his eyes. There
would be women, travel, women, Victoria, other women, maybe Madge, and old man Cabot
would be kissing his ass.

He had taken the first step.

Having set the point-spread at an unheard of 15½, Mickey had accepted every dime and
dollar the hometown rubes could beg, steal, or borrow to wager on the rivalry. What cracker
could resist lopsided odds that favored the home team? The yokels could not pass the opportunity to show Riverton pride and at the same time put it to Mickey Black and his wallet.

Fix and all, it had been a hell of a game. In the final minute of play he'd pounded his
thigh sore with a rolled up program. Shot after Riverton shot had circled rim, but never quite
fell until a Haverhill player ended the suspense with a defensive rebound at the buzzer and
an elbow into Arnie's teeth. The ref missed the call, and Mickey mentally noted that the next

time he needed to orchestrate a killing, he'd bribe a ref, too.

Beyond Daddy Kane's front plate glass, the Riverton streets glistened with light rain. No account, no-name kids elbowed their way to the stainless steel counter; they ordered burgers, fries, malteds, and frappes. Happy as a Hoover, the jukebox sucked in dollar bills. A few pinheads danced in the cramped spaces among Daddy's tables.

Where in hell was Bughouse? Months ago, Bughouse had planted the seed that this night had flowered into Mickey's exquisite triumph. Where the hell could Bughouse be on a rainy night?

Last April, they had been in the sun behind the chicken wire backstop at Riverton Field. Observing batting practice was no casual pastime; Mickey carefully assessed each player each week for any hint of injury. A limp, a touch to a sore elbow, a creaky swing—little things revealed a lot. Smart guys looked for every edge, and Mickey Black was one smart guy.

On the pitcher's mound, from behind a protective waist-high screen, Arnie hurled pitches fat as grapefruits for his teammates to slap high and far over the outfield fence. On the second row of the aluminum seats, Bughouse skulked like a vulture, his head lower than his shoulders. Mickey sat one row higher and behind Bughouse, his weight resting back on his elbows, his face lifted to the sun to begin the exacting work of developing his annual summer tan that made his smile appear even whiter. By mid-July he would appear "swarthy"; the word made him feel dangerous.

Big Juice cracked a sky-ball that had the leftfielder loping to the warning track before he lazily waited for it to settle into his glove. A few feet from the player, Mary and Victoria were wiggling onto the field through a hole in the cyclone fence someone had snipped with wire cutters long ago. The outfielder's attention went astray; he dropped the ball.

The girls each extended a long, bare leg through the hole, followed it with a hip, a full, perfect ass, then the other leg. First the blonde; then the brunette. Bent at the waist, they backed onto the field before wobbling erect. When Mary's white t-shirt snagged and rode up enough to expose the plain of her pale, hard belly, despite more than 100 yards, Mickey's eyes had no choice but to linger.

Victoria's and Mary's entrances were uncalculated if not innocent. They believed that being the perpetual center of attention was just how the world was structured, something managed by Divine Right, like nobility. Baseball might be baseball, but they were who they were. Why challenge how the universe had been made? What possible good could it do to be aware of other people? Why step aside if someone was in a hurry? A person's hair might be burning, but Victoria and Mary would stare tiredly at whomever had the nerve to interrupt them in some stupid frantic search for water.

The blonde and brunette wore matching red short-shorts, white T-shirts, and pale blue high-heel sneakers. They wore little else. With every step they took closer along the foul line, their bodies quivered like gelatin dessert.

Another fly ball landed with a thump onto the grass behind the outfielder before it rolled slowly to the base of the fence where it came to rest.

Mickey planned to marry Victoria's trust funds, and he looked forward to fucking his gorgeous brunette wife, but he acknowledged that blonde Mary's feather-brain was set atop a body that could send a Visigoth out to savage whole civilizations merely to earn the chance to lie an hour between her thighs. Poets could pen odes about her ass. Painters could immortalize those blue, blue eyes. Sculptors might envision her legs, belly and breasts in blocks of marble, and they would slowly, painstakingly, spend fulfilling lifetimes chipping at the rock to release a polished image of that perfect form.

It was an odd irony: though Mickey Black admired Mary and planned to marry Victoria, he lived for his secret nights with Madge. He did not dare to share his sexual triumph with Bughouse; if he did, in days the memory of his nights with Madge would vanish and he'd be back to holding his own. Either that, or Big Juice would rearrange his anatomy in less than optimal ways.

Mary was prettier, and Victoria had far more money, but Madge was the real deal; she delivered. In a town where being simple-minded was a badge of honor, Madge Klink was complicated. He'd trade both the tarted-up professional virgins for an hour with Madge. The fact that Madge was Big Juice's girl was just another inducement. Risk hung on Madge like a cape, so every time he screwed her and remained unscathed, Mickey Black was assured of his invincibility, the precursor to his inevitable triumph. When it came to Madge, he kept his mouth shut.

From the pitcher's mound, Arnie also noticed the girls wobbling their way down the third base line. To impress Victoria, Arnie threw heat, and since Big Juice never expected a fastball at batting practice, he swung, whiffed, and nearly sank to one knee.

Mickey leaned forward, eager to see Juice club Arnie into raspberry jam for making him look foolish, but Juice just said, "Take it easy, Arnie," and tapped imaginary dust from his cleats.

Where *was* Madge, anyway? The library? Madge read too many books, but Mickey saw no percentage in it; all reading did was make Madge unhappy.

Some punk sophomore appeared out of nowhere, climbed the aluminum seats, and forced five dollars into Mickey's hand. Mickey pulled away from the kid as if the bills were coated in rat shit. "Take it easy, cocksucker. You want to get us busted?"

The jag-off with a brown and gold Riverton cap on backwards looked away, and from the side of his mouth muttered *Riverton*. Mickey scribbled on a page of his blue pocket spiral notebook, tore out the sheet, folded it, and handed over the betting slip. "Settle with me later, shithead."

Bughouse, who never bet, asked Mickey how he could be so sure Riverton would fold to Lowell in baseball's season opener.

"I'm not. Makes no difference to me. Bettors play against each other, not against me, Bug."

"I don't get that."

Juice swung from his ankles and whacked a second towering hit to left. The ball seemed to rise and then pause in mid-air before it gathered speed in a descent that carried it beyond the fence to plummet to the school's parking lot. It bounced twice off the concrete before coming to rest in the center of Miss Grimley's windshield. The glass splintered like a spider web.

Arnie roughed up a new ball and laughed like a drunken mule: *Kyuk, kyuk, kyuk.* Grimley's windshield was shattered every spring. It was as predictable as the first robin. Every year, Arnie laughed the same way, his hands on his knees as if nothing had ever been funnier. Mickey could not remember an April when Grimley's windshield was not shattered by a baseball.

At the third base coach's box, Mary and Victoria paused to clap.

"I can't lose," Mickey said. "I take action from both sides."

Bughouse scowled. "That's the part I don't get," he said.

Why did Mickey know these things? Where had he learned them? When? Ask a fish when it learned about water.

Mickey explained point spreads, middles, and how if the action was balanced on two sides of any proposition, the more action, the more profit. Bughouse heard nothing. He was captivated by the shape of Mary's breasts, hanging like cantaloupes beneath her clinging T-shirt as she bent to tie a shoelace.

But Mickey persisted. "It's not about the teams; it's about the odds. Set the odds so the contest looks even, and the money rolls in on two sides. If the book goes out of whack, all I have to do is lay-off risk with Danny, this guy I know in Haverhill. He's got connections." How did he know Danny? He had no memory. It was one of those trivial details that seemed drained from his mind like water from a squeezed sponge. He knew only that losers provided the money for winners, and that for every dollar he handled, a few pennies stayed with him. "The vigorish sticks to my fingers. My only risk is that if I miss a spread, the book is lopsided. Then I am on the Poorhouse Express."

"Which is why we watch batting practice?"

"Which is why we watch batting practice."

Bughouse shook his head with admiration. "It would be something if you knew in advance who was going win, though, wouldn't it?"

So in the sun, on the bleachers, behind the Riverton Field backstop, even as Mary and 'Toria sidled onto the seats behind them, at that precise moment, while Bughouse had all the willpower of a salmon struggling upstream on a river that flowed between the banks of Mary's thighs, a vision like a rose blossomed in Mickey's mind.

A man with brass balls could take it all. Forget middles. A real killing could be made if he rigged a game, set a ridiculous spread to get every sucker in, accept every bet, and make damn sure the outcome was the correct one.

He waited for his opportunity. Months passed. Another school year began as summer bled into fall. And then in early November two weeks ago, Mickey loitered near the school until basketball practice ended. When Chukker Washington emerged through the big metal doors of the high school gym, Mickey fell in behind Riverton's All-Star guard.

Two stars glimmered in the sky near the waning moon, while the heatless sun, already below the horizon, tinted the high clouds in the west a startling gold. As they spoke, the sky deepened to crimson and then to black.

Mickey thrust his hands into the rear pockets of his slacks. He tried to look like any other Riverton student who lingered late at school. That was hopeless; who else wore slacks? Besides, why would Mickey Black be at school after classes? He played for no team; he edited no school publication; he marched in no band; he'd wrap his own head in a poly bag and duct tape before he'd attend a pep rally.

Everyone, including Chukker, knew this about Mickey Black. Nevertheless, the two played out a script; they were just two clean-living American boys who met by chance. How could larceny come up?

Mickey offered Chukker a ride home in his modified Honda Accord. He'd ripped out the muffler, so the car buzzed like an angry hornet. Chukker declined. "I'll wait for Janee."

Mickey said he was happy to keep Chukker company. He asked, "Chukker, why does Arnie get all the credit when you do all the work?"

"What do you mean? We are teammates."

"I know. I know. But here you are, last man to leave practice. Probably first to report, too. You work hard, Chukker. You work hard."

Chukker said, "Arnie is an okay guy."

"But he's not half the player you are. Not half."

Janee might show up any time, but some things cannot be rushed. It was a dance. Mickey felt the rhythm.

Strictly hypothetically, just for the sake of conversation, he asked if a guy like Chukker

Washington, a guy everyone respected and knew had talent, a guy people loved—yes, *love* was the appropriate word—could a guy like that ever play less than one hundred percent, maybe because of a cold, or a bad night's sleep, or maybe because of problems with his girl? How did it happen that a star athlete might suffer an off night?

Chukker admitted that, yes, a star athlete might have an off night. Everyone knew that.

Mickey jacked his collar higher, clapped and rubbed his hands together, then blew into his palms. They stood uneasily beside the reproduction of Rodin's The Thinker, a statue Mickey passed daily but never understood. In the center of a lawn surrounded by the semi-circular driveway to the high school's main entrance, a naked guy propped his head on his fist. What was that about? He looked like he needed to crap is what he looked like.

Mickey said, "Everyone knows Haverhill is going to win this one. If Riverton had five guys like you, Chukker, things might be different, but everyone knows you are alone out there. It's funny how Arnie gets all the credit while you do all the work.

"So what I wonder is whether a smart player, a really good player, a player with all the moves and brains to match, could that player choose his night to leave his best game in the locker room? Why not keep his best game ready for a night when it will matter?"

Chukker shifted his weight. The guy teetered on the edge. Mickey could blow on his chest and he'd fall backward over the cliff.

Without turning to Mickey, Chukker said, "My Dad is a coach, Mick. He could lose his job."

Mickey pursed his lips and nodded as if he were sympathetic. What was it with these guys? Basketball was a fucking game, not a moral code. Satin shorts, a jock strap, and sweat, sweat, sweat. Players stank like barnyard animals. It was a freak-show, nothing more.

He said, "Right. Right. Your Dad is proud of you. We're all proud of you. But are you going to tell your Dad you *chose* the night to leave your best game behind? I am not going to tell your Dad. If you don't tell him, and I don't tell him, how will anyone ever know? You aren't going to tell him, are you?"

"No."

"All right then."

Mickey resisted the urge to coil an arm around the guy's shoulders. He could not put the arm on him, not yet.

Washington drew a deep breath. "Cut the bull, Mickey. How much?"

"Fifty," Mickey snapped.

Washington licked his lips. "Make it a hundred, Mickey. A hundred. Christmas is coming. Janee likes nice things."

"I like Christmas. I like Janee. A hundred it is."

"I need it right away, man. Up front."

Mickey showed him the folded bill in his palm. Waiting for Washington, he'd taken the time to fold it small. Just the denomination showed. He'd also taken the precaution to fold a fifty in the same way. The fifty was stashed in a different pocket. There was no telling where the negotiation might have ended—either bill or both.

"Don't make a mess of it, Chukker. Play your game, just don't try so hard. Riverton doesn't have a chance for this one. Your best game; your worst. Makes no difference to Riverton. Haverhill has five players and Riverton has just you. It's a hummer."

"A hundred doesn't buy that much."

"It's a hundred you don't have. Get Janee something nice. Maybe something gold with a little stone in it."

"A diamond?"

"Maybe not a diamond. But something nice."

"I want something for me. Shoes. The high top Nikes."

"The white ones? You don't already have a pair? That's not right. An athlete like you needs those shoes. Absofuckinglutely."

Washington nodded, still peering into the gathering gloom and unwilling to look at Mickey. "Size twelve," he said. "A hundred dollars and the Nikes."

Mickey idly reached out to touch the icy metal of The Thinker. One more thing needed to be said before Janee appeared.

"Look at me Chukker. I need to see your eyes and you need to see mine." Chukker turned to him. Chukker's eyes were slits. Mickey said, "If you don't want to do this, I don't want you to take my money. There is still time for you to change your mind. No one will ever know we had this conversation. No hard feelings. No problem. Five minutes after you leave, I will forget we ever spoke."

Janee's blue Toyota Corolla whipped into the high school's long circular driveway. The dome light shone as if she had been looking for something in the passenger seat but had forgotten to extinguish the light.

Mickey risked his index finger on the athlete's chest to make his final point. "Once you take my money, you have to deliver, Chukker. Don't take my money and fuck me. Once you take it, people will have expectations. Stuff can happen."

"What people?"

"People." Mickey shrugged. "Janee is a pretty girl. No one likes to see anything happen to a pretty girl."

"Don't threaten me, man. I don't like that."

Mickey dropped his hand from Washington's chest, turned his palms up, and shrugged.

"I'm your friend, Chukker. I'd never threaten you. I am protecting you. I am telling you how it is. If you have any doubt, I am begging you now, do not take my cash. No problem." He clapped his hands and held them forward like a magician after a playing card vanished.

The Corolla's brakes squealed. Mickey's hands returned to his rear pockets and he bent to look into the open car window. Janee was thicker through the middle than a willowy girl like Victoria, but nevertheless, definitely, definitely a potentially lively piece of ass, black, skin the color of a nut, exotic in Riverton. "Looking good, Janee," he said.

She smiled tartly back at him. "You seeing much of Madge these days?" she teased.

"Madge is Juice's girl. Do I look that brave to you?"

Straightening up, he tried to give Washington the black handshake—grasp, knock fists, grasp again—but he screwed it up and endured Chukker's sneer of contempt. Still, the tightly folded hundred dollar bill moved from hand to hand.

Washington folded himself into Janee's car. His knees touched the dashboard. Mickey pushed the passenger door and shut him in.

Janee's hand waved above the car roof to Mickey. The stones in her bracelets and rings glittered with reflected light. She must have had five or six rings on her left hand. Maybe three jangling bracelets, and her boyfriend, Chukker Washington, would leave his best game in the locker room to buy her yet one more bauble.

So the word had gone out. Crazy Mickey Black was giving 15½ points! There were boosters in town who'd take Riverton and 15½ against the Celtics.

Schoolboys robbed their mothers' purses. They raked leaves. They washed cars. They stole from their baby sisters, and if their sisters were too tough to steal from, they took their sisters in as partners. Schoolgirls sold cookies door-to-door and peddled lemonade on the street. Daddy Kane coughed up three yards, triple his biggest bet ever, and though the runner who showed up from Horatio Cabot's cardboard box factory with a near dime in bills said all the money was from line workers, Mickey suspected at least five yards of the action must have come from the pocket of his future father-in-law, old Horatio himself. Grownups sold the family farm and pawned Grandma's silver. You walked down the center stripe of Main Street, you heard the sound of shattering piggy banks. All week, the suckers lined up to wait for him at his booth at Daddy Kane's; they left notes on his windshield; they slid notes into his locker. He was more popular than tutti-frutti on The Fourth of July.

But at the game, just three hours ago, Mickey near puked with fear.

How could a hundred and a promise of a lousy pair of Nikes do the trick? So much could go wrong. Suppose Haverhill went cold? He held more than five hundred in paper slips and well over a thousand in cash. He had not laid off ten cents. For all Danny in Haverhill knew, the Riverton Gymnasium this night was hosting a Girl Scout Bake-Off. Mickey had deliberately created a lopsided book, but if anything went wrong, he was naked, riding it flaming into the earth.

He'd put his neck in Chukker Washington's big hands. If the guy was a moron, how smart did that make Mickey? At the very least, Mickey should have told the guy the point spread, maybe invested a few more dollars on a ref. Jesus. What if Arnie developed a hot hand? What if a Haverhill starter on the opening jump ball came down and broke a leg?

At the Riverton gym, Mickey floated through the crowd with all the confidence of a balloon in a pin factory. Banks of Riverton fans in the wooden fold-away bleachers helicoptered brown towels. In the mezzanine, on the four-lane indoor track, the fifteen members of the marching band rocked the gym with fanfare after fanfare. The place was a cauldron of heat and noise.

The crowd screamed itself silly during warm-up drills. On his toes and peering over a dozen people's shoulders, Mickey saw Mary sitting prim on a floor chair beneath the midcourt game clock. She sat at the timer's table. Her date that night, none other than the team captain, Arnie, started at forward, and Arnie's selected girl of the night received a privileged chair.

What was it about that guy? A totally crap athlete, he stank up the joint, but he started at every sport. And the girls loved him. He wasn't smart, he wasn't talented, he wasn't clever, he was not handsome. Mickey and Arnie took gym class together; Arnie was hung like a hamster. The asshole had freckles all over his back and ass. What was it about the guy? As if 'Toria and Mary weren't enough, Cherry, the DuBois girl with all the money ever printed who went to private school, that hot redhead, Cherry left a wet seat whenever she saw Arnie, too.

Arnie had the blonde; he had the brunette; he had the redhead. What else was there?

Mickey had no time to puzzle it out. The buzzer sounded, and the Riverton Gym, already hushed as a steel mill at noon, rose to decibels to humble a ramjet.

In the first period, Chukker Washington dribbled and spun past three defenders, faking one off his feet and simply stepping around two others, but under the backboard instead of taking the easy lay-up, he whipped a pass to Arnie at the top of the key. Arnie was so startled, the ball smacked him in the face and his nose bled. The ref called time while Arnie sat on the bench and put his head between his knees. Mary tried to help, but the coach scowled at her until Mary skulked away.

Did Chukker manage that, or was the pass just too much for Arnie to handle?

The Riverton boys tried—they really did have heart—but they were outgunned and outclassed. Once Haverhill had a solid lead, the game ebbed and flowed. But if Chukker had left his best game in the locker room, it was damned hard to tell. The knot in Mickey's belly rose to his throat where it lodged like an orange.

At the halftime buzzer, Arnie sank a desperation shot that cut Riverton's deficit to only six. Swish. Perfect. Nothing but net, from half-court no less. His eyes had been closed. If the crowd surging onto the court had given him space enough to fall over, Mickey would have fainted.

The halftime show featured the Riverton cheerleader squad stomping their saddle-shoes like Clysdales, the rubber-soles pounding out an intensifying rhythm for the team chant. Every starter got his due, and they ended with:

> *Arnie, Arnie,*
> *He's our man,*
> *If he can't do it,*
> *No one can!*

Jesus, high school sucked. It seemed to go on forever.

At each player's name, some dork in a white seaman's sweater with a big gold R on his chest tossed Victoria to another dork wearing an identical white sweater. 'Toria sailed though space, her long dark hair whipped around her before she was caught in a perfect split. The two imbeciles playing catch with the heir to Horatio Cabot's fortune had to put a forearm between her thighs and catch her, a palm flat against her waist.

Mickey could imagine a dozen better ways to grab Victoria Cabot.

He stood online to pee and then to get an orangeade. Fluids out; fluids in. The purpose of life was to flush kidneys. "We have your ass this time," someone whispered in his ear while he shook his dick dry, but by the time he turned around, the guy was gone.

If anything, the gym was even more crowded for the second half.

Riverton burst through a paper hoop into the gym. Chukker Washington soared into the air to win the tap clean, and the ball floated to Arnie, who whipped it back to Chukker, who broke away, put on a spinning move, and without a single defender within four feet of him banged a brick off the backboard.

Mickey moved off the doorframe where he'd settled to wait for death, raised a fist, and leaned forward. "My man," he breathed, as the crowd groaned.

Coach threw his towel onto the floor and jumped on it. Thirty seconds later, Washington bounce-passed the ball into the hands of a Haverhill player, a turnover that could happen to anyone having a bad night. And a few minutes after that, after being fouled in a way that should have brought a charge of felonious assault, Washington went to the line for two.

Mickey tracked player stats in his head. It was his business, no hobby. Chukker Washington's free-throw percentage was a luminous 92 percent. But his first try hit the back of the rim and arced back; the second try was an impotent airball. This from a guy who spent days and nights practicing nothing but free-throws, whose father was a coach, who'd grown up on a basketball court, and whose cradle was likely filled with all manner of rubber spheres where other kids had had cushy teddy bears. Screw *Momma*, figure Chukker Washington's first words were *pick and roll*.

As the red numbers on the digital clock raced to zero, Haverhill had the ball, shot, missed, and Mickey forgot to breathe for thirty seconds until Haverhill came out of a scramble with an offensive rebound, scored, and managed to tie up Riverton for eleven seconds before Chukker missed a shot, got his own rebound and missed again, Arnie missed, dribbled out of the paint and held the ball, seemingly unable to pass or shoot despite the fact that all the Haverhill players had their arms at their sides and were shouting, *No foul! No foul!*

Mickey's program near shattered his own femur.

The buzzer sounded. 63-47.

One point more for Riverton, one point less for Haverhill, and Mickey would have been a skydiver kissing an anvil. He'd have needed to sell his car, and never mind Victoria's trust finds, his future would have been about wearing pee-stained boxer shorts, defrosting frozen dinners, and eating off a rickety foldout bridge table in a two-room basement in downtown Buffalo.

But he was Mickey Black, winner.

Hours later, in the warmth of the afterglow, Mickey massaged his leg and sipped his coffee, no milk, three sugars, hot enough to blister an unwary customer's palate. Daddy Kane's coffee was served in honest crockery, cups and saucers that clattered and had to be washed. No cardboard, no Styrofoam, no wooden stirrers. Good, honest coffee. Best in town.

Arnie and Mary, two points of Riverton's eternal triangle, perched beside each other on rotating stools. One strawberry ice-cream soda, two straws. Arnie never had to order it; Daddy Kane started shaking the whipped cream canister as soon as Arnie's car parked out front. The scene was so sweet, Mickey's teeth ached.

Victoria must have been hostess at an exclusive post-game party at the Cabot Mansion. The cheerleaders would be eating crab dip off hundred dollar bills while old man Cabot ogled the pink-with-excitement teenage girls in their short skirts.

Delbart Dellingham jangled the front door sleigh bells, stuck in his head, looked quickly around and vanished. Riverton's puny genius had put up fifty on credit, but Mickey knew he was good for it. Dellingham was smart in ways Mickey did not care to be, so smart, no one knew what he was up to, but not so smart as to pass up 15½. If Mickey ever needed brains, he'd rent Dellingham's.

Mickey pretended not to notice when Madge and Big Juice came in, but he could not stop unreeling his private inventory of mind movies. His memory teased his nose with the rich smell of her when he licked the salt taste from her neck, and his hands tingled with the feel of every recess and curve of her bare back and hips. But it was Madge's walk that broke his resolve not to look. He lifted his eyes to take it in once more: Madge never ambled, never strolled, but went across a room like a heat-seeking missile locked on target.

As Big Juice paused to greet his good buddy, Mickey, Madge and Mickey exchanged a meaningful look. Big Juice would not have noticed a large pink elephant wearing an orange tutu. Mickey wet his lips. Once you've seen a person naked, the mind cannot recall them any other way. Madge's eyes told him all he needed to know about where he would celebrate this night.

Things were winding down when Daddy Kane tried to freshen Mickey's coffee, but Mickey held his palm over the cup, refusing caffeine after 10 o'clock. Daddy said, "You beat me good this time, Mick."

Mickey shrugged. "Dumb luck, Daddy," he said. "Just dumb luck. Have you seen Bughouse? We were supposed to arrange a trip tomorrow."

"This is Riverton," Daddy said. "There are a million things for a healthy, young boy to do. He could be up to anything."

Arnie and Mary were already gone. There had been no sign of Chukker or Janee. Juice ran out the door into the rain to bring his car around for his girl. Briefly free, Madge hurried to Mickey. She hissed, "We have to talk," and rushed again to stand near the door.

Short, darker than most, heavy in the chest, three times smarter than she was willing to let anyone know, Madge was deep in ways that Mickey would never fathom. When he finally did make his life with Victoria, a little something on the side with Madge would not be out of the question. All he'd need to do was persuade Big Juice to enlist in the French Foreign Legion.

Talk meant vigorous fucking followed by a long, boring new theory about the Shadow. Madge was obsessed with that shit. What good could did it do to think on it? The best way not to think was to get naked. He'd have to pretend interest, get laid, sleep, and then start the cycle all over again.

So midnight at the No-Tel Motel it would be. Cabin #3, the cabin closest to the river. He'd surprise her tonight and not ask her to split the cost of the room.

The shower had no mildew and the linens smelled of bleach and boiling, but, best of all, Cabin #3 had a parking space hidden from the highway, no small asset when you considered that Big Juice would not lightly accept Mickey bending his girl over armchairs, setting her ass on sinks, or having her kneel on a pile of cheap pillows. While most Riverton kids believed the library's computers were the work of Satan, Madge was online all the time. She'd once discovered an Internet site about Kundalini Yoga, printed out the pictures, sealed them in a manila envelope with no note, and gave the envelope to Mickey. One picture, "the Oyster," was circled in red.

It had taken her weeks with his hands on her to stretch her hamstrings enough to lock her ankles behind her neck. Madge was one determined girl. If she was resolute about exploring the cosmic reaches of her soul through controlled, hours-long sexual encounters, what else could Mickey do but help out his friend with his available erect dick for her every spiritual journey?

As he stood to leave, the Shadow swiftly attacked him. Mickey shook like a wet dog. To steady himself, he held the lip of the table. The brain freeze felt as if he'd eaten too much ice cream too quickly. The pain centered between his eyes. He fought to keep the details of his life. He would see Madge this night. He gripped the roll of bills in his pocket. The next step had something to do with Danny in Haverhill. That was what the money was for.

Sin was Mickey's ally. His clients had to pay their bets. So, like Madge, the Shadow was his enemy. Unlike Madge, Mickey did not give a shit what it all meant. He just wanted the cash.

Madge had discovered that as long people did not disclose their secrets, they could keep them. "If I blow a goat in a barn, I can keep that memory forever," she had explained, "But if word gets out, in a day or two no one will care. Even I won't remember. It will be as if it never happened."

"Why would you want to blow a goat?" he'd asked.

The memory was interrupted when Daddy said, "I know. I know." Somehow, he had made his way to Daddy's counter. Daddy Kane rang open the register and grudgingly handed Mickey three hundred dollars in wrinkled tens and greasy fives. As Mickey folded the money, the Shadow receded.

Mickey squeezed the bridge of his nose. He quickly snapped Daddy Kane's money under the three red rubber bands that held a fat roll of cash in his pocket, and then stepped out The All-American Burger Shoppe door. Sleighbells jangled behind him. The cold drizzle peppering his face felt fine. He would be all right once he got to the motel. He's have Madge begging for it.

THE MORNING BEFORE THE NIGHT JUICE DIED, CLOSE TO THE SPOT ON THE bank of the Merrimack River where the All-State fullback leapt from the shadows with a baseball bat over his head, just hours before Danny Donnelly near ripped Madge's tits off, Mickey bounced on his toes and blew warm breath into his loose fist. He clapped his hands and pressed them in his armpits while he waited for Madge. His ass leaned on his Honda's fender.

The November morning sun was a white, heatless dime a finger's width above the horizon. Tendrils of gray mist shimmered over the river. Mickey's tan, pleated slacks were too thin to afford him warmth; neither did his yellow Oxford shirt nor his Italian shoes. The shoes had been an irresistible indulgence, rich, supple leather, and the soles so thin Mickey could feel the separate pebbles in the motel driveway.

His fingertips stayed in contact with the roll of bills in his slacks' pocket. Big as a tennis ball, his Chicago bankroll's solidity reassured him; his victory was no dream. Quickly, he inspected all three red rubber bands as he shifted the bills closer to his heart in his jacket's inside breast pocket. He tugged his jacket's broad brass zipper snug to his chin. The Shadow would have hard work to erase any memory of Mickey's money.

Mickey had owned the brown suede and wool jacket since forever. He liked the bulky knit cables and the zipper that never fouled. The threads of the jacket's big patch pockets were unraveling, but there was no way to fix that, and he could find no replacement. The hole in the left pocket allowed loose change to slip to the ground; he kept his car keys in the right. The jacket's elbows were thread worn, too, but the time his mother offered to sew patches on the sleeves he'd sworn at her so hard she'd trembled. What kind of jerk wore patches on his sleeves? Looking good in Riverton was enough of a struggle without his mother making him look like a refugee. Keep the fucking patches off his elbows, dammit.

Invisible from the highway, Madge's mustard yellow beat-up Subaru huddled beneath the trees. Though the transmission sounded like a coffee grinder, she adored the thing. You'd think Riverton was on the Alaskan tundra the way Madge went on about the four-wheel drive. The most difficult surface she drove was gravel. Four-wheel drive was worth fuck on ice. Everyone knew that.

Slow as if awakening, the inky river beyond the cabin flowed sluggish and cranky.

There was no time when Madge had not been in his life. They had not "met"; they had each forever known the other, and at some time neither could recall they'd become lovers. A weird kind of futuristic nostalgia made him sentimental in the present. A soft spot formed in his heart when he imagined the day he would look across a breakfast table and ask Victoria, his adoring wife and mother of his two magnificent children, "Whatever happened to good old Madge?"

The rusted spring of the cabin's wooden screen door squealed open and then clapped shut, a noise like a rifle shot shattering the morning. The room key and its green plastic disk dangled from the doorknob lock.

"Why the fuck don't they take off screen doors in fucking November?" Madge asked. "What in fuck is that about?" Arms pumping, breath a silver cloud before her crimson lips, eyes set on the ground a few feet before her, Madge strode toward Mickey. Her gait made her seem much less pliant than Mickey knew her to be. Her flesh, anyway. Madge was not so pliant when it came to what she wanted. Sex with Madge was an Olympic competition where the scoring judges were thin-lipped, disapproving old-maids from Hungary.

"We should go," Madge said, tip-toeing just enough to peck at his cheek. She groped in her black clutch bag for her car keys. "I'll race you home." Her dark hair had already trapped the aroma of her morning's first cigarette.

"Breakfast?"

She twisted his wrist to look at his watch. "I don't think there is time, Martin," Madge said, and smiled. "We played around a little too much." She bumped her hip against his side.

Not even his mother called him *Martin*. He detested the name, but Madge could roll the R like a purring tigress. He said, "Denny's would be good. It's right up the road."

"I should let my parents see me this morning, dear heart. I have to get home, sneak in, climb the stairs, undress, tuck myself under the blankets, and let my mother wake me."

Mickey's parents had stopped checking on him ever since the day he'd bloodied his father's nose and kicked him three times when he fell to the ground. He covered up, but Mickey still broke the man's rib. How was it the old man's business to ask where Mickey was at night?

"See you at school," she trilled in the schoolgirl sing-song voice Madge affected when she wished to sound carefree. Madge last night had fucked like a randy pagan, but this morning she flirted like blonde Mary doling out ambrosia at a church social.

Madge was half in the Subaru when Mickey stupidly said, "No. No, you won't see me."

Madge quickly stood.

Returning home undetected really was no trick, but Madge never cared for the game she played. Her father managed line production at Cabot Enterprises, and so he was gone long before sunup. As for her mother, Mrs. Klink was oblivious to everything except insipid TV shows. The Klink home had five TVs, the living room, her parents' bedroom, the den, a smaller set with a seven-inch screen and plastic top handle for easy portability that had nevertheless never moved from the kitchen breakfast table, and the inoperable set in Madge's room. The sets were always on. Three were flat screens. Madge's mother drifted from room to room, and though the sets were tuned to different channels, she found continuity among helpful talk show hosts and judges who pronounced justice on combative trailer trash. The television in Madge's own room had ceased working one afternoon when Madge had been cutting herself with an Exacto, and in an inspired moment without first unplugging the thing, she'd looped the television power cord in her hand and neatly sliced it in two. She was disappointed not to receive any electrical shock, but watching the screen implode into permanent darkness had been more satisfying than cutting her arm. The death of the TV ended any risk of Madge becoming like her mother.

"Where are you going?" she asked Mickey. "Come on. Where? Tell momma," she purred.

"Haverhill. There's a guy. Danny. Danny is a guy in Haverhill."

"I'm in." It was no request. Any chance to leave Riverton, even for few hours, was not going to pass her by.

"I thought your parents needed to see you."

"Fuck that. I lied."

Mickey laughed. "You don't even know why I am going. Come on, Madge. Let's just get breakfast. I need to keep my strength up."

Madge hated Riverton. Riverton was so fucking predictable, the place totally creeped her out. Arnie was forever cool, Mary forever a giggly flirt. 'Toria was whimsical, Juice jealous. Delbart was smart, Mickey crafty. Bughouse was lazy, Chukker an athlete. Cherry a flirt, and Madge...Madge was a cutter. She could slice and dice herself into quarter-inch cubes and nothing in Riverton would ever surprise her. It was as if their lives had been written with a two-page script.

She would die this day if she did not go to Haverhill. Sure, she could drive to the drab mill town any time she wanted, but traveling with Mickey, something might happen. How could she miss it?

"Why are you seeing this Danny?"

"You don't want to know."

Madge sidled next to him until their hips pressed together. Mickey thought she'd try to persuade him with a kiss and a little sweet-talk, so he grimaced with surprise and pain when she gripped his balls through his thin slacks.

Her dark eyes looked up into his as she whispered, "Don't make me hurt you, lover."

"Jesus, Madge," he groaned.

She twisted her grip. Mickey winced. Slacks were one of the things Madge liked about Mickey. He dressed like a tango-dancing pimp. Mickey never wore jeans. She did not think he owned sneakers.

"It's just business. Madge, that hurts." His eyes watered. He placed his hands on her shoulders, but Madge did not flinch.

"What kind of business?" Mickey was developing an erection despite his pain, maybe because of it. Madge filed that fact away for further investigation another day. She repeated, "What kind of business, Mickey? Talk to me, lover, or I swear you'll have to untie a knot in your dick."

"Danny is a guy. In Haverhill. He came to Riverton. Maybe twice." Mickey was gasping. He spoke quickly. "I can't remember. Daddy Kane might have put us next to each other. You know. Business. My business."

Madge held tight. "Martin, now tell momma. Does this have to do with last night's basketball game?" Juice said Mickey had made money on the game. Juice said he himself had lost three whole dollars. He'd ruefully noted he'd need to mow a lot of lawns to earn that kind of money again.

Mickey lifted his left leg and placed it slowly down again. There was no relieving his pain. "Danny said if I ever came into money I should look him up."

Madge loosened but did not release her grip. "So this is illegal?"

"Maybe. Yes, I don't know. Probably." Mickey winced as he squirmed.

Her nostrils flared. The scent of danger was in the air. She flexed her grip. "How much money?" she asked. Mickey hesitated. Madge squeezed and repeated, "How much?"

Mickey gasped, "A thousand buy-in. Two hundred for Danny. It's an access fee."

"Twelve hundred dollars?" Startled, she released him.

Mickey exhaled.

"You have twelve hundred dollars? Holy fuck! How much did you make on the game?"

"Leave it alone, Madge."

"Just tell me you did not steal it. If you stole it, they'll be after us."

"I did not steal it."

Madge gnawed her lip. There was no way she would be left behind. Not this day. "I'm going with you. I have to get out of Riverton. The place makes me nuts." She came near to sharing with him her last night's newest terrors, but this was neither the time nor place to talk about Tantric yoga, mass psychosis, or her yearning to suffer. Two hours earlier she'd had Mickey's dick in her mouth, and, dammit, that ought to be worth a little trust.

Mickey walked around his car to the driver's side. She stayed beside him. "Madge, it's not you. You know how I feel about you."

Now this was just so much bullshit. She knew exactly how Mickey felt about her, and neither of them could pretend that was much. If Mickey had a heart, it was home in a bureau drawer, and there was no telling from whose chest it had been cut. She had even less feelings for him. For a girl who was going places, feelings were bubblefuck.

Mickey said, "What about Juice? I'd hate to pick my teeth up off the sidewalk."

She mimicked him. "'What about Juice?' 'What about Juice?' Fuck Juice. Just fuck him."

"Do *you* fuck him?"

"Not like you, lover," Madge said and lifted her knee into Mickey's hamstring. His leg went numb.

Madge could pound him hollow, he'd never lift a hand. Boys in Riverton were made harmless. Madge never saw a girl in Riverton with so much as a bruise, if you did not count the purple marks on her own thighs, and those were hardly from malice. Besides, her bruises vanished in hours.

Madge played her last, best card. "Baby cakes, tell momma true. Did you enjoy last night?" she asked.

Mickey toed gravel. "Don't be like that."

"*Fuck*. How should I be?" She stamped her foot. "Mickey, I have got to get out of Riverton. To-*day*." She stamped her foot a second time. "How plain can I make it for you? I will fucking scream all fucking day that Martin Mickey Black raped me. I swear to God I will. You'll have Juice so far up your ass that when you yawn, people will say, 'Hi, Juice.'" She stamped her foot a third time and inhaled to release her first scream. They'd hear her in Lawrence. They'd hear her in Boston. They'd hear her in the fucking Boston Garden while the Bruins skated in overtime.

"You can't smoke in the car," Mickey said quickly.

His shoulders sagged a little.

The front seat of Mickey's car was too far forward and was grimy beneath a McDonald's fries cup, several grease-smeared burger wraps, a crumpled newspaper, nameless crud, and a half Butterfinger. She swept the garbage onto the ground; the greasy wrapper fluttered toward the trees. She'd have taken the stuff to the cabin's trash, but Madge Klink was no fool: not only was Mickey capable of running out on her, he'd laugh about it when she next saw him. So fuck being a litterbug. She'd live with it.

Mickey slid behind the Honda's wheel. "Do you want to go home and change?"

Her crotch was sodden and grungy. For warmth, Madge wore pantyhose but nothing else beneath her jeans. She'd washed herself and smoked that blissful first cig of the morning while Mickey waited for her, but she was funkier than a forest critter in estrus. If she went home to bathe, Mickey would leave her flat. She said, "Let's just go. We can pick up my car when we come back."

Mickey gunned his engine. Gravel spit into the wheel well like buckshot into a steel drum.

"You are going the wrong way, scumbag," she said.

"Bughouse."

"Bughouse? What about fucking Bughouse?"

"Bughouse is coming with us. He's like my advisor. We're going to scoop up Bughouse."

"We don't need fucking Bughouse."

Mickey looked at her while he drove. "What is this 'we' shit? You are along for a joyride. That's it. There is no 'we.' There is you; there is me. You and me are taking a drive together, but when we get anywhere, there is no 'we.'"

"All right," she said. Why fight this? She agreed in principle. When it came to her and Mickey, there was no "we."

He must have thought she gave a shit, because he added, "I am serious, Madge. Don't fuck this up." He patted his chest where the bankroll nestled in his jacket's inside breast pocket. "I need to show Danny the color of my money, so if I say Bughouse is coming along, Bughouse is coming along."

"Bughouse is your protection?"

"Yeah."

She stifled her laughter. "Oh, that's fucking great. Just fucking super. I feel all warm inside."

When Mickey throttled down in Riverton, Madge slid off the seat and ducked below the glove box. Better to be out of sight than be seen by Juice.

"That's my smart girl," Mickey said, and patted her head.

Looking up from the Honda's floor, if she could have bitten his hand, she'd have drawn blood.

The only way for Bughouse to climb the hill before the final three blocks to Riverton High was to stand on the pedals. His bike was too small for him. Bughouse bent forward from the waist to keep his hands on the grips, his spine parallel to the earth and the bike's banana seat. Weight on his wrists, bony ass in the air, Bughouse felt like a fool.

Knowing that made it no less humiliating.

His book bag was empty except for a ham sandwich on white, but the nylon bag's weight slopped over to one side or the other of his back, chafing his neck as he strained to make just one more rotation of the crank to carry him just two feet more.

The hill was torture. He climbed it every day. His back stiff from where he'd struck the ground when he fell from the maple tree in Mary Swenson's backyard made it no easier.

Mary had known all along! The fact raised whole new universes of thought. Was her little show for him? Or did Mary just like to show herself? Women who liked to show themselves were all over the Internet, but they had elaborate tattoos, which flawless Mary most definitely did not. Her immaculate flesh was unsullied. He thought he knew her; he did not.

Either that or he did not understand women, an explanation that seemed fully possible.

The deep stirring began in his groin. Why would struggling and sweating to muscle the bicycle up the hill change anything? His ever-ready monkey glands were independent of such factors as fatigue, injury, or the terrain that lay between him and Riverton High. His dick lived in a separate world.

Bughouse wore heavy jeans to hide his perpetual erection. He never raised his hand in school—not that he did not know the answers to Miss Grimley's questions, but Grimley's iron-clad rule was that a student who spoke was a student who stood. He couldn't. He just couldn't. It was too humiliating. He looked like a scarecrow with a police flashlight strapped to its thigh.

Battered and sore, soaked and cold, last night Bughouse had crawled into bed, but sleep never joined him. As soon as he closed his eyes, a willing, wanton, depraved red-lipped Mary haunted him. He'd drowse, but then awaken, humping his pillow. In his fantasy, Mary had no body part he did not penetrate. She bent to his will in ways that were anatomically impossible. At four in the morning, he'd awakened with a third sticky mess in his boxer shorts. He groaned and rolled to his hip. Lying still while his heart slowed, he tried to recapture his lurid hallucinations, so superior to grim reality. It was like trying to embrace smoke.

Showering before breakfast, he'd grown hard again. He turned off the hot water and stood shivering until he his boner subsided, but as soon as he began to towel himself dry, he had to touch himself. So he painfully bent himself to get into his jeans, hoping he would not have to have to strap his dick down to his leg with the Red Cross adhesive tape again. The last time he'd done that, he'd limped through the halls of Riverton High as if his knee was broken, and for two days he'd suffered a rash.

The strain of pedaling raised the taste of his strawberry Pop-Tart breakfast to his lips. A car passed loaded with sophomores who shouted, "Loser!" and one kid in the rear seat opened the window and bared his ass at Bughouse. Bughouse lifted his middle finger. The gesture cost him forward momentum and the bike toppled. Bughouse's shaky legs propped him enough to prevent his completely keeling over. He straddled the fallen bicycle and cursed, savagely kicking his bike. The pedal dug a divot in the soft ground; the bike itself hardly budged.

That was when Mickey pulled up beside him. He leaned across the seat, the passenger window rolled down. "Need a ride?" he asked.

"No, Mick. Why would I want a ride? I am having a terrific time here," Bughouse answered. He kicked the bicycle again; his sneaker came away with a grease spot on the toe.

Mickey grinned. "Ditch classes today," he said. "Daytrip to Haverhill. I'd have told you last night, old buddy, which was why I waited for you at Daddy's. Where were you?"

"Busy," Bughouse mumbled. "Sorry."

"Oh, you're a busy guy, you are."

"When are you going?"

"Right now. Breakfast first, and if we boogie maybe a stop at the Haverhill mall before some business in beautiful, downtown Haverhill. What would you say to breakfast, Bug?"

After a Pop-Tart, real food had appeal. Bughouse thought about Miss Grimley, the stupid homework he had not done, and this day's lesson, the causes of World War I. Bughouse was pretty sure it was every day's lesson, but for reasons he did not like to think about, he was unsure of that. The best Bughouse could make out, 100 years ago, older guys conspired to kill younger guys by compelling them to charge into machine guns, the most lethal technology available. To keep it interesting, they made them do this through clouds of poison gas across muddy fields strung with barbed wire. He'd figured it out by playing a computer game where he'd died forty-seven times before leaping into a trench and bayoneting the Kaiser. Searching for game clues, he'd inspected textbook pictures of trenches and doughboys. They'd been real people who when they died did not rise to fight again.

History was nothing more than a litany of the dead.

He said, "I could check out some music at the mall. Not that I have any money. Just look."

"No sweat. I can spot you," Mickey said. "What do you want to do with the bike?"

Bughouse grasped the car handle. "Anyone steals it, deserves the thing."

Mickey laughed and straightened up behind the steering wheel. "You'll need to ride in the back," he said. The car door swung open. Madge was huddled in a ball under the glove compartment.

Maybe Madge had a dozen pairs of jeans and always wore men's white Oxford shirts, the same outfit he'd seen her in yesterday at lunch. She also wore the same woolen black jacket with the white leather sleeves she'd worn, a team jacket with no school logo. It was possible she just liked to wear the same clothes two days in a row. Why not? Bughouse did it all the time.

But Bughouse was not as stupid as a World War I general. Given sufficient data, he could draw a conclusion. Mickey's threads were also far from crisp. Maybe Mickey and Madge had been together since yesterday; maybe not. Maybe someone was getting laid, which meant even Bughouse could have hope.

Bughouse kept the few friends he had because he kept his mouth shut.

"How're you doing, Madge?" he asked, as if seeing the girl hugging her own knees at Mickey's feet was ordinary. "Looking good."

"For fuck's sake, Bughouse, get in the fucking car. Is Juice anywhere?"

Bughouse shaded his eyes and rotated 360 degrees, slow as a lighthouse. "Nope. No Big Juice in sight. You want I should shout his name?"

"Fuck. Just get in. Fuck."

Mickey laughed at Madge's panic. *What could Juice do? Really?* he thought.

Folding like a penknife, Bughouse's head touched the roof in the rear seat. He slipped his shoulders from his book bag harness and he put his legs up. Amputees might sit comfortably in the rear seats of Honda Accords, but gangling boys like Bughouse folded like safety pins.

Out of town, Madge uncoiled to ride shotgun. She swiveled Mickey's rearview mirror to check herself out. She blew up at her bangs, but her hair fell immediately again across her eyes. "Fuck," Madge said.

She applied a little lipstick. The faint aroma of cosmetics wafted back to Bughouse. Madge reddened her ripe lips; staring at her, Bughouse had to cross his legs, hard.

Denny's was mostly silent, filled by tired waitresses happy to have jobs, but hating their work. Their eyes betrayed their exasperation: why wasn't it possible to be hired and go straight to payday without all the stupid labor in between?

Bughouse ate, Mickey drank too much coffee, and Madge slouched so low on the bar seat of a Denny's booth, she could see Bughouse and Mickey's knees beneath the table. The final remnant of Bughouse's Triple Slam breakfast was a thin yellow smear of yolk left from three eggs sunny-side up, three strips of bacon, three sausages, three slices of rye toast and a mountain of ketchup-smothered home fries. Now he eyed Madge's leftovers.

Bughouse must have had a tapeworm. Where in fuck could he put it all? Staring at him under the table as she had so many times before in school, she wondered again if the size of the package in Bughouse's pants meant he stored all that food in his dick. Did he stuff his briefs with sweat socks?

Mickey shared a little of his plans, so vague, Madge did not know whether to cry or punch his face. How did she get hooked up with this short stack?

"Danny has connections. He told me to look him up if I ever scored."

"What connections? This Danny. He's just a nice guy who can't wait to give you money?"

The itch in her crotch was making Madge a bitchy skeptic. The world would always disappoint her; she knew that. Last night in a seedy motel she'd been doing a boy she only mildly liked; at the moment she lacked any underwear other than pantyhose, and she was developing an itch that promised yeast in her future. She disgusted herself. No one could confuse Madge Klink with a tragic heroine.

"Why does this Danny need you?"

Bughouse did not look up from his food when he said, "Volume," through eggs and toast. "Doesn't matter what the deal is, as long he does more business, he makes more profit."

Mickey patted Bughouse's shoulder.

Fuck. Bughouse was smart. Money and dicks were similar. No one ever had too much money; no one ever had too much dick.

Madge drained the last of her bitter coffee. There were at least twelve hundred reasons to think Mickey knew what he was doing. She'd thought of taking his money and just leaving, though she had not gone so far as to think how she'd get Mickey to release the cash. Blow him, watch him sleep, take his money and drive? She was not about to blow Bughouse, too. If the package in his jeans was what she imagined, she'd need two hands and she'd still break her jaw. The real problem was Bughouse himself. It would be like doing her kid brother, if she had one. How far could a girl travel from Riverton with twelve hundred dollars? What would she do if she ran out of money before she saw everything in the world there was to see? The idea of going down on a man every time she needed bus fare was pathetic.

"What do you say, boys and girls? We're out of Riverton. A little shopping?" Mickey looked at the time; no one in Haverhill got out of bed until noon.

They waited while Bughouse sopped up the last of his eggs and ketchup. Then Mickey drove them to the Haverhill mall, Madge hanging out the passenger window to honor her promise not to smoke in Mickey's car. Not smoking after breakfast was out of the question. She must have looked like a happy mutt with a cigarette.

She smoked another as they walked from the car across the mall parking lot. Was this the feel of real danger? Would Anna Karenina have worried about nicotine cravings and yeast infections after eggs and pancakes with two boys who never needed to shave?

Inside the mall, they split up.

Twenty dollars of Mickey's money in his pocket, Bughouse found a music store. He flipped through racks of budget CDs, used crap. No one bought CDs anymore. Daddy Kane had a jukebox filled with vinyl records. *Horses* by Patti Smith stopped him. It was an old recording, probably vinyl once long ago. Shag-haired, sunken-cheeked, thick-lipped, Smith stared defiantly into the camera, an odd mixture of pride and vulnerability. She wore a man's shirt, black slacks, and black suspenders. The photo was by some guy named Mapplethorpe. This Patti Smith was not sexy, just the opposite: a woman of frenetic elbows. How could a photograph make a person look as if she might explode? She was a serious artist. He could tell. Serious artists were neither sexy nor well fed, but desperate and obsessed.

The cashier cracked gum. Maybe it was the red platform heels, but she was taller than Bughouse. The left half of her head had been shaved to the scalp where she had a geometric blue tattoo. Her scalp, it must have hurt like hell. Maybe she, too, was desperate and ob-sessed. Her remaining hair was an unnatural black. Three small metal posts topped by three small metal balls pierced the register girl's eyebrow, a new-moon crescent went through her nose, and when she said, "Thank you," the gold ball through her tongue clicked against her teeth. "I like this old shit, too," she said. "But I really like emo. I could be, like, a suicide girl."

Bughouse could not speak. His mind-movies detailed the uses of a gold ball in the girl's tongue. No girl in Riverton had anything like it. He had to walk pigeon-toed to hide the bulge in his jeans. He never scooped up his change. Mickey's change. Someone's. He dived into a bookstore.

At the other end of the mall, Madge lingered a long while in front of Frederick's of Hol-lywood, gathering the courage she'd need to enter. It was just a goddam pair of panties, she told herself. If Mary or Victoria had been with her, they'd have giggled and challenged each other into buying something slutty, maybe the red satin with black lace peek-a-boo bra. But wouldn't taffeta be irritating? Of course, the point would not be for a woman to wear it for very long, so what the fuck would Mary or Vicky do with it? What would Mickey do if she wore that honest-to-god white lace garter belt with the magenta ribbon stays? Fuck. What was the deal with men and underwear, anyway? It was underwear, not fucking gift-wrap-ping. Tarting up was a waste of time. The point was the fucking.

With no girlfriend to crank her courage, Madge did as she always did, which was to draw a deep breath and just go forward. Do it. Oh, just do it.

The saleswoman was decrepit and old, maybe 35. When Madge said, "Cotton pant-ies," beneath her false lashes, the saleswoman's eyes glazed. "Maybe you should go to Sears, dear," she said.

Madge forced herself to laugh, a lame attempt to appear as though she had made a deliberate joke. The saleswoman's smug superiority made Madge spend far too much on two thongs, one crimson and the other electric blue. She used her father's credit card, risking the possibility he'd look at the bill and she'd be caught. If the Shadow did not swallow the charge and have it vanish. She shrugged: tomorrow's problem could wait for tomorrow's solution. Right now, her pussy itched.

In a stall in the Ladies' Room near the food court, Madge peeled off her jeans and panty-hose. She waited until she was alone. A cig was out of the question. Smoke alarms were everywhere. Nude from the waist down, she dashed to a sink and splashed her crotch with cold water, then dried herself with coarse brown paper. After she stepped into the blue thong and drew up her jeans, she balled her soiled pantyhose into a sodden mass and pushed it into the wastepaper basket. Then she crumpled the red thong and pushed it into her back pocket so she could ditch the plastic Frederick's shopping bag. Wearing a thong felt like something was trying to crawl up her behind, but she'd get used to ass-floss.

Her profile in the Ladies Room mirror showed no panty line. Thongs might have their uses. A little discomfort was worth her perfect ass. Not as great as Mary's, maybe, but Madge's ass was nothing to be ashamed of, world-class at least.

At an isolated table in the food court on the second floor at the mall's center, Mickey idly observed young mothers and their baby strollers. The mall's carousel played Dutch organ music, and Mickey's toes tapped the rhythm. In Sports Shoes storefront he'd seen Washington's high-top Nikes. $175, but Mickey held off. Why invite questions from Bughouse and Madge. *Size 12 basketball shoes? What for?*

The real challenge was how to greet Danny. Suppose the guy had forgotten who he was. Since Mickey could not remember when they last met, easy confidence would be his best bet. Self-confidence bred confidence in others. He's read that somewhere. Confidence was contagious. He could do confidence.

When he saw Madge carrying a small package dart into the lavatory corridor, he checked his watch. When he looked up, Bughouse popped out of the air. It was as if the guy dropped silently from the ceiling. Spooky.

Bughouse was clammy-pale, perspiring, and wide-eyed.

"Where's Madge?" Bughouse stammered.

Mickey jerked his thumb over his shoulder, and as if by magical summons, Madge herself emerged, without the package. "Sit down, Bug, you look as though you've seen a ghost."

Like a kid who needed to pee, Bughouse danced from one foot to the other.

Madge drew close and said, "Can we get the fuck out of here? Bughouse, you have that lean and hungry look, but you can't need lunch yet. It's not possible."

"Look at this," he said. Bughouse slapped a magazine onto the table.

Thick, printed on rough, porous paper, more of a booklet than a magazine, the garish cover was printed in bold reds, yellows and blues. *The Archie Digest: America's Favorite Typical Teenager.*

Mickey fanned the pages. "It's a comic book. What's your point?" He tossed the thing to Madge. The cheap paper fluttered like an injured sparrow.

Beads of perspiration trickled from the edge of Bughouse's scalp to creep down to his jaw. "Look at it. Look! They *sell* these. It's about *us.*"

Madge studied the cover. A red-haired character named Archie was strutting with a blonde girl named Betty on one arm and a brunette named Veronica on the other. The girls had impossibly full hair. They'd need to spend hours brushing it out with blow dryers. They'd have time for nothing else. Betty had a ponytail; Veronica had a pageboy, though hair that long would never hold a flip without lacquer and sleepless nights taped around beer cans. Who would endure it? For what? The muscles of Madge's cheek twitched, trying to imitate their broad smiles, their teeth a sheer white wall in grotesquely distorted mouths. The biggest grin was Archie's. Why not? He carried outstanding pussy on each arm. In the foreground, to make the comic even stupider, they'd put in a furrow-browed character named Big Moose. Anyone named Moose had to be an idiot, so, sure, he said, "Duh, that's what Archie calls a double date!" A dark-haired character named Reggie slapped both sides of his own head, an act that generated expanding concentric circles that Madge supposed meant chagrin or envy. Reggie's black hair was perfect.

That was the entire joke. The whole fucking thing. A single unfunny panel, all for "double date." It was so sappy that Madge was embarrassed. Life was more earnest than this; on the rare occasion when life became odd or funny, well, it was funnier than this.

Insipid shit trickled through her life. For a woman with acute sensibilities, life should be more than a season in an unventilated sewer. Why in fuck was Bughouse personally delivering her more shit?

She said, "You have to admit, Martin, that Reggie goon has hair slick as yours." She thought of running her fingers against Mickey's part. If Mickey had looked as much like a gigolo from Paraguay as this cartoon Reggie did, Madge would have gone down on him on the mall's food-court carousel. He could pick his pony. She'd do his zipper with her teeth, no hands. She asked, "Who is this pencil-neck Jughead pecker-head?"

"That's *me*," Bughouse said. "Don't you see it?"

Mickey groaned. "Come on, Bughouse. That's impossible." He snatched the booklet back from Madge and flipped the pages. Nothing but short crappy jokes where the Reggie character took it in the neck. It was bullshit, was what it was, but being a careful man, one who respected Bughouse's instincts, Mickey searched for any stray panel that showed a Chukker-Washington-type talking with the Reggie-dude about basketball. Mickey found a black character, all right, but he went in and out of the plot so quickly he did not even get a name.

In panel after panel, the characters yakked about the redhead, Archie. At least that made sense; Archie was the title character. Just like Arnie, Archie seemed always to triumph. Either the book was a preposterous string of coincidences, or Mickey, Bughouse, Madge and the rest of the Riverton gang were imaginary, someone's bad idea of what life was supposed to be like.

The pain of a brain freeze formed in the center of his forehead. He had had no ice cream.

Madge snatched the comic from Mickey's hands. She flipped wildly through the pages in search of a waif-like, tragic, devoted girl who cared for Big Moose, but all she could find was a total woose named Midge who passed in and out of two or three panels with a cheerful wave. Her entire role was to wave as she went by. What kind of life was that? Where in fuck was she going? This cartoon Midge wouldn't fuck a rock star, much less this Reggie creep. Who in her right mind would fuck anyone named "Moose?" He was drawn so muscle-bound that he had to be taking 'roids; his balls would be shriveled to raisins. There was no panel of this Midge cutting herself, either; fat chance of that. And thank God. It would not do to have her most private secret become public. If it did, the Shadow would descend, Madge would forget, her Exacto knife retired, and then she would be done, unable forever to feel alive.

She grew dizzy. Without letting the boys know about her sudden vertigo, she sat and gently placed the book facedown on the table. Mickey abruptly flicked the damned comic back to Bughouse.

It hit Bughouse's chest and dropped open on the floor to a page where Jughead had fallen down the stairs of Riverton High; he was being scowled at by Miss Grimley. But the school was called Riverdale and the teacher's name was Grundy. Jughead landed on his head. Little blue birdies circled him.

Bughouse moaned. This trip to Haverhill had become a nightmare.

Bughouse's voice sank an octave. "There's a whole rack of these at the bookstore. One of them is named *Jughead.*"

Mickey rubbed the bridge of his nose. His brain freeze was radiating outward, nearly encasing his skull. "Buy them all. Autograph them. Give them away."

"Is there a *Midge* comic?" Madge asked, already knowing there would not be. She'd never be a main character. Was the Midge in the book smart? Did she ride a motorcycle, go ice climbing or skydive, or do anything thrilling? Had she been to Amsterdam or Karachi? Did she say *fuck* a lot? Did she give good head? Was she noble? Heroic? Did the fake Midge in the fake Riverdale suffer? Or was her happiness as phony as Madge's own? Madge lacked the nerve to search the pages again. The characters all kept their clothes on. What would there be to see? The spot on her arm where she most liked to cut prickled and itched from a million flea bites. Her skin wanted to slough off. Maybe she could return to the lavatory with one of the plastic serrated knives from the pizza stand. They were dull, but her need to be alone with her blood was raging. If she had her Exacto with her, in half an hour she'd peel herself down to a fucking anatomy chart.

Cripes, you set Bughouse loose for an hour in the mall, and he came back with a metaphysical can of worms.

Trembling, Bughouse bent to pick up the book. He held it between two fingers and dropped it into his book bag to nestle against the Patti Smith CD and his Saran-wrapped ham on white with yellow mustard. He'd had no lettuce when he packed his school lunch. What earthly use was a ham sandwich without lettuce?

"Maybe we should get going," Madge said, relieved that the magazine was out of sight, but already scheming to steal it from Bughouse.

"We should go this way." Bughouse pointed to the far exit. "I shoplifted the book. I think the bookstore guy saw me."

"Oh shit, Bughouse," Mickey said. The pain in his head was subsiding. He could think again.

"Why in fuck would you do that?" Madge breathed, thrilled by his audacity. Shoplifting? Why had she never tried shoplifting? Why pay for thong underwear if it fit so neatly in a pocket?

"I had to show it to you. I am sorry, Mick. I screwed up. When I bought the CD, I forgot my change."

Mickey made fast decisions. Suppose the mall's rent-a-goon was on the way? *Hi, Danny. Good to see you again. We just were busted by the Haverhill cops and so we came straight here. Do you think they are after us?* The risk was too great.

Mickey gripped Bughouse's upper arm, took Madge's hand, and force marched them to an exit. Outside, under thickening clouds, they circled back around the parking lot to Mickey's black Honda.

They took off, three shoplifting desperadoes who'd scored a comic book and carried a substantial roll of cash.

The business-minded Puritans who founded Haverhill in 1640 purchased the land near a bend in the river from the Pentucket Indians for 3 pounds, 10 shillings, a fair deal all around, especially so for the Indians whose notion of private property did not exist. One may as well sell the sky. They bought rum and flintlocks and laughed themselves giddy at the stupid Europeans.

Roughly fifty years later, one Hannah Duston, a week after giving birth to her twelfth child, Martha, was taken from her isolated home by a party of roving Indians who, by all reports, were roaring drunk. They dashed the infant's brains out on a rock and then turned to the more earnest business of gang-raping Hannah. This proved so satisfactory a diversion that, rather than simply cutting her throat and discarding the woman, a war party of braves dedicated to theft and speed chose to take her with them on a 45-mile forced march upstream to the future site of Concord, New Hampshire. After two nights of further revelry, Haverhill's daughter awakened to find herself unguarded, unbound, and surrounded by several snoring and farting heathens. A lesser woman might have fled; Mother Duston, however, bludgeoned each of her ten captors to death.

So goes the official tale, but skeptics wonder. How or why would the Indians leave their prisoner unguarded and unbound within handy distance of a deadly weapon while they slept? Consider: a tomahawk is little more than a pointed rock strapped by leather to a hefty stick. A glancing blow would certainly awaken a victim; he might cry out. Any alarm would surely have led the Indians to decide that Mother Duston was far more trouble than she was worth, and they'd have cut her throat before rolling over to complete a good night's sleep. Unguarded and unbound; why would they have trusted her?

The story has it that despite the risk of discovery, death, and further depravations, Hannah stayed her course. She did not simply flee. Vengeance steeled her unerring arm. It rose and fell ten times, each blow instantly lethal, each blow delivered in total silence, each blow crushing another Indian's skull as easily as a robin's egg.

Ten murders, ten blows. No sleep disturbed except by Death itself.

Though mass murder and escape might be deemed sufficient for most, Mother Duston was from Haverhill.

With no tool sharper than an edged flint, humble Christian Mother Duston then ripped flesh and hair from the heads of ten corpses. Butchery would be among the valued skills of any colonial woman, and the Puritan town fathers of Haverhill who were civilizing the New World with smallpox and Christianity paid a goodly bounty for scalps of the indigent population—man, woman or child. Practical Mother Duston was not one to leave easy money moldering on the forest floor.

A cynic might wonder if Mother Duston's ruthlessness was necessary to still any suspicion that in a fit of postpartum depression she'd skedaddled into the bush with an itinerant band of ordinarily peaceful savages for a dance and a howl. Perhaps ruthlessness ran in the family; her sister, one Elizabeth Emerson, was hanged for sewing her illegitimate twin infant daughters into a bag and burying them in her backyard days after giving birth to them, unassisted. Who can guess at the madness that burgeoned within hardy pioneer women scratching a brutish life from the ground in the shadow of the ever-brooding, virgin forests of North America? With a smirk and a leer, only a filthy revisionist would reduce Hannah's heroism to a sordid sexual diversion followed by guilt, remorse, and mass murder.

Whatever the source of her courage, mottled with gore, Mother Duston floated downstream to Haverhill in a stolen canoe, ten bloody scalps hanging from a tree limb propped in the bow, the irrefutable evidence of her courage and virtue.

The temperament of all Haverhill women forever after was set. Enshrined at the center of modern Haverhill, the first statue in the New World erected to a woman still stands. Mother Duston of Haverhill holds a raised axe in one hand, the sleeping winos nearby safe in her long shadow. Pigeons show unrelenting affection.

Danny Donnelly knew little of Haverhill's history, less than most of his fellow citizens, in fact, though since his boyhood he'd shared the almost universal impulse of the populace to want to get out of town. George Washington came and went. Louis B. Mayer came and went. R.H. Macy came, organized an ill-attended parade on Thanksgiving Day, and then went to New York City. The entire shoe industry began its Haverhill exodus after World War II, leaving only chronic unemployment and toxic soil in Shoe Town America. Departing Haverhill was an ongoing, honorable tradition.

Danny Donnelly, however, would never budge. One thing and another, though his Irish heart longed to wander, he was mired in Haverhill to stay. He'd sunk roots early in life.

Danny was 27, and his loving wife, Margaret Mary Theresa Harrington Donnelly, was heavy with child, gestating their third brat in five years. She prayed daily for a daughter, a girl to be christened Charity, thus completing the Trifecta begun by her previous issue, Faith and Hope. The gender of the next Donnelly offspring was a matter of prayer only because Margaret Mary liked surprises; she instructed her obstetrician to keep the cursed sonogram pictures to herself. If the Lord in His wisdom had wanted mothers to know the sex of the children growing in their wombs, He'd send messages on the wings of doves.

Truth, Danny would not have minded a boy. A son might accompany him to the occasional Sox opener, though he'd knock down any man who suggested he did not love his girls with a full heart.

Sadly, Danny Donnelly saw no winning outcome to this pregnancy.

A boy, and his beloved Margaret Mary would insist on a fourth attempt to birth a third girl; "Faith, Hope, and Danny Jr." had insufficient rhythm to it. A girl, the gates of pleasure might be closed to him forever after. Not only would he never know a son, his sex life might take a certain turn for the worse. Not exactly a modern girl, Margaret Mary believed the road to Hell was paved with birth control pills and condoms. Rather than ruin her girlish figure with uncontrolled pregnancies, she'd opted for her own method, which was to take a small square of black paper, place it on her left knee, and hold it in place with her right.

Ryan, who owned and operated The Clip Joint, the one-man barbershop in the shadow of the rail station on the line that ran to Boston was merciless. "You're a button-hole maker, you are," Ryan said. He brushed hair from a customer's shoulders.

Ryan was handsome, trim, and from his years on the beaches of Plum Island was tan as George Hamilton. When teenage girls walked by the store, Ryan favored them with a dirty remark, and if any of them were stupid enough to gawk into the shop window, they unfailingly received the full tongue waggle. The Clip Joint's walls and mirrors were pasted with autographed record album covers and musicians' publicity photos. Hung above the antique cash register was Ryan's prize possession, a tiny perfume vial taped to a handsomely engraved, notarized certificate that testified to the authenticity of the vial's contents: a droplet of Elvis Presley's sweat shed in Memphis, Tennessee, on July 25, 1957. Ryan would not have traded it for a bit of the True Cross nor a thimble of the Savior's Blood. Indeed, a customer expressing doubt about the fluid's authenticity might leave with uneven sideburns and hair down his shirt. In extreme cases, insistent disparaging remarks about the King's perspiration were quieted by a scissor accidentally closing on an earlobe.

Danny was one of the few people in town who knew that Ryan was Ryan's surname and that he hated being called Francis, Frank, Frankie or anything else that referred to some fucking hippie saint who spoke to birds because his mother had liked a certain crooner from Hoboken. "Just Ryan," he said. "Like Fabian, Sting, or Madonna."

In the backroom of the overheated barbershop, in addition to the music memorabilia, Ryan stored tangles of assorted power tools, radios, stereo players and the occasional small flat-screen television, the kinds of objects that fell off delivery trucks. They moved quickly, however, never gathering much dust. It was a well known fact that laborers committed miscounts that resulted in minor discrepancies on bills of lading. Such goods made their way either to the far side of the moon or to Ryan's storeroom. Fifty cases of scotch might in the hurly-burly of commerce be discovered to have been only 49, a fact that sent no merchant into the spiral of bankruptcy. Good business practice built in an allowance for breakage. Prices were set accordingly. Where was the harm?

Since Ryan never moved anything worth more than a few hundred dollars, and since Ryan never accepted merchandise from anyone who knew the uses of a crowbar, thus excluding unsavory B & E men, not even the cops who came in for a trim troubled Ryan. In fact, a few of Haverhill's finest had been known to exit The Clip Joint with a green fifth of Tullamore Dew tucked in a deep pocket. Law enforcement was a noble calling, but good Irish whiskey was altogether something else again.

The kid who near one o'clock ran through the glass door of The Clip Joint needed no haircut. Trying to remain invisible, Danny peeped over the upper edge of his *Herald*. The kid looked as if Danny should know him; then it came to him, Mickey something-or-other, a squirt from Riverton. Years ago, Danny had journeyed to Riverton because Aunt Sosha, his employer, had a friend who had a friend, a guy named Kane who put the occasional nickel on a football game, but the total play in that town was so small that she'd asked the guy to recommend someone to be her Riverton bagman. Danny had gone to make the initial arrangement, but after that they had never again heard from this Mickey, the bagman-elect, so they figured he'd gone freelance, which no one cared about as the handle was too small, or that old man Kane had died, which was sad, but was in the way of the world and would cause no one in Haverhill to break out purple crepe.

Danny hated Riverton. The place was so clean it gave him nightmares. The last time he returned from Riverton he took to his bed for two days and could keep down nothing but tea and toast with thinly spread strawberry preserves. He was like those Sherpas who lived way up in the mountains; if they ventured to sea level they sickened and died in the richer air. Danny's system was conditioned to Haverhill soot and grime; Riverton's squeaky cleanliness was unnatural, a shock to his constitution. Despite appearances, Danny was delicate. He suffered frequent head colds and earaches. Even now, his eyes itched. His two little ones had noses that forever ran thick rivers of green muck; they may as well have been full sisters to Typhoid Mary.

This Mickey Something-Or-Other strode across the barbershop swift as dear, departed Ted Kennedy when he'd eyed a babe in a voter's arms, maybe as swift as Ol' Ted just eyeing a full-grown babe. Danny was terrified: what if the little dandy hugged him? Saints, he'd have to kill him if he was a hugger. Worse yet, this Mickey weirdly looked no older than the first time they'd met, his face unlined, the bloom of youth still fresh in his cheek, while he, Danny, had since married and sired two daughters. Some guys had the gift of looking forever young.

Could Mickey Something-Or-Other be a vegetarian? Margaret Mary believed that red meat trapped in the bowels secreted all manner of poisons; from time to time the entire Donnelly family ate nothing but cauliflower, beans and potatoes until the farting became so unbearable that the family headed for the golden arches to gorge on Big Macs. It was a well known fact that vegetarians never grew old until the day they sickened and fell dead. Perhaps Margaret Mary was right. The nectar of life might not be Pabst, but carrot juice.

Aunt Sosha had arranged for Danny to occupy the only chair with all its springs intact in The Clip Joint just as Danny's career as a smash-and-grab car radio thief was proving insufficient to support his growing family. Aunt Sosha was a true daughter of Haverhill in the cast of Mother Duston, despite being born somewhere near Odessa. When she needed someone trustworthy, not too bright, but forceful enough collect the vig due her from her money that worked up and down Merrimack and Washington Streets, she'd called on Danny Donnelly.

A natural for the job at six-four and 240 pounds, Aunt Sosha needed Danny to replace her nephew, a guest of the governor at Walpole after a misunderstanding about whether the nephew had been putting out a restaurant fire or had set the place ablaze himself. Margaret Mary bought her husband a used black leather jacket and a porkpie hat so he could look like Sylvester Stallone in *Rocky*, an old movie she knew he liked to rent again and again. "If you are going to be a knee-breaker, you should look the part," she said, and each dawn, often be-fore the crack of noon, Margaret Mary sent the love of her life and father of her children out with a kiss on the cheek and the same heartfelt advice. "Don't fuck up, baby-cakes."

Not seeking Aunt Sosha's advice about this Mickey might conceivably be deemed *fucking up*.

Danny was troubled by ambiguous situations. On the one hand, pounding the pissant from Riverton into paste would require minimal effort and might add amusement to an otherwise dull day; on the other, there was the connection to Daddy Kane; who knew how highly Aunt Sosha might value that?

Aunt Sosha was, in fact, a sentimental woman. She held a soft spot in her heart for him because of Danny's grandfather, may Tim Donnelly rest forever in the close embrace of Our Lord and Savior, Jesus Christ. Grandfather Tim had been one of Aunt Sosha's business companions in the old days, and perhaps he'd been something more, though the complete nature of the relationship, like history, remained a veiled mystery to Danny. Danny only knew that when he was three his parents had challenged a bridge piling with a speeding pale blue Chevrolet Malibu, the bridge piling winning easily. Grandfather Tim raised him on a diet of beer, boiled potatoes, and Chef Boyardee Ravioli, but Danny had been saved from beriberi by Aunt Sosha's roast chicken, *kreplach* soup, kasha *varniskes*, and, at Christmas, what Danny called *latkes* until he was twelve and learned the rest of the world knew them as potato pancakes, a customary food for what Sister Agnes at the Sacred Hearts School whispered to him was Hanukkah, the holiday the Hebrews celebrated because they stubbornly refused to worship God's only Begotten Son sent to Die on the Cross for Our Sins, and so they hated Christmas. Sister Agnes' hurried whispers had rung with capital letters as she crossed herself three times, kissed her crucifix, and fingered her rosary beads.

Penniless at his death, Grandfather Tim nevertheless left Danny with a priceless legacy: an Irish sense of fatalism, a manner of talking that made Danny sound like the old days Aunt Sosha dearly missed, and three specific bits of wisdom worth far more than money: first, never bet a filly among colts in the spring; second, always consider the leading apprentice jockey for a run at second place; third, remember that horses are herd animals—they dislike running in front—and that was why horses were smarter than people.

"I did it," Mickey said as Danny stood and took the guy's damp hand.

"Did what?"

"What you said to do." This Mickey grinned like the cat that downed the canary with pickles, relish and mayo, and then washed the bird down with a double JD and water back. "I just came from Riverton."

"Would zootsuits be in fashion in Riverton? Could I interest you in a four-foot gold key chain?" Ryan asked, with a raised eyebrow taking in Mickey's shoes, his neat slacks, and the cable sweater.

Mickey seemed not to hear the barber, but whispered, "I've got the cash."

News of cash was always welcome, but sadly Danny was clueless as to what the little peckerhead might be talking about. He said, "That's good." What else was there to say? Mickey sounded as if they'd talked two weeks ago.

Then the kid withdrew his bankroll, and the tone of the day took on a new cast. He turned his body so Ryan could not see, a futile gesture as Ryan knew the angles of the barber shop mirrors better than a 3-cushion billiards champion knew his home table. When Ryan leaned a little forward, his face appeared in a sidewall mirror. Ryan's lower lip protruded as the kid peeled bills off a roll big as a man's fist. The genuine article, all right. The twenties had lots of company, and their older sisters with those lovely portraits of sad-eyed Benny Franklin were not orphans, either.

Mickey handed two hundred dollar bills to Danny. Just like that. "Your access fee," Mickey said. "As we agreed."

Danny had outgrown being able to be bought for two bills, but the rest of the roll beckoned to him. Danny had a duty to Faith and Hope to provide for their futures, and here was Mickey from Riverton presenting an opportunity for responsible fatherhood. It would be negligent to kick his bony ass out the door without first separating him from his money, tantamount to child abuse.

So Danny reached for his coat near the shop's front door. "We should go somewhere private. To talk," he said. Ryan softly whistled Pop Goes the Weasel.

Mickey's grin grew broader. The guy had enough teeth for two crocodiles, but they were straight, white, and possibly the result of drinking nothing but Riverton water and soymilk. Mickey would want to preserve those teeth; the opportunity before Danny looked easier and easier.

But as his hand closed on the shop's brass doorknob, Danny remembered that Mickey knew Kane, and Kane knew a friend who knew Aunt Sosha. A light glimmered. What if the kid was simply carrying Kane's money? It would not do to piss off Aunt Sosha. Had Margaret Mary been there to advise him, his beloved would succinctly advise: "Baby cakes, do not fuck up."

Heeding the inner voice that never failed him, Danny echoed, "I have to check with Aunt Sosha."

"Who's Aunt Sosha?" Mickey said, but Danny knew well enough not to answer. He told the boy to wait.

Alone in Ryan's backroom, behind the blue painted door of the filthy rust-filled toilet,

Danny flipped open his cell phone and thumbed Memory #1. A young man with a thick roll of bills who wanted to dispose of his money presented opportunities, but Walpole was populated by lads who could not distinguish opportunities from snares.

Ari, Aunt Sosha's housemate who scared Danny spitless, answered. Aunt Sosha was cooking, hardly uncommon. Danny heard her shout in Russian and English that she couldn't be bothered with details. A potato kugel was in the oven. "Tell him it has plenty of pepper, the way he likes," she yelled, and Ari said, "You hear this?"

Ari spoke rarely; as far as Danny knew, only on the telephone. His eyebrows were so pale they might not have existed; his lashes, the same. His eyes were shallow cornflower blue pools of terror, his lips bloodless, and he had the hands of a concert pianist who liked to strangle people.

Danny quickly told Ari about Mickey, leaving out the part about the two hundred the kid had already given him. Ari said something in rapid Russian. He heard Aunt Sosha say, "So tell him to bring the boy. We'll eat. What could it hurt?"

When he emerged from the back room, Mickey from Riverton was asking Ryan, "What is that music?"

"That's The Rolling Stones. 'Satisfaction.'"

"Must be new," Mickey said. "Catchy."

Danny shrugged into his black leather coat, adjusting his shoulder to accommodate the weight of his pistol on the right and the brass knuckles on the left. He wrapped his muffler around his throat, a flimsy defense against the cold that ravaged his system. He sniffled.

"Will we walk there?" Mickey asked as they stepped onto the sidewalk. "'Cause if we do, my friends maybe should get out of the car. They can wait someplace warmer." He pointed at a black Honda parked up the street where two shadow shapes climbed from a tiny auto.

Here was proof of his sainted wife's wisdom. Danny was a big man, but if he'd accompanied Mickey into an alley, the two in the car surely would have followed, and adjusting the attitudes of three guys without drawing the gun from his coat might have proved challenging.

There was the thing about guns. Once drawn, they had a way of going off. No one "showed a gun" for respect. That shithead move was on a hundred television shows; Danny had to laugh each time he saw it. Suppose the other guy was also carrying? Better to draw and fire with no notice of intention. A careful man would pull the trigger until a weapon clicked on empty. Guns made little men brave, big men vulnerable, and left stupid men dead.

Aunt Sosha had gifted Danny with a .38 Special Smith & Wesson Centennial revolver. It was a woman's gun, though that fact did not bother Danny. Most of his work was accomplished with the brass knuckles, and he rarely needed those. He'd never fired the pistol in anger. Aunt Sosha required that Danny be able to defend her money, so she'd given him the gun with strict instructions. "Make no trouble, boychik, but if you take it out, don't be slow and don't be fancy. Aim here and here." She'd poked two stiff fingers into his chest and belly. Ari, later, had instructed him on the efficacy of a final shot into a fallen man's ear.

Since Aunt Sosha seldom left her big old house on the better side of the river, Danny said, "They should come along. We can go in your car."

They drew close. One of the two people standing beside Mickey's car was a girl, smoking. That made Danny no more trusting, but Aunt Sosha would be pleased; she liked people who smoked. At first sight, the girl seemed older. When Danny looked a second time, he saw she was a kid. Then again, she talked as if she were older. It confused him, but no matter what her age, he had to admit she had one fine shape, a rack on which you could set dinner service for two.

They exchanged short introductions, but Danny shook no hands. He'd studied *The Godfather*. Taking the hand of a stranger was an invitation to a sudden, violent death.

As Madge bent to get into the rear seat, a loop of red elastic peeked from her back pocket. This Madge could not be a strong believer in proper underwear. What's more, even if her underwear had been where underwear belonged instead of in her pocket, her taste went to red. While Madge climbed into the car, Danny reminded himself he was a loving husband, soon to be the father of three. He forgave himself, looking at this Madge was only a venal, not mortal, sin. Perhaps an act of contrition would keep him square with God.

With his back to the Honda's front door, his posture seemed conversational, but it also allowed him to keep an eye on the lot of them. Another lesson from *The Godfather*. The boy in back, Bughouse, had arms and legs like twigs, but there was no telling what he carried in his backpack.

Mickey drove. Danny thought they must have looked like the Clown Car at Ringling Brothers as the little Jap rice burner buzzed them across the stone bridge that spanned the Merrimack.

Aunt Sosha's nondescript Federal backed the shore of a pond in a Haverhill neighborhood built in an age when mill owners ordinarily had five and six children. The poor had larger families, but less space. The bricks were painted white, the wooden shutters black, and two red brick chimneys stood at each end of the structure. A finger of light smoke snaked heavenward from the chimney on the right.

Aunt Sosha's four visitors climbed five steps to the gray-painted porch where Danny raised the brass knocker on the oak door, but the door silently swung open before the knocker made a sound.

Ari had been waiting for them.

He shuffled back into the interior shadows. A gaunt, middle-aged man with dead flat blue eyes set so deep in his skull Madge thought they might glow. His waxen skin was translucent; his white hair spare as a baby's; his enormous ears were thick with wiry tufts. His powder blue golf shirt was buttoned to his chin under a hound's tooth sport coat. Ari wore cuffed gray slacks and fine brown shoes. Mickey wondered why he never thought to wear a sport coat.

Those shallow blue eyes balefully examined each of them. Ari searched Bughouse's backpack, grunted, and then politely returned it to Buggie. For a terrible moment Madge wondered if he would pat them down, and the moment was terrible because she knew that if that man's hands were laid on her, she would have to scream, but after his half-closed eyes raked each of them, he shuffled back to the shadows He sat beside a low burning heatless fireplace, his two hands gripping the arms of a Queen Anne chair. He faced no window; he lighted no lamp.

On Aunt Sosha's first floor, opaque drapes covered every window. The polished floors were distressed cherrywood that shone beneath a high gloss finish. The area rugs in the two main front rooms were Persian. The walls were painted a subdued burnished red; the wooden trim, moldings at the floor and ceiling, a glossy white.

Mickey stepped across Aunt Sosha's threshold like a triumphant marathon runner. Bughouse kept his gray sweatshirt, but Madge and Mickey shrugged out of their jackets. Danny hung them beside his own on a pine pegboard by the entryway. He kept his porkpie hat.

Bughouse went to his right, drawn by the art suspended on coarse filaments of fishing line anchored in the ceiling. Paintings were hung on every wall. He recognized Chagall. That was easy. He knew the plates from books in the library, but he'd never seen anything quite as vibrant as these prints. He drew closer and saw they were not prints, but must have been genuine copies. Real paint; real canvas; real brush strokes. He knew enough to keep his hands in his pockets. It was all he could do not to extend a finger to feel the texture of the paint.

Of course, the paintings could not be originals. That was impossible. Paintings such as these were only in museums, not private homes in Haverhill. In the room's center was the Vermeer, "The Concert," certainly no print. The deep, elaborate gilt frame was made of real gold. In the shadows up the stairwell, Bughouse thought he saw "Storm on the Sea of Galilee," Rembrandt's only seascape. Aunt Sosha's walls were better than the big books in the Riverton High School Library. Someday, Bughouse wanted skill enough to paint Mary just like Goya has done the Maja. Mary was far prettier than that fat old whore.

The short woman who emerged from the recesses of the house wiped her gnarled hands on her rumpled white apron. "Aunt Sosha," Danny said. Her thick stockings were rolled at her calf just below the hem of her gray dress. Her black shoes were blocky, the kind a podiatrist might prescribe. Heavyset, she walked with a slight waddle.

Danny dutifully kissed her wrinkled cheek.

"You know from art?" she said to Bughouse. She brushed cigarette ashes from her ample chest. Except for a few stray wisps stiff as wire that floated above her face, her gun-metal gray hair was knotted in a severe bun.

Mickey said, "Hi. I'm Martin Black," and thrust out his hand. "People call me 'Mickey.'"

Aunt Sosha walked past him as though Mickey was invisible.

"You know from art?" she asked Bughouse again.

Bughouse managed to say, "A little."

Her lips pursed and she shrugged. "A *bissel* is better than *bupkis*. History remembers only artists and generals. You know from Chagall?"

"The stained glass is very famous."

Aunt Sosha smiled. "Ach! A *mensche*." She turned to a grinning Danny. "This is rare in a boy so young anywhere. In America, it is unheard of." She stepped close to peer into Bughouse's eyes. "You have a name, sonny?"

She gripped his arm. Bughouse blushed and tried not to wince from the pain near his elbow. "Bughouse."

"*Bughouse*. This is a name for a person?" She shook her head as if the world was bringing her a new marvel.

"It's his nickname," Madge said. His name is Reynard Danton Smith. We just call him *Bughouse*."

"This is a name?"

"A nickname," Madge said.

She shrugged. "And these are your friends?" she asked Bughouse.

He nodded.

"These are *my* friends," she said, and waved her hand at the wall. "My Papa, he should rest in peace, the schmuck, he loved art. He lived for it." Her knuckles rapped a mahogany table and rattled the small bronze cast of a Pan that stood in the table's lip. "He couldn't afford crayons, but he made sure all his children knew from art. A lifetime cutting herring don't make you rich, but if he had a dime, he bought a book. A man should have passion. You understand this, Bughouse? *Fishdeit?*"

Bughouse nodded. She put her arm through his and she guided him to the next canvas.

"Come. Maybe you maybe know from Malevich? How about Chaim Soutine or heaven forbid Pinchus Kremegne?"

Bughouse shook his head.

"No. Of course not. Don't feel embarrassed. What could I be thinking? America, this is. In America, time for art there is none. Here, they are crazy for the French impressionists, but the *Yiddische* Russians who went to Paris? Who has time to know from this? After the Revolution, they went. You know from history?"

Bughouse swallowed hard and said, "World War One. The Bolsheviks."

"Ach, Danny, a regular genius to your Aunt Sosha you bring!" She pronounced the word, *regallah*. Aunt Sosha's smile was filled with brown stained teeth, no two of which pointed in the same direction. "These Yids knew Chagall, also a Yid. Chagall outlived them all. They came from Bialystok, Kiev, and my own Odessa, into the ocean it should sink." With a single finger, careful not to touch the canvas, she removed dust from the inner lip of a frame.

Bughouse knew that Rembrandt was most definitely not a Russian Jew. Neither was Vermeer. What were the masterworks on the stairs doing there?

Aunt Sosha pinched Bughouse's arm. "This one, Danny, the intellectual, he don't talk so much. But smart, he is. On him, you can see it." She stood on her toes and peered into his face. "A young man, but such old eyes."

Aunt Sosha released Bughouse's arm and turned to Madge. "And you, girlie, which one is your boyfriend?"

Madge did not hesitate. "Neither."

The woman smiled. "Danny, another one is smart!" Her laugh was a low cackle. "Her I like. What do they call you, darling?"

Were any Jews in Riverton? Had she ever met a Jew? Why were there no Jews in Riverton? She'd never thought about it. She said, "Madge. Madge Klink. Magda, actually."

"What kind of name is this? 'Klink?'"

"I don't know. It's just a name, I guess."

"Hungarian? I think maybe your grandfather maybe took this name, 'Klink.' Not a gypsy, are you? Magda. This name is not American. My brother in Brooklyn, the *goniff*, may he live until he pays me what he owes and then have a heart attack, he tells me people come to America and change their names to something short. In America, everyone is snappy." Her lips smacked pity. "Magda, you and I will drink a glass tea while the men discuss business. For business, I have no head. I don't want to know from what they are doing. What could I understand? My friends take care of me. This is all an old woman can ask."

What was it like to have a grandparent? Why had she never thought to ask her parents about her own?

A third time, Aunt Sosha passed Mickey as if he were not there. "You will all stay for dinner, yes? I made plenty. You have time?"

It was no question. Madge nodded.

Aunt Sosha smiled. "*Gut*. After dinner, you'll go home. Where is home? You shouldn't be out late. I would not want your parents should worry."

"Riverton," Mickey said, "We're from Riverton."

Aunt Sosha paid him no mind. She was already whispering to Danny.

Danny shrugged, turned to Bughouse and Mickey, and said, "Follow me, boy-os," as Aunt Sosha gently took Madge's arm above the elbow. "Come, Magda. We'll talk girl-talk. You have secrets? Aunt Sosha loves to hear a girl's secrets. You'll call me 'Aunt Sosha.' You'll do this?"

Madge nodded. It was not as though anyone knew the woman's complete name. She was *Aunt Sosha*, nothing more and nothing less.

The second floor back corner bedroom's parquet floor had depth. Mickey and Bughouse were to learn all they'd need to know about OxyContin, Rohypnol, and what Danny said was Ecstasy, though it had a more complicated chemical name that no one knew or gave a fuck about. There was more, of course. There always is. But Danny would explain all they'd need. "Nothing but Oxy, today, boy-o. It's neat and not a party pill. Learn all you need, earn, and we'll see about expanding your product line."

"It's addictive?" Mickey asked. "A narcotic?"

Danny did not answer.

Mickey had imagined Haverhill would present clean opportunities, maybe like an investment, or a tip on a horse, but now that he was here, there was no turning back. Drugs. Well, all right. Everyone starts somewhere.

Bughouse was fascinated by the floor. How was simple wood made to have such luster? His squeaking sneakers were desecration enough, but Mickey and Danny heedlessly allowed their shoe heels to click sharply on the hard veneer. Bughouse's fingers touched the corner bedroom's only real piece of furniture, an antique oak printer's cabinet. Marred and pitted, it seemed terribly old, the kind of object people prized for its proof of a past. The gracefully curved legs were carved with lion's heads and ripe grapes still on a leafy vine, the squat legs ending in a claw. Oiled, the honey oak had depth suggesting mystery. Like fine art, the floor crafted dimension to otherwise flat reality.

The room's only horizontal surfaces were three unfinished planks of pine set on two sawhorses. Four gallon-size Ziploc bags, each containing hundreds of colored pills, sagged lopsidedly in its center. One bag held white, one green, one blue, and one yellow.

A little guy with small eyes and very little remaining dark hair combed flat back from his widow's peak sat on one of two deep easy green vinyl chairs with chrome tubular arms, the kind that belonged in a dentist's waiting room. He had greeted Danny with a nod, then eyeballed Mickey and Bughouse. Danny thrust his thumb over his shoulder.

"New recruits, John-boy," he said, and John-boy echoed, "New recruits."

Mickey handed Danny his Chicago bankroll, the big man tossed it to Johnny, and the recruits began their educations. Your whites, the smallest dose, held ten milligrams of oxy. Mickey was getting a break. A major break. Like maybe the kind of break where he should drop to his knees and thank God who must love him because with no reason other than her sentimental heart, Aunt Sosha was allowing him to start a career with 500 whites. "You charge one dollar a mil. Do the math."

"A lot of money," Bughouse said, and grinned. The weasly guy in the easy chair smiled. He had a gold canine tooth.

"What we need least is a wiseass," Danny said, turned to Mickey and added, "It's all in the attitude. This is serious. Don't fuck with Aunt Sosha's money."

"Five thousand dollars," Mickey said, trying to suppress his awe. You could put that many pills in your pocket, and it was enough to buy a car. All right, a piece of shit used car, but a car. It could buy a flat screen plasma television, if there were anything to watch. What did a Rolex cost?

"Fine arithmetic, boy-o," Danny said. "But I need you to repeat what I said. This is school, every word is a test, and I am Hell's own headmaster."

Mickey stood dumb.

Danny snatched his black leather porkpie hat from his head and slapped Mickey with it, hard. Mickey's cheek flared red; his eyes teared. Bughouse quickly said, "'Don't fuck with Aunt Sosha's money.'"

"Bughouse, here, is the fast learner, I see. Your turn, boy-o."

"'Don't fuck with Aunt Sosha's money.'"

"Go to the head of the class." Danny's hat resettled squarely back on his head. "You pay first what is owed to Aunt Sosha. Your kids are starving. You pay Aunt Sosha, then maybe feed them. I don't care if they turn off your lights and your gas in February and you are dying of the pneumonia, you shiver in the dark and cough blood knowing you did right because you paid Aunt Sosha. Is my meaning clear?"

"Pay Aunt Sosha, first," Mickey said, eyeing the leather hat.

"Smartly done," Danny said and handed Mickey four empty sandwich bags. "Help yourself. One-hundred twenty-five to the bag. Count them out. We will weigh them for accuracy when you're done. We could weigh it out for you now, but I do so like to have a man learn his trade from the bottom up. Do they teach dandies to count in Riverton?"

Mickey parted the Ziploc slide. Danny spoke as if to the air. "I don't know why she does these things. She has a good heart is all. You'll not disappoint my aunt, Mickey. It would personally offend me to see my aunt disappointed. The woman says she has a feeling about your girlfriend, the one with the ass and tits I pray to God you are doing because if you are not, the waste is a sin. God did not put such women in the world for us to ignore. Me? I trust no one right off, but Aunt Sosha claims to have radar about the worth of people. It may be true. My Margaret Mary can detect falsehood at a thousand yards. The loving wife detects a lie faster than you smell stink on shit.

"Careful with the counting, Mickey. Pay attention to the task before you, my Grandfather Timothy used to say, and all else follows. 'Mind your P's and Q's.' That's 'pints' and 'quarts.' He was a drinking man, and I sorely miss the nasty bastard."

Bughouse could not imagine missing his father, another nasty bastard.

The tiny pills slipped from Mickey's shaking fingers. When they fell to the pine, they took on life, rolling and fleeing from him. A circle grew on his back where he expected to be struck.

"Review. Be sure we understand each other. In three weeks, you return to Haverhill with five large. Not four weeks. Not ten cents less than what is expected. Is my meaning clear?"

Mickey forced himself to ask, "How much will be mine?"

Danny's shoulders slumped as he sighed. He stood close to Mickey's back. "Now did I ask you a question or was I talking to myself?" He sharply lifted his knee into Mickey's thigh. Mickey's leg numbed from hip to ankle. He nearly toppled. Sensation slowly returned, but he lost count. He emptied the second half-filled sandwich bag to begin again. "Three weeks, five thousand," he gasped.

"That's the spirit. Far better. Despite those shoes and the trousers look like they came off the Salvation Army shelf in 1946, you may be smarter than your average gigolo, Mickey. I truly hope so. Deliver five large, boy-o, and we'll figure out your cut. Do not dream that for a shitty fifteen hundred front money Aunt Sosha will make you a partner. We don't get out of bed for a thousand dollars. We wipe our asses with hundreds. But she is a generous woman, understands incentives, and is civic mind enough to encourage youth. Learn, you earn; earn, you eat; earn enough, we all dine well.

"All you need do is show us that in Riverton people are mad for oxy. Money will flow through your life like cheap wine flows in a French whorehouse. Do not think too much, and you will make out like a bandit. What is needed is what is called proof of concept. We'll not be fooled again."

"Again?" Bughouse managed.

"It's Mickey's pants, Bughouse. The pants remind Johnny and me of a man we knew. You remember that spic, Johnny?"

"Torres, wasn't it? From Lawrence, I think."

"That's the man. A bantam weight, and a ladies man like our Mickey here. He wore such pants. But he proved himself tough in the end, though it did neither him nor his wife any good."

Johnny sucked on his teeth. "He put up five K, didn't he?"

Danny put a finger to his chin. "That he did. Nothing wrong with your memory, Johnny. You may be older than dirt, but never let them say your mind is gone." He suddenly spun about. "Johnny, are you sure it was not Figueroa? The Spanish with their names, I can't tell one from the other."

"No. Figueroa is our associate in Lowell. This was Torres. You have it right, Danny."

"That's right. That's right. It was surely Torres." Mickey was bent over the table, and Danny planted his elbow on Mickey's spine as if Mickey were a bar and Danny's big hand circled a pint of good stout. Pills tumbled from the Ziploc. Mickey restarted the count a third time.

"'Manny,' we called him, that being short for Manuel, naturally. Well, things went smooth for a month or so. It looked like Manny would be handling five large a week and be in rice and beans for life. Lawrence is a mean little city; not at all like fucking Riverton. But despite his success, our Manny suddenly became silent. It was as if a radio tower had fallen in an earthquake. First we had regular contact, then nothing. Not a word. Now, unless a man is dead, such treatment of one's associates is just inconsiderate. And even if dead, a man should make every effort."

Johnny barked a sharp laugh.

"Aunt Sosha became concerned. Suppose our associate Manny had come to a dreadful end? Not everyone in Lawrence is upright and fair-dealing, and perhaps Manny had run afoul of such men and would need to be avenged. He might be sick, needing our help, which is indeed how associates support each other. So Aunt Sosha requested that Johnny and I make inquiries. You remember that first day we went to Lawrence, Johnny?"

Johnny nodded again. This time, his grin fully exposed his gold canine. "Rained all that week."

"It did. It did rain. That's true. The rain, Manny tells us, is why we find this Manny hiding from the weather in the back room of a *bodega*. He claims the market for Oxy has dried up worse than a nun's privates. From the rain, he says. Demand is gone.

"We try to imagine how one week, the whole city is pimping their sisters and mothers to raise the cash for one more pill, and the next all of Lawrence for lack of umbrellas has joined

12-step programs. We wonder: is it possible the good people of Lawrence have discovered religion? Perhaps the priests are working overtime with the congregation lined up five deep at the confessional, and they are granting dispensations at a rate to evacuate Hell.

"But our friend Manny says if it is not the rain, he cannot explain it, and since Manny is our friend and associate, we want to believe him. We sincerely do. So we merely request that he work harder, rain or shine, maybe go out and make deliveries to nodding Lawrence junkies who are shut-in by bad weather, run a delivery service like from your pizzeria, and we leave our visit at that. We do not disturb a hair on his head. At the base of every good business relationship there must be trust. Do you get my meaning, Mickey?"

"Trust," Mickey said, waiting for the stinging blow to his neck, but none came. Danny's elbow lifted, and Mickey straightened up for a short moment before returning to his counting.

"That's the ticket, boy-o. We are fair men, Mickey. This is not a clean business, to be sure, but we are not unfair. We do not force ourselves or our product on anyone. We want to do business, and maybe this Manny indeed has a bad week. But what do you suppose happens just two weeks later?"

Mickey sealed the second bag with a twisty and lifted both bags. They felt as if they weighed the same.

"By my hairy white Irish ass, I swear this is truth: our good friend Manny again goes silent. So off we go again, and this time when we visit his wife greets us at the door. Her English is spotty, but she tells us how Manuel has flown to the Dominican Republic. There is a sick uncle, the retired baseball star with his 92-mile per hour fastball. She does not know how to find him, and she knows nothing about any money. She is a little bit of a thing, dark as bitter chocolate and maybe twice as sweet. She stands in the apartment door with a babe in her arms and another pulling at her cotton skirt. Maybe two or three more little ones are running around in the flat, screaming their nappy heads off. The television is blaring. So is a radio, playing that Spanish music, what is it they call it?"

"*Salsa*," Bughouse said. "It means *hot sauce*."

"Are you a music lover, too? Bughouse, you are indeed one formidable little prick." Bughouse stared at his own feet.

"It seems unnatural. Our Manny has not only gone and left his wife and little ones to fend for themselves, but he has left us no forwarding address. Do you think we believed that, Mickey? Do you?"

"I guess not." He was near done with the third bag.

"Right as rain, Mickey, right as rain. Trust is a terrible asset to squander.

"Johnny and I make further inquiries. After all, Manny would not be the first husband to tell his wife one thing and do another. We wonder if our Manny's sick uncle is in fact some high school tart with tits like apples and a taste for older, pock-marked men with an endless supply of E. Suppose she and Manny are holed-up in an apartment listening to that *salsa* music while Manny neglects his obligation to Aunt Sosha? You wouldn't ever consider such carryings on, would you, Mickey?"

"No. Yes. I don't think so."

"Well said, Mickey. Give no product away, not even to yourself. It's what is called inventory control in the world of business, and to be sure, we are businessmen above all else.

"Well, wouldn't you know it, but the first street junkie we ask where we might purchase smack or weed points out a dark blue van on a lot just off Lawrence's fabled Canal Street. The junkie offers to blow us both at a discount, but being on business, we refuse. We do gift her with twenty dollars as a finder's fee. You see, we are not bad men. Fair dealing all around.

"You remember the van, Johnny?"

"I do."

"A Chevy it was, dark as midnight. The metallic paint finish. Glowed like a sapphire. Lovely machine. Treat it right, change the oil, I say a Chevy will run forever. Dodge makes a fine machine, it's true, but it's Chevy for me.

"But I ask you, what could we think of our Manny now? A man who will lie to his wife will lie to anyone. Manny, it turns out, is far from some balmy sand beach where he might be twirling those little paper umbrellas in a drink with the cherry and the orange slice. Nor is he in mourning for his uncle the retired All-Star; our Manny is right there in a van parked a mere block from his own wife and children, pissing out the sliding side door into the streets of Lawrence when he feels the call, rather than going home.

"Johnny and I, we express our disappointment. Still, we never lay a finger on him, as that is not our way. No. What we do is invite him for a private interview with our other associate, Ari. I drive the van, and Johnny follows in our car. You met Ari downstairs, you'll recall?"

Mickey wanted to finish, but his hands shook and he kept losing pills. Mickey thought of Ari's depthless cornflower blue eyes, and he lost count.

"Johnny, would you care to tell our new friends about Ari?"

Johnny shuddered and waved away the privilege.

Danny said, "I have it that years ago our associate Ari resided in Israel where he was an interrogator with the Mossad, which is what your Hebrews call their secret police. Perhaps you've heard of them?"

Bughouse had. He'd read awful things.

"Aunt Sosha, she is a great supporter of Israel. They should name a high school for her.

I admire the Hebrews, myself. Plucky bunch of bastards, they are. My grandfather claimed that when he was a lad, the Jews and Irish stood shoulder to shoulder against the British. Brothers in arms, they were."

This was not wholly true. Bughouse said, "The IRA allied with Hitler."

Danny exhaled a great sigh. "From art critic, to musician, to history professor in the blink of an eye, is it? I would not know about that, Bughouse my friend. All I know is what I have been told by my grandfather, Timothy. Do you think old Tim lied to me?"

Mickey prayed Bughouse would shut up, but Bughouse was a runaway bulldog with a bone. No matter the danger, the ramrod up his ass that adored Truth turned into a lightning rod. He lectured on the Irish Republican Army and its odd history with the Jews.

When Bughouse finished, he said, "I'm sure of that. Positive."

Danny sighed. "All I know is that the Jews are now surrounded by camel-fuckers who'd rather kill a Yid baby than eat lamb stew. There is Israel, maybe the only real estate in that piss-hole desert lacking oil, and every one of their Arab neighbors wants to murder and rape their women, their babies, and, given your average towel-head's tastes, rape the men, too.

"You might imagine the Mossad has its hands full, what with lunatics wanting to jam plastique up their own asses, sneak onto a bus and blow themselves and fifteen schoolgirls to Kingdom Come. You'd understand why the Mossad has very little patience. These are men who understand the complex relationships among the uses of electricity, fire, consciousness, and a man's tolerance for pain. Here's the simple lesson for you, Mickey. You never want to be interviewed by Ari."

"I never want to be interviewed by Ari."

"Again."

"I never want to be interviewed by Ari." Mickey's heart sank. He emptied the third bag a third time and started counting once more. It had been near full. A hundred? A hundred and ten?

"I'm told interrogation is a fine art. When it comes to administering pain to make a man forthcoming, while limiting his pain to keep him conscious and lucid, our very own Ari is the best among the best of them. Aunt Sosha herself told me that our Ari was asked to leave the Mossad for excessive zeal. Imagine that! Fired for doing your job too well!"

Mickey sealed bag three.

"Out of kindness, the goodness of her heart, Aunt Sosha has equipped a private sound-proofed room in this very house where Ari can practice his art. And it is indeed an art. I am told he employs nothing but common kitchen utensils, a self-imposed discipline, like a sculptor who welds only discarded iron. Have you ever been through the door to Ari's studio, Johnny?"

Johnny crossed himself. "No, and I pray Jesus keeps me from crossing that threshold."

"Come, Bughouse, you're a thinking man. What do you suppose is the effect of a garlic press on a testicle?"

Bughouse said nothing. Mickey breathed a prayer of thanks for his silence.

"Well, where was I? Oh, yes, our friend, Manny. Manny, I gather, proves to be a man of unforeseen determination and will. The Dominicans can be stubborn. Perhaps Manny saw his children's good fortune in his own, bought them the trust funds or something, saving up to send his kids to Harvard. Or maybe Yale."

He turned quickly to Johnny. "What would it be for you if God someday blesses you with children, Johnny? Harvard or Yale?"

"Yale," Johnny answered. "No question."

"A man after my own heart. Yale for me, as well. But we'll never know about Manny's Ivy League ambitions for his children because after two whole days as Ari's guest, Ari reports that Manny is doing very little to help his situation. He won't reveal where Aunt Sosha's money has gone. So Ari asks Aunt Sosha if she would like to hurry things along, and she admits she is growing anxious. Who can blame her? Her money is her money.

"Johnny and I are dispatched once more to Lawrence." He paused to sadly shake his head. "This time we bring back that sweet little brown woman, Manny's wife."

Mickey finished the fourth bag and snapped back like a rodeo cowboy who has roped a calf. Danny tossed Mickey's four bags to Johnny, who lifted a heavy druggist's brass balance scale from the closet. He put three weights on the left and all four bags of pills on the right. The four men anxiously watched the balance needle settle precisely on zero.

"Lovely," Danny said.

Johnny handed the four bags back to Mickey who slid them into his trouser pockets. "Now how does it work?" Mickey asked.

"Wait," Bughouse said. "What happened with Manny and his wife?"

Danny stared at him. "I see our Bughouse here likes a story to have its conclusion. It's the artist in you, I'll wager. Shortly after we delivered Mrs. Torres to Ari, we heard the banshee. Forget your soundproofing, I never heard such a sound before and pray to Heaven I never hear such a sound again. Manny must have witnessed something never meant to be seen by any loving husband."

Johnny crossed himself three times and spit to his left.

"I believe the children went to an aunt. But I wonder about the van, I do. Fine vehicle. Only Ari knows, and he'll not tell."

Danny's hat rode at the back of his head. He stepped to his left, and grabbed Bughouse's arm. "Story hour is over and school is back in session. Watch closely, Mickey."

He lifted Bughouse by the neck without choking him, holding him easily. Bughouse squirmed like a beetle on a pin. Mickey realized Danny could probably dropkick Big Juice over a fence. On long boring afternoons, he probably bent iron bars to interrupt life's monotony.

With his free hand, Danny plucked a single twenty milligram pill from the table, squeezed Bughouse's cheeks between a thumb and forefinger, and when Bughouse's lips parted, as if Bughouse were a flintlock, he shoved the pill in Bughouse's mouth. "Don't swallow it, professor," he said and moved his hand to Bughouse's throat. "Chew it." He turned to Mickey. "It takes but a minute."

Bughouse near ruined his pants. The chalky pill crackled in his mouth. He had so little spit he could not have swallowed if he wanted to.

"Your oxy is a pain reliever, but don't confuse your oxy with your Advil," Danny explained. The time release mechanism of the pill was the coating. Swallow an OC whole, and it lasted most of a day. To accelerate the effects of the opiate, it needed teeth.

"How's that first pill coming, professor? Open up, now. Give us a look." His big fingers closed on Bughouse's throat ever so slightly and Bughouse's mouth opened. "You do lovely work, boy-o," he said to Bughouse. "Swallow it, now," he said.

Danny spoke to Mickey as with one arm he held Bughouse aloft. "It is a beautiful thing I am told, that since OCs dissolve in water, with a simple drop in a spoon and a little heat, we could have had Bughouse suck it up in a syringe and mainline it. That's quite the rush. But I'd be careful of that one. While it is all the rage in Lawrence and Lowell, Riverton doesn't seem ready for junior high school kiddies on the mainline, what with needles and the AIDs. An aroused citizenry is bad for business, and should the people of Riverton get their shorts in a knot, well, there is little we can do for you, Mickey, very little indeed."

Though Bughouse felt inflated as a party balloon, Danny inserted a second white pill in his mouth as if he were a vending machine. Then Danny gently lowered Bughouse into the chair beside Johnny.

Danny said, "No need to worry about our friend here. No one becomes a junkie from one or two pills. Most don't even get addicted after five. But they will chase that first rush. It's like pussy. Nothing ever feels that good again. So they will indeed come back." He peered into Bughouse's eyes. "Feeling fine, I'll wager, professor. Would you care to correct me again about Irish history? Perhaps you have a lecture for me about Rohypnol and the end of gentility among youth who take it in the ass."

Warmth emanated from a place just below Bughouse's stomach. The warmth was the blossom of a precious flower, a rose or lotus. His nipples stiffened, his forehead numbed. His upper lip was a vague memory. No, the warmth was not a flower, it was a vine. Yes, a vine. The vine crept from his shoulders into his arms and down to his fingers, right to the tips. The vine extending into his legs was like an early morning dream of Mary Swenson, a dream that lingered when he was half asleep and half awake, the covers tented over him, a dream that made everything feel good at once. But this was no dream. He was weightless; he had the crazy idea that from foot to crown he was a giant erection waiting to be stroked. Or licked. The thought made him giggle. His father often called him a prick—what would the old man say now?

"You might give a first taste away," Danny said. "What's good for Ben and Jerry's is good enough for us. I tell you, that Chunky Monkey is more addictive than any of this crap. Build a little volume, and if you need, put a few trusted agents on the street. You cannot be everywhere at once. The girls, they buy Mary Kay Cosmetics and vibrators on this system. Every customer becomes a seller. Every seller returns money to his supplier. People at the pyramid's top get rich.

"But choose your sales force with care, lad. That nice girl you figured was the best lick in town and would come across because you gave her fifty pills on consignment who decides instead to take your money and fly to Miami to work on her tan is not our problem. You owe Aunt Sosha what you owe."

"I owe Aunt Sosha what I owe," Mickey repeated, and Danny smiled. Bughouse's eyes were pins. "How long will Bughouse be like that?"

Bughouse mumbled, "Like what?"

"Maybe six hours," Danny said. "Your oxy goes direct to the brain. Big person, small person—all the same. I hear a woman on oxy is a rare opportunity, if you like them quiet and cooperative. They think the knee pads you loan them are for roof work." Mickey had no idea what Danny was talking about. "Do you think that Madge of yours might like oxy? If they all look like her in fucking Riverton, I might have to rethink the little shithole."

Johnny smiled, and his gold canine tooth gleamed.

Danny's voice dropped an octave. "Now this is serious, Mickey. You'll be dealing with me," Danny said. "You never come to Aunt Sosha again. Never. Forget this address. Forget Aunt Sosha's name. You deal with me and me alone. If I am not at Ryan's, Ryan will know where I am."

Mickey nodded. "Ryan," he said.

"Now what's your cell?" Danny asked.

"My what?"

"Your cellphone. You aren't leaving here with product in your pocket and me with my dick in my hand. I'll have a call from you every day, or I will have your balls on a tin plate."

Bughouse wondered what it would be like to touch Mary's perfect skin, and then he wondered what it would be like to be Mary herself, to shower with lots and lots of hot, soapy water and explore with her fingertips those places Bughouse longed to know. Everything in him tingled. His hair felt good.

Mickey said, "Cell phones don't work in Riverton." Danny looked at Johnny, who shrugged. Mickey added, "I swear it," cringing, expecting the leather hat. "It's the iron ore in the hills," Mickey added, repeating Delbart's hypothesis about the awful radio reception.

"Oh, kiss my hairy Irish ass," Danny said. "Iron ore in the hills? Does this look like fucking Colorado to you?"

Johnny said, "Give the guy a break. Maybe there just are no towers."

"Nah. They use those satellites up in space. There's no need for towers any more."

Danny and Johnny discussed wireless technology. Mickey was clueless as to what they were talking about. Bughouse was only vaguely aware of his surroundings, captivated by a vision of the flat plane of Mary's belly and her navel that was the center of the world.

Johnny opened a stubborn drawer of the printer's cabinet. Nestled among power cords coiled on each other like a nest of vipers were dozens of silver and black phones. He carefully matched a cord to a phone, tapped in a number, and said, "Memory dial number one. Fucking Riverton, It's always fucking 1952 in fucking Riverton."

He pulled his earlobe and gave the phone to Mickey. "Do I need to tell you to never, ever, mention product on the phone? You must know that much. No one could be that stupid. It is discouraging to work with people who are stupid."

"Sure."

"And never use a landline. Use a landline, you may as well just call the FBI in Washington and ask for the director himself. They have feebs do nothing all day long but eat donuts and listen to landlines. You can't fart while you are on a landline without the feebs pick up the scent, come to your door to ask what crawled up your ass to die, and wonder if your mother didn't teach you to say 'Excuse me' when you break wind."

What were landlines? "Sure," Mickey said. "No landline. Do not mention product."

"When we talk, any listener will think we are in business selling paper airplanes and party hats. Anything else will get me very, very angry. Johnny, did you ever see me angry?"

Johnny said he never had.

"Of course not. And that is because anger blinds a man. Angry men make mistakes. A cool head is a sure business asset. Can you believe I had an anger problem once? But I have attended to it. Does that surprise you, Mickey?"

Danny held his hat in his hand. What was the right answer? "Yes," Mickey said, "It would surprise me."

The hat went slowly back on Danny's head. "Ari attends to my anger," he said. "He's my private therapist. I tell Ari my troubles, and after that, I am free of all concern."

Aunt Sosha shouted to them from downstairs. Danny picked up five green pills and stuffed them into Mickey's pocket. "A bonus," he said. "Put one in a girl's drink, and have your way with her. Though she may awaken bleeding from her asshole, she'll remember nothing. Roofies are a wonder drug."

Danny turned to Johnny and asked, "Will you be dining with us, Johnny? It's *shabbos*. My Margaret Mary has not seen me on a Friday night in months."

"Plans, Danny-boy, plans. I hope to get my dick sucked. You know how it is. You spend a fortune on dinner, and then while you slip the coat-check girl another five, they go off to the loo to stick a finger down their throats and put the filet mignon in the toilet. Two shakes of Binaca, they come out smiling. If they liked the steak, you get your dick sucked. What I can't figure out is whether the steak has to be good going down or going up. You'd think I could buy the steak and throw it in the toilet, save some time, but that is women for you."

Danny nodded. "The girls will be your death, Johnny. Mark me." Danny pointed to Bughouse and said to Mickey. "You'll want to help Bughouse navigate the stairs."

As Mickey slipped Bughouse's arm around his shoulders, Bug whispered to him, "Do you see the birdies?" Bughouse's legs were water.

They staggered into the hall. "What's a *shabbos*?" Mickey asked.

"Jew Sabbath," Danny answered. "You light your candles, say a few words in Jew-speak, and eat chicken."

Danny asked Mickey if perchance he was a vegetarian. When Mickey said he was not, Danny muttered something about good luck and good looks, and advised him to go easy on the kugel which could block a man like concrete in the bowels, but to help himself to browned potatoes with an unstinting hand. Aunt Sosha trusted no man who did not eat.

At the same moment the boys were learning the size, weight, and color of all manner of Oxycontin, E, and Rohypnol, Madge took the tour of Aunt Sosha's kitchen.

It was a temple for food preparation. Between recessed gold ceiling lights and a floor of ivory terra cotta Spanish tile, the kitchen occupied half the first floor. A bleached white granite countertop flowed around twin porcelain sinks. The huge stainless steel refrigerator, the freezer, and the dishwasher were decorated by chevrons of hard, black rubber. Iron pots and pans hung from chrome gratings suspended from hooks in the ceiling. A humidified bread drawer, a refrigerated wine rack, a trash compactor, all manner of small appliances for which Madge knew no use, were cunningly crafted to be invisible behind panels and cabinet doors that hid Lazy Susans. Doors held shut by magnets swiveled silently open at a touch. Despite the array of devices, the room seemed spacious and uncluttered.

At the kitchen's spiritual center was a six-burner black cast iron stove. Stolid as Aunt Sosha herself, it emanated heat and the rich fragrance of pepper; two iron pots on its top simmered with broth redolent of onions. "*Tsimmis*," Aunt Sosha said, as if the word might explain something. She then rapped the glass of the floor-to-ceiling glass rear wall that over-looked a wooded yard. "Bullet proof," she said, as if that explained something more.

Beyond the maple and oak trees, down a gentle slope of land covered with fallen leaves, a pair of Canadian geese rose to soar above the silvered rippling surface of a lake.

Madge boosted herself onto one of the two high stools beside the serving island. The island's top was inlaid with hand-painted white tiles, a whirling delicate abstract design in blue. Handmade, no two tiles were exactly the same. The tiles surrounded a square of deeply scarred butcher block.

Aunt Sosha cracked opened the oven door, clucked at what she saw, turned down the heat, and sat opposite Madge. Leaning on her elbows, she asked, "You smoke, Madgellah?" and when Madge nodded, Aunt Sosha sighed and added, "I knew I'd like you. Here, take."

Aunt Sosha shoved a crumpled soft-pack of Kents toward Madge and ignited one of the two gas burners at the island's edge. She held her wispy hair back with her free hand, and leaned to light the cigarette quivering between her lips, then passed it to Madge. Madge lighted her own from the tip of Aunt Sosha's. They shared an enormous glass ashtray. It was a kind of communion.

"Arthritis," Aunt Sosha said as she shifted herself to find comfort on her high stool. "Hitler should have had my hip." Her hand waved dismissively, as if to pre-empt any con-cern Madge might have, a gesture she repeated time and again. "Long ago. A terrible winter. I slipped. I fell. I was never the same. This is life for you. One minute, one thing. The next, something else."

Just not in Riverton.

"As for my shoulder..." Aunt Sosha shook her head disgustedly and raised her arm until it was horizontal. "Your see this? No higher. Not since I was a little girl." She coughed and inhaled.

"Why wouldn't you talk to Mickey?"

The older woman shrugged, then sat back to hold Madge in her gaze. After a half-beat too long, she said, "Smart, pretty, and brass balls, eh, girlie? But a bad combination I admit maybe this is not. Truly, tell your old aunt, this Mickey is your boyfriend?"

Madge had been fucking Mickey last night, but she said, "No. No. I don't think so. No."

Aunt Sosha plucked an imaginary shred of tobacco from her tongue tip. "But you are with him, no? Maybe there is for you someone else?"

Thinking of Juice almost made her laugh. This was not like gossiping with Mary or

Victoria. No gush of giggles, no whispered secrets. Simple, plain talk, woman to woman. "No," she said. "No one."

"Pardon an old lady who puts her nose where it has no place, but this Mickey, you could love him?"

No one in Riverton ever asked such a question. Madge's mother thought Madge's life was about pep squad meetings, not about slicing at her own flesh in the shower to watch blood trickle down her leg into a drain, much less sweating in sheets with a boy she did not love just to deliver herself from solitude and numbness.

Madge tapped her ash. "No. I never could."

"Smarter and smarter. Then you won't mind I should give you advice. This Mickey, he is not for you. Don't ask me how an old lady knows such things. I just know. This kind never knows from peace. Like my brother, Dmitri. Always there will be something more he must have. He is proving something, but has no idea what or why. There is always more to prove. You should have someone who can know happiness. Be patient. Men are like the bus. Wait long enough, another one comes along."

"Not in Riverton."

Aunt Sosha raised an eyebrow. "Even in Riverton. It's the waiting that is hard."

"Riverton is strange. I never feel right."

"Girls your age never feel right. There is no place for women with brass balls." Aunt Sosha laughed so hard she coughed.

Madge was encouraged by the intimacy. She said, "I can't figure out who I am. I am always the same. Nothing changes."

Aunt Sosha eyes held Madge while she put a finger to the center of her own swollen lower lip. "There was a Chinaman long ago, Chuang-Tzu, who dreamed he was a butterfly, and when he awoke he did not know if he was a man dreaming he was a butterfly or a butterfly dreaming he was a man."

"Yes! Yes! It's just like that!"

Aunt Sosha tapped her ash. "This Chinaman was a schmuck, Madge. *Meshuggah*. What a person does is get up in the morning and struggle. Then you do. Your hip hurts, your shoulder hurts, but you do. Let the butterflies be butterflies; you be a person." She barked a laugh. "And let Chinamen be Chinamen."

"I'm not pretty."

Aunt Sosha's crooked finger lifted Madge's face. "Where did you get such an idea?" She critically examined Madge. A thick river of blue smoke snaked from her lips into her nose, then out from her mouth again. "Stupid talk. With your Aunt Sosha, don't be modest. With me, only be honest. Always. Yes? Only in this way can we be friends."

"Then you be honest with me. Why didn't you talk to Mickey?"

Aunt Sosha brushed ashes from her chest. "Who would want to talk to someone so eager to break the law?"

"He wants to work for you."

Aunt Sosha held up her palm. "Now, my darling, you are confused. Mickey wants to work with Danny, no? I know Danny since he was a *pishah* and his parents died, may they rest in peace, the idiots," she rapped her knuckles against the butcher block three times, "but I am not Danny's mother. He was raised by a good friend of mine, something like your Mickey, but with more heart. Now we are like family, but we are not family. You understand this?" Madge nodded. "So Danny invites his friends to my home and I am happy to receive them. But Danny is a man, not a child. What he does with his friends is not my concern." She leaned across the counter in new intimacy. "Tell me, Madge, if anyone should ask you if I spoke with your Mickey, with your hand on the Bible, your answer must be 'No.' Am I right?"

Madge nodded.

"Do we have an arrangement of any kind?"

Madge shook her head.

"Your Aunt Sosha is just an ignorant old woman." She inhaled and held the smoke, speaking as she exhaled, "Now if you are as smart as I think you are, you understand."

Madge allowed herself to smile. "You're not ignorant. I don't believe that."

"'Ignorant' is not 'stupid.'" The older woman reached to Madge to nip her cheek between two fingers. "Like I said, smart and pretty. And balls of brass."

Aunt Sosha slid from her stool to light candles. She withdrew an ornate silver candelabrum from a cabinet and set it on a silver tray near the window, then set five white wax candles in their places. "You know from this?" she asked, and when Madge did not answer, she added, "*Shabbos*." The silver tray was etched with Hebrew letters and what looked like a goblet of wine.

Aunt Sosha draped a kerchief of filmy gauze over her hair and eyes and lighted the center candle. With that, she lighted the others. The candle flames expanded into globes of golden light. Aunt Sosha gently covered her eyes with her palms and then waved her hands as if ushering the candlelight to come to her. She chanted a near-inaudible prayer in Hebrew. When she was finished, she refolded the lace kerchief and set it back into a drawer.

They returned to their high stools. Aunt Sosha said, "Not so much for God as for my mother and father, may they rest in peace. For them, I do what they would want. Not for God. If I should meet God, there are things for which He must answer. To be a Jew in Stalin's Russia was no better than to be a Jew in Hitler's Germany. I was not yet born, but for a Jew, history is more than a memory and the past is forever the present. My aunts, I am told, were little girls asleep on the ground in Stalin's work camp. It snowed. They did not wake up. Not a tent did Stalin give them, though the Jews were communists since before there were communists. Russia was *Gehenna*." To answer the question in Madge's eyes, she added, "Hell. Not with little devils and pitchforks, just suffering. To be denied the face of God. This is Hell. My mother, on her deathbed we held her up so she could say the prayer for the candles. This is her silver tray, that was her kerchief. The candleholder ... ach, who knows?" She waved her hand. "Her mother's and maybe her mother before that. Time swallows everything."

The Jew wore History like another woman wore a coat. Everyone in Riverton came from Riverton, except the funny little man who swept out the high school, and he was Swedish or Norwegian or something and had no stories to tell.

"My parents rest in the Jewish cemetery near Odessa. To go back to see their graves before I am dead, this I would like. At least, they tried. Them, I owe an explanation. But to God? No, I owe God nothing."

The moon rose. Red, blue and yellow lamps set in Aunt Sosha's backyard shrubs glowed and cast dark, animated shadows among the trees.

Aunt Sosha seemed to make a decision. She said, "I will tell you something, Madgellah. Your Mickey, this boy you do not love, this Mickey is going to ask you to try drugs. Tell him 'Drop dead.' He will tell you it is harmless; he will tell you that all it does is make you feel sexy and that everyone loves you. I know you sleep with this boy, don't deny it. I have eyes to see. I also know this is not the same as love, so this is why I speak to you. He will tell you the drugs will make the sex better. He is not lying. But still, turn from poison. Promise your aunt you will keep your soul."

Madge nodded.

"Say it."

"I promise."

"*Gut*. Not even your Aunt Sosha can help a girl with no soul. Now, about this Mickey. Tell me some things. Can he be trusted?"

"What do you mean?"

"If a person gives him money, can a person expect Mickey will pay it back? Does he mean what he says? Does he lie?" Aunt Sosha's finger tugged at her lower lip.

"I've known Mickey for as long as I can remember," Madge said. "He has more ambition than anyone in Riverton."

Aunt Sosha's head lifted. "Ambition? Ambition I can trust even if I cannot trust the man. He will always follow his own self-interest. To know this is good. Is your Mickey violent?"

Madge laughed. "Mickey? Mickey talks. There is another boy, Juice, who can be angry. But when he is angry at Mickey, Mickey runs."

Aunt Sosha slapped both her knees, disappointed. "*Ach*. So he is a coward?"

"No, no. I don't think that. Just smart. Juice is too stupid to be angry for long. It's better just to run away."

Aunt Sosha placed her finger at the center of he swollen lower lip again. The interrogation lurched forward.

"This Bughouse, the artist. Tell me."

Bughouse an artist? Madge supposed it could be so. "Bughouse is Bughouse. No one understands Bughouse. Not even Bughouse. He is like a character I read in a book. Pierre in *War and Peace*. A searcher."

The older woman's chin snapped up like a fish caught by a lure. She hopped from the stool and waddled to the stove to turn down the heat, then hurried back. Dinner was set to slow cook.

"*Oy, mein shayner maidelah!* You know from *War and Peace*? Where is there a girl today that knows from *War and Peace*? From Tolstoy? Books? You read?" She became newly animated. "Can you read Russian?"

Aunt Sosha's arthritis vanished. She scurried about the kitchen hastily finishing what needed to be done. With a potholder in each hand, she slid a huge roast chicken from the stove and set it to cool on the stove top. The aroma of rosemary filled the kitchen. "Conversation like this I never get. Let the chicken cool! It will be easier to slice. Pish-tosh on Mickey and Bughouse and Danny. An American girl who smokes cigarettes and knows from Tolstoy in my kitchen sits! Let the men wait. Let them wait. Next will be the messiah himself!"

They agreed Anna Karenina was a fool, but blameless. "Should Vronsky walk through a door and into your life, what can you do? Madgellah, it's thanks be to God that such men are rare," Aunt Sosha said, "and thanks again that they exist at all."

"So they do exist?"

"Pray your Vronsky never comes, because then you life is not your own. Then pray he comes soon."

"It's the suffering," Madge said.

Aunt Sosha shrugged at such self-evident knowledge. "We are made to suffer." She tapped her fist three times against her chest. "But this does not mean we should seek misery. Misery comes on its own. The *goyim* who think suffering is some sort of way to appease God puzzle me. You are a Gentile. Come. Tell me. Do you think suffering appeases God? The Jews know better. There is no mystery. Suffering is nothing but suffering."

The peppery potato pie came out, crusty and stiff, what Aunt Sosha called *kugel* as they moved on to *Crime and Punishment*, which they both admired, though Madge admired Sonia more than Aunt Sosha, who believed Svidrigailov, a character who hanged himself, was far more tragic, the more so for his unrepentant sins and lack of any moral compass. "But you, my new *shiksa* friend, you must know *The Brothers Karamazov?*" Madge confessed she did not. "Oy, Madgellah, this must be your very next book. Tonight, whatever you are reading, throw it away. To not know *The Brothers Karamazov* by that gorgeous anti-Semite bastard, Dostoevsky, is to know nothing. It is about sin. It is about redemption…it is about everything." Aunt Sosha filled a bowl with steaming string beans and pearl onions and inserted a long-handled silver serving spoon. "It's true. The son-of-a-bitch despised the Jews. But still, in Russian, *oy*, the words make you weep." She tapped her fist against her own chest again. "I am telling you, weep! Real tears on your face." As if she was telling secrets, she whispered, "And then you must read *Zhivago*. And then … and then you must come back to visit your Aunt Sosha. Don't trouble yourself with Sholokhov; Stalin's apologist is a waste of time." She made to spit. "But Pasternak, yes. Pasternak you must know. The man understands love. The man was a Jew. Of course."

Aunt Sosha turned a tiny window crank; cigarette smoke and cooking aromas were sucked out into the night.

They set six places at the long, mahogany dining room table. The walls were papered with mint green silk and huge gilt-framed paintings, peculiar landscapes under dark brooding clouds, imminent storms above flocks of sheep and shepherds who carried crooks and pipes. The six-armed chandelier above the table was looped with crystal. The serving platters came from a china cabinet that had belonged to Czar Nicholas. "Not in the Kremlin. Just a summer *dacha*. But think, think, Princess Anastasia herself may once have touched this very spot." With her hand over Madge's younger fingers, they together traced the line of the cabinet's grooved beveled edge and its inlay of mother of pearl. It was slick with lemon oil and history, and Madge, who'd never understood the appeal of antiques, now did.

The embroidered linen tablecloth covered the entire dining room table. The dishes were bone white Lalique run with a gold trim, each plate painted with a small flower in green and blue on a single edge. The glasses were Baccarat goblets; the heavy silverware came from a maroon velvet-padded box.

Treasure. Madge's ignorance of the greater world came crushing down on her. She had to leave Riverton.

Aunt Sosha looked at their work. "All right," she said. She waddled to the base of the stairs, but before calling to the men she turned to Madge and hissed, "When you are done with this boy, you must leave him."

Aunt Sosha took one look at Bughouse hanging on Mickey's arm like a drunk clinging to a lamppost, made as if to slap Danny with the back of her hand, stopped, pinched his cheek, and told Danny to put Bughouse on the couch in the dim front room.

Aunt Sosha cleared Bughouse's place setting. "An empty place? No, we do not invite the dead."

They ate. Madge was always served first. Danny heaped huge portions on his plate, and, encouraged, so did Mickey. It was hard to tell if Ari ate at all.

Kugel was sharp and peppery, but left her mouth unburned. The potatoes, rubbed with chicken fat and sprinkled with paprika, were soft and delicious. After a prayer, each of them touched a goblet of red wine to their lips. Only Mickey drained his.

To her best memory, the wine was Madge's first encounter with alcohol. Were there bars or liquor stores in Riverton? Might the Shadow take Pasternak and butterflies and Karamazov from her?

She was certain she'd never lose any memory of Ari, though. When those limpid blue eyes fell on her, she felt more than penetrated, as if her flesh peeled from her bones.

Like any family saying sad farewells, skipping coffee or dessert, soon after Madge and Aunt Sosha had cleared the dinner table, they all returned to the wooden porch. Mickey and Madge pushed their arms into their coats. Aunt Sosha stood in the doorframe. The yellow electric lights of the interior cast her in silhouette; her face was invisible. Danny wore Bughouse on his arm, limp as a scarf. The night, warm for November, was ripe with the heavy aroma of decay bubbling up from the lake. What secrets lay beneath its silvered surface?

Aunt Sosha thumbed at her lower lip and said to no one, "Why should Bughouse travel? No. The boy should stay until he feels better."

Mickey said quickly, "No problem-o! Bughouse is not driving."

Ari materialized from the interior shadows, his bony fingers closed around Bughouse's elbow, and Bughouse was pulled back to Ari's dim room and was swallowed by darkness.

Aunt Sosha said to Madge. "In a few days, Bughouse you can pick up. We'll talk more, yeah?" It did not seem to be a question. "Books to you I can lend. Bughouse...such a name... Bughouse and I can talk about art. He'll be fine, as long as everyone plays straight."

Madge said, "His people in Riverton…"

Aunt Sosha waved her hand dismissively. "It's decided, Madgellah. Look at the poor boy. Too thin. Ari will take care of him. Maybe he plays chess? Later, when Bughouse is more himself, he can call his parents."

"His father," Mickey said. "He only has a father."

But Aunt Sosha went on as if she had not heard. "Bughouse will be my guest. It's decided." She dropped her lighted cigarette over the porch banister and turned to re-enter the house.

The door began to close, but then Aunt Sosha seemed struck by a new thought. She raised herself to her toes to cup her hand around Danny's ear to whisper.

Danny shook his head *No*, but Aunt Sosha pinched his cheek and with his flesh in her grip lightly made him nod *Yes*. Danny went inside with her and returned alone.

The front door snapped decidedly shut behind him.

Madge, Danny and Mickey stood in a cone of bright light. The collar of Danny's black leather jacket was hiked up around his thick neck. He reached into his pocket and withdrew a pistol. Its nickel-chrome finish flashed.

Danny said, "It seems I am to educate you once again, Mickey lad. Aunt Sosha wants you to carry a piece. She doesn't think you are a coward, but she wants you to know how to protect her investment without running off. Don't ask me how she has come to such a conclusion, but there you have it, and there will be no two ways about it. We'll deduct the gun's cost when next we meet."

Mickey stammered that he had no idea how to use a weapon.

"And there's the thing. Just as I warned her. Nevertheless, I am to teach you, and that's the long and short of it, and no dispute. Have you never fired a firearm, Mickey? A hunting rifle?"

Mickey was too nervous to speak.

Danny nodded sorrowfully. "I can teach a monkey to pull a trigger. To handle a weapon, correctly, though, you have to be a man." He tossed his revolver to Mickey. "Hold my gun while I fuck your girl."

Danny spun Madge so her back was to his chest. Before she could make a sound, his hand clamped over her mouth. His other hand went into her black team jacket. The fasteners unsnapped, sounding like so much popcorn. Danny's big hand roamed roughly over her chest.

"Well are you going to stand there, boy?" he roared. "The first lesson about a weapon is to discover whether you have the balls to use it."

Mickey's arms were rags. Madge struggled to breathe through Danny's fingers as his free hand tore at the buttons of her white shirt. He pulled her bra to her throat, filled his rough hand with her left breast, and squeezed, hard. Madge struggled, but Danny's rough grip was iron. He hurt her. Mickey trembled. The gun remained pointed at the earth.

"Holy Mother Church, boy! I am about to rape your girl right before your eyes! I'll tear her tits off! Will you stand there until pigeons shit on your head? Do you need to see my dick in her arse before the spirit moves you? That's a goddam pistol in your hand! For the love of God, what will you do?"

Danny's hand plunged across her bare belly. Madge kicked out as the hand jackknifed beneath her waistband, but all that accomplished was to make Danny rear back and then settle forward again, bending her double. The brass button at her jeans' waistline popped open; her zipper rasped. The hand over her mouth suffocated her, but when she bit the soft flesh at the base of his thumb, Danny seemed to feel nothing. His hand smelled oddly of lilac soap.

Madge gagged on her own vomit. His erection pushed against her through his pants and the seat of her jeans. His hand roamed from her crotch to her back pocket where he snatched at the red thong. How did he know? Had he seen it? When she gasped for air, he stuffed the thong into her mouth. Madge tried to spit the thong out, but Danny forced the elastic between her teeth. *Shoot him! Shoot him now!* Mickey's wide dark eyes glowed with indecision. *Shoot him!* Mickey's forehead glistened with the green and amber lawn lights. What in fuck was he waiting for? Madge struggled, helpless.

She near passed out as Danny locked her wrists in one of his big hands and lifted her arms. Her knees buckled as she was forced to bend forward. Her arms felt as though they were being ripped from her shoulders.

"Here now. A clean shot at me, boy! What's it going to be? Does Madge not wear under-wear, Mickey? Or is it in her back pocket for show? The kind that go commando is the wild ones, I hear. Always at the ready." His hand went under her and across her belly once more, further down than before, jackknifing under the waistband of her jeans. While he held and lifted her wrists behind her, his other hand slipped beneath the triangle of fabric of the blue thong she wore. He squeezed her. It was no caress. Her eyes watered with pain.

Shoot him! Shoot him! She could not spit out her gag. *Shoot him!* But her dumb fuck lover held the gun pointed at his own feet! Madge struggled uselessly. She tried not to wet herself. Her vision clouded dark.

Before she could faint, Danny spun her away. Madge collapsed to her knees and seized the porch railing as she spit the thong from her mouth into the darkness.

"For crissakes, boy! Have you no balls at all?" Danny roared.

He snatched the gun from Mickey's trembling hands and slapped him three times smartly across the mouth with his leather hat. Quick, just like that, one, two, three! Just like that, bitch slapped him as he might slap a hysterical girl. Danny raised his hand to do it again, but visibly grabbed hold of his own rage before he murdered the little dandy.

Madge's vision cleared. She heaved two more great gulps of air, stood unsteadily, straightened her bra and buttoned her shirt. Her hands trembled. "Let go of him," she said with more courage than she felt. "Let go of him, or I will shoot you myself."

Danny looked at her and released Mickey's shirt. "There's a woman with stones! More than you, God knows."

Madge could not fully catch her breath. She was not going to cry. No. She would not give him the satisfaction. It was all she could do not to run. Besides, there was nowhere to go. Her heart hammered at her ribs.

Danny pulled Mickey into the center of the porch light. "Now you watch close, you little prick, because school is back in session. With God as my witness, if I hear someone robbed you, it's me you'll have to deal with. I'll rape Madge before your eyes, then I'll rape your mother, too, and only then put a cap up your ass. Is that what you want?"

Mickey's tongue swiped at the trickle of blood that leaked from his lip.

Danny slapped him. "What? I did not hear you."

"No. That's not what I want," Mickey said.

"This is a Smith and Wesson.38 Special, as fine a revolver was ever made. It holds five shots in the cylinder." His arm rigid around Mickey's neck, he snapped the gun open with his wrist and held it inches before Mickey's eyes. "There's not a bullet in it, you dumb dipshit. So the first thing you need to learn is how to load the damned thing." Danny fished a box of shells from his coat pocket and handed them to Mickey. "You slide them home, one to the chamber. Just like in the movies."

When Mickey's shaking hand had done its work, in a practiced move, Danny snapped the revolver closed. Still clutching Mickey by the throat, Danny showed him the two safeties, one a simple slide and the other a pressure plate on the stock. "You point at what you want to kill, and you pull the trigger, here. You note I said 'kill.' If I hear you took this little beauty out to impress some jagoff with how important you are, I will travel to Riverton for the pleasure of ripping you a new asshole. Is my meaning clear?"

"It's clear."

"Good. Now, the action moves slick as crap through a goose." He held the gun up as if to shoot it, pointing the barrel out to the darkness, making Mickey peer down the short barrel. "Can you handle that?"

"Yes. Yes, I can handle it."

Danny's voice lowered. "What I've seen, I doubt it. You'll need practice. For the love of God, don't go discharging a weapon in the city limits. It makes the civilians nervous. Go somewhere deserted. The riverbank will serve. And forget what you've seen these assholes on the television do. You hold the damn thing straight up, not sideways. Two hands if you can. Shoot like a killer, not a pimp."

He released Mickey from his grip. Madge's breathing slowed. Danny spoke in near whispers.

"A gun will kick like a mule gone mad, so hold it sideways and you will either snap your elbow or clip yourself in the chin. But if you ever whip it out, Mickey, just like your dick, you fire every single shot. Hear me, boy? Every fucking shot, or else why in God's name did you draw the weapon? Do you get my meaning?"

"I get your meaning."

"Do not let the shiny finish fool you; this is not a show weapon. This fine, fine pistol is for killing. It will fit in your pocket. What you don't have in stopping power, you trade-off for size. You want an ankle holster, God bless you, but don't buy one until you know what you are doing. You'll want your weapon close at hand. Your pants pocket is too thin, unless you want all of Riverton to know you carry a piece. Better to think about a heavy coat, or use the pockets in that sweater-thing you have on. You look like a country club golf hustler, you ask me, but what the fuck do I know about fashion in Riverton? Whatever you do, for the love of God, Jesus, Joseph, Mary, and all the saints, don't push a revolver into your belt unless it is your intention to shoot your dick off."

"Not in my belt."

"You point and squeeze. That's not overly complicated, is it? Try not to jerk it unless you are in a hurry. A small gun like this is for close work, so you fire as fast as you are able, but try to squeeze. If you can grab a man with one hand, hold him still, and shoot him with the other, that's best. Put the gun against his belly. It will be difficult to miss. Are you getting all this, Mickey? Am I going too fast for you?"

Mickey nodded. Then shook his head. Then nodded again.

"I need to get home to the ever-loving wife, so I have no time for bullshit or a demonstration. Listen well. A single shot won't stop a charging man unless you have the luck to hit his heart or head, but two shots will indeed slow him down, and three will have you home free and clear. That leaves you two more. Put at least one in his head once he is down. That's right. Finish the job proper. It's you or him, and it may as well be him. Stand clear, put one more behind his ear, and try not to splash brains on your shoe. Is my meaning clear? Is there any part you'd like to review?"

Mickey nodded. Then he shook his head. Then he nodded again. He needed to pee.

"I can't hear you. Do you think I am joking?"

"Yes. You're clear. It's not a joke. No."

Danny shoved Mickey away, shook his head, and hocked phlegm off the porch into the darkness. He tossed a small box of bullets to Mickey, seemed to hesitate, and then handed him the revolver, barrel first. "What you need most of all, boy-o, is the balls, and on that there is damn little I can do to help you."

His big fingertip settled against Mickey's chest. "Five large in three weeks," he said, then turned to Madge. "If this sorry piece of shit does you wrong, Madge, you come to me. I truly regret what I had to do, but Mickey's the kind that wants focus. My wife, God bless her, tells me I should have been a third-grade teacher. It's a gift, she says, a gift."

Danny shook his head with sadness. "Holy Mary, a woman with an ass like that is wasted on a dickless boy," he said, spun about and disappeared behind Aunt Sosha's paneled oak front door.

Three minutes later in Mickey's black Honda, just beyond sight of Aunt Sosha's porch, Mickey puked. He pulled over to the side of the road, flung open his door, and fell into a row of low hedges that fronted the lawn of a gloomy Haverhill house. He dropped to all fours and threw up, full bore, the kind of heaving that left a man helpless as a sick cat.

Madge sat rigid. His spleen could wriggle out of his mouth, and she'd not move. Her shoulder hard against the door, her knees clasped tight to her chest, she stayed as far from Mickey as she could. Let him retch. Good. If he puked blood, even better.

She might slide into the driver's seat and leave. Not back to Riverton. Just go. It was a big world. She could do that. Why not?

Her bruised breasts ached. Cigarette smoke bothered Mickey, so she lighted a Marlboro Light. She'd have smoked two at a time just to make his eyes sting. The 'grette calmed her, a little. Fuck him, if he did not want the tobacco smell in his car. Just fuck him. She hoped his eyes bled.

Back behind the wheel, Mickey wiped his mouth with the back of his wrist and asked Madge if she had any gum, which she did not. He took Main Street to the highway, and as the car looped around the entrance ramp and Madge helicopter-flipped her glowing cigarette out the window, he said, "Quite a day."

Madge launched from her seat. She punched his shoulder. That felt so right she did it again, both her hands flailing, her whole weight behind each blow. "Oh you fuck. You dumb fuck. *Quite a day.* You dumb hopeless fuck!" Her throat clogged with mucous. Fuck. She was crying, damn it. Fuck.

Mickey cringed while she rained blows on him, fists bouncing off, and coming right back. The car swerved. "Hey, I'm driving here."

Kneeling on her seat, she pummeled his closer arm. "Your best friend is a hostage held by a sadist. My tits are purple. Your fucking dream-plan makes you a dope peddler. You're carrying a gun, fuckhead! It may be the only gun in Riverton. You won't make a fucking dime. Oh, you dumb fucking loser fuck! Jesus fucking Christ, how did I get hooked up to such an asshole? What was I thinking? I'd be better off with fucking Juice and his two-inch dick, you arrogant total fuck moron. Juice would have shot him. Juice would have torn off his arm and beat him to death with it!"

"The gun wasn't loaded, Madge."

"You didn't know that! How could you know that? You didn't know that! His hands were all over me, Mickey. I've never felt so … so fucking *helpless*." She squeezed her eyes tight. "Let me plant my foot up your ass. Just to give you the idea of what it felt like." She climbed over the seat and fell sprawling into the back. "Shit," she muttered. "Shit, shit, shit, shit, shit."

She could choke him from behind. She weighed her chances. Would he die before they crashed, and if he did, could she get control of the car?

Mickey said, "Everyone has to start somewhere. I am at the bottom of a learning curve."

All she needed to do was lace her fingers at his throat and squeeze as hard as she could.

"They gave me five hundred pills." He patted his pocket. "They're called Oxy. Every great fortune in America begins with a bandit. The Rockefellers had an illegal monopoly on oil, the Kennedys ran liquor...,"

She laughed. "Oh, you've studied up on it, have you? You dumb fuck. You're right, Mickey. I'm the village idiot. Today was all steak and butterscotch ice cream." She peered into the gelatinous night. Mickey alive might be worth more than Mickey dead. She said, "Let's just go away. Let's just you and me go away to New York or something, baby. They'll never find us. Throw that shit out the window and head south with me. Please, baby."

"South?"

She knelt on the rear seat. "Boston. New York. Maybe Florida. We're just kids. They'll never look for us."

"Everything I want is in Riverton."

"And what is that?" she asked.

Mickey did not respond. They drove through thickening darkness. But after a few more miles Mickey asked, "Do you want to leave Bughouse? How about Bughouse?"

Madge thought, and then said, "Cut our losses. Bughouse is fucked. Do you think they are done with you? They own your ass, Mickey Black. Bughouse is yesterday. *Learning curve?* More like a fucking learning mountain, and the shit is sliding down on us, you stupid shit." She slapped the back of his head, mussing his hair. It was no love tap. She did it twice more and stopped only when she noticed that Mickey had a five-o'clock-shadow. He needed to shave. Imagine that.

"Do you want to try a pill? It might calm you down. Free."

Aunt Sosha was a crone seer. She knew everything. She knew Mickey would offer her drugs and what was it, twenty minutes? Predicting what Mickey might do was that easy. "No, I don't want to try a fucking pill."

"It will work out. You'll see," Mickey said. "Everybody starts somewhere." He stroked the rough stubble at his chin as if he had felt it there all his life. One day breathing the air in Haverhill, and he was a different man. "Bughouse will be fine. You know Bughouse."

"Oh, sure, Bughouse will be in great shape. Peachy keen. Danny is a fucking choir boy.

Bughouse and Danny will be playing Rummy Cube all this week, as long as Ari doesn't eat his liver."

As they drew nearer to Riverton, like a tide receding into the sea, Madge's adrenaline high abated. She fumbled through Bughouse's book bag, looking for something with which she could choke Mickey. Just enough to make him see her point. If not Florida, maybe Texas.

Mickey decided not to mention what he knew of Ari's special skills. Madge might vault back into hysteria, and she seemed to have an intuition about Ari. Women were a mystery. Things could be worse: he had to make a daily phone call, never mention product, sell pills, get back with five thousand dollars, and Bughouse would be fine.

What could go wrong?

One exit shy of Riverton, Madge withdrew the CD Bughouse bought at the mall. She held it up to the passing automobile lights. "Look at this," she said. "Bughouse bought *Wayne Newton: Live in Vegas.*"

Mickey concentrated on the road to the motel. Would Madge want to spend another night in Cabin #3? They'd never been together two nights in a row; it was too much like being married. But maybe for the first time he could remember, Mickey wanted sleep more than sex. He was genuinely weary. "Wayne Newton?" he said. "Go figure Bughouse. We cart his ass out of Riverton, but he comes back with Wayne Newton."

Madge tossed Bughouse's soggy ham sandwich out the window. "Didn't he buy a magazine?"

"No. He stole a magazine."

"Whatever. It's not here. There is no magazine here."

"Did he take it into Aunt Sosha's?"

"I didn't see him take anything into the house. It just disappeared. What was it again?" She turned the book bag inside out and shook it. Nothing.

Mickey saw the familiar glow of the green highway sign: *Riverton: Next 3 Exits.*

Magazine? Comic book? He could not be expected to remember every little detail. His head hurt. There had been something, though. He was sure of it. He asked Madge to remind him.

"I can't think," she said. "It was peculiar. I remember that. I just can't think," she said again. "God, what a day."

What she wanted was her bed. Even girls who live for sex and danger need rest.

At the No-Tel Motel's gravel driveway, Mickey's headlights probed the shadows of the distant trees. At Cabin #3, he cut the engine, and they stepped out of the car.

Juice charged from the shadows.

Events flickered like a silent movie. Madge smelled gunpowder, heard the explosive sound of the gun, felt the night, felt her terror, was blinded by red flashes, saw Juice dying so damned slowly, and then Mickey was on top of her and he would not allow her to run and run and run and run and run and run, his legs scissor-locked around her, his one arm pinning two of hers, and his other hand on her mouth. Mickey whispered through his clenched teeth into Madge's ear, "Will you scream?"

She shook her head.

Her eyes bulged. Her breath was hot on his hand. Mickey slowly released her, ready to slap his palm back down if she made the smallest sound.

The faint far off light from the motel's office was too much illumination. Mickey wanted the night's thickest cloak. His legs unlocked from around her waist and hips. Madge gulped cool air.

Mickey might have been a pussy with Danny, but these moments were about survival; Mickey Black would survive. His thoughts were never more clear and swift.

Mickey said, "We're doing good, here. We are doing fine."

Madge pushed herself to her knees. The dark, still hulk that had been Juice lay on its back, one leg twisted grotesquely under it. Him. It. Under *it*.

Little was left of his face. Looking at Juice was a mistake. A scream bubbled up Madge's throat. She swallowed it. Juice used to make her feel safe. She forced herself to breathe slowly. All was illusion. This was karma. All was illusion.

"What are we going to do, Mickey?" she hissed. "What will we do?"

"We can't leave him here."

"No. God, did you hear the sound in his throat? That was a death rattle. I always thought that was made up, but I heard it. Fuck. It was real. It was real. A death rattle."

Mickey spoke quickly. "We have to move him out of the light."

"Did Juice say anything? I thought I heard him try to say something. He must have been trying to say something." The night closed around them. The night was suffocating her. That was not possible, was it?

"We have to move him."

"What do you suppose he said? I never heard anything like that. That sound I mean. I never heard anything like that. It was a death rattle."

"We have to move him now, Madge. We have to drag him out of the light."

She cocked her head to one side. "Shhhh. Do you hear something? I think I hear something down there."

They froze, still as deer in headlights. Trucks hummed on the distant highway. They heard a faint murmur of old women whispering secrets far, far away. Mickey muttered, "That's the river."

"Maybe we should call an ambulance."

"He's dead, Madge. An ambulance can't help him. No ambulance. He's dead."

"I didn't shoot him. You did."

"Don't go simple on me. You held him; I shot him. It's as good as if you held the gun yourself."

She nodded. Maybe she had held Juice. She did not remember. It could be true. "But it's Riverton. No one dies in Riverton."

"Juice might disagree."

As if Madge had run a great distance, she was panting. She was a smart girl; why couldn't she think? Mickey would have to be smart enough for both of them, and Madge knew Mickey was a fool, but that was it and there were no options. "All right, all right. We move him. We can't put him in a car, though, can we?" She rose unsteadily to her feet.

"No cars. He'd bleed all over the cars. You don't want that, do you?" Mickey stood with his feet at either side of the mess that had been Juice's face.

"But they'll find him. Eventually they'll find him," Madge said.

"The river."

"He'll float up, Mickey. Downstream, someone will find him. Let's call the police. There was a man with a gun, see? That's it. A horrible man. Someone not from Riverton. A drifter. You throw that fucking gun away, see? Dump the pills. Some crazy fuck came out of nowhere, shot Juice, and jumped in his car..."

"Madge, I am not dumping the pills. Do you want Bughouse dead, too? He won't die pretty."

Madge needed to pee.

"We'll stuff rocks in his pockets." Mickey bent to grasp Juice's two wrists, but his hands slipped on blood. He wiped his palms on his pants legs, realizing his mistake as he made it. "When you get home," he said, "burn everything you are wearing. Don't throw it away. Burn it. Every stitch. Don't forget the shoes."

He seized Juice's wrists again. "If you have any better ideas, Madge, now's the time. Otherwise, a little help, please. Grab his ankles."

Juice had thin ankles. It surprised her. She'd been Juice's girl since forever, but she did not know the terrain of his body, not like she knew Mickey's. Juice had ankles like a racehorse. Her hands closed on his skin, still warm, and since that was too horrible, she shifted her grip to close around his socks.

Juice weighed a ton. Mickey's grip slipped again and again. Mickey wiped his hands on some leaves and grabbed Juice by his sleeves, but nothing worked. There was too much blood on Juice. He said to Madge, "Come up here." Madge stood beside Mickey. "Grab the cloth, not his wrist. Ready? On three," Mickey said, counted cadence, and they tugged. Nothing. He repeated the count, they tugged harder, and Juice's body budged a few inches across the pebbles and rocks. When his skull hit a stone, it made a hollow sound like a gourd. For a half second, Madge thought his head had come off and was rolling toward her.

"Again."

"He's heavy, Mickey. I never felt anything so heavy. I didn't know Juice was so heavy. I swear to God, how can he be heavier dead than he was alive?"

"Did you ever fuck him?"

"Go to hell."

"Did you?"

"No, I never fucked him."

Inches at a time, they dragged Juice into the pines down by the river behind Cabin #3 of the No-Tel Motel. Safer in the darker shadows, Mickey said, "Wait here."

"Don't leave me here with him. Please, Mickey. Don't leave me."

"I'll be back in a minute. Juice can't hurt you."

The night seemed animated. Everything was alive, especially Juice's corpse. Tree limbs reached for her. The moon looked on, impassive. Things that had no name lurked just out of sight. Despite the moon, Madge was unable to see her hand in front of her. She realized she still held Juice's jacket sleeve and let go. Juice's arm slapped the earth like a sack of wet shit dropped from a high window.

Mickey found Juice's bat, a Louisville Slugger. Wood. The real thing. He found Madge's purse and threw it into her car. He wondered how Juice had come to the motel. There was no automobile. Had he walked? How would he have known to come here? Someone must have given him a ride, maybe spent the day with Juice looking for Madge. Washington? Chukker Washington would have reason to help Juice. Arnie? Arnie would stoke Juice's rage for shits and giggles. Maybe both of them. Arnie and Chukker would have egged Juice on. Nothing else made sense. They'd have spent the day looking for Juice's girl, the big guy getting more morose and sliding into deeper sullen rage by the minute, which Arnie that prick bastard would have loved, and when they found her car, they left Juice behind with his Louisville Slugger and a fireball of fury growing in his belly. Big joke. Big fun. *Kyuk, kyuk, kyuk.*

Who might know where Juice had spent his last hours? He'd have to take care of them, eventually. Who else might know?

Mickey returned to Madge.

"Juice was talking to me," she said.

"Don't be crazy."

"He's talking to me, Mickey. I hear him. I swear, he's talking to me. I can't make out the words, is all. Don't the dead get last words?"

Mickey knelt to put his ear to Juice's chest. If Juice was still alive, rather than risk the sound of another gunshot, he'd have to smother him, but it was like listening to a brick. "He's dead, Madge."

"The soul migrates and is reborn."

"We don't have time for that crap. We're two of us under the gallows. We don't have time for that crap."

He hurled the bat spinning through the darkness. It splashed into the river. This close to the sea, the Merrimack rose and fell with the tide and was salty to the taste. Mickey wished he knew about tides, but the only person in Riverton who knew about such things was the master of Horatio Cabot's yacht anchored downstream at Newburyport.

They tore stones from the ground with their fingertips. Madge's nails ripped ragged. The biggest rocks they could pry loose were half a foot in diameter, no more. They pulled twenty or thirty stones from the mud at the water's edge. They were difficult to unearth, but there were plenty of them, and when they came free and emerged from the muck they made a sucking sound.

Mickey placed his knee firmly on the "R" of Juice's Riverton team jacket, square on the guy's chest, and separated the jacket's grommets. Madge undid the belt at Juice's waist. The last time she'd unfastened Juice's belt his response was not much different from now. She started to giggle. She tried to share the joke with Mickey. It was no good. Then she had to sit down on the cold ground because she was giggling uncontrollably. It was funny to think in this way. She could not stop giggling.

Mickey slapped her. "Cut that crap out."

They stuffed Juice's loosened clothing with rocks until no more fit into Juice's jacket, and then they pulled the jacket closed. Would the current carry Juice unseen out to sea with the bat? Or would he float to the surface in a matter of days?

There was no telling. So *this* was risk. *This* was danger.

Where was the thrill?

They rolled Juice off the soft bank into the river. He bobbed face up in the shallow water. Mickey balanced himself carefully. With one foot on the riverbank, he stepped on Juice's chest, pressing down while air bubbled up from Juice's clothes. The river water was warmer than Mickey expected. His best pair of shoes was ruined.

Black water closed over Juice's face, the current took him, and Juice was gone.

Mickey said, "Go home. Go home like it was any other night. Any night. I'll smooth the ground over. It will look like nothing happened."

There would be drag marks on the ground. Mickey planned to scatter leaves. This was not going to be perfect. He needed rain. A soaking downpour, lightning, and wind. That would do it. He looked up and cursed; the stars were hard pins in the cloudless night. No luck. No one had ever put the words *luck* and *Mickey Black* in the same sentence without adding the word *bad*. Mickey never had the luck. "It's you and me now, Madge. You and me. No one can know."

"Just another night," Madge said.

The girl who cut herself never felt more alive. She sucked in great draughts of cool night and the cloying rot smell of the river. Her own blood thrummed in her ears. Her senses became one. Madge could roll the universe on her tongue for flavor and texture, and then spit it out. Her nipples were stiff.

Her lips locked onto Mickey's.

They collided like rocks hurled together. Had she grabbed him or had he grabbed her? They stank from mud, sweat, terror, and Juice's blood, already crusty on her shirt. Mickey's mouth was sour. His stubble of beard chafed her throat as he buried his face against the soft skin of her neck. Her hands tore desperately at his back as his hands found her aching breasts.

Mickey pinned her against a tree. Her jeans dropped around her ankles, and she lifted one foot clear of the puddle of cloth. Her filthy fingernails raked him through his open shirt. She nipped at his neck and ears and lower lip as he lifted her left leg and raised her thigh to his waist. He gripped her ass in his hands as she groped for him, found him, and urgently pulled him into her, writhing as she bit his tongue for the pleasure of tasting his blood, and then she came, shuddering with the power and speed of it, and then she came again, twice, quick, shuddering under the force of it, the hard tree at her back, Mickey hard in her, his hand over her mouth so no one could hear her cry out, his mouth at her delicate throat, their hot breath mingling, Madge cumming so hard, so utterly, that she unequivocally knew that the surging force flowing through her could be nothing less than the breath of God, His promise she would live forever.

Madge spent three days in her room. She never cut herself once. Saturday and Sunday it rained and rained.

She did not call Mickey; Mickey did not call her.

By Sunday, her bruises were gone. She inspected herself in a bathroom mirror. Her skin was flawless as ever, and her hymen was once again intact.

Monday she told her parents she was unwell, and when she suggested to her mother she was having her period, Mrs. Klink whispered something to Mr. Klink, who kissed her on the forehead after breakfast and left her alone with Mrs. Klink and all their televisions.

During the afternoon while her mother watched Oprah, after the rain was finished, in the Klink backyard she put her clothing from Friday into an aluminum trash pail, not forgetting her shoes, covered the heap of clothes with a stream of charcoal starter fluid from a plastic bottle she found in the garage, and tended the fire. It smoked a lot at first, then burned clean. She stirred the ashes, covered them with more fluid, reluctantly threw in her little clutch bag, and burned the whole mess a second time.

"Having fun, dear?" her mother called from a rear window.

"Science homework," Madge said.

Tuesday, Madge returned to school. During Study Hall in the Riverton High School library, she found an old leather-bound copy of *The Brothers Karamazov*. The gold gilt on the spine flaked at her touch.

In a quiet corner under a window beside a radiator, Madge immersed herself in the story. Russian names did not trouble her. A novel that mentioned gloomy and tragic death in the first line could hold her attention, so she read more until she felt a weight beside her on the soft seat.

Juice's big arm circled her shoulder and pulled her close. He said, "How's my best girl?"

Madge's eyes rolled up into her head. When she fainted, it was as if she plunged headlong into a dark, dark bottomless well lined with the finest black velvet.

PART II

A MONTH PASSED. MADGE HID IN HER HOUSE.

The Shadow was unable to find her, but she might have welcomed it.

Juice was dead, then Juice was alive. This was the reverse of the natural order. Could someone be too stupid to die?

New terrors filled her. Juice had made her feel safe. *Safe* was an illusion. She saw that now. She would never feel safe again. Madge stared deep into the abyss; the world was strange and risk lurked everywhere. Fools sought suffering. Madge had been a fool.

While Madge hid, she recharged, and like a caterpillar ready to emerge, a chrysalis, she dreamed of what she might become with no certainty of what she was.

Mrs. Klink awakened from her narco-TV haze long enough to ask if her daughter were ill. She rediscovered Madge daily, startled each time she saw her. "It's called the curse for a reason, dear," she'd say, evade looking at her in the eye and softly close her daughter's bedroom door behind her before lunching on cucumber and tomato sandwiches on Wonder Bread slathered thick with mayonnaise.

From the safety of her room, Madge cruised the world on a bogus cable Internet hookup Del Dellingham had installed for her long ago. Juice was no zombie; dead or alive, he had no hunger for brains. The stupidity of zombie lore appalled her, but googling words like "undead" or "resurrection" brought her to screen after screen about the soulless undead and their hunger for the living. Cripes, a zombie would feel perfectly at home in Riverton. Worse than the zombie sites were the millions of web pages devoted to Jesus Christ. *Ecce Juice!*

Madge had no use for religion and never thought much about western deities. She was at heart a pagan. She had gone to church, but like everything else from her childhood, the recollection was a certainty lacking all sensory memory. She had only a syllogism; Madge was a good girl; good girls attended church; Madge must have attended church.

Religion had to be just so much crap. *The Brothers Karamazov* might well be the best novel ever--Aunt Sosha was a lot of things, but none of them was stupid--but in that book when Jesus shows up for forty pages the Christ stands mute, uttering not a syllable. God demanded faith but gave no sign. *We get it, Fyodor, but fuck off!* Madge hungered for answers, not Divine silence. Faith held nothing for her. What would a Jewish woman gangster find in such a book?

No administrator from Riverton high school pursued the absent Madge, a truant. She was not missed. She could stay home forever for all it mattered to the Riverton social whirl.

Periodically, Madge stepped hesitantly onto her back porch for a cigarette. It was late November, nastier by the day. Pewter clouds formed an impenetrable dome above her. One morning, perfectly white snow fine as ash dropped on the perfectly groomed streets of perfectly picturesque Riverton, and Madge slid into perfect despair.

Mary and Victoria would be breaking out their sweaters, hats with bright knit pompoms and matching scarves and mittens, and Victoria would have a fur muff, mittens being for common folk. Mary's flushed rosy pink cheeks would enchant every boy in town. The two girls at the center of the Riverton universe would be fulfilled and happy.

Madge extinguished her cigarette into two inches of perfect snow, then mounted the stairs to her room, undressed, ran the shower as hot as she could stand it, and with her Exacto sliced a line that ran on her inner thigh from her crotch to just above her knee. The cut was deeper than usual; more painful than she remembered ever having before endured. Her breath rasped shallow and sharp. The hot water burned. Madge panted, but that did not stop the progress of the blade.

Could she pull a Juice? Why not die and come back with a new deal? Riverton could have advantages. She leaned her throbbing head on the tile wall and realized that if she had committed suicide, she might have returned from the dead without knowing. She could have been dead and resurrected once before. Perhaps several times. She'd never know it. Might she have left herself a note?

Madge:

You killed yourself. If you are reading this, stay dead, please.

Love forever,

Madge

She stepped from the shower stall long enough to check the fogged bathroom mirror, but if she'd killed herself and scrawled a note with lipstick, it had vanished.

Back in the shower, her very red not terribly reassuring blood mixed with hot water and ran over her foot. Blood did not stain water pink, but swirled in thick curling crimson streamers through water. Madge sliced a second long line along her left arm, from her armpit to near her elbow. She cut her other thigh with a cross-hatched checkerboard pattern.

Arteries lurked in her somewhere. How close could she get without relying on the Shadow to restore her?

Skin is the largest single organ in the body, flexible, semi-permeable, threaded with nerves that alert us to pain, an alarm system for danger. Madge was a loose sack of organs. Cut enough holes in the sack, she would splash apart and slither down the drain.

Her thickening blood flowed over her foot.

Each long, slow, and deliberate slice into her flesh was an exercise in purpose, no slash of despair. Knowing pain proved her control and steeled her against numbness. Her life *would* not be fulfilled by pom-poms and cheerleading and flirting and boots and giggles.

Her Exacto was defense against oblivion. The dead felt no pain; she felt pain; she was therefore alive.

Even near unconsciousness, she was good at syllogisms. The dead do not bleed.

Lightheaded, soaking wet, she spread the big blue towel on her bathroom floor and rested. After a time, the room stopped spinning.

When she awakened, though she should have looked as if she'd run through a plate glass window, her flawless skin had the texture of a baby's ass.

Instead of puddles of blood, her bath tub was immaculately white, smelling of Ajax cleanser. Madge searched her room, on the walls behind the pictures of her parents, inside her closet, behind her mirror, under her bed, under the mattress, in every drawer in every bureau.

No note.

The next morning Madge ripped the cellophane on her last pack of cigarettes. If she rationed them, the pack might last two more days. Then, she'd have to go out.

She cried, a little.

Why or how Madge stayed addicted to nicotine was a mystery. Her hymen could grow back and her cuts heal, so why didn't her body renew at the cellular level? There was no fucking sense to it. Nicotine was a private sin, no different from blowing Mickey in a motel room or the debts owed to Mickey by gamblers, so why did her very private cuts heal?

Murder ought to make any list of sins, public or private. Mickey had blasted most of Juice's face into goo. Blood had percolated in his throat. They'd listened the whole time while Juice died, then dragged the big dead fuck into the black river, Madge pushing rocks into his pants and Mickey standing on his chest until streamers of air no longer rose around him and the black water closed over Juice's face.

Shadow or no, Madge was not forgetting any of that horror. Not any time soon.

She savored one of her two final cigarettes on a late afternoon when the air on her back porch was crisp and clear. Darkness fell earlier each day, but what daylight there was sparkled. Beyond the snow-covered back lawn and open field behind the Klink home, just over a small rise, yellow light tumbled from the small window of a cinderblock garage.

Delbart Dellingham was at work in his laboratory.

Delbart, the genius, was her neighbor since forever. No one knew exactly how smart Del was, but everyone knew he was a shrimp. Five-two, if that tall, he probably did not weigh one hundred pounds. If his mind was intimidating, Del was not.

In the same way Madge knew she attended church, Madge knew Del. They must have shared history, though she could not summon a single concrete childhood memory of her and Delbart doing anything in particular. The tree house on the Dellingham property was a sheltered platform in a tall elm, the platform weathered gray, a frayed rope hanging limp as an old cat's whisker, but if Madge and Del had ever played there together, Madge could not recollect those carefree, childish days. They must have been carefree—that's what childhood was supposed to be, and since this was fucking Riverton, that's what childhood was.

In that precise moment on the back porch, the Riverton paradox opened to her like a lotus. In Riverton, every talent was coupled with a compensating defect. The pair made a person ridiculous.

Brilliant and puny, Del could be the butt of any joke, despite the fact that he had more brains than the rest of town combined. He was gifted but ridiculous.

Shrewd Mickey was a total loser. He just thought he was a winner. The disconnect made him ridiculous.

Shy Bughouse had a dick like a normal man's forearm; any girl who glanced at Buggy's crotch had to wonder at the package. But Buggy was pathologically tongue-tied around girls. His gift was worthless, except to make him ridiculous.

Gorgeous Mary was dumber than a pile of broken bricks; the moment she opened her mouth, if she could find her way to the end of a sentence before something sparkling distracted her, she betrayed herself. Always a victim, always second best, she would be forever sad and ridiculous.

Wealthy Victoria was so self-centered she embarrassed herself. Immense wealth should be matched by generosity in heart and spirit, all that power to do good, but 'Toria's empty heart made her vain and ridiculous.

Powerful Juice, constructed like a locomotive and hung like a squirrel could not cross a street without a map, a compass, and someone to lead him. He should have been admired and feared; he was ridiculous.

And Madge herself? Bold, smart, ambitious, inquisitive, sexy as hell, she was made of Awesome, but no matter what she did, up to and including killing the big fuck, she was attached to a sexless moron for no reason anyone could understand, least of all herself. She would always and forever be *Juice's girl*.

Her life was worse than ridiculous; it was hideous.

Hands laced behind her neck, Madge lay awake on her bed, staring up into total darkness, because then there was Arnie.

Despite having all the charm of a steaming turd dropped on a Thanksgiving table, Arnie was never ridiculous. *Kyuk, kyuk, kyuk.* Arnie got to laugh at them all.

An idea took shape in her mind. She put it aside for a while, but in the morning, the idea lingered, the sure sign of its value. She would not be free until she killed Arnie. She would have to kill him in a way he would not show up three days later. Arnie had to be irretrievably dead.

Madge held her clawing need for nicotine at bay a half day more, but the craving eventually overcame her fear. She could give up cigarettes, but then how alive would she be? She saved her last cigarette for breakfast, knowing after that she was fucked.

She could not bear the thought of going out alone. She would have to trust Del.

That evening when the yellow light once again fell from the tiny cinder block garage window onto the snow-covered field, she tugged a shapeless black sweatshirt over her head and examined herself in the mirror. It would not do. She changed into her usual men's white dress shirt. She had a closet full of them, neatly hung in line like Marines on dress parade. Then she pushed her head into a baggy Kelly green rag wool sweater with its roll collar and a zippered neck.

Madge easily crossed the snow between the Klink and Dellingham backyards. There were few fences in Haverhill. At the garage door, she pulled her sweater collar higher and undid one extra button at the top of her shirt, just enough to expose the very top of the lace of her bra cup.

Del's laboratory door cracked open at her touch. Without turning his head or sliding off the four-legged wooden stool on which he sat staring into a binocular microscope, Del greeted Madge as if he saw her every day—which he did at school, but neither could recall the last time she'd called on him in his lab. Del gestured that she should make herself comfortable, lifted his eyes from the 'scope, and turned to his workbench. His concentration disallowed speech. That was Del. Mr. Intensity.

It was sexy.

Fixed with a loft and a sleeping alcove, like a photo darkroom, Del's lab smelled of corrosive chemicals. The walls were raw pine wood on which loose notebook pages fluttered, each held by a single tack. Light might have come through the skylight, but the skylight was shaded, and since the sun had already set, the lab's only illumination came from a single foot-long fluorescent bulb, one of what could have been four in a swinging fixture that was mostly dark. The homemade computer on the table's far corner was a tangle of wires and boards. The monitor was dark and there was no keyboard.

Madge asked why Del kept the place so murky.

"Murky?" He looked up. "I guess it is pretty dark. Organic compounds can be photo-sensitive," Del said.

"Mind if I smoke? I am taking a walk for some more cigs, saw your light, and wondered if you'd want to come along. We could talk, like old times."

Del said without looking up. "Smoke? I don't care if you burn."

What in fuck was she talking about? Old times? What old times?

Del then spoke to the computer, addressing it as Isabella, and the monitor glowed into life. He said things Madge could not understand, and she saw characters etch themselves on the screen. Then he said, "Isabella sleep now," and the screen imploded dark. He said to Madge, "I've got to finish up, but, yeah. Give me a couple of minutes." Del slowly hand-printed notes in pencil, stared at the page, erased a phrase, and wrote again.

Madge with two hands boosted herself onto a workbench, easy to do because the top had been set so low for Del. She gently pushed pipettes and assorted glassware out of her way as she held back her hair and leaned to insert the business end of her cigarette into a lighted Bunsen burner. She lifted a beaker. It contained a fish.

"Be nice to GIGO," Del said. "Goldfish and science have a lot in common: 'Garbage in, garbage out.'

She inhaled deeply. Her final smoke soothed her nerves. She'd need more. She tapped GIGO's bowl, but the black, bug-eyed fish hardly stirred. "Black goldfish? It doesn't seem natural."

"I bred her that way. Don't startle her. GIGO likes to hang motionless. I bred her that way, too," he lied. He lifted GIGO's beaker. GIGO was the only creature on the planet who had ever traveled through time, but Del was not ready himself to take a jaunt to elsewhen, not quite yet, and he had no intention of explaining how he'd dabbled in time travel to Madge. Not that he did not trust her, but he hated having her know he was wrestling with a problem he had not yet solved.

He would tell her someday, but not just yet.

He had sent GIGO thirty minutes forward, waited for her to appear, briefly enjoyed watching two fish who were one fish stare at each other, then saw one GIGO vanish. Ever afterward, GIGO, who used to swim restlessly clockwise, hung suspended in water unin-terested in movement until she was hungry, at which time she swam in the wrong direction.

"She hardly swims. Very little oxygen passes through her gills, and I bred her for that, too. GIGO is hardy, but I'm afraid she has had a few shocks to her system."

Madge tapped her fingernail on the glass. The fish remained motionless. "How do you know it's a she?"

"Parthenogenesis and gene splicing."

"Partheno-say what?"

"Parthenogenesis. Asexual reproduction. Females only."

"Fish can do that?"

Del shrugged. "My fish can."

"So you are telling me I can fuck myself and make a baby 'cause I am a girl."

Del had to look up to see that she was smiling. He cleaned the lens of his glasses with the tail of his dirty T-shirt. "It could be arranged." He leered at her, "It just seems a terrible waste."

"Why the hell would you want a goldfish that won't fuck?"

Del slapped shut his notebook, slipped it into a drawer and locked it. Madge wondered if he was going to swallow the key, but he stood on a stool and placed the key on the lip of the door jamb. "No one ever searches up," he said, brushed a shock of unruly black hair from over his eyes, hopped from the stepstool to the floor, smiled crookedly, and explained he would scan the pages later. "My notes are digital."

"Why didn't you dictate to Isabella?"

"You can't dictate diagrams of molecular structure, Madge. You have to draw them."

Del was in the habit of relating facts. His voice stayed expressionless. "It's good to see you, Madge. How long has it been since we chatted? I can't remember you ever visiting me in the lab. What's on your mind? Cigarettes? Just cigarettes?"

Del emitted nervous energy like sparks flew off a flint wheel. It was difficult for him to stay with a single topic. Sentences weren't necessarily in sequence. There was too much to think, too much to say, too much to do.

Madge decided to trust him. They'd both forget it all, someday, anyway. "Do you think I am crazy, Del?"

"Like insane? Gibbering and drooling? Howling at the moon? Crazy like that?" He flipped a lever under his chair, tilted back, and laced his fingers on his chest as his feet went onto a counter top. He wore olive green blocky suede shoes, Hush Puppies. "No," he said. "You are not crazy. In fact, Madge, you are pretty smart."

"*Smart* and *Madge* are rarely paired in a sentence, Del, but thanks. I hear 'tits,' 'ass,' and 'pep,' maybe." She was happy to see his smile broaden. Del had good teeth and dense, dark eyebrows. They shared the same hair color, dark, India ink black. When he leaned back, his T-shirt rode up and exposed his flat stomach. "I hate fucking *pep*. But I don't hear a lot of *smart*, and it is refreshing. You may be right, Del, but I am not smart like you."

"Few people are," Del said and blinked. His glasses made his eyes look large. His un-buttoned white lab coat's left sleeve looked like Swiss cheese from an acid splash. He was barefoot, and bent forward to examine the spaces between his toes, then produced a pack of Black Jack licorice gum from his lab coat's pocket.

Madge declined his offer of a stick. She leaned forward. Del got the full view of what was under her sweater. "A person going crazy would not know she was going crazy, would she?"

"One of the comforts of insanity is knowing one is insane. Except at the worst moments. Are you having self-destructive thoughts?"

"No," she lied.

"Periods of intense depression? Like you can't get out of bed?"

"No," she lied again. "Nothing like that."

"Blackouts?"

She paused on that one. "Maybe. There's stuff I can't remember."

"'Stuff'?"

"You know what I mean. Don't play stupid on me, Del. It's not your nature. I know you know what I am talking about. Let's be smart together. And let's be dead honest. It's that Riverton thing. Private sin is remembered; as soon as it is shared, the memory is wiped out. Maybe you and I should sin someday. As an experiment. You could take notes."

"Strictly for science."

"Anything for science."

Del touched his lips and chewed his gum more slowly. "I would not call the Riverton singularity *sin*. The theological overtones are a distraction. How about *shame*? That locates the phenomenon in people, rather than a deity. Private shame versus public shame. I can deal with psychological, cultural and even chemical—but I draw the line at Divine." Del was so damned smart, she thought of just throwing him to the ground to have her way with him— strictly for science. "It may not be just in Riverton, too. We don't have sufficient data. Maybe there are a dozen other places where people forget stuff. But if we are being honest, this is old stuff. What brings this question on today?"

She exhaled a final great cloud of blue smoke. Did total honesty imply complete disclo-sure? "Nothing, really. What's your take on reincarnation?"

"Geez, this must be my week. In Chem class, your boyfriend Juice asked me the color of Heaven."

"He's not my boyfriend."

"I stand corrected. You'll want to tell him that yourself." Del spread and relaxed his toes.

"Fuck you, Del. What did you tell Shithead?"

"I gave him some fairytale about silvery clouds and he nodded his head, happy as a bobble-doll on a jackhammer."

"Is that what you think? Reincarnation is a fairytale?"

"More or less," Del said. "It's a matter of faith. More in the east than the west, but faith is the same everywhere. Where no evidence exists, people impose what they need to believe." Del rose from the chair and crossed the room to a small sink. He rinsed glassware and set test tubes on a wooden drying rack over a folded dish towel. "Reincarnation presumes an immortal soul for which there is no evidence, and since the versions of reincarnation I have seen always include amnesia from one life to the next, even if reincarnation existed, what would it matter?" He watched Madge think, and added, "Why? Who died?"

"Nobody fucking died. Did I say anyone died?" Madge's eyes flashed and she stubbed what was left of her cigarette into a Petri dish. "Okay, genius-boy, bear with me. I am eliminating possibilities. Tell me about naturally occurring psychotropic substances."

"Jeez, Madge, where do you come up with this stuff?" He smiled. "You are not going to tell me you are not smart again, are you?" Del flipped open an autoclave and after placing each of his sterilized instruments into flannel sleeves, placed the sleeves in a drawer. "You mean Psilocybin? Stuff like that? You did not learn that stuff at Riverton High. The end of Science at Riverton High is the difference between animal and plant cells. They've never heard of DNA. If I ever have to do another diorama of the water cycle, I'll power it with spit, I swear to God."

"When you swear, is that the God you do not believe in?"

"That's the one."

She grinned. "I read a lot, Del. I've been online looking into mass psychosis." Madge lifted GIGO's beaker to her face again. To GIGO, Madge must have looked more bug-eyed than the fish looked to her. A motionless fish should have been a dead fish. "Suppose magic mushrooms grow near the reservoir?" she asked.

"No chance," Del said. "Riverton water is purer than glacial run-off."

"Test the water," Madge said, idly scratched her knee, and then touched the soft spot at the base of her own throat.

"I would, just to please an old friend, but there's no point to it, Madge. It's a waste of time. Even if a field of psychedelic mushrooms were growing beside the reservoir, they could never leech enough toxins into the water to poison a whole town. Besides, Riverton aerates its water, and psilly is delicate stuff, a big honkin' molecule that degrades even without being pushed through pipes. The molecules break down before the water table can carry it to your faucet."

"'Psilly' is it? You say that like you are old friends."

He shrugged. "I cooked up some synthetic. Just to see if it could make me think in a different way. For science."

"Of course, for science." Madge laughed.

"No. I'm serious. Did you know that Sherlock Holmes took cocaine to sharpen his deductive powers?"

"Did it work for you?"

"Not really. If you want to try my synthetic psilly, there's still some in the refrigerator over there. Reds look more red. Yellows more yellow. Everything is more intense. Hyper-reality."

"Would it make sex better?"

"I'd have to conduct an experiment. For science. I'd need a volunteer. How did we grow up together and miss playing Doctor?"

"It may not be too late for that. But yes. Of course. For science."

Del added, "But why would everyone in town share the same illusions?"

Madge said, "Delbart, you're a pain in my pert ass." Delbart's crooked smile and uneven teeth pleased her again.

She shook her head resignedly. She knew no more than before. When she hopped off the workbench, her short hair and bangs jounced. At Del's door, she turned to ask, "Do you want to walk with me? There's more I need to know, and your opinion matters," she said.

Del slipped into a pair of moccasins and shrugged into his Riverton team jacket, probably the smallest size they made. It still looked big on him; it had no varsity letter.

They walked with their hands in their pockets. Del ignored his cold feet. You'd think a guy with an IQ over two hundred would know the uses of socks. Their breath hung in misty clouds before them. "Del, I need to check whether I am crazy. You'll check for me, right?"

"If you really need me to. Just tell me why."

So with the new snow gently crunching beneath their feet, she told Delbart a little of how she, Mickey, and Bughouse had gone to Haverhill. She left out the parts about her growing certainty that Mickey had rigged the basketball game, everything about Juice, Danny Donnelly's hands on her, and Mickey's gun. When she finished, as they arrived at the convenience store, it sounded like they'd gone to Haverhill to meet a nice old lady named Aunt Sosha, and she felt like an idiot talking to Del. But God bless the genius, he listened to every word.

Every girl needs a person who listens.

"Have you seen Buggie lately?" she asked as the convenience store clerk handed her four packs of Marlboro Lights. Madge never wanted for money. She never asked the universe where her money came from.

"Come to think of it, no. Haven't you?"

"I've been in the house."

"Sick?"

"Something like that. But you have not seen Bughouse, right?"

"When I am into my work, I don't notice much."

Del had not reported to school for two weeks. He saw no point in telling Madge. He was hot onto a bio-chemical solution that could bring him five figures.

On the walk back, Del explained how a company named Hemenway Drug offered a bounty for a new refining process that Del guessed was the intermediate stage of a new drug in development. The first person or organization that delivered it would get ten grand. As a registered researcher, he was in the race. "They think I am a whole lab," he said. "I beat Stanford and MIT now and then." It was no boast.

"That's how you got that nifty car?"

"That's my baby, my Austin-Healy 3000 Roadster. I did the restoration by hand. Re-plated every bit of chrome. Damn near skinned a cow to cure my own leather."

Madge suddenly increased her pace and Del thought how watching Madge walk away was a vision of her second best feature, or third, depending on how one tallied her two best features. Madge could not know that on the wall beside the lab's sleeping shelf Del kept a photo of Madge taped to the wall, one he'd shot with a telephoto lens, though he could not re-call when or how. It was a simple photo of her on her back porch, her hands on the balustrade, staring up and away from her house.

"Del, let's go to Haverhill. I want to check on Bughouse. I can persuade Aunt Sosha to give Bughouse a break. She liked me."

Madge waited for Del. His short legs made it hard for him to keep up. She'd have to walk slowly when she was with him. "A guy whose IQ was double his weight has certain advantages," she said, "worth waiting for," and she flashed him her best smile.

The smile was sincere: Del perceived connections where no one else did. Smarts were sexy as hell. What would he make out Danny and Ari and Aunt Sosha? For the first time in weeks, she felt hope.

Del, for his part, believed Madge was *interesting*. The girl had read a few books; her questions were profound. He'd never be able to feed her bullshit; she'd chew up any soothing crapola answer and spit it back in his eye. Just because she was an adrenaline junkie who might not work Diophantine Equations, it did not mean she might not be fun to ride with.

Besides, when Del looked at Madge he wanted to take off his shoes and run across her chest like it was fresh cut grass, throw her on her back across his workbench, lock her ankles behind his neck, and do her so hard she'd think her cervix had been pushed into her liver.

Del was a genius; not a choirboy. His IQ was 212, a three digit palindrome that also happened to be the same as the Fahrenheit boiling point of water, more than double his weight of 102 pounds.

How often would a girl with a perfect, symmetrical, inverted valentine ass, never mind a girl who lived behind a chest that could distract the Pope from Mass on Easter Sunday, ask him to go for a ride? Sure, some significant bounty money was at stake at Hemenway, and, sure, the online discussion boards were filled with rumors that a group at Ann Arbor neared a solution, but every one of those turkeys in Michigan would leave their wives and sweethearts for the privilege of a ride with Madge; one look from those jade green eyes was worth any number of dollars.

He said, "Your car or mine?"

By ten the next morning, early for Madge, they were in the Subaru. Del buckled himself in, though he noted that Madge at some time must have sliced through the vinyl of her safety belt. The driver's seat had no such nuisance.

Before the tires gripped the highway, Madge inhaled deeply and said in a rush, "I have a theory about why Riverton makes no sense."

"A fresh hypothesis? Not more about psilocybin?"

Madge described her theory of grand talents paired with defeating defects. "We've been made to be ridiculous," she said. "You too. You're a world-class genius, Del. What in fuck are you doing in high school?"

"I try to ignore that. I can't take school too seriously, but I feel as if I have to show up. It's not easy to get rid of the feeling."

"How do you mean?"

So he told Madge about his days when long after he awakened he felt as though he'd emerged from a trance, those shorter days with fewer hours of consciousness, those days he felt as if he should know more than he did, those days when dawn was not the beginning of his day. "Do you dream, Madge? I don't think I ever dream."

"Maybe you just don't remember," she said. "Everybody dreams. Even caterpillars and butterflies. Maybe we are sleepwalking."

He shrugged. "Coming awake in the middle of the day is distressing. We're like drunks emerging from blackouts."

"We could spend a night together. I'd watch you. Make sure you are not sleepwalking."

"For science."

"Of course."

Del frequently awakened at the top of the climbing rope in gym class. He told Madge of how the damned rope was snaked around his ankles and waist like a boa constrictor. His first thought was always, *How in fuck did I get here again?* Mickey, Bughouse, Chukker, Coach Kennedy, and Arnie were below, laughing. They wore those puffy cotton brown Riverton gym shorts and their gold T-shirts. Arnie pointed up and laughed and laughed: *Kyuk, kyuk, kyuk.* Coach turned crimson blowing on his metal whistle. Arnie slapped his knees with joy. The mere thought of it pissed him off. "Arnie is a talentless, brainless, perfect freckle-faced sub-prick asshole," he said to Madge.

"Don't hold in your feelings just because I am a girl," Madge said.

Del slumped against the door. "Fuck him."

The Subaru roared through the crosswalk in front of Riverton High. Yellow school buses were unloading, their red lights flashing. Madge swung out into the oncoming lane, and her reflexes spared the lives of several emerging sophomores who dropped their book bags and scattered in wide-mouthed terror before Madge floored the accelerator. The bus driver honked angrily, but Madge did not so much as glance in the rearview mirror. The world was in front of her; drive fast enough, pass everyone and you never need to look back. Del rolled down his window and held out his arm, the middle finger raised.

Madge scratched her leg. "What happens at the top of the rope?"

"Your boyfriend, Juice, gets sent to rescue me. He hauls me down on his shoulder like a sack of fertilizer."

"Juice is not my boyfriend. Stop saying that."

"Oh come on," Del said. "Everyone knows Juice is your boyfriend."

Madge took her eyes from the road long enough to look into Del's eyes. "I'd fuck a guy who was my boyfriend, Del. I'd remember it. God knows, he would."

"Really? You'd fuck a guy?" Del held her challenging stare.

"Bet your bony ass. You think everyone in Riverton High is a virgin? We just look like kids. You are no kid when it comes to brains. I have my talents, too."

"Scientifically speaking, strictly for science, I'd love to learn the details."

"Well, for the sake of science, maybe we'll investigate someday."

"For science."

She laughed. "You and your rope remind me how in Riverton every summer the girls go skinny-dipping at the quarry and come out of the water to discover their clothing is gone. Every fucking time. I can't remember going in the water—but there I am with Mary and Victoria totally bare-ass behind a bush. We don't get raped; we just blush and squeal and run barefoot. I have no idea who takes our clothes. Fuck, I am not even sure how we got there."

"Next time the girls go skinny-dipping, you be sure to let me know."

"Count on it, genius-boy. Next summer, I just might. Bring your binoculars."

Talking helped. Everyone needs someone to trust. Life alone is just too hard. Madge turned to Del and said, "We exist to be humiliated." Conviction filled her. "Maybe I am Juice's girlfriend for the same reason you weigh...what?"

"One-twenty-five," Del lied.

"See? I get the best rack in town, but I also get a dickless imbecile for a boyfriend; you get brains and the body of an eleven-year old. No offense. It makes us pathetic."

"No offense taken. It's not quite a theory, but it's not a bad bit of observation. Science, Madge, science. You sound like a mystic. You need a theory."

"So far all I have is observation," she lied. Her heart knew the answers, but she did not want Del to think she was crazy. She could not lose her only ally. "Here is Mary, gorgeous, but dumb as a post. Juice has the strength of ten men, but he needs help tying his shoes, he is so fucking stupid. Trust me on this—the boy is not only brainless, but sexless. Bughouse is pathologically shy around girls, but the poor bastard has a hard-on all the time. His pants look like the main tent at the circus."

"You look?"

"Fuck you, Del. Grow up. Of course I look. Any girl says she doesn't has defective ovaries. Listen to me. Just stop being a dork for five minutes. Just listen. Mickey hatches schemes and dresses like an Italian pimp, but he is a perpetual fuckup with great plans. Victoria Cabot has money and drop-dead gorgeous looks, every advantage, but her arrogance always puts her into deeper shit."

Del worried a fingernail with his teeth. He might have to reassess Madge, yet again. *How did she explain her own existence and ability to doubt?* Every skeptic had to account for himself. You could not be in the system and at the same time claim to be out of the system. But Del had to admit, not only did Madge have the best rack in town but she understood the Singularity in ways he had never considered. Maybe they were all at the top of their personal ropes. He said, "What about the adults?"

Madge bit her lip. "I haven't worked this all out, Del. It's not a fucking equation. Give me a break. I am trying something here. Trying. But notice how older folks get one quality each. No contradictions. Daddy Kane is jovial. Grimley is stern. Horatio Cabot worries about Victoria's purity. People in Riverton are about as deep as sidewalk puddles after a light rain."

"And then there is Arnie."

Her palms slapped the wheel. Del was coming around to where she already was. "That's the thing. Arnie *is* a total dork-wad. But Arnie always wins. All the rest of us lose, but fucking

Arnie always wins." She was shouting.

Del said, "He does seem to beat the odds. But there has to be a reason. Maybe he is just the outlier. You know what Einstein said about chance?"

"No, but I'm sure you'll tell me."

Del had never before noticed the dimple on her right cheek. It seemed to wink at him.

"'God does not play dice with the universe.' Einstein thinks there must be cause and effect."

"Fuck old Albert. Old Albert never visited Riverton," Madge said. "In Riverton, God is down on one knee in an alley blowing Divine Breath on three watchamacallits. You know, those dice with twelve sides?"

"Dodecahedrons?"

"That's the ones. But they are loaded."

Del said, "We have to be missing data. There are always two ways to understand everything. We are missing the data to explain it by logic, that's all."

Driving to Haverhill with Del was more fun than she'd imagined it could be. The talk was getting her somewhere. This was nothing like being with Mickey. Every day need not be the same as every other.

"I'll tell you an old story to make a point."

"I'm listening," she said. "Make your point."

"Suppose two guys are in a lifeboat in the middle of the Pacific Ocean."

"Got it," she said and lighted a cigarette with the butane lighter she picked out of her purse. She kept the purse on the floor between her legs. Enough crap was in her bag to stock a convenience store, but Madge didn't need to look, just reached in, snared the lighter, and lighted up.

"Those things will make you sick," Del said and cracked his car window.

"Not in Riverton, but get on with it, Del. You left me in a leaky rowboat with two guys in the middle of the fucking Pacific."

Del resolved to investigate Riverton cancer and stroke rates. He watched Madge's thighs work the clutch and the accelerator; immortality rose insistently between his legs.

She slammed the shift into high. The Subaru's transmission ground. They were doing ninety. Madge did not so much drive as fly at low altitudes. They swerved around an eighteen-wheeler at the base of a grade and raced it to the top. Madge steered with her right wrist; her left hand flicked ash out the window. The remnant of her cut seatbelt flapped unfastened near her shoulder. Except for a wisp of bangs over her left eye, the wind hardly rustled her short, black hair. The Subaru's ashtray overflowed with crushed butts. Madge shouted to be heard over the wind, the Subaru's engine, and the truck's diesel belching black exhaust. As they crested the hill, they opened distance on the truck.

Ashes settled onto Madge's cranberry sleeveless denim top over her broadcloth white shirt; her hands left the wheel and her eyes left the road to brush her chest clean. They didn't slow down, though. Easing up on the accelerator was an act of cowardice. The landscape charged at them as Del told his story.

"One guy is a minister, the other is a scientist. It's been three days and they are out of water and food. There's no land in sight, and no ship on the horizon."

"Okay, so they are fucked."

"Beyond fucked. 'Fucked' would be a step up. The minister says, 'Let's pray,'" and the scientist figures he has nothing to lose and joins him. They kneel in the bottom of the boat, lace their fingers, and raise their hands to Heaven.

"Twenty minutes go by until a whale surfaces just under the boat. Whales are mammals, so they have to come to the surface to breath."

"No shit. Fuck it, Del, don't let these boobs fool you. Tits are not inversely proportional to brains. I am not a total fucking idiot. I know whales are mammals. So are dolphins. They've got tits, too. Don't fucking patronize me, okay? And try looking at my eyes when you talk to me. I'm up here."

She touched her chin; the speedometer crept to 95.

"Point made."

"Two points." She laughed wildly and then lowered her voice. "If I have a question, I swear to God I'll ask you. Do I seem shy?" Wind whipped a stream of cigarette smoke out her window; they passed three cars on the right. Her head swiveled and her green eyes flashed. "Well, fucking get on with it. There's a whale."

"Right. The lifeboat balances on the whale's back and the animal carries them for hours, swims to land, and submerges. The boat floats, of course, and the two castaways wade to the shore as the whale disappears.

"The minister drops to his knees on the beach and shouts, 'Praise God! God be praised!' but the scientist looks at him in shock."

"In shock? What's he in shock about?"

"He says, 'Don't thank God, thank the whale, you jackass.'"

Madge said, "I like that. 'Don't thank God, thank the whale.'"

Madge veered onto the icy right shoulder to pass a truck on the right, the left lane being blocked by a Toyota SUV creeping at a mere 75. The SUV may have been hauling half a third grade soccer team. Madge muttered, "Baby on board, my ass... Fuck you, fuck your baby, and fuck that bus you drive." She pumped the accelerator, and raised a cloud of gritty dust and ice particles—the stuff of a comet's tail. The faster she drove, the faster Del chewed his gum.

Then she turned to Del and said conversationally, "If you are going to ride on the shoulder, there is no better car than a Subaru." At 100 mph, with less than ten yards to go before they'd have collided with the stone piling of an overpass, she jerked the car back onto the road, lowering her window to flip her middle finger to the trucker and the soccer Mom.

But then Madge slowed to 70. It felt like reentry to the atmosphere. She chewed at her lower lip. "Wait a sec, Del. Take me back to this island."

"I'm with you. We're back on the island."

She lighted another cigarette and peered at a road sign. "I think we want the next exit. It's hard to remember. Mickey was driving... Okay, the minister and the scientist disagree on why the whale showed up. Answer to a prayer, coincidence, or maybe just what whales like to do. They can never agree. I get that. No matter how much evidence the scientist offers, the minister will believe God put the evidence there. Your dinosaur bones, your mutating viruses, nothing proves anything except that nothing means nothing, or the Good Lord is forever fucking with us. The deity spends eternity hanging red herrings in the living room to see if we are stupid enough to believe with our lying eyes instead of our bleeding, sacred hearts. And this sadistic, mad, Grifter in Heaven threatens us with hot pitchforks and brimstone up our asses forever if we are stupid enough to yield to the temptations God Himself created."

"Right. The reverend and the scientist are an old story, Madge. I did not make it up. You got it. No matter how much they know, they will account for the world differently. They are both right, or they are both wrong."

"That's the part I don't get. How can they both be wrong?"

"It's like Schrodinger's cat."

Her palms slapped the steering wheel. "Give me a fucking break, Del! What does someone's pet kitty have to do with this? I know kittens and I know pussy, but what's with this Schrodinger dude?"

How could anyone as smart as Madge not know about Schrodinger's cat? "Schrodinger was a man," Del said and explained how Schrodinger performed a thought experiment to explain quantum states. Place a cat in a box and bombard it with neutrons. Don't open the box. Maybe the cat is dead; maybe it is alive. You have to treat the box as a system in which the cat is both dead and alive at the same time, equal chances for both. "Like the cat in two contradictory states, whales either do what whales do, or God wills whales to do what whales do, but in terms of what we can see, *dead* or *alive* look the same. We are outside the system, so we cannot know."

Madge contentedly exhaled a blue-gray cloud of carcinogenic poisons. "I guess this Schrodinger guy is not up for any PETA Award, but I got it," she said, "I got it."

They'd driven only a little more before Madge said, "My turn, genius-boy. Let's suppose now a tribe of cannibals crawls out of the bushes."

"Cannibals?" Without discarding the old, Del inserted a fresh stick of Black Jack into his mouth.

"You said it's an old story. Okay. Let me add some new stuff. Fuck the cat. If this Schrodinger dude can do a thought experiment, so can I. I know the difference between fake pussy and real pussy, but right now I want cannibals. By the way, how are you on pussy, Del?"

Del pretended to ignore what Juice's girl asked him, but said, "Okay. You have cannibals. How many do you need?"

"All I can get."

"You get a tribe."

She laughed and squeezed Del's knee. No calculus could ascertain the risk of accepting what Madge offered. Del discounted the rumors about Mickey, not so much because Mickey was not a hound, but because even Mickey could not be so stupid as to think he could steal a kiss from Juice's girl and not suffer consequences. Still, watching how Madge drove with her whole body, her legs, her arms, leaning left and right, Del recalculated the risk-reward ratio.

Madge said, "The cannibals come out of the trees, scoop up the minister and the scientist, and drop them in a pot. The cannibals start beating tom-toms or whatever in fuck it is that cannibals beat, they set a fire, and every cannibal on the island grabs his honey for a serious evening. Feast first, jungle juice second, fertility rites by dawn."

"Got it," Del said. "It's party time on Cannibal Island."

Madge kissed her fingertips. "Exactly," she said. "The minister and the scientist are waiting to come to a boil, and so they have a few minutes to discuss the situation. The scientist says, 'Bad luck.' I mean, what else can he blame? Days at sea, a whale ride, and none of it means dick because he will be suet as soon as the cannibals can locate a turnip. He could know all there is to know about wind, tides, whales and cannibals, but he still ends up in the pot. Karma is karma. Fucked is fucked."

Del nodded. He saw where she was going, but waited for her to take him. Good conversation was like good sex — a slap, a tickle, and then on to higher intensity. What good lover hurries his partner?

"But what can the minister blame? Who put the cannibals on the island, and why in fuck did God's whale take them there? I mean, how can the minister accept that God is fucking them over like that? If you have an answer for me, I am all tits and ears, Delbart. Just do not tell me 'God moves in mysterious ways,' because that's an answer to soothe children. I will not be soothed. Fuck soothing. This girl does not go gentle into that good night. And I will dropkick the testicles of any pinhead who tells me the minister blames the Devil. I could not stand that. Not from you, Del. I like you. Don't give me the fucking Devil because you know what I will ask, and after that I will have to hurt you."

"'Who put the Devil on the Devil's evil mission?'"

"Damn, it is refreshing to be with a boy with a brain that matches his balls. If your dick is half as good as your mind, we might have a hell of a time someday. A hell of a time."

"For science."

"Absolutely. For science."

"Why do you hang out with Juice?" Del asked, but Madge stomped the accelerator to the floor, the Subaru fishtailed around a curve, and inertia's heavy hand on his chest pushed him into the seat. They were verging on 100 again. If standing on the accelerator could make a car go faster, Madge would have driven standing up.

The exit ramp to Haverhill was a long, slow curve around a pale yellow grass field crusted by filthy snow. Downshifting hard enough to launch her piston valves through the engine block, Madge said, "You have to wonder, though. Suppose the cannibals had been hungry. Fresh out of missionaries and coconuts, maybe they did a dance, rattled some bones, threw a spare virgin into the volcano, and this whale swam up with lunch. Sort of like dialing out for a pizza, but by prayer."

"So the minister and the scientist are asking the wrong question."

"Right. Right. That has to be it. They are asking, 'Why did this happen to us?' and the story is not about them. The story is about the cannibals. The cannibals are inside the box with Schrodinger's cat. They know what is what. We are outside, clueless."

The ramp delivered them to a Haverhill street near a dingy Dunkin' Donuts. Madge braked beside a police car in the donut shop's black macadam parking lot. She rubbed her temples. "Is that it, Del? You and me, we're the minister and the scientist. I see that. But who in fuck are the cannibals?"

"We can't know, Madge," he said.

"I want to be a cannibal, Del. I need to be a cannibal."

She violently cracked open the car door, and when it bounced back at her, she kicked it open with more force. It swung and dented the police car.

GRANDFATHER TIM OFTEN CRACKED A CAN OF PBR, TOOK A LONG SWAL-
low, belched loud enough to scare the birds, and said to no one in particular, *What was life if
not one damned thing after another?* And here was the despised Riverton heaping surprise
upon surprise on Danny Donnelly's head faster than a flock of pigeons could shit on a statue
in the park.

If a month ago you'd have asked Danny Donnelly Mickey Black's fate, Danny would
have predicted lead pipe water wings and tank-free scuba lessons in the dark lake behind
Aunt Sosha's home. Danny himself expected to have been dispatched to Riverton to explain
to the boy how his friend's unfortunate disappearance was precursor to his own, and Danny,
for the record, had looked forward to that, not so much because he wished to pound Mickey
Black to a smudge of grease than for the faint possibility of once again encountering sweet
Madge Klink. The number of women in Danny's life enamored of red thong underwear was
few, and the clean scent of her hair lingered in his memory.

Surprise number two was that seven times in four weeks, Mickey Black had appeared
with a bag of cash in one hand and his other eager hand extended for yet more product. He
sold better than Girl Scouts offering free head with every box of peanut butter cookies.

Despite being a first class earner, Mickey Black's regularity and obedience had en-
gendered no fondness in Danny. The lad was off center in that Riverton way. It left Danny
twitching with the heebie-jeebies. Why, just yesterday, Ryan and Danny passed lunch specu-
lating on whether the little dandy with immaculate black hair would appear wearing beige
or olive slacks.

"Beige, it will be," said Ryan, withdrawing a five dollar bill from the antique cash reg-
ister, and slapping Abe Lincoln flat with certainty onto the marble shelf beside a full line of
Clubman Pinaud tonics, lotions, talc, and colognes, the sweet aroma of Lilac Vegetal being
Margaret Mary Donnelly's favorite.

Danny matched Ryan's bill with his own.

After Mickey Black appeared and then departed with fresh supplies for the eager youth
of Riverton, as Ryan folded his ten dollars into his breast pocket, Danny asked, "What if he
had worn black? Or blue?"

Ryan thumbed his lower lip. "A push, Danny-boy. A push. But he's so predictable, I feel
almost sorry to take your money."

"As long as they suck down pills in Riverton, and so long as our good friend Mickey earns, he can wear cellophane drawers if it pleases him." Danny riffled the roll of wrinkled cash Mickey had given him. The boy was up to three large a week, and growing. Who'd have thought Riverton was a market for the kind of painkillers dock workers in Boston and fishermen in Gloucester sucked down like M & Ms? What the hell were they about in Riverton?

"It's the pomade keeps his hair so perfect, you know. You can smell it on him. The boy is a throwback to a better time, Danny."

"It's Riverton."

"No doubt."

Danny had been about to speculate on the backward nature of all that emanated from Riverton, but at that very moment two high school sweeties in the tartan skirts and saddle shoes of St. Brendan's Academy appeared outside Ryan's glass door. They huddled safe from the wind in The Clip Joint's breezeway, taking the opportunity to bend and peel off their bulky woolen socks and then tug on pantyhose they withdrew from their book bags.

Ryan crossed himself.

As the father to daughters, Danny saw the wisdom of boundaries impeding the lust surrounding jailbait, though in the case of Madge Klink, who seemed at once a child and at once a fully grown woman, the boundaries blurred. As his sweet, pregnant, Margaret Mary grew larger than Connecticut and found all manner of marital congress to be awkward if not unsavory, Danny too gazed upon the young girls' bared thighs outside the Clip Joint's glass with the kind of longing that if indulged led a man only to a cellblock, a jailhouse dentist who removed canine teeth with a pliers, and a roommate named "Bubba."

Ryan sighed, "There ought to be a law."

Danny replied, "Ah, my friend, but there is."

Madge Klink's firm breast had neatly filled Danny's large hand; that perfect inverted valentine ass had pressed firm to his hip as he'd taught the gutless Mickey the use of a revolver. Think of things he might teach young Madge! Fresh as a child, mature as a woman, ripe as a summer plum and twice as sweet.

They grew them strange in Riverton, they did that.

While Mickey was one surprise, and his persistent longing for Madge another, it was Bughouse who filled Danny Donnelly with ongoing wonder. Mickey Black had made good on all he promised, and by rights Bughouse should have been sent home to Riverton, but complications had arisen.

The miracle boy lived the Life of Riley in the small two-room windowless apartment Aunt Sosha had Ari construct in her basement. Though he dined lavishly on her cooking, Bughouse gained no flesh. Bughouse was supplied with all manner of books and videos, had the 50-inch flat screen TV, an X-Box game console, HD cable, and was learning to play a fair game of chess against Ari.

That, however, was not the miracle.

Ari was not one to leave a job incomplete. The webcams he'd placed throughout Bughouse's quarters were hidden. The lad had not been with them two days when Ari gestured to Danny to join him to observe the boy. In dim light, Bughouse lay on his back caressing what appeared to be a baseball bat between his legs. Danny let out a low whistle and mumbled the *Pater Noster.*

Ari, whose utterances were rare, held up four fingers. "Just today," he said

The two men breathed more deeply and watched.

After two days of performances that shamed the legendary donkeys of pre-Castro Cuba, Danny, who would rather endure Hell's own imps than chat with Ari, asked the former Mossad interrogator, "Should we tell our good aunt?"

Ari tugged at his lower lip and then slowly nodded.

That very afternoon, Aunt Sosha watched a DVD Ari made for her. "*Gevalt,*" she said. "Every day?"

"More like all day long," Danny replied. Ari concurred.

At the subsequent dinners they enjoyed at Aunt Sosha's table with Bughouse in attendance, Bughouse became an honored guest. He sipped Aunt Sosha's Rothschild '93 while they whispered and giggled like school girls, and they laughed aloud while discussing the merits of Kandinsky versus Chagall. Now and again, Aunt Sosha placed a friendly hand on Bughouse's knee, a gesture whose complete meaning Danny chose not to consider.

Plans were made and plans were set in motion. Bughouse's talents precipitated a call to Aunt Sosha's brother in Brooklyn, Dmitri the *goniff.* Dmitri had at first disbelieved. Danny himself had taken the DVD and two more like it to the Fedex office. Hours after the DVDs arrived in Brighton Beach, an agreement was struck between Massachusetts and Brooklyn, but all depended on one Moscowitz. Moscowitz was a man of indefinite origins who could most often be found in Los Angeles. He was creative director of Spank the Monkey Films. Spank the Monkey specialized in talent from far away Myanmar and the slums of Bangalore, places where poor nutrition made girls of legal age appear far younger. The younger the girl, the larger the gross.

Nothing was possible without Moscowitz; everything was possible with him.

Moscowitz was chagrined to learn that circumstances made it ill-advised to place Bughouse on a jet bound for the sunnier climes of California, as Moscowitz himself had a morbid fear of flying toward snow. "Pish-tosh," Aunt Sosha said. "It will be easier to keep an eye on the boy here. Come, Moscowitz, personally I will go to the airport to greet you." After he viewed copies of the now fabled DVDs, mollified by a first-class ticket from Aunt Sosha, Moscowitz himself boarded an American Airlines jet bound for Boston and snowy New Eng-land—strictly for screen tests and an understanding there would be no one on the set other than local talent. Why pay for importing starlet power when willing girls advertized their availability on the Internet in every city in America?

Aunt Sosha generously offered to rent all necessary technical equipment at her personal expense in exchange for an additional ten points on all future profits. She settled for seven. Moscowitz believed in spreading risk when there was plenty of money to be made as there was little point to grasping at every last dime while in the negotiation stage. Besides, while this Bughouse looked like the real deal, Moscowitz had been down the path with potential male stars who, despite fluffers and a diet of nothing but raw eggs, beneath arc lights had the strength of overcooked *kreplach*. Bad enough, he was flying into the cold, overinvesting in unproven talent was the road to ruin. So giving away seven points of money not yet made was a simple business decision in a business where he himself would keep the books. Seven points could be made to be three or two with the stroke of a red pen. Gross? Net? Who could say?

While it was common practice to surgically repair the anatomical deficiencies of women, especially Asian girls whose eyes might be too narrow or breasts too small, gifted men were admittedly rare. There was only so much that could be done with camera angles and lighting, though stamina could be chemically managed. The fag market was lucrative, but not every well endowed boy could be drugged into a performance with a male partner or three, but a weeping female could always be penetrated and suggestions of rape could sell that that much more.

The call from back east came just as Spank the Monkey was contemplating diversify-ing its product line, and here was this Bughouse Smith who might be the centerpiece for any contemplated marketing initiative that might remove the heat from UNESCO. A male star was rare, and white male stars unheard of. If this Bughouse was the reincarnation of John Holmes, Moscowitz would brave a plane ride even into the blizzards of New England.

Moscowitz the skeptic flew east; Aunt Sosha herself had this very day gone to the air-port to greet him.

So things should have been all steak and vanilla ice-cream in Haverhill, but a conun-drum stared Danny Donnelly in the face. All he was able to do was stare back. Danny parted the curtain over Aunt Sosha's sitting room window a third time to peer into the gray Haver-hill day. Across the street, light snow capping the roof, engine running, sat the conundrum, a brown Subaru.

Its presence taunted him. Grandfather Tim was a man of wisdom: *One damn thing after another.*

House-sitting was a task that should have provided Danny an opportunity to nap; it was leaving him with an ulcer.

Should he go out and confront the occupants of the Subaru, call Aunt Sosha for further instructions, or do nothing at all?

The first stratagem, confronting the occupants, left no one at the ready, strictly forbidden. Aunt Sosha's home was never empty. Feebs thick as biblical locusts might seize even the briefest opportunity to infest Aunt Sosha's home through an unguarded rear door. Indeed, the mystery Subaru might have been planted with the express purpose of drawing Danny Donnelly onto the front porch so legions from the FBI, ATF, CIA, DEA and who knew what other alphabetized scumbags might invade unimpeded to plant microphones and cameras in places smaller than the crack of a cockroach's ass.

The second plan, a phone call, put Danny and Aunt Sosha on the airwaves, a situation that was inconceivable. Danny Donnelly carried multiple cell phones and found them indispensible for his main job of tracking Aunt Sosha's working capital on the streets of Haverhill, but Aunt Sosha herself stayed strictly off the grid. Even the telephone in her house was an old-fashioned wired phone with a corkscrew cord forever tangled. There was only the one, the wall-mounted yellow phone in the kitchen. True, Danny in fact would be calling Ari, but that had all the appeal of fastening one's testicles and tongue to a car battery, a posture Ari had once kindly sketched for Danny who had doubted it was possible. The pencil drawing featured a figure sporting a leather porkpie hat; this may have passed for humor in the Mossad, but Danny failed to appreciate the joke.

Yet Danny's third option, to keep his thumb firmly up his own ass and do naught, might prove most disastrous.

Danny loathed hard choices. Daily, the voice of the light of his life, Mary Margaret, reverberated in his mind as he parted from her: *Don't fuck up.*

Danny looked away, squeezed his eyes shut, and counted to one hundred. But when he parted the curtain again, the damned Subaru and its double-damned occupants still sat stolidly across the street.

The Subaru's window cracked open and a puff of smoke curled heavenward. Danny wondered if perhaps their colleagues were Apache Indians awaiting smoke signals.

The two dark shapes within could not be local constabulary, as the Haverhill police were a cooperative lot and relied on Aunt Sosha for the perquisites that made life as a pubic servant bearable. She contributed to any number of official police causes, several others less official. Danny doubted these could be feebs, as federal agents were Republicans, and as such would prefer total freedom for serial killers, towel-headed terrorists, drug smugglers, and child slavers before they would be caught in a rusted Subaru. While their masters favored Lincolns and Cadillacs, the feebs themselves traveled about strictly in black Buicks or Chryslers, the better to impress the criminal elements in our society of their majesty and might, and the necessity to buy American.

Nor might the Subaru hold Mickey, the Riverton pissant. Last seen, gutless Mickey Black drove a buzz-bomb Honda Accord, though he'd been talking about moving up to a Jeep Wrangler. Besides, he'd never appeared at Aunt Sosha's, knowing full well that should he do so, Danny would have taken enormous pleasure in pounding him to the width of a dime.

The light snow had delayed Boston-bound flights. If God in his wisdom had wanted men to fly, why had He invented railroads? Moscowitz would be filled with terror and loathing, and even Aunt Sosha might be in a foul mood.

The decision facing Danny was a wet sack of shit. He could not put it down, but if he held it too long, it would shred apart of its own weight, and leave a mess on his shoes.

He looked once more across the street and decided there was nothing more for it then to don his black leather coat and with a 9mm Sig in each pocket sally forth to make innocent inquiries. He was double-checking the back door locks when, with the luck of the Irish, Heaven intervened to save him.

Three hours late, but not a moment too soon, Aunt Sosha's black Cadillac Escalade spun dirty slush from its tires as it climbed the rise into the long circular driveway. What demons of marketing managed to call such a vehicle an SUV? Just what sports did Aunt Sosha and Ari engage that required so handsome and imposing an automobile?

Moments later, with her gray sweater's sleeves rolled above her elbows, Aunt Sosha ran water into a steel kettle for tea. Moscowitz was claiming jet lag, impossible as he had flown east, but he needed to sleep off the Valiums he'd swallowed as his flight endlessly circled burning fuel before a long, slow approach Moscowitz was certain would end with his jet sliding on ice and snow into Boston Harbor. Would he freeze to death or die in fire?

Aunt Sosha listened to Danny's suspicions about the Subaru, smoked, scratched her head, and then rose to her toes to reach up and pinch his cheek. "You did good, *boychik*. You did good."

Ari and Danny slid like skiers in dress shoes on Aunt Sosha's snow-covered front yard, making their way to the Subaru, unsteady, their hands deep in their coat pockets, their shoulders hunched, a posture not conducive to balance but ideal for swift lateral movement and returning fire if needed. "Snow calls for better footwear," Danny said. "Is there much snowfall in the Holy Land?"

Ari lowered his chin into his ermine collar.

Danny stepped sideways down the three broken concrete stairs to the sidewalk. He wore his black leather coat and his porkpie hat; Ari wore a black cashmere coat and matching fedora. Danny carried two 9mm Sigs; Ari favored the Glock. Neither man wore gloves.

Madge watched them come. Could the Subaru gather enough traction to leap forward over short ground and break both of Danny's knees? She reached for a cigarette from the bag between her feet but fumbled the grab, her hands shook so. Del had never before seen her miss.

"Maybe we should go," Del said.

It was too late for that. The two hoodlums flanked the Subaru. Danny's wedding ring rapped the driver's side window. When Madge lowered the glass, cold air stung her eyes.

"Fuck you," she greeted Danny.

Bent to examine the car's passengers, Danny's flat Irish face split with a broad smile. "Madge! Is that you? Game as ever, I'll warrant. All this time in the cold when I could have made you tea? Oh, the pity." The supple leather coat sagged from the weight of his guns. He spoke to Ari across the car's top. "You'll remember Madge, Ari. Our aunt took a shine to her, she did, and bid that she return. You'll remember Ari, Madge."

"Fuck the ghoul, too."

Beside Del, Ari the ghoul wiped a clear droplet that hung from the tip of his nose. Danny clapped his ungloved hands. Madge stilled her trembling long enough to light a smoke; then with more courage than she felt exhaled at Danny's face. His grin never wavered. Madge was prettier than he remembered, and he was pleased to see her spirited as ever. As Grandfather Tim observed, with women and thoroughbreds, the ones with fight in them were always worth the struggle of breaking. Danny's colorless eyelashes slowly blinked. "I pray you've forgiven me, Madge. I did only what was required, and I swear by the saints I took no pleasure in it. I know you'll respect that. Nothing was personal." His heart swelled with hope.

Madge vividly remembered the prod of his erection as he'd bent her forward. "It was as goddam personal as it gets, you stone-headed mick." She spat into the snow at his feet. "Where in fuck is Bughouse?"

"You've brought a new playmate. Are you a jockey, lad?"

"I'm not a jockey," Del said.

Danny grinned. "Well, bantamweight, then. You'll do us the favor of stepping from the car. Both of you. Smart, now."

It was no request.

Madge killed the engine and stood with her back to the Subaru's open door. "If you touch me, I'll kill you," she said through gritted teeth.

"It brings me sorrow to hear you say that," Danny said, his hope diminishing, if not extinguished. He peered into her green eyes and saw no forgiveness. "But search you now I must. If I tell our good Aunt that none other than her dear friend Madge waited hours only to decline her kind invitation to come in to rest by the fire, she will be disappointed with me. But should I deliver you to her without first assuring her safety, she will be even more disappointed. Why would you have me disappoint our good aunt? She speaks of you often, and by my children's eyes, I swear that's true. The books and whatnot and those that like them are never far from her mind. It may be she sees herself in you. So come. Which will it be? Shall you be searched by me or by Ari?"

Madge flicked her cigarette into the snow, turned to the car, and put her hands on the roof. "Just do it," she said.

With no real pressure, Danny's foot tapped her ankles wider. The shape of her ass was all that he remembered. As he frisked her, though Danny's hands moved gently, Madge's skin crawled. He popped the grommets on her team jacket only long enough to trace a fleeting edge of his palm through the space between her breasts, patted her ribs, ran his fingertips the length of her legs, and skipped her crotch completely. Madge was not the type to keep a shank in her snatch.

"Thank you, Madge. I take no pleasure in this."

"Fuck you, you lying fuck."

Ari with far less delicacy patted down the bewildered Del. Madge had said they would be checking on Bughouse; who were these people?

Danny asked, "Does the jockey pass?"

Ari held his empty palms up to Danny. He gestured to the rear of the car. Danny reached behind Madge to flip the trunk release. "Trust the Jew to be thorough," Danny said. "Tell us Ari, any sign of diesel fuel and fertilizer?"

Ari slammed the trunk closed and they made their slippery way back across the front yard.

"I'm not a jockey. I'm a scientist," Del volunteered.

"And if the queen had a pair of balls, she'd be king," Danny said, but as they stamped their feet free of snow on the wooden porch, remembering Riverton's potential for surprises, Danny asked, "And what kind of scientist might you be?"

"All kinds." The question startled him. Del had never thought of having a specialty. He knew what he needed to know whenever he needed to know it. "Physics, chemistry, organics, whatever."

Fucking Del seemed to think he was on a class outing with Grimley rather than trapped in a snowstorm with a professional sadist and a leg-breaker. Maybe they'd all slice up a cheddar cheese and have some Saltines. Del should shut the fuck up is what he should do. Where was Juice when a girl needed him? Where were Juice and his trusty baseball bat? So what if she had killed him once? He was back, no hard feelings, and right now good ol' Juice could even the score with the simple service of mashing to a bloody pulp the man who tried to tear her tits off.

When Ari spoke, his lips barely parted. He had the voice of a frog who'd never be a prince. "You cook?"

"Mostly I defrost."

Ari almost smiled, an effort that could have disintegrated his face like a hammer on a plaster death mask. Danny said, "Lad, I believe Ari was inquiring about your chemistry skills. Methadrine is commonly cooked from cough medicine. It requires your ether and whatnot."

Del said, "That's one way. You mean methamphetamine, I suppose. There are two isomers, actually...."

The lecture began. Maybe Del was nervous. Maybe Madge should have included some of the teeny details she'd omitted about her last trip to Haverhill. Del prattled on about the cascade of serotonin and dopamine that methamphetamine released in the brain, "Well documented phenomena," he added, "powerful psychologically *and* physically addictive."

"Is that right?" Danny nodded sagely.

Del, the dumb fuck genius, was going to get them killed if not worse; that was Madge's fault. She'd given Del no warning and placed him in harm's way.

Cripes, without the assistance of a whale, they had delivered themselves to fucking Cannibal Island, and now they were being waltzed into the pot.

The oak front door swung open on well-oiled hinges. A cloud of warmer air laden with the smell of lemon oil enshrouded them.

"Just tell us where in fuck Bughouse is," Madge said, calculating if while the door was still open she might bolt from the house with at least a crumb of information. She realized her challenge was not to run quickly, but only to run faster than Del. If they chased her, all she'd have to do was trip him up to guarantee that extra, needed second to start the engine.

Then, smoking a Kent and wiping her hands on a green-checkered apron, Aunt Sosha herself appeared in the dim hallway.

"You'll have a glass tea," Aunt Sosha said, "Then, Madge-ellah, you have to be on your way. Aaaach, you should first call. I have a guest, Moscowitz, but he is already asleep. So much to discuss, so little time. You read the books?"

Madge nodded.

"Today is business with Moscowitz that my brother sent all the way from Los Angeles in California. Mr. Moscowitz must return in just two days, which is why he naps before we begin work this very night. With the snow and the traffic at the airport...there's just no time.

You'll stay, have tea, I have oranges and halvah, and then you and your little friend must go. You know from halvah?"

"Del here is a chemist," Danny said as he shrugged out of his coat, relieved to be rid of the weight of the twin Sigs, still in the pockets. His heavy, cable stitched white bulky sweater came to his chin.

"This little *pisha*?" Aunt Sosha peered closely at Del. "Is Riverton filled with boys who are men, or is it filled with men who are boys? Danny, *boychik*, downstairs go and check that everything is as it should be so we are ready the minute Moscowitz opens an eye. Bring back if it is not too much trouble a carton of cigarettes for Madge. Marlboro Lights, yes? Let me make you a gift, *mein shayna maidelah*. I have to ask you, though, don't share. We have not yet had a chance to apply the tax stamps, and without the stamp, questions get asked. What I give you is a present only for your personal use. *Fishdeit?*"

Madge nodded and Aunt Sosha led them down the hall. In minutes, Del, Madge and Aunt Sosha sipped smoky tea from a samovar in the big kitchen. Madge and Aunt Sosha lighted cigarettes. Del peeled thick-skinned blood oranges. The marble halvah had pistachio nuts in it. Madge had never tasted anything quite that sweet. It made her teeth hurt. Del aggressively chewed a stick of Black Jack gum.

Aunt Sosha noticed as he slipped the pack into his shirt pocket, and gestured that he hand it over. She laughed.

"They still make this? I have not seen such chewing gum since I was a little girl. It comes too in cinnamon, yes?"

"Sure," Del said. "They sell it all over Riverton. You want one? Take the pack."

"It would take the fillings from my teeth," Aunt Sosha said, and gave the chewing gum back to Del. She turned her attention to Madge. "So, tell me, how is it going?"

"I'm suffering," Madge said. "I worry all the time. It does not feel good at all. It's not like books."

"This is truly a discovery for you?"

"I thought suffering would feel differently. Good for the soul."

Aunt Sosha patted the back of Madge's wrist. "Some lessons everyone has to learn for themselves." Aunt Sosha held Madge's gaze a long moment. She said, "Madge, the books are made up. Life is different. You know the *Kabala*? No, of course not. *Kabala* is a holy book for my people. *Kabala* says we are God's dream."

"I want to dream my own life."

Aunt Sosha poured golden tea and with a silver spoon stirred in three sugars. "Who could hope for such a privilege? We are History's dream; all Jews know this. Such questions have no answers. Better, Madge, tell me about your new friend. Is it 'Del'?"

So they sat on three high stools set around the kitchen island, Del's legs hanging like a ventriloquist's dummy's. Del explained that he rarely did more than go to school and work in his lab, and when Aunt Sosha looked skeptical, as if he were talking to an old friend, Del explained his bounty work for pharmaceutical companies.

"On the Internet?"

"Yes."

"Such a marvel. I wish I understood it. I am a simple woman." Aunt Sosha turned to Madge. "He tells the truth?" she asked. "He does this?"

Madge nodded, and Aunt Sosha turned again to Del with new respect. "So from this you make a living?"

"A good one," Del said. He described how he'd bought and reconditioned his 1968 Austin Healy 3000 Roadster after finding one for sale, buying it, and shipping it from Iowa.

"This sounds expensive."

"More than your Cadillac Escalade."

"I would not know. A friend gave that car to me. People give me things all the time. Go figure." Aunt Sosha shrugged and then questioned Madge about Riverton, whether everyone was as peculiar as they seemed or if anyone had recently changed. When Madge said, "I've been out of it, lately," Aunt Sosha asked her no more.

Twice Madge asked after Bughouse. But when she did, Aunt Sosha found a new topic, lighted a cigarette, asked Del his opinion about trivia, or laughed as if Madge had told a joke.

Buggie, she concluded, was dead. She'd cry in the car, later. Maybe. Maybe Bughouse would come back, like Juice. If that had really happened. She doubted her own memories, now.

More likely she was crazy. That could explain a lot, too.

After an hour of pointless conversation that Aunt Sosha totally controlled with a shrug here, a grunt there, a wave of her hand, or raising her eyes to heaven, Aunt Sosha slid off her stool, filled a plastic bag with dried pineapple slices and apricots, and walked the two Riverton kids to the front door. She apologized for not feeding them a proper meal.

"Business," she said, then whispered in Madge's ear, "This one I like," before she ushered the two of them out and onto the porch where Danny Donnelly waited, shivering. Aunt Sosha pulled her close, speaking too low for anyone to hear except Madge.

"My phone number," the old woman said. "Don't write it down. Remember it." She added, "Only if you God forbid need it because if you call this number, I will answer, but after that I will have to change the number. You can only use it once. The world is filled with ears."

As the front door silently closed behind her and Danny, Danny said, "Madge, if I can ever lend a hand, you'll be sure to let me know."

Madge flipped him the finger and pulled up her collar. She felt Danny's eyes on her back as she and Del walked to the car.

Darkness had fallen. From the Subaru's driver's seat, Madge saw a lighted window on the ground floor in the house go dark. For good measure, she rolled down the window and flipped Danny the bird once more, sure it had been him at the window.

She began to explain to Del that Bughouse must be dead, but then she realized she did not know that for sure.

Bughouse was Schrödinger's Cat, alive and dead all at once. She was no wiser than when she and Del had left Riverton. What had she been thinking? She was a kid, not equal to the world. Not yet.

Driving back to Riverton, the snow imposed a hush on the land, one they reproduced in the car. New ideas like wind-blown snow whirled through Madge's mind.

"Don't be pissed at me, Del."

"You should have told me these people are dangerous. What happened to 'honest'?"

"You're right. I promise—nothing but the truth," she lied. "I'll make it up to you."

"For science, I am sure," he said, but there was nothing amusing in the phrase any more.

Dashboard lights cast green and amber highlights in her eyes and hair. How long could he be angry with the neighbor girl who'd played with him so long ago in that tree house they built? They must have had fine times—those times were just hard to recall. And all the times they'd played were dear to him, even if he could not recollect them. Memory in Riverton was a function of i, the square root of negative one, an imaginary number.

"Open a pack of cigarettes for me," Madge said as they neared Riverton.

Del tore at the carton. He said, "Didn't Aunt Sosha say these had no tax stamp? She must have made a mistake." Del separated the blue stamp to open a pack.

Madge paid him no attention. Her thoughts would not straighten. "Del," she said, "You heard what Aunt Sosha said about *Kabala*? What if that's right? Suppose it is all a dream?"

"What is?"

"Everything. Us. Riverton. All of us. Aunt Sosha, too. Bughouse."

Del was smart; it was always worth talking to Del. Why had she wasted herself on Mickey Black?

"It's an unproveable premise," Del said. "Suppose I am in your dream. Or you are in mine. How could either of us prove either of us is real?"

"I could kick your ass. For science."

"But I could be dreaming that you kicked my ass. The argument is subject to infinite regression. Like God Himself."

Over a snow-covered interstate, Madge drove at near mortal speeds, the Subaru churning through miles in four-wheel drive.

"Tell me your dreams, Del."

"I told you, I don't dream."

"Exactly. I don't remember any, either. Dreams cannot dream."

"Dreams to the second power? You're weirding me out, Madge. But I'll accept your working hypothesis. Then who is our Dreamer?" he asked.

As they slowly circled the highway exit ramp back into Riverton, they simultaneously looked into each other's eyes and said,

"*Kyuk, kyuk, k-fucking-yuk!*"

After several days as Aunt Sosha's guest, Bughouse had acknowledged the benefits. They had plans for him!

Needing to shave every other day seemed a small price for not having his father regularly beat the living crap out of him. The omnipresent tension in his shoulders slacked, and he actually felt taller. He dined most evenings with Aunt Sosha. With her index fingertip flapping at her extended lower lip, she considered his opinions on whether Tintoretto or Titian was more accomplished, they agreed that Caravaggio was fiery, they debated whether representational art had any future after the inventions of the digital camera, all while she educated him to a thousand fine points of brush and canvas technique. He absorbed it all quick as she could deliver it. "As smart as a regular *yeshiva brucha*," she said, and when Bughouse asked what that meant, she said in a voice laden with respect, "Scholar." It did not hurt Bughouse's growing sense of well-being that Aunt Sosha's roast chicken was succulent and crisp, better than anything he'd ever eaten. Cooking, it seemed, was also high art, something that could go far beyond opening the cans in his father's doorless kitchen pantry.

Every three days, they supplied him with fresh white T-shirts and white shorts that smelled of Clorox. Bughouse did push-ups and sit-ups, and though he did not bulk up, his arms, shoulders, chest, and abdomen became toned as an Olympic swimmer's.

He never doubted that Mickey and Madge would return for him, eventually. People who knew each other since forever did not simply vanish. Right?

Trust good ol' Mickey to cut a deal without telling him the details! Mickey was always a step ahead of everyone, even these sharpies from Haverhill. Bughouse took pride in his role as a bargaining chip. It would all work out: everything in Riverton always did, and if he was now in Haverhill, well, what difference?

Things began to look up when Aunt Sosha's guys customized the place just for him. Mr. Ari said he had personally entertained any number of guests in these two soundproofed basement rooms, but agreed with Aunt Sosha that the accommodations were too Spartan for a guest of Bughouse's stature. They installed a shower and replaced the stained canvas cot with a mattress on a genuine wire bed frame.

"Our boy needs his rest. We expect great things from Bughouse," Aunt Sosha said one night at dinner, and Bughouse beamed.

Though windowless, the two rooms no longer seemed like a dungeon. The walls remained putty white, the color of the plasterboard beneath, and the concrete floor had a six-inch circular drain, but they hung a 50-inch flat screen TV on a wall that received every cable station. They surprised him one afternoon with an X-Box game system. "A gift for my honored guest," Aunt Sosha said. "Such trifles cost us nothing, and we want you should be happy." Then she added, "Happy and healthy. Health, that's the most important thing for a boy like you. Keep up your strength." She stood on tip-toe as if to whisper the secret of life into his ear, curled her hand around his ear and breathed, "Eat broccoli."

People cared. The feeling was new.

Mr. Ari placed a small white vitamin pill on his daily breakfast tray. It calmed him. Mr. Ari also often brought cereal and toast and a fried egg. Bughouse disliked eggs, but Mr. Ari waited while Bughouse ate and checked that Bughouse took his vitamins. "Protein," Mr. Ari said, waiting. Like a bored cat, his pale blue eyes blinked twice.

In afternoons, as long as someone was with him, Bughouse had the run of the house, except for a few days when they conducted business upstairs. Then they closed his door behind them and the padlock clicked closed. "Rest, lucky boy," Aunt Sosha said, her voice sounding muffled through the door. His vitamins kept him from panic.

Playing Call of Duty or Skyrim online, Bughouse wore a headset with a microphone, but when he interrupted the trash back-and-forth and told other players he was being held prisoner in Haverhill, Massachusetts, they told him he was full of shit. What kind of prison included an X-Box?

Bughouse joined an online posse called The Badaaassss. They won more often than they lost, and they admired his cyber handle, "Buggie." Bughouse, it turned out, as he'd always suspected, was a talented sniper, the kind who lingered in the rear and from long range picked off enemies who carelessly exposed themselves in the crosshairs of his telescopic sights. Badaaasss placed the guys with fastest reflexes up front, armed with bazookas. Sometimes Bughouse manned the chattering machine gun mounted at the rear of the jeep-thing. He liked doing that, but the dumb shit who drove the jeep flipped them twice and got them all killed. Now his own teammates killed the dumb shit before every game.

No matter. In cyberspace, everyone came back to play again. Death was inconsequential.

His memory of the day Mickey abandoned him remained a blur. Mr. Ari said he should not dwell on it—a thing past was a thing past. Bughouse recalled a powerfully pleasant sensation, and he would have liked to try the drugs one more time, but Mr. Ari said they wanted him healthy and he should just take his vitamins. Like anyone from Riverton, Bughouse tolerated ambivalent memories.

But he missed Mary. Thinking of her, his mind charged his body. Having utter privacy had its advantages; at Riverton High after a day with Mary, Madge, Victoria, and a thousand unnamed sophomores, his blood percolated, but in Aunt Sosha's soundproof rooms he dimmed the lights and administered relief.

He least missed Riverton High. Screw Grimley; screw the causes of World War I; screw especially Arnie and perpetual ridicule. At Aunt Sosha's, any library book he asked for was his in a day or two, and there were so many of those they finally bought him an e-reader, but without e-mail.

His continuing education was guided by Aunt Sosha and entrusted to Mr. Ari. Bughouse did not care for the novels she recommended, but he read deeply in Art History, particularly biographies of the Impressionists. *Letters to Theo* made him weep. Mr. Ari, too, had ideas about education. Wordlessly, on the same tray as his Cheerios and sliced banana, Mr. Ari left a paperback book about a girl who'd been taken captive by bad men. The book was illustrated with crude pen and ink pictures by someone who signed his name, Bishop. The paper was porous and grainy. The binding glue soon cracked.

Bughouse tried not to read it too often, but the pictures on pages 14, 44, and 122 haunted his sleep and invaded his waking hours. After reading and rereading the five page passage that started on page 82, Bughouse tried to lock his own ankles behind his own neck like the captive girl, and after several tries over several days, he succeeded. In his daydreams, Bughouse became all three of the men in the story, and several times, just reading, without touching himself, he became so excited that he sprayed his shorts. This proved he was a pervert; in his imagination, the kidnapped girl in the drawing looked like Mary

At least he was in private.

Mr. Ari also taught him chess. They sat on two three-legged stools on opposite sides of a low table. Mr. Ari tugged at his chin and muttered in Yiddish. "Who could play chess in English? Russian, maybe, but English? Pfui," Mr. Ari said. He derided Bughouse as a wood-pushing *potzer*, and as a matter of education he allowed Bughouse to retract his weakest moves, saying that so feeble a maneuver was too easily refuted, so his generosity was nothing for to make a *tsimis*. When at dinner Bughouse asked what *tsimis* was, Aunt Sosha's tears of laughter streaked her quivering cheeks. The very next night she prepared a delicious stew of carrots, sweet potato, and onion. "This," she laughed, "this is how you make a *tsimmis*." When Aunt Sosha laughed, her entire body laughed.

That night, Mr. Ari and Aunt Sosha poured him a shot glass of cherry-flavored Slivowitz, a kind of brandy. "Take just a little. Wet your lips," Mr. Ari said. The drink scorched his throat and left him dizzy, which was more cause for laughter, but this laughter was not at all like the daily dose of ridicule doled out by Arnie or the girls at Riverton High.

These people *liked* him.

One morning Mr. Ari left Bughouse a DVD. Bughouse dropped it into the X-Box. It held nothing but short videos, the kind Bughouse had never had the nerve to watch in the Riverton school library. Not that he could not find them: they ran too long and he knew he'd go out of control in a public place. Scene after scene on the DVD put him in a fever.

He fast-forwarded through the scene that was exclusively men. The scene where women were with women held only mild interest until one of them stepped into a strange belt that she fastened at her hips that enabled her to behave like a man. But the scene that haunted him was the last on the DVD, a scene with a woman who was with two men and several pieces of elaborate apparatus; she seemed to enjoy all manner of humiliation with stocks and handcuffs, though Bughouse thought the part with electricity had to be fake. It looked phony, but that did not mean the scene failed to arouse him.

He'd never have thought of such things on his own. Mr. Ari must have realized that Bughouse's education as a man was stunted. Mr. Ari was far nicer to him than his own father had ever been. Mr. Ari understood boys and all they needed to know.

Bughouse lost track of time and decided not to shave, but then Mr. Ari told him he must. Aunt Sosha had plans for him that required him to be clean shaven. In fact, they might someday shave his entire body, except his scalp, of course. He'd look clean.

"Plans?"

"Eat your poached egg. You must have endurance. What does not kill you, makes you stronger. A philosopher said that."

"Which?" Bughouse asked and washed the whole egg down with a double orange juice.

Two days later, Mr. Ari brought a paperback edition of *Beyond Good and Evil*. The philosopher's beard and face reminded Bughouse of a hairbrush. Did Nietzsche's friends ridicule him too? The book made him think, but Bughouse never got to finish it.

One morning Mr. Ari brought two raw eggs, tomato juice and two new kinds of pills. Mr. Ari broke the raw eggs into a drinking glass. They looked slimy. He shivered to swallow them, but he did. It was like swallowing jellyfish. Then he downed three new vitamins with the tomato juice.

Mr. Ari left him without saying a word. When Bughouse called, "Ari?" the padlock outside the door snapped shut.

Later that same day, Bughouse heard more movement than usual on the floor above.

Business, he assumed, but he had no curiosity, being absorbed in his book, underscoring in pencil *And if you gaze for long into an abyss, the abyss gazes also into you.* What could that mean? How could such nonsense move him so deeply?

When Mr. Ari and Danny Donnelly came for him, Danny Donnelly said, "Have no fear, boy. We mean you no harm. Today is your day, and you'll thank us, later."

But just as he had done the last time Bughouse saw Mickey, Danny pushed him into a chair, held open his mouth, squeezed his nose and forced him to ingest a pill. It was the second time Danny Donnelly confused Bughouse with a vending machine.

Bughouse's heart raced, not from the drug, but with fear. Would they hurt him? With Donnelly's large hand over his mouth, he could not speak. He caught Mr. Ari's pale blue eyes, but Mr. Ari ran a freckled hand over his bald head and looked away.

"Should the world suddenly seem blue, lad, worry not. It's the way of the medication." *Blue birdies? Bughouse hated the blue birdies.*

They flanked him on the tiny chess stool, Donnelly talking all the while. "There's little time to waste, as Mr. Moscowitz insists on a strict schedule, so you'll have to don this now. There won't be time later, and he wants your unrehearsed reaction. The Yid thinks he is the second coming of Fellini, I'll grant, and to hear some people tell it, he is. It's Bergman for me, but there is no denying Fellini's talent, and in his circles, Moscowitz is who he is. Will you have my help, Bughouse, or can you manage to don your costume unassisted?"

The folded robe Danny withdrew from a clear vinyl bag was a forest green and gun metal gray kimono. The black silk sash ended in strings with knots.

"That's it?"

"Every bit of it."

"But where are we going?"

The drug put his fear on a sailing voyage over a sea of pink clouds. He was aware of his terror; it just made danger seem far off, like an ice-pick wrapped in thick white cotton.

Bughouse obediently turned his back and peeled off his T-shirt and his boxer shorts. Before they could see him, he shrugged into the kimono.

"Well done, lad," Donnelly said, and then as if Bughouse were a helpless cripple, Danny Donnelly scooped him up in his two big arms easy as a baby and carried Bughouse up and out of the basement, through Aunt Sosha's kitchen, and down three wooden steps into the garage.

Aunt Sosha was already in the front bucket passenger seat of the Escalade. Mr. Ari drove. Bughouse sat beside Danny Donnelly on a bar seat behind Aunt Sosha. His door was unlocked.

"We have been good to you, Bughouse, yes?" Aunt Sosha asked, turning in her seat to face him. His sash came undone and the robe fell open, but Aunt Sosha did not avert her gaze to his nakedness. His skin tingled pleasantly.

Bughouse's head lolled with the car's motion. He'd never felt anything as soft as the black leather seat under him. He almost fell against Danny Donnelly. It would have been nice to sleep.

"You've been good to me," Bughouse slurred.

"So you'll want to do as we ask, yes? You trust us, no?"

Unsure of the right answer, Bughouse nodded. These were good people. They cared about him.

"There's our Bughouse," Danny Donnelly said, his big hand resting like a throw rug on the boy's knee as he closed the kimono. Donnelly loosely belted the sash.

Warmth emanated from somewhere under his stomach and went out to every part of his body. This was just like the final day he'd ever seen Mickey and Madge. If he never saw them again, it would be all right, as long as he could always feel like this. Mickey, Madge, Riverton—they were all long, long ago. Every inch of his skin on every spot on his body felt like the softest and best places on his body.

No, the softest and best places on a girl's body. A sweet and eager and flexible and agreeable and adventurous nineteen-year old girl. Bughouse wanted to touch himself.

The Escalade roared through Haverhill, its big wheels spitting filthy snow behind them. Melting flakes streaked the car's windows and made globular halos around the faintly green streetlights. Bughouse lost his sense of time. It must have been night; there was no sun. That was all he knew. Maybe they drove a long time; maybe a few minutes. There was no way to be sure, and who cared, anyway?

Every time he reached to touch himself, Danny Donnelly gently took his two wrists in one big hand and said, "Patience, lad, patience."

Aunt Sosha turned to him from her seat. "You're comfortable?" she asked. Bughouse nodded. Aunt Sosha stared at his lap. The kimono covered very little. "You look comfortable," she said, lighted a cigarette, and turned to face front. She said something sharp that sounded nasty in Yiddish to Mr. Ari, and he laughed, at least as much as Mr. Ari ever laughed, a kind of croak that emerged from his bloodless, thin lips. "Who'd think a fortune is in such a *schlong*?" she said. "Moscowitz estimates a hundred thousand units at fifty dollars each. *Oy vey iz mir*." When she laughed, Aunt Sosha's whole body quaked.

They penetrated the hushed night, passing Haverhill's abandoned red brick factories, their large windows blind and empty of life as the glass eyes of a carousel pony. They rumbled over a wooden bridge, went upriver, then turned down a long half hidden street that snaked back to the riverbank, passing several two-story houses decorated with Christmas lights. Bughouse waved to Santa. The black Merrimack was frozen; river ice glimmered with reflected green, yellow, red and blue lights.

The Escalade abruptly backed into a driveway that led to a loading dock of what had once been a shoe factory on the bank of the Merrimack River.

Danny said, "It's time, lad," and gently pushed him out the back of the SUV onto the dock. Mr. Ari and Aunt Sosha went to a front entrance. The cold dock floor stung Bughouse's bare feet, so Danny carried him up a green grated steel staircase into a small room that was antechamber to another larger, well-lighted room. A dark green curtain, not more than a filthy rag, really, hung over the entranceway. The wooden floors were unpolished, gritty, and dull. From beyond the curtain, Bughouse heard people shouting and arguing. Light seeped around the curtain into the antechamber.

"Where did Mr. Ari and Aunt Sosha go?"

"They'll be with you soon enough," Danny said. "Now, listen sharp, Bughouse, as we do not have a lot of time, and a lot of effort and money have been invested in you. It is time for our risk to become our reward. That's a principle of business, and there can be no argu-ing with business, not with those two old Jews. Mind you, I love them with all my heart, but blood cannot be denied."

Why would anyone invest in him? Everything was spinning. "It all looks blue," he said.

"That's expected with Viagra, my boy. Don't let it distract you from the task at hand. On cue, when you are called, you'll step beyond that curtain, and there, I promise you, no harm will befall you. By God, you'll thank me, I think. Expect no pain, as this is not the dentist's office, though there is drilling enough. Beyond that curtain, just do whatever Mr. Moscowitz directs."

"But which one is Mr. Moscowitz?"

"The one with the goatee who fancies himself a great man for holding a camera at eye level."

Someone yelled *Roll tape.*

Danny peeked out from the curtain. "You're a lucky bastard, you are," he said, and unceremoniously pushed Bughouse forward into stark light.

He was instantly blinded by arc lights, so bright he could feel their heat. Bughouse blinked. All he saw were blue-tinged shadows. He put his hand above his eyes for shade, but that did nothing, and the voice that had to be Moscowitz yelled, "Stop with the hand!" There were a lot of voices.

"Can someone get this *schlemiel* to go forward? What is his name? 'Bughouse?' We'll have to change that. Just take a few steps, Bughouse. Find your mark. It's just a screen test. No one expects miracles from an amateur."

Bughouse took a step. The world seemed to be wrapped in crinkly blue cellophane, but he saw an adhesive tape cross on the wooden floor. On a wooden futon a few feet farther, her back to him, sat a totally naked girl with long, blonde flowing hair.

Maybe the futon bed was white and he just thought it was blue. Her shoulders tapered to a tiny waist.

"OK, sweetheart, do your stuff," Mr. Moscowitz said, and the girl, totally naked and totally gorgeous, hair the color of a Chardonnay, skin smooth as buttermilk, stood. She dropped two yellow throw pillows at Bughouse's feet and knelt.

Bughouse's kimono parted of its own accord. Everyone in the room drew a sharp breath and held it. Moscowitz muttered, "*Mein Gott*, we are rich," and then whispered, "Are you getting this?"

The robe slid from Bughouse's shoulders into a soft puddle of cloth behind him. The girl eagerly grasped in her two hands all she could of Bughouse.

Though he was light-headed, Bughouse dared to look down. The world was as blue as the girl's perfect purple eyes. She blinked, smiled up at him, and with a twice pierced tongue licked her crimson, rounded lips.

"Ooooooh, Buggie," Mary said, sweeping back her hair for an unobstructed camera angle. "Who would have thought there was so much of you!"

And then she went to work with far more talent and skill than ever Bughouse had imagined.

And why not? She'd been tutored by the best.

Just as Bughouse was becoming reacquainted with Mary, Del sat beside Madge in her Subaru, slowly steering their way back to Haverhill. Slow for Madge, that is. She drove like an acid-dosed hallucinating gerbil. Fuck the snowstorm.

But not even the vision of Terror and Death hurtling toward him at 80 miles per hour through the windshield on a snow-strewn highway could distract Del's focus. Parallel wheel ruts were impressed into the snow in the center lane where drivers slowed by fears of mortality proceeded in a line. Madge spun her steering wheel wildly to the left and right, passing eighteen-wheelers inching up even the slightest rise. Calculating mass and momentum, no slide rule at hand, Del concluded that a traction-free truck in a sideways skid would crush him and Madge to the height and consistency of a fried egg.

Snow fell, but within his slight chest heartburn raged like prairie fire in a dry wind. Del quickly chewed Black Jack gum, folding a fresh stick into his mouth with every knot of logic his mind encountered. Del's thoughts were as reckless as Madge's driving -- breakneck speed, scattered all over a slippery landscape, heedless of danger, risking everything at every turn. Occam's Razor, the logical principle that a hypothesis that accounted for all known phenomena was likely correct, was worth dick; Del required Occam's Chainsaw.

As undeniable as the oncoming blizzard, Madge could not be telling him all she knew. Mickey and Aunt Sosha and Danny Donnelly and Bughouse were connected, but how? What had gone down between Madge and Danny? And that Ari guy…he had all the charm of a boa constrictor with none of the warmth. Where the hell was Bughouse, anyway? Why were they leaving Haverhill no wiser than when they'd left Riverton?

With a fresh stick after stick to help him think, the wad of gum in his mouth grew to the size of a softball. The larger it grew, the slower Del chewed; the more slowly Del chewed, the faster his mind raced. With his IQ that matched the Fahrenheit boiling point of water, Del's ideas hissed like superheated steam.

All right. All right. He was the Scientist, and Madge was the Minister, so now that Del had sipped tea with Cannibals, he ought to be able to name Who or What moved the whale.

They skidded over the last hill to Riverton. The snowfall intensified. They were driving blind, which seemed totally appropriate because God was down on one knee in Riverton, blowing Divine breath on three dodecahedrons. They were coming up triple snake eyes every time.

Del begged off Madge's suggestion that he go with her to Daddy Kane's.

"Help me put it to that prick, Arnie," she said. "We've got him by the balls. We know. There's no stopping me, Del. He's the fucking Dreamer," she said. "You know it. I know it. And now that prick needs to know we know. I want my life. He's the Dreamer, Del."

"What if you wake him up?"

The Subaru slid to a halt at the base of his driveway, spinning a full ninety degrees perpendicular to the roadway. Madge's palms slapped the wheel. "Oh who gives a flying fuck? Anything is better than this. I want my life back, and if I have no life, I need this fucking dream to end."

Del stood beside the Subaru's open door. Snow drifted into his collar. He said tiredly, "Do what you think you have to do, Madge, but I need to think about it."

"You think too much. What if I *do* wake him?"

"Then whatever I think won't matter much."

Madge shook her head. "There was so much we could have been doing for Science."

The Subaru fishtailed on the snow twice, and then disappeared behind the curtain of snow.

Del's hands shook, but not with cold. He unlocked the padlock on the lab door. Inside, he slapped ham and American cheese onto dry white bread. He was out of mustard; he despised mayo. Crumbs of a rye cracker still floated at the top of GIGO's beaker.

Maybe they were all sealed in a box named Riverton? Were they alive and dead all at once? Did Schrodinger's cat know Schrodinger was a maniac?

His answering machine insistently winked a pinpoint of red light at him. He threw the half-eaten sandwich into the trash and he touched a button. Some Brit flunky was calling for Colonel William DuBois. The Colonel desired to confer with Mr. Delbart Dellingham. *It may prove lucrative.*

Lucrative to Del or to the Colonel? Freelance science for profit was a goddam dogfight. He hated distractions. He needed a major score for a decent electron microscope. A half-decent, used machine was only fifty grand or so. He could modify it for another ten. Figure in two years, it would pay for itself twice. How in hell could he be expected to compete without one? Meanwhile, over at Riverton High, Chemistry classes were dropping zinc into hydrochloric acid, thrilling moronic children when the teacher lighted a bubble of hydrogen. Every. Fucking. Day. *Pop!*

But Colonel DuBois, all the rich for that matter, bored Del comatose. Put Del in a room for long with a Cabot or a DuBois, he'd have to be put on suicide watch. The Colonel and his here-again-gone-again kid, Cherry, did not interest him. Money bought an illusion of safety, so the children of the rich had fewer life skills than GIGO, his black goldfish hanging motionless in clear, still water, mouth puckering, gills undulating, stupidly waiting to be fed.

Heartburn burbled like molten magma forcing its way up a volcanic flue. Del's heartburn was an old friend, the telltale proof he was on the verge of a breakthrough. Reason was one thing; his gut another. Del Dellingham thought with his brain, bowels, and balls.

He swirled sodium bicarb in a water flask. His belch generated concentric circles rippling on the surface above GIGO.

He'd ponder the Colonel's summons later. Del was evolving a new theory, and he knew what that meant: even when he was not thinking, he would be thinking. What was the point of being a genius if you could not train your subconscious mind into working for you while you slept, read a book, or looked at greenish telescopic photos taken through a nightscope of Madge?

Could a person escape Riverton by traversing time? Might Madge go with him?

For Science.

Del had in fact never believed time travel particularly worth thinking about, though he'd played with the notion now and again. Really, what could you do with it? Sell front row tickets at Waterloo? *See the Crucifixion! Talk to the Disciples! Check out the rouge on Cleopatra's nipples!* The paradox was an old one: if you traveled through time and engaged the past, you might foment events that would strangle your grandmother in her cradle – in which case, how did you generate the events?

All right. Throw that thread-worn paradox out. All it did was get in the way.

Dogs hear ultrasonic sound; hummingbirds see ultraviolet light. Suppose we merely lack the perceptual apparatus to apprehend time. Del drew. It was a problem in projective geometry. We exist in three dimensions; time is a fourth.

Symbols boogied in his mind. He drew sketches that looked like regenerating fireworks. He converted his sketches to equations on his green chalkboard. When he smelled something really foul, he realized it was himself, but decided not to bathe. Who had time for hygiene?

Hypothesis: Riverton rocketed through existence on a time stream where cause and effect were disconnected, one that left Riverton kids ageless, adults idiots, one that had talent-free Arnie Appleton laughing like a fucking loon that swallowed a hyena who ate a jackass.

Madge's notion of a Dreamer was simpler, perhaps more elegant—but it required a leap of faith. She was the Minister; he was the Scientist. He needed an explicable cause to account for the Whale. What made things happen? He needed a Dreamer, but by another name, one that could be established by reason, not faith.

After 4 am, his calculations collapsed into rubble. He pinched the bridge of his nose and then stretched. He glanced out the lab's sole window. The snow stopped. Stars were shining steel pins in the moonless black velvet night. He climbed the rickety ladder to his sleeping loft and looked at his photos of Madge.

Sleep did not come.

Suppose the Dreamer inhabited only one of the infinite firework bursts of Time, one where cause and effect were unmoored, only tenuously related. Might he and Madge roll Riverton back to a moment before the Master Dreamer dreamed?

The sun had not yet risen when Del climbed down the ladder to take another pass at his chalkboard. GIGO watched Del sweep his straight black hair from his eyes as he reinvented the laws of time and space.

Del Dellingham was down on one knee in a Divine Alley to shoot Craps with God. The dice might be loaded, but God ran the only game in town.

At the precise moment Del heard the message from Colonel DuBois, Madge helicoptered a burning cigarette into a bank of perfect white Riverton snow outside the glass door of Daddy Kane's.

She pushed in with her lowered shoulder, sleigh bells jangled, and Daddy Kane's roared. The place was quieter than a fighter jet runway, but louder than a subway tunnel.

Madge had been away, all right.

Two familiar rattan fans still spun lazily suspended below the tin ceiling, but the shoulder of her jacket came away streaked with grit. Daddy no longer wiped the windows. A green neon sign buzzed: *Daddy's Bar and Grille.*

The All-American Burger Shoppe was gone, and with it the bubble-machine Wurlitzer that had played Frankie Avalon and Fabian at a dime per tune. A CD jukebox was on the wall, and it played music that seemed half chant, half scream, and all hatred, sucking in bills at a dollar per tune. It never went silent.

In her heart, it all seemed wrong, but her mind insisted Daddy's had always been like this.

Slot machines trilled a constant racket, and if the crowds standing before them were any measure, they took in far more money than any jukebox ever had. People lined up five deep to play, and they jostled each other to sneak ahead in line. Faux Tiffany lamps hung over two pool tables. Girls bent low to line up shots, elevating their hard asses into the air. They wobbled on heels and wore not much below their waists other than skirts that were pussy belts. When two guys went at each other, a peroxide blonde shrieked with laughter. Daddy Kane showed a sap he withdrew from his apron. The gesture stopped the tussle.

Sap. A sap was a hard rubber truncheon. Why would Madge know that word?

Behind the zinc bar, Daddy wiped a row of Old-Fashioned glasses. He placed them mouth down on a neatly folded white towel. Madge braced her knuckles on the bar to lean close to Daddy's ear. She shouted, "What in fuck is this?"

Daddy Kane smiled broadly. "Madge, baby! Long time no see!" and drew a draught of Sam Adams ale, the thick foam pouring over the sides of a Pilsner glass. "The usual for my old sugar!"

Sam Adams was long her favorite. Madge was equally sure she had never had a beer in her life. How could old memories be new? "Daddy. What happened?"

Daddy Kane's wet palm smoothed back non-existent hair on his bald head. "Why worry? Madge, this is Riverton! Enjoy!"

The bitter brew was ice cold, delicious and tart. Noise encased her like a tight wet cloth that was shrinking. It became difficult to think.

The ale struck Madge's forehead like a sledge hammer on a church bell. The Shadow was at work. Three ice cream headaches and a double cluster migraine could feel no worse. Madge's mind was under siege. Pain radiated over her scalp; the Shadow's bony fingers dug into her skull through her eyes.

Madge drew shallow breaths. She focused on what she knew had to be true and what she could see despite narrowing tunnel vision.

Over in his booth, Mickey's wraparound sunglasses and his shag-cut hair hid most of his face. That was normal. Or was it? She'd always liked his hair, but she'd forgotten why. His neck rested back against the seat cushion, his Adam's apple prominent. He had one arm around Victoria. She looked totally wasted. When did Madge start using a word like *wasted*? Madge focused on the indisputable memory of that lovely salt taste on her tongue as it traced a line from the soft flesh just under Mickey's ear down to his hairless chest. She'd licked him like an envelope. Memories of Mickey drifted through her like unmoored boats in a flood. They collided with each other. Some sank.

The dot of pain above her eyes broadened. Mickey's hair. She focused on Mickey's hair. If she could understand Mickey's hair, she'd understand everything.

Behind her, Daddy Kane distracted her as he rambled on about the widening scandal at Riverton High; Grimley and two freshman boys in a detention class had become a sordid episode the whole town was working to put behind itself now that Grimley was doing time. Daddy did not believe the three other teachers who were involved claiming the boys had initiated a rape gang and Grimley was a victim. "For Heaven's sake," he said. "This is Riverton." He was less sure about the allegations swirling around Chukker Washington, and no one would ever know the whole truth since the poor boy hanged himself from a basketball hoop. Daddy sorrowfully observed, "Arnie is our last best hope to beat Haverhill now." He nodded sagely as his shot glasses lined up neat as soldiers on parade.

Mickey's hair was wrong. That was it.

Madge rubbed slow circles at her temples and squeezed her eyes shut. Her alleged memories scattered. She captured one image: Mickey straining above her, she gripping him with her thighs, he fucking her, he filling her, their always private, always delicious sin, but his hair…it had been different. Sunken memories floated to the surface again, wavered, try to right themselves, but remained cloaked in darkness.

The flesh along her thigh and on her upper arms itched like fire ants. She risked a deep swallow from her ale. Mickey had never looked as if he needed a haircut. That was it. She'd loved to muss his always perfect hair. His pomade made it brittle to her touch. Now it looked soft as fur.

She asked Daddy for ice and a hand towel to make a cold compress to press against her eyes. Daddy offered her a refill; she held her shaking hand over the Pilsner glass.

Hadn't Daddy's mustache always looked like a black caterpillar wriggling like hooked bait on a sea of rosacea? Her nausea was fading, but now she felt giddy. She dug in. Madge was tougher than the fucking Shadow. She could prevail. Caterpillars. The little fuckers crawled through all her thoughts. Caterpillars became butterflies, and those fuckers could wake up from dreams and not recall if they were butterflies or men.

Breath whistling in her nostrils, Madge deliberately eased her clenched fists. Her knuckles had gone white. Cripes, she practically had gouged finger marks into the zinc bar's top.

At her left, Juice, who thank God was not coming toward her, sat on a wire-back chair too small for him at a tiny, black, iron table. His face was expressive as the inside of a baked potato, but Madge had no trouble recollecting the ragged hole where the bullet had ripped out his throat, how he had slowly rolled face-up in dark water while Mickey in his very best Italian shoes stood on Juice's chest until the inky water closed over Juice and the final bubbles escaped Juice's clothing to linger at the edges of Juice's corpse. Juice had been very, very dead, and though she and Mickey had rolled in the dirt and he'd fucked her deliciously hard against a tree, Mickey's hair had been stone perfect.

That was it. No moon; no light; hot with murder and blood, Mickey's hair stayed perfect. That shag cut she saw was utter bullshit.

Fighting the Shadow required minute-to-minute running of a life inventory. What did she still know? Bughouse was in Haverhill with Aunt Sosha and big Danny Donnelly. Danny Donnelly had tried to tear her tits off. She was not forgetting that any time soon. The Shadow could not take that from her. Yes, she and Del had gone to Haverhill earlier that very day, and Del had shared with her how he too often awakened paralyzed with fear and ridicule at the top of a rope. Madge had explained to Del that she needed to be a cannibal. Or was it a whale?

Daddy said, "You look pale, Madge."

The pressure in her skull rose again, full force, so hard it made her gasp. Grappling with the Shadow was like a boxing match, and this was the final round. Her shaking hand clumsily withdrew a cigarette from her bag, the little gold lame thing she toted everywhere. The cigarette tax stamp read, "Massachusetts." Now why was that extraordinary? What was the big deal? Daddy Kane struck a wooden match and held it to her cigarette. Harsh smoke and the match's sulfur satisfyingly clawed at her lungs.

Her breathing slowed. Her back under her jacket ran damp with cold sweat. Cutting her flesh was her best defense. She could exert control. Whatever it was that had gripped her mind receded like a tidal wave after crashing ashore, rubble in its wake. She rubbed the soft flesh under her arm above her elbow.

Daddy Kane's smile was expectant and empty.

She needed to move. Mickey had left his booth and was slapping palms high and low as he crossed the floor to see a man about a horse. That left 'Toria alone.

Madge felt the crush of being alone in a crowd. The place teemed with strangers. Madge's other option for company was Juice, his big freckled hand dwarfing a mug of what looked like lemonade. His wide, unblinking eyes stared at nothing. No, she was not going there.

'Toria was a friend, or at least once had been. They had been girls together. They had attended pajama parties and played with makeup and giggled over silliness. Somehow. Sometime. Somewhere. Madge's memories were frayed at the edges.

Her thighs pressed the booth's table's edge. 'Toria arched an eyebrow.

"I have no money," 'Toria said. "Fuck off."

"Who said anything about money?"

"Good old Madge, my main biffle." 'Toria's voice rasped in a strained whisper. "Any cash you can loan me? I'll pay you back, I swear. I'll pay you back the day I turn twenty-one." 'Toria's dull black hair swooped over one eye, but vine-like fell forward when she spoke. Her pupils were large as plates. Her lipstick was plum, her eyeliner matched. The black leather metal studded dog collar at her throat seemed menacing. "Give a bitch a cigarette," 'Toria said and reached across the table to drape her cold hand, limp as Daddy's Kane's wet towel, onto Madge's wrist.

Madge dropped her 'grettes onto the table. She had plenty. A carton from Aunt Sosha was still in her car. Del thought they were odd, but she could not remember why. Had Victoria Cabot always smoked? It was hard to recall.

'Toria groaned at the effort it took to reach the smokes. Her chest rested flat on the tabletop. Her shoulder bones stretched her skin, translucent as a rubber. Little flesh was left on her. 'Toria wiped her running nose with the back of her wrist. Her false nails were lacquered crimson.

Madge slid into the booth where Mickey had been.

'Toria's black camisole was topped by lace. The spaghetti straps slid loose off her bony shoulders. She wore no bra, and Madge saw that her left nipple was pierced with a fine, platinum ring set with a ruby. The camisole exposed her hip and midriff. 'Toria's navel was pierced by a second matching ring, but the ruby was replaced by a diamond. A line of fine black hair, a treasure trail, ran from her navel to beneath her black leather silver-studded belt. The tattoo on her pelvic bone was a Celtic knot. 'Toria's black jeans were skin tight. She wore open-toed blocky four-inch heels, the ankle straps undone, her toenails painted the same crimson as her fake fingernails.

Madge slid into the booth.

Daddy Kane refilled 'Toria's coffee. She ripped four sugar packets at once with her teeth, then swirled her spoon through the muddy brew.

"Nice outfit," Madge said. "The shoes must be killer in the snow." She shrugged toward the storefront window; snow glistened like jewels on Riverton's main street.

'Toria shrugged. "Mickey likes CFMs." She rounded her lips and emitted a smoke ring. Then, as if the effort of sitting up was too great, extended her arm across the table and rested her head on it. Her eyes fluttered shut. The camisole gapped. There was another tat on her breast, a sketchy pentagram.

"CFM?"

"Come Fuck Me. Where'd Mickey go?" 'Toria asked, forced open her eyes, and by great effort pushed herself to sit up. When Madge shook her head, puzzled, 'Toria breathed, "Ass out, tits forward, calves tight. Come Fuck Me."

'Toria's perfect teeth worried a ragged cuticle. When her finger spouted a pearl of blood, she tongued it clean and then whipped her bleeding hand down beneath the table as if she were hiding evidence. The nail polish was chipped. 'Toria clicked her nails on the table. "Are you sure you didn't see Mickey?"

"He was sitting where I am now. You were sitting with him. He's taking a leak."

Someone hit a slots jackpot, a siren wailed, and a spinning red light strobed the room. Despite the din, Madge heard the front door's sleighbells jangle.

Arnie, a redhead hanging on his arm, went to the bar.

"Goddam, it's the bitch," 'Toria said. "I am gonna fix her ass good as soon as my father gets over this shit-fit and gives me my money. That asshole thinks I have to do what he says. Fuck him. Mickey gives me everything I need. Mickey has plans. But they are my trust funds. The day I turn twenty-one, I am in the clear. Why can't the bastard give it to me now? What is the difference? If he keeps this shit up, I will shoot the motherfucker and get it all. It will take forever for me to turn twenty-one. It feels like forever."

"You're with Mickey?"

"Yeah. So? You have a problem with that?"

"He's all yours. How's Mary?"

'Toria shrugged. "Mickey says our favorite blonde bimbo left town for a business opportunity. If it works out, he says I can join her, soon. He needs me to pay him what I owe him, first, and since my father the tightwad prick motherfucker won't give me money anymore, I have to start earning. My father is such an asshole. Everything is fucked up. It's that Cherry DuBois, you ask me." 'Toria nervously spun her studded black rubber bracelet. The titanium barbell stud in her tongue clicked against the back of her upper teeth. "Riverton does just fine without that bitch, but as soon as her ass gets kicked out of her private school she comes wiggling back to us. She's a goddam shark. I hear this time she did her English teacher. Do you think she's doing Arnie? I think she's doing Arnie. Did you ever do Arnie, Madge?"

"No."

'Toria patted the back of Madge's wrist. "Smart." 'Toria held up her finger and thumb up about an inch apart and giggled. "Just stay with Juice. Nice boy. Keep your legs crossed and he'll have to marry you just to get into your pants. Good ol' Madge. Good ol' Madge will be just fine, as long as she keep her legs together. That's all that matters. You take that Cherry bitch. Cherry sucks donkey dick, okay? She's not around much, but as soon as she shows up,

Arnie gets stiff nipples. Private school, my sweet ass. Private cathouse!" She raised her voice, but no one could hear her. 'Toria wiped her running nose. "Thinks she's too good for us," she mumbled as she checked her profile in a cracked compact mirror. "Do I look all right? I think I look all right. Do I look all right?"

The uneven plum lipstick made her look like a vampire after feed. Madge said, "You look perfect."

"Good ol' Madge. Where in fuck is Mickey? I need to see Mickey. Mickey has my medicine."

'Toria gnawed a knuckle, seemed startled to discover she had inserted more of her own flesh in her mouth, and abruptly pulled her clenched fist away. Then she touched her ear and chin. She did not know what do with her hands.

Madge said, I never realized Cherry was Arnie's type."

"Does she have a cunt?"

"What kind of question is that?"

"She has a cunt, then she's his type, is all." 'Toria's tongue wet her lips. She fell forward on the table, in some sort of near-sleep, restless and covered in a sheen of cold sweat.

"'Toria's quite a pip," Mickey said. Like an imp from thin air, he'd materialized and slid into the booth beside Madge, trapping her against the wall. "How's my main squeeze?"

"Fuck you."

Mickey grinned, removed his sunglasses, placed them on the table, and rubbed his jaw. "Same old Madge. We've had some times, you and me." He jostled 'Toria awake. Her sleepy head rose and her eyes blinked. Her hands embraced his arm as if she were going to make his hand her pillow.

Mickey was having none of that. "Give us the booth, 'Toria. Madge and I need to talk."

Victoria Cabot sat uncomprehending until Mickey dropped two glassine envelopes in front of her. "On your account," he said.

"Jesus, thanks, Mickey," she breathed. She dropped the two envelopes between her breasts. As she slid from the booth, he grabbed her wrist. She said, "You're hurting me."

"Don't thank me. Just pay me. I'm too good to you."

"I know."

"The deal with me is always the same, no matter who you are. Everyone knows this about me." She winced as he twisted her arm. "If you don't want to pay me, I have no problem with that. Return my product and there are no hard feelings." He slapped his palms together and spread his hands, empty and clean.

"I'll pay you," she said and rubbed her wrist. "You know how I feel about you, baby."

Mickey shrugged. "Just a reminder."

Victoria wobbled unsteadily away on her high heels. The whitish flesh at the small of her back was decorated with still more body art.

Mickey gestured to Daddy Kane who with short, hurried, steps brought two coffee mugs and a small, steaming metal pot.

Madge said, "What's happening, Mickey? Don't give me that dumb-ass look. I know you know what I mean."

"It's good to see you, too, Madge. What do you say? Meet me at Cabin #3 tonight? For old time's sake? You need to try some of this new stuff Danny Donnelly gave me. Amazing shit. You remember Danny?"

"I remember Danny. I remember all of it."

Mickey brightened. "So we'll get together?"

"Fuck your fist."

Mickey laughed. "I don't need to do much of that anymore. But I'll tell you Madge, you'll always be the best."

Madge hated that she liked hearing it. Mickey had been a sweet boy. She'd been able to tell him anything. She said, "The town, everything. It's all changed."

"Changed how?"

"Cut that shit out, Mickey. Do I look as dumb as Mary?"

Mickey sipped his coffee while his free hand squeezed her knee. She gently, but decidedly, moved his hand away.

"That's you all over, Madge. Always the same. Why not go with the flow? It is what it is, and I am on a roll, here. Why mess it up? So what if Riverton changes? As long as we come up winners, where's the harm?"

"'We'?"

"You were always part of the plan. You know that."

"I thought the plan was to get Victoria Cabot's money?"

"You were part of that, too. Why would I ditch the best lick in town?"

"Fuck you."

"That's the first good idea you've had since I sat down. All you'd need to do is stop with the Shadow bullshit," he whispered. "Just drop it. Did you ever think that bringing up the Shadow is what made it happen? Did you ever think of that? Of course not. All you want to do is understand. Just forget that shit. Accept. Cut that shit out, Madge, and who knows what you'd have. Do you really want to wake up tomorrow and have all this vanish? I'm the King of Riverton."

"What comes after being King of Riverton?"

Mickey lower lip extended as he thought and pushed his spoon through his coffee.

"What else is there, Madge? Maybe there is no 'What then?' You've got what you wanted."

"What I wanted?"

"Suffering. Purpose. Significance. The crap you'd whine about after you screwed me blind."

Fuck Mickey. Just fuck him. He was too goddam accurate.

His hand wandered to her knee again. Madge bent back one of his fingers until he cringed. "Martin, tell me true. Chukker's really dead?"

"Dead as a post. Like moldering and stinking and rotting-in-the-grave dead." His eyes went mercury gray, depthless. "Chukker is not coming back. The dumb shit stretched his neck and strangled 'cause he did not step off a chair high enough to have the fall snap his spine. He fucked up his own suicide. Think of it; the last thing you do, and you fuck that up. He used his Riverton school tie, the one Coach makes players wear with a blazer and gray slacks at the season dinners."

"And you know this how?"

"A guy hears things, is all."

She bent his index finger back further. Mickey said through clenched teeth, "Let go of me you cow-bitch or I will hurt you, Madge. Hurt like damage. Old times or not."

Surprised by his vehemence, she loosened her grip.

"You cannot mess with me anymore, Madge. I'll put up with a lot, especially from you, but there is no Juice to protect your ass, anymore. I am dangerous. Things can be arranged. Figure a guy like Chukker, a guy with all the skills, maybe he had his reasons, but he was being a pain in the ass. You've got no Juice, Madge, unless you think that sorry-ass lump of zombie shit sitting over there can help you out."

Mickey had been the boy who'd joyfully screwed her two and three times in a night. He'd been almost shy. He had helped her feel alive. Where was that sweet boy now?

Mickey whispered to her, "The big guy is spooky. I feel bad. I gave him a job. Him and his baseball bat. Now Juice collects for me. It shows how generous I am. All he ever wants to do is talk about a bright fucking light he thinks he saw."

Madge hissed, "You asshole. You shot him. You killed him."

Mickey shrugged. "No. You held him, I shot him, *we* killed him. The fine points matter. You still don't get it, do you, Madge? The Shadow saved our asses. We're off the hook. Your Shadow took us off the spot. Juice is not smart enough to shake his dick after he takes a leak, but who is to say that's not because his football helmet was too tight? He was not too bright before we killed him. Look around, Madge. Look around. You and I are different. We know a little more. We risk more. But where I am different from you is that I don't need to understand the world; I just have to live in it."

"What about Bughouse? Your good buddy. What about Buggie?"

"Oh, give it up, Madge. Bughouse is with Mary. The two of them are fucking great."

Madge perked up. Was it possible to run from Riverton? "Did they elope?"

Mickey's finger stroked the side of his nose. "I have no idea what they are up to," Mickey said. "I just know they are doing fine. You know Aunt Sosha. Would that sweet old lady hurt anyone?" His hand drifted a third time to Madge's knee. "Relax, Madge. There is no evil at work, here. Danny asked me to bring Bughouse a friend, for company. Mary volunteered. Danny tells me they have gone off into the great wide world. You know how that Irish prick talks. Acts like he just got off the plane from Dublin and his shit is green, but he is just a fucking leg-breaker in a black leather coat who was born Haverhill." Mickey touched his ten fingertips together, a spider on a mirror. "That's really all I know, Madge. I swear." He then poured a refill for himself from the metal pot. "What do you say, Madge? For old time's sake. A quickie. Look, I saw you staring at 'Toria's ass. You want to arrange a threesome? Just say the word. She'll go for anything I say. She's not so high and mighty these days."

Madge saw Juice's big freckled hand still curled around the same mug of lemonade. The ice in the mug was melting. He stared into the distance, though there was nothing before his eyes. He stared at nothing, nothing at all. Madge had forever been *Juice's girl*. She shivered. "Martin, listen to me, Just listen."

"I love it when you call me 'Martin.' No one else calls me Martin. My mother called me Martin once, but I let her know I would not take that. I take it only from you, Madge. You think maybe it's the way you say it? I don't know, when you call me Martin, I don't get pissed off. You trill the R and I remember how your tongue...."

"Shut up. Just shut up," she said, and then Madge told Mickey how she and Del had gone to Haverhill despite the snow. The words tumbled out of her, fast as she could think. She had to tell him while she could still remember it, and while shared sin was quickly forgotten, maybe that was less true for Haverhill events.

Mickey did not like hearing they'd been to Aunt Sosha's. "Don't fuck me up," he said.

"We talked about horseshit, I swear it. Books, a little. She liked Del. Thinks chemistry is a great field and maybe will offer him a job. We were there maybe half an hour."

"The old Jew-bitch still won't admit I am alive."

Madge explained cannibals and whales, dead cats in boxes, God, Einstein and dice. The more she spoke, the stupider she sounded and the more she wanted to cry at Mickey's growing lopsided smile. Despair like molten lead filled her belly. "It's Arnie," she hissed, finally. "Arnie is the Dreamer! Don't you get it? Arnie always wins!"

Mickey laughed. "Not lately, Madge. Not lately." His coffee cup clattered on its saucer. "Look, just a quick blow-job. Why go to the motel? Right here, right now, in this booth. Who'd notice?" Madge punched his arm. "Okay, so Arnie is your dreamer. What does that change? An asshole is an asshole forever, and we are what we are, whatever in fuck that is. If this is his dream, I'm turning it into his nightmare. If you want to wake him up, you'd better hurry. Cherry is already gone and Arnie is halfway to the door." He shrugged his head toward the bar. Arnie fumbled in his back pocket in search of his wallet.

Madge dropped her cigarette in Mickey's coffee. The butt curled like a dead locust. 'Toria was side-stepping through the crowd back to Mickey's booth. Madge pushed at Mickey, and he obligingly stood to get out of her way. As she left him, Mickey grabbed her wrist and held her, just as he'd grabbed 'Toria's.

"Look, if Arnie doesn't wake up, you meet me at Cabin #3. Doesn't the idea just make you tingle?" He rubbed his jaw.

Her knee lifted into his hamstring; he winced, but he laughed. "I love it when you hurt me," he said as 'Toria wiggled her ass back into her seat in the booth. Mickey sat beside her, whispered in her ear, and her head fell into his lap under the table. Mickey placed his mirrored sunglasses over his eyes and leaned back, content.

Like a man who knew no end of woe, Arnie sat at the bar and cupped his head in two hands like a golf ball on a tee. His elbows were propped at either side a melting strawberry Daiquiri. Two straws drooped like limp dicks.

"Arnie Appleton, we need to talk."

Arnie hopped off his bar stool. His mile-wide smile contradicted the distrust in his green eyes. He looked like a trapped squirrel. "Gotta go, Madge. Gotta go. A date with Cherry!" His eyes rolled like a ventriloquist's dummy's; he squealed like a balloon being pinched empty of air.

"You can make all this go away, can't you? You can, I know it."

Arnie carefully counted some bills onto the bar. With two fingers he gestured a cavalier *So long* to Daddy Kane. Daddy sliced limes with a paring knife, too busy to look up.

Madge snatched Arnie's elbow.

"I know your goddam secret, you red-headed piece of shit," she hissed. "Talk to me, motherfucker!"

"Ma—aaadge, cut it out. I can't talk to you. You are Juice's girl." Arnie giggled. One at a time, he uncurled her fingers from his sleeve.

"I am Madge, dammit. Not Juice's girl. Not anybody's anything." Arnie struggled to get away. She clutched again at his team jacket, missed her grip, and, desperate, called after him. "I'll never cheer for you at a Riverton game again!"

The threat stopped him, cold. Nothing could be more horrible.

"Ma—aaadge. Not that. You wouldn't do that. Everybody cheers for me. Everyone loves Riverton. I am Arnie."

His mouth was filled with perfect teeth, little gravestones in a new cemetery. Could Danny introduce Arnie's teeth to a ball-peen hammer? If she asked him nicely, that is. As a favor. Payback for bruising her. Not so much to knock his teeth out, but just shatter a few.

"Appleton, you prick. I know your secret. You are the Dreamer."

"The what?" Arnie danced from foot to foot like a kid who needed to pee.

"You made this up. You made us up. Undream us Arnie. I can't take this any more. Wake up. Wake us all up."

Arnie placed his two hands on his cheeks. His mouth opened to a perfect circle. "*Kyuk-kyuk-kyuk!* Good old crazy Madge! You make me laugh so hard! Dreamer? I love your jokes. Hey, everybody! Madge thinks I am dreaming." He slapped both his knees and bent forward, then lifted one hand to point at her. "*Kyuk, kyuk, kyuk!*"

When Arnie was happy, Riverton was happy. Daddy Kane's place rocked with laughter. Madge felt like she had awakened naked at the Riverton Prom.

Mickey stood to get a better view of her humiliation. 'Toria came out from under the table, wiping her mouth on her wrist.

Madge seized Daddy's paring knife and slashed at Arnie. She caught his team jacket's forearm, ripping a four inch gash in the leather sleeve. Fiber gushed, but Arnie was unhurt.

Of course not, it was his dream. How could he get hurt?

Big Juice shouted, "Madge is *my* girl!" But Juice neither stood nor faced them. He was less animated than a block of concrete. He sipped more lemonade and stared stolidly at something only Juice could see.

"I'd love to stay, Madgie, but I've got to see Cherry-o. Whooo-hoo!" Arnie explained breathlessly. "She's just sooooo terrific!"

Arnie sprinted for the door.

Madge caught Mickey's eye, a line of site like a taut rope. Maybe for old time's sake; maybe in hopes of a rendezvous at Cabin #3, Mickey reached into his sweater pocket and produced the Smith & Wesson.38. She was on the move when he tossed it to her, and she caught it with two hands as if they'd practiced pass completions at the football field.

Mickey had never destroyed the weapon, the stupid shit. The evidence that could have sent them both away forever was in his pocket.

But Arnie was in her sights, now. Could you go to jail for killing someone who would rise from the dead?

Madge plunged into the Riverton night. The sidewalk lay beneath four inches of powdery snow. She slipped, righted herself, and slipped again, stopping her fall with her hand on a car's fender before she went ahead. Snow stung her naked hand. Beneath Riverton's subdued eerie greenish streetlights, she saw Arnie's receding shadow turn a corner.

As she ran, Madge struggled with the revolver. Hell's own teacher, Danny Donnelly, had barked instructions at Mickey about safeties. Slide *this* here; that *there*. All she remembered was the pain as he pulled on her tits and her fear that he'd damage her, but now the lesson from Hell's own teacher was coming back.

She managed a shot into the air. Snow-shrouded Riverton muffled the sound, though her ears rang. She ran on the slippery snow. Gunsmoke teased her nose, the aroma oddly sweet.

Madge skidded around a corner in pursuit, but saw nothing. Then Arnie's Ford betrayed him. Every car on the street looked the same as every other under a cowl of snow, but Arnie's brake lights glowed, twin red eyes shining at her. That shit hard-top Mustang, the worst automobile ever made, stirred to life. Dress it up—it was still a Ford. It had to be Arnie. Who else would be out in this snowstorm?

Madge slid and ran, slid again, ran again. She lurched to her Subaru, jerked the door open, and tossed the reassuring weight of the gun onto the passenger seat. She'd not thought the gun would be so heavy.

Arnie said he was going to see Cherry. DuBois Hill was on the other side of town. There was only on way to get there. She had the carrot-top son-of-a-bitch.

The Subaru coughed, hesitated, and started. Madge waited one swipe of the windshield wipers and hunched her shoulders to see through the only clear spot on the glass. Good enough. Once she was moving, wind would do the work to clear all her vision. But she clipped the car in front of her, and Madge's front right headlamp shattered and went dark. Tough shit, somebody.

She kept going.

Madge was sweating, clammy under her jacket. Her eyes were adrenalin-wide. Heat flared in her cheeks. This was it. This was the limit. The little prick was running from her, but she knew where he was going. There was no escape. Not this time.

Wake the butterflies. Crush the caterpillars. Tell the little worms it was over. Fuck everything, just fuck everything. She had the Shadow-loved fuck by the balls.

Arnie's headlights punched twin white cones in the windblown snow; Madge's one headlight followed. No one was out in a snowstorm, not even doctors or ambulances. No need. No emergencies. This was Riverton. How long might it be until Chukker Washington came back? Basketball season would come around; the never-ending dream would continue. In Riverton, defeat was celebrated as victory; in Riverton, no one grew old; in Riverton, no one suffered. In Riverton, no one knew what it was to be alive. In Riverton, star basketball players came back in season.

When she banged the Subaru into four-wheel drive, it bucked like an unbroken horse. Snow be damned; Madge drove flat out, wrestling with a steering wheel that was a live thing struggling to escape her grip. She could not smoke. She saw no road under the snow and guessed where the road was, needing both hands to steer. Madge was fearless, but skidding off the road would delay her, and if the little prick made it to the DuBois estate, he'd be beyond the iron gate. The Riverton nightmare would continue forever and forever. Who knew how badly the Shadow might shred her mind between now and when she next saw Arnie? No, now, today, this night, this hour, it had to end.

The Subaru closed on the Ford. DuBois Hill was just over the old stone railroad bridge. Madge's wheels gripped the snow. On the seat beside her, the gun's nickel polished finish reflected amber and green dashboard lights. She was going to put the fucking gun in Arnie's fucking mouth and if he did not admit he was the Dreamer, his fucking brains would spatter the interior of his shit Ford.

Mickey was a lot of things, but none of them was especially stupid; had he figured out that Madge would eliminate the last obstacle between him and the Cabot fortune? Mickey Black had the survival instincts of a cockroach, with none of the class.

Where do dreams go when they are done?

Arnie must have spotted her in his rearview; the Mustang suddenly opened distance. He was running hard from her. He was scared.

"I've got you now, you son-of-a-bitch!"

She pumped her accelerator. The two lane blacktop road hugged the hill like a roller-coaster, dense woods on either side, eerie and quiet as driving through a sound-deadening tunnel. The Subaru fishtailed; it took another curve and spun a full donut before the rear wheels banged into a shallow ditch off the shoulder. The four-wheel drive saved her. Madge cursed at the lost seconds as she muscled her way back onto the road, spun her steering wheel, and charged forward toward DuBois Hill.

When the night sky parted, clouds like an evaporating curtain scudded across the moon. The revealed stars were pins, the night crystal, pure and cold. Snow no longer fell. Before her lay the one open road that led to where Cherry DuBois lived with her father, the Colonel, behind white-washed walls and the black iron gate that surrounded the DuBois mansion.

Arnie would have to stop at the gate.

Madge's thin-lipped grimace relaxed into a mean smile. She only had to pace him. Arnie had to pause at the gate. She owned his ass.

Just to scare him a little, was all. That was her real plan. Just scare the living crap out of him. She'd come up beside his car all nice and cozy, and stick the motherfucking barrel in his motherfucking ear and soft as could be just explain how she'd blow his motherfucking brains out if he did not own up to being the origin of the nightmare that defined her life, if she even had one. What could go wrong with a plan as simple as that?

Who was she? What was she? The fucker had to talk. He could not have imagined her from nothing. Someone, somewhere, was the real Madge. Could she meet her? Could they talk?

The Subaru crested a hill. The moon shone like a dull pie plate. Silver light flamed from pine trees bending bent by the weight of heavy snow.

From fifty yards behind and above, Madge saw Arnie's Mustang spin out, almost straighten, and then carom like a pinball trapped in a rubber-band chute formed by the sides of a steel bridge. The bridge crossed a railroad track. The Ford crashed through the iron bridge's railing and teetered half a heartbeat on the bridge's lip. Arnie tried to crawl through the shattered windshield, so his car door must been bent jammed shut. But Arnie was out of luck. The car fell end over end the hundred feet into the gulley below. It landed on its roof, four smoking tires spinning in the air, pathetic as a dead rat.

Madge stood on her brake, damn hear killed herself as the Subaru slalomed to a sideways halt on the bridge's slick metal surface. She grabbed the revolver and hurled herself from her car. As she leaned over the broken railing, the first small flames licked at the carcass of the Ford.

Madge ran to the bridge's end where she dropped to sit on the snow-covered ground. She slid down the embankment. It was too steep to walk; there was nothing to hold on to.

The car lay obliquely across the abandoned tracks. The fire had grown, and heat was palpable and terrible on her cheeks; her nose filled with the stench of burning vinyl, rubber and the nauseating perfume of gasoline. Trapped, Arnie gestured pleadingly to her. Maybe she could have saved him, but it was too late in too many ways. Flames licked at the gas tank.

The car exploded.

Madge was hurled backward off her feet by the fireball. Her forearm shielded her eyes. Her eyebrows singed. On hands and knees, she crawled to safety. Then she stood.

Beneath the silver full moon floating among the scudding clouds, yards from Arnie Appleton's pyre, Madge carefully lifted the pistol, aimed with two hands, and just as Danny Donnelly had instructed, held her breath as she aimed at Arnie. His back bowed as he burned, surely already dead, but that did not stop her. She squeezed one round into the burning wreck. The gun kicked violently, but she held it steady. Now she was ready; she shot three more times. The flames grew higher than the trees. Madge breathed gunpowder, burning gasoline, and scorched rubber, then hurled the empty pistol as far as she could into the uncaring, black forest.

And nothing, not a damn thing, happened.

They say no one can die in their own dreams.

Arnie was dead. But Riverton, fucking Riverton, persisted.

PART III

THE MORNING AFTER ARNIE CRASHED, BURNED, AND WAS SHOT FOUR times, several hours after Danny Donnelly stared with longing at the departing Madge, some time after Bughouse reunited with Mary, but well before Horatio Cabot signed the papers that formally disinherited his daughter, Victoria, the drug addicted slut, shortly before Del met Cherry DuBois in a way even the Shadow could never erase, Del awakened from three hours of restless sleep. He never seemed to need much more.

He lay in the loft above his lab. He had no memory of climbing the makeshift wooden ladder the night before. His loft was a palette of pine planks he'd suspended by thick rope from the garage ceiling, then propped with a few two-by-fours set as braces into the walls below. Every engineer knew that triangles created the strongest possible construction. The loft hung three feet below the A-frame of the uninsulated garage roof; it held a bare, stained mattress and a colorless woolen blanket that smelled mildly of mildew. Five white thumbtacks pinned three photos of Madge to the ceiling over his face. Del had shot the pictures with a telescopic lens; all three showed her smoking on her back porch. The pictures were grainy, black and white. Del took no photos that were sordid, never thinking to violate her with his eyes or with a 'scope fitted with night vision aimed at her bedroom window.

Del rose with the sun and slid his ass off the edge of the sleep palette. He fell to the concrete floor and landed lightly on his feet. Del awakened daily at dawn as if an alarm was in his head; why fight a million years of evolution imprinted in DNA? The sun was up; so was Del. He wore sagging gray sweatpants and a white T-shirt with red and green ink stains above a breast pocket. Del was barefoot.

He scattered a pinch of dill over an egg he scrambled in a cheap aluminum pan he placed on the lab's cherry red hotplate. While the egg sizzled, he held a piece of rye bread in forceps above a Bunsen burner. Del saw no use for plates in his lab; he dropped the pan and a fork into his small sink. He inspected the cool amber drops that were slowly collecting in a retort, sublimating slower than he wished, but quickly enough. He set a coil down two more degrees and made a note. If the cooler temperature did not destroy the substance, he'd beat that band of bastards in Michigan, for sure.

GIGO floated close to the surface of her bowl to receive a few crumbs of rye toast. The fish swam slowly clockwise when she swam at all. She'd swum in the opposite direction before Del had zapped her for thirty seconds into a yesterday that from GIGO's perspective required a return journey back to tomorrow. Did Del dare time travel? Might he come back left-handed? What if he returned thinking backward? He'd not met himself yet, so he was certain he'd not worked up the courage, or his older self to come had perfected such a trip but did not deem it safe to meet his younger self. He was waiting for his older self to show up and tell him it was not a problem, but that made no sense, for if he did not initiate a first trip he could not go back to reassure himself. Time travel made even a genius's head hurt.

GIGO's changes were surely at the cellular level; fish did not change how they swam as a matter of fashion. But Del lacked the heart to dissect his pet to do the needed histology analysis. Content to remain ignorant, he realized it was one of the ways he differed from Madge. The black goldfish hung suspended in clear water, gills undulating, eyes huge with trust.

Del dropped to the lab's floor to bang out fifty full sit-ups. With his ankles braced and locked on a short stool, he cranked out an additional one hundred crunchers. He rolled to do twenty pushups, donned a gray sweatshirt so large he could cover his fists by grasping at the sleeves, tied on a battered pair of running shoes, and jogged two miles. His running path shone black between pure white piles of shoveled Riverton snow. No one knew who shoveled it.

It was a fine Riverton winter morning. A cloud of his own breath preceded him. Coming home, Del hurdled the white picket fence that surrounded his parents' home, stretched his hamstrings and calves with his palms against the garage wall, and back inside banged out twenty-five more sit-ups for the sheer joy of it.

While he'd exercised, he'd reviewed all the data and theories he had about Riverton. In his cold shower, he reviewed his review.

Because he had run in this new Riverton morning, because dawn had come, and because the sun rose, Madge's mystical notions were demonstrably false. Either she had arrived at Daddy Kane's and failed to awaken Arnie, or Arnie was no Dreamer.

But Madge was right about one thing: causality was out of kilter in Riverton. And while Madge attributed anomalies to an all-powerful deity, some Dreamer, Del knew that the world was explicable. Facts required a theory, not denial that they were facts.

His speculations had begun one day in Grimley's class. The red sweep hand of the clock on the pea-soup-green wall over Grimley's head not only stood still, but Del was sure it ran backwards. He'd always attributed that to an illusion of boredom, but what if duration, time itself, was a psychological phenomenon?

It was plausible.

Grimley delivered the same lesson daily, the causes of World War I. Did the other kids need review? Could the lesson be the only thing Grimley knew?

The skinny old woman in her pale green turtleneck tops often called on him. No matter what she asked, Del stood and said, "Militarism," and Grimley crossed her arms on her flat chest and held him with that thin-lipped stare that could wilt celery. Grimley smiled with the pleasure of absolute power, a facial expression that exposed no teeth. He'd feel compelled to say more.

Time crept, slowed by psychology.

At about that moment, to his left, Mary Swenson would swoon into a giggle fit and develop hiccups; to his right, Victoria would put her head on her desk and theatrically snore.

There had to be a reason Riverton was strange; exceptional intelligence was an embarrassment and genius was always suspicious, not to mention frequently being socially fatal. There might be something to Madge's theory of ridicule, the kind of quantum symmetry that had matter and antimatter in absolute balance.

Take the many times they were in the lunchroom when Mary might notice *The Quarterly Journal of Astrophysics* in his stack of books. She'd bend sideways from the waist to read the title from the spine. Admittedly, getting Mary to bend over was never a bad thing, but as Del admired the outline of her hanging breasts beneath her turquoise knit top, two perfect conic sections, he saw her lips move as she read.

When she straightened up, in that breathless whisper she had, she gushed, *Tell me my future, Del.*

Del was weak. Forget that her lips moved; so did the flesh of her arms, legs, and thighs. The sight of her quivering body parts filled his mind with vain hope and his dick with blood. Mary sprayed longing like a honeybee sprayed pheromones and hints of clover.

At such a moment, time galloped.

Like a fool, Del explained to her how astrophysics was different from astrology. Mary's pink tongue wet her lips. The more Del spoke, the deeper his heart settled toward his ankles. He had the same futile feeling when he awakened at the top of the gym rope. A punch-line like a downhill runaway locomotive was coming at him.

Del tried to sidestep. He'd tell Mary that her stars predicted she would live forever and always be happy.

Mary's eyes rounded to perfect orbs. She bent to peck his cheek, and the view before him down her blouse was the road to Paradise flanked by pink nipples. Del drew in her perfume. His face grew hot. Her lipstick was imprinted on his face.

But of course, that was what Arnie had been waiting for. The carrot-top fuck yelled, *Hey, everybody, Del is telling fortunes! Kyuk, kyuk, kyuk.*

Del would have given twenty IQ points to have a girl like Mary. Thirty. But he'd spare a cool hundred for a good, unobstructed kick to Arnie's nuts.

It was time to visit Colonel William DuBois.

Del leaped into his Austin Healy 3000 Roadster, yanked his tweed cap down onto his ears, slung the yellow and maroon scarf his mother knit for him around his throat, rolled up his sweater's collar, slid his feet onto the wooden blocks he'd pasted to the brake, accelerator, and clutch, and sat on the two telephone books he kept on the driver's seat. By 9:30, snow was melting away all over Riverton. He pulled out the choke and pressed the starter button.

The morning was unseasonably warm, the kind of day skiers bragged about if they were lucky enough to get one. The first powder snow remained on slopes of New England, but the storm itself had moved out to sea, leaving in its wake air so pure and sharp that the world seemed new. It would have been a lovely day for early April; it was mid-December.

The closer the Austin drew to the DuBois estate, the warmer it became. Del stopped to take down the car's top. He stuffed the supple black vinyl into the battery well behind the two black leather seats. His cap and scarf would keep him warm enough. The rich blue sky was cloudless.

Del had to stop a second time for fifteen minutes at the old railroad bridge. Emergency vehicles spinning mournful red lights had chains and grappling hooks on the burned hulk of an automobile. It was being hauled out of the ravine. While he waited, he removed his amber sunglasses and turned his face up to the sun. The fireman who loitered near him on the bridge span said, "Nothing to get excited about, sir. We have it under control. This is Riverton, after all, and if a bunch of high-spirited kids have a little too much fun with an old abandoned car, well, we can certainly handle that!"

The sun licked his face. He was to see the Colonel, but he thought about the daughter. He knew Cherry; he knew he knew Cherry; he believed he had always known Cherry. He recalled little personal history. A wrinkle in the Singularity?

'Toria's only competition for Arnie was supposed to be Mary. As Madge the Mystic might put it, Mary and Victoria were the yin and yang that balanced Riverton.

But Cherry's disruptive appearances made the Riverton High social climate more volatile than horseshit and diesel fuel. With legs that started at her neck, Cherry DuBois was eye-candy for the boys and had every girl in town on suicide watch. When she descended on Riverton, boys lifted weights and nursed hard-ons in tighter pants; the girls tarted up.

Lipstick grew moister; heels became higher; bras had more uplift, and skirt hemlines rose to heights that generated church sermons. When Cherry materialized, she stalked Arnie Appleton like a heat-seeking Sidewinder locked on a ramjet in Arnie's ass. She did that thing with the fake beauty mark on her cheek, and she wore that see-through blouse, the filmy, tight yellow number, and she wore it with one extra button undone, a black lace bra beneath, and a grim curl to her lips that could give a wolverine a case of the willies.

Single-minded, rich, and unscrupulous, Cherry had the same character as 'Toria, but in spades. For his part, Arnie thought it was great that Cherry's long flowing hair was the same color as his crewcut.

Del could not remember ever meeting her. He just knew all about her. It made no sense; he would have to live with the contradiction.

The Colonel himself was a frail widower in failing health, a recluse whose fortune came to him the old-fashioned way: he inherited it. There was some disagreement in town whether Cabot or DuBois sat on the bigger pile of dough, but the only real debate was which man's brat daughter could spend a fortune faster.

On the far side of DuBois Hill, the turnoff from the paved blacktop to the DuBois estate was an unmarked space between leafless arching elm and oak trees. The rutted dirt path approach to the estate itself was clean of snow.

The gates of the DuBois estate swung open. The Austin Healy bumped forward in second gear. Del drove on a gravel lane, up a gentle hill, the road flanked by vast meadows that would be lush and green in spring, but now were yellowed with tall, dry winter grass.

Maybe the rich could buy better weather.

Del shed his hat and scarf as he passed a weatherworn gazebo, once a gay yellow, now gone to a weathered gray. Beyond the gazebo stood a blue and white cabana, a faux Greek affair beside a small, rectangular pink gunite pool that held only crackling brown leaves. A half dozen freestanding Ionic columns looked as if wind left them standing after having blown off the top of the Parthenon. Chaotically arranged skeletal white chaise lounges without cushions looked like the shells of giant dead insects. One chaise rusted at the bottom of the empty pool. A tall cyclone fence enclosed two net-less clay tennis courts, the kind that need constant rolling and maintenance from a dedicated house staff.

The courts weren't getting any care.

A redheaded woman in tennis whites and a white cotton zippered sweater leaped from a tattered rattan chair in the gazebo and shouted at him to stop, but though Del saw her waving to him in his rearview mirror, he continued forward. Cherry DuBois seemed to be all he'd been able to recall, but Del had been summoned on business by the Colonel. Business first. When Cherry flung her racket after him, it whirled like a boomerang before harmlessly hit the ground. She slapped her elbow and raised her fist.

Del waved his cap.

The Healy emerged from the dappled shadows and circled a pink marble fountain, twin goddesses, their arms supplicating to the sky, half draped, bare-breasted. Dead leaves and brown dust choked the empty fountain basin. There was no sign of last night's snowstorm anywhere on the estate.

Del ratcheted up the emergency brake and vaulted from his car. He loved doing that; he practiced the move, and he was good at it, but the one time he'd dared to do it in front of Madge, 'Toria, and Mary, his foot hooked the steering wheel and he collapsed to the sidewalk like a marionette with cut strings. Naturally, that impossible prick, Arnie, enjoyed the pratfall. *Kyuk, kyuk, kyuk.*

The DuBois home was a Palladian mansion, white, three columns on the portico, two wings to the house, two stories on each wing, black wooden shutters nailed open at every window. Thomas Jefferson would have felt comfy once he'd whipped a few darkies into scraping the peeling paint.

Del walked beside a bed of dead peonies to take the portico stairs two at a time. As he dropped the polished brass knocker on the front door, a uniformed butler silently swung open the big white door.

Del was ushered in. The DuBois place smelled like an abandoned bank where old money slept contentedly in secure, lightless vaults. He followed the portly butler to a door the butler said was the library, but did not follow as Del stepped over the threshold.

Del was bludgeoned by sudden humidity, an oppressive soupy miasma of fish and decaying plants that filled his nose thick as cotton. Library, nothing. This was an aquarium. Vague light through the glass ceiling cast hot spots on the oak paneled walls and floor where empty shelves that once held books held only tanks of water. Del's back trickled perspiration. The fish tanks glowed eerily blue with ultraviolet light. Most were the standard twenty-five gallons, but several were large enough for a terrier to swim laps.

Colonel DuBois was balanced on a stepstool beside one of the largest tanks, the sleeves of his white dress shirt rolled nearly into his armpits. His skinny arms were deep in water. He threw dank, brown grasses limp and rotted as a drowned heiress's hair onto a sheet of newspaper spread on the parquet floor.

"What do you know about Siamese Fighting Fish, Mr. Dellingham?" the Colonel asked without looking up.

"Not much," Del said. "When she swims, my goldfish swims counterclockwise in her bowl. That's all I know about fish." Del leaned back against the oak door and wiped a line of salty perspiration forming over his eyebrows. "They are called Bettas, aren't they?" He breathed through his mouth.

"*Betta Splendens*. The very same. Remarkable creatures. They seldom grow longer than a man's finger. Native to the shallow rivers of Southeast Asia, so they require more heat than most, water temperature above 75. They have a special organ called a labyrinth. Right at the top of their heads. Imagine that. They can breathe air. They also have gills, so they have all the options, but their air-breathing apparatus is called a *labyrinth*. Isn't that marvelous? A labyrinth."

"I didn't know that," Del lied.

Colonel "Red" DuBois expected people to hang on his every word. He was smart enough to know that his money commanded their attention, but not smart enough to understand that the attention was not his due.

The old man's piercing green eyes were the only part of him that did not seem worn with overuse. "Bullshit. Of course you know it," the Colonel said as he gingerly stepped down the stepstool.

Del reached to help the Colonel steady himself, but the older man slapped his hand away. "There is not a lot you do not know, Mr. Dellingham. I've the means to know what you know. So let us agree to be frank."

"I'd like that," Del said.

The Colonel was slender, but not slight. His shirt wanted starch and the frayed collar ringed his neck as if the Colonel were a boy playing in his father's clothing. Under the rough whiskers of his throat, his Adam's Apple bobbed like a trout float. The crow's feet at the corners of his eyes spoke of years at the tiller of sailing yachts. His wrinkled linen shirt was tucked into stained khaki pants cinched by a worn brown dress belt with three raw holes punched through the finished leather. His brown penny loafers were spit-shined. "Good, Dellingham, we will abandon false modesty."

"If you like. Call me Del."

The Colonel rolled the newspaper tightly around the dead grass and dried his hand on his slacks. "The male of the species are at constant war. All the display, the colors, those marvelous fins, it is all nothing but display to attract females and propagate the species. Put any two males in proximity, they will fight until one is dead. Divide them by a glass barrier, they will hurl themselves at the glass until they are both dead. No female need be in sight. Consider that. No female need be present. Remarkable."

"Like some people I know," Del said.

Colonel William DuBois's toothy grin was filled by receding gums and yellowed gapped teeth. "You're a poet, Mr. Dellingham. You see my metaphor," he said. "We are going to get along, sir. We are going to get along." He snapped his Rolex over his slim wrist and extended his hand. The watchband was too large for him; the watch face flipped face down.

Colonel DuBois's handshake was the grip of a man who'd once been stronger. The smooth hands had never known any work more arduous than pressing the keys of a piano.

"Nothing but Fighting Fish?" Del asked.

"All except that large tank there. Piranha. They are unhappy unless they are in schools. But come. I will have my brandy. Join me."

They escaped the cloying stink of the aquarium by passing through a short hallway and out a pair of white French doors to a bricked patio. The patio was enclosed on three sides by glass; the fourth wall was the house itself. They may as well have been fish in a tank. At the base of DuBois Hill, the gray Merrimack River, an estuary this close to the sea, was broad with black water flowing downstream. The tide was running out. At their backs, beyond the wall of glass, beside the front lawn, Del saw his car beside the pink fountain.

They sat at a small glass table where a silver service tray waited for them. The December sunlight heated the glass enclosure like a hothouse. The Colonel poured two fingers of Calvados into a brandy snifter, but when Del turned down alcohol, the Colonel touched a bell and the liveried butler brought Mr. Dellingham a pitcher of iced tea, a bucket of ice, tongs, and a tumbler dressed with a sprig of fresh mint.

"I've not seen an Austin Healy for quite a while," the Colonel said. "My, my, my. In BRG, no less. That's the 3000 Roadster, isn't it?"

"You know your antique cars," Del said.

"I have a few. You'll have to see my Morgan sometime. The twin rearview mirrors on the Healy at the ends of the fender always puzzled me. They'd make far more sense if they could be controlled from the driver's seat, but they certainly look sporty. No, they do not make cars like that any longer, do they?"

"I had to do some restoration, especially the leather seats. And I set the mirrors on gimbals. I control them without having to get in and out of the car."

"Of course. How did you manage the expense?"

They'd agreed to be frank. Del told the Colonel how he'd awarded himself the Healy after refining an intermediate carbocation process for a large pharmaceutical company.

"Which?"

"You're not suggesting I violate my nondisclosure agreement, are you?" Del said and smiled. "They needed a Fries Rearrangement of a specialized ester. It's an intermediate stage to a final product, and since I needed a decent ride, I did the work for them."

"You make it sound simple." The Colonel's eyes narrowed. "Can you offer me the layman's version?"

"I'm a registered freelance research organization. Companies post needs on the Internet and offer bounties. On this one, I got there first with the most. I was lucky."

"Quite a business model."

"It's nothing new. Napoleon offered a prize for a way to preserve food, and a man named Appert invented canning. He used vacuum-sealed glass bottles. To this day your tuna lasts forever in the can because Napoleon wanted to feed his army without pissing off the local population. He forbid pillaging, and the people he conquered cheered," Del said. He peered into the old man's eyes. "Don't tell anyone you heard it from me, but I suspect that by next year, you may be able to buy an aftershave that will make women trip over themselves to bear your children. Human pheromones."

"Wholly unnecessary. A large bank balance works wonders."

They touched glasses.

The Colonel dragged his chair close. He swirled the Calvados, his hands cupping the snifter to warm the brandy and evoke the vapors that teased his nose. He wet his lips, color crept into his pasty face, and he leaned in. "Dellingham, you are something of an engineer as well as a chemist?"

"I can make a thing when I need to."

"I like practical men. Let's not pussyfoot. We've agreed to be frank. Frank and practical. A most excellent combination." He placed his hands on his bony knees and leaned even closer. His voice rasped. "Dellingham, I've made some mistakes in my life."

"We all do, Colonel."

"Not like mine. But I want to correct them. I'd like to start again, so to speak. I do not have enough time to make it right."

Del sipped his tea. The mint was like a pinch on his tongue. "I am sure you can do a lot of good, Colonel. You are fortunate to have the means. I am sorry about your health."

"I don't mean charitable work, Dellingham. I have no guilt, just regrets. I am not in debt to God. Dellingham, you miss my meaning. I want to start again."

"Colonel, I am a scientist, not a leprechaun."

"Ha. That's quite good. 'Not a leprechaun.' You think I make an idle wish?" The Colonel took a bolder swallow of his brandy. He cheeks colored red; his fingers became more animated, floating in the space before his chin like warring fighting fish.

"Build me a time machine," he said. "I want to go back."

Del set his glass on a coaster. "That's not possible," he lied.

"Oh, come. We agreed to be frank. Surely, you've considered the problem." The Colonel was unused to hearing his wishes so lightly dismissed.

"Colonel, no matter when you went, you'd be the same person, just as old."

The Colonel sat back. Then his eyes brightened and he leaned forward again.

"Cloning then."

"That's arguably possible, I'll admit."

The Colonel slapped his knees. "There you have it. Just what we need. I knew you were the right man for the job."

"Now, hold on Colonel. There's no 'we' here yet. You are talking about creating an infant. That's a clean slate, a baby with no knowledge or experience. A genetic duplicate isn't the same entity as the mature donor organism."

"But it is close."

"Yes. There is that. And there's speculation about chemically implanting memories. Memory may be just a string of peptides that form and persist in the brain. But that's just speculation."

It occurred to him that Madge would want to know that. Del planned on telling her.

"But if you could clone one organism, you could clone several?"

"Well, of course, but other than lab rats, why would you want an army of identical organisms?"

The Colonel laughed. "I've not explained myself, Dellingham. That's not it. I meant clone just two selected individuals, one with memory and one without. The plan is to have them come of age simultaneously." He scratched his unshaved chin and drained his Calvados. "I am a romantic. Two people who could discover each other. It's a dream I have."

A metal gate clanged shut. Still in her tennis skirt, Cherry DuBois sauntered toward them. Her hair was held back by twin Kelly green barrettes and a matching scarf. The pompoms on the heels of her socks bobbed. Cherry DuBois seemed used to entering a room and having conversation stop. Del figured it was the bare thighs the color of maple syrup and soft Irish butter on hotcakes.

Her tennis racket clattered onto the glass table and she sat on her father's lap, her arms encircling his neck before she wetly kissed the top of his balding head. She toed off her Tretorns. Five slim fingers lazily went back through her father's thinning hair. The old man grinned like an inspired corpse, canines glistening.

"Mr. Dellingham, this sweetheart is my Cherry." The old man's skeletal hand rested on the very fair skin of his daughter's very bare lower back.

"Call me Del," he said.

Cherry extended her hand as if it were to be kissed, limp at the wrist, manicured, pink lacquered fingers wavering like sea anemones. "Red, now why would you think you could invite Delbart Dellingham here and utter not a word to me? Not the teeniest word. You know you are no good at secrets." She leaned close to her father and pinched his sunken cheeks as she stared into his sallow eyes. Swiveling on her father's thin knees, Cherry said to Del,

"Do you only drink iced tea? Will you stay for lunch?" She lifted his glass from the table and sniffed it with annoyance. Her pert nose wrinkled. "Daddy has been pouring me wine ever since forever," she said. Cherry tipped a generous splash of the Colonel's Calvados from his snifter into Del's tumbler, darkening the tea, then thought for a heartbeat, and poured in the rest. "It tastes like apples," she said. "Not the sweet kind."

"Tart," her father said.

"That's right, Daddy, tart."

If Cherry DuBois stood at a roadside, she could stop an ambulance. Her hair was rich hue of single filament copper wire. If her nose had ever known a freckle, it had been banished to join the freckle party on her chest. The green loosely knotted scarf at her throat did little to cover her pronounced décolletage. She squirmed and twisted on her father's lap, chattered, touched the old man on his chin, his eyes, his chest, and his arms. She talked about her dreadful, boring, restrictive, horrible old-fashioned private school, and how she'd much prefer Riverton High, but her father just did not like the vulgarity of the people there. "You don't think Mr. Dellingham is vulgar, do you?" she asked, but without waiting for an answer immediately went on. The girls at Riverton were all right, and there was that dreamboat, Arnie, did Del know him? Del could tell him for her that Cherry had been deeply, deeply disappointed. She pouted. "He was supposed to meet me last night, but he stood me up."

"Don't get too enamored of the Appleton boy," the Colonel said. "He's totally forgettable."

Cherry cupped his chin in her two hands and wetly kissed his brow. "Red, you have to stop saying that. He always says that, Mr. Dellingham. He says that about every boy I ever mention. Don't you, Red? Don't you always say that?"

The old man grinned like a cat with scratched ears.

Cherry DuBois' full and luminous hair shimmered and flowed around her bare shoulders, an undulating wave of silk astir in clear water. She hastened to explain her name was from the French. "It has nothing to do with fruit. It means, 'Dear one.' Isn't that right, Red? Aren't I your dear one?"

She paused to wet her full lips with the tip of her tongue; then she asked if Red had bored poor Del with unending details about Siamese Fighting Fish.

"I thought the fish were pretty interesting," Del managed.

Cherry held her fingers to her chin and pretended to be scandalized. "Red, I begged you not to bore our guests with your stupid fish." She inserted the tip of her thumb into her mouth up to the first joint, just under her front teeth. Cherry lifted her Lalique choker into her mouth. Pink coral beads clicked one-by-one out and over her perfect teeth.

A tennis outfit in December, no matter how warm a day it was, filled Del with wonder. Cherry DuBois would not know the uses of an athletic bra, far too binding. She had the muscled shoulders of a female athlete. Her exposed stomach was flat, but after she had touched her own damp hand to her abdomen, her skin shone with a dull sheen. Her narrow waist flared out to unembarrassed hips. The pleated skirt was short as a stupid rumor. Her legs, though, took a while to take in. They tapered where they should and broadened where they should from her hips to her slender ankles. Each time she crossed those legs, small bells in the laces of her sneakers chimed like a Tibetan prayer wheel.

Del now understood what those monks prayed for.

"You are short," Cherry said abruptly as if she discovered something no one else knew. She filled her father's brandy snifter to the brim, drained it in a single swallow, and then re-filled it. Her lips left a crescent of coral color on the glass. The Colonel's snifter was roughly the volume of GIGO's bowl; Cherry DuBois empted it twice. "Now why should I be astonished you are short? Haverhill boys are always so odd. That's why I love them all so much, you know. So few things are what one imagines, and here you are, Delbart Dellingham, exactly as your advanced billing had it, but shorter. Are you as smart as they say, Mr. Delbart Dellingham? Tell me truly."

"I do what I can. Do you play a lot of tennis in December? I didn't notice any nets on the courts."

"I do what I can," she said. She spun on her father's lap to face Del and take up the conversational gambit. Dellingham had responded to her teasing. She followed the scent of fun like a bitch bloodhound. "Do you play, Mr. Dellingham?"

"Not tennis."

"What is it you do? For exercise, I mean."

"As little as I can," he lied. "Walking across a room makes me faint."

"You're joking with me, Delbart. You look trim and fine. We shall have to perspire together, someday. I always say, you never know a person until you've perspired together. Don't I always say that, Red? Don't I? My personal trainer attends to my needs. He's a talented masseur. Extraordinary hands, and thoroughly versed in the maintenance and cultivation of all the human body can do."

She worried her thumb tip with her mouth again, then brightened and asked, "Did you notice my statue, Delbart? Red had me pose," she said. "The sculptor wanted a second model, but Red insisted that I become twins. Isn't my father just so marvelous?" She cupped her father's chin in one hand and kissed the Colonel's bald head once more before wiping the mark of her crimson lipstick from him with a cloth napkin she moistened with her tongue.

"'Red?'"

"My nickname from when I had hair, Mr. Dellingham. Cherry, as you can see, inherited it."

The Colonel reached for his brandy, but Cherry kept his glass from him, tipped back her head and slugged the entire contents down, four, five fingers worth in a single swallow, her third full snifter in as many minutes. Her breasts quivered inches from her father's face. "It's a pity we cannot run the fountain in December. My pink marble ass looks so much better with a cascade of clear water shining on it. You'll have to see that, sometime, Delbart."

"I look forward to it."

"I don't doubt it. I'm sure you'd find my polished behind memorable. I'm not a goddess, mind you. Just a water sprite." Her smile held the whitest teeth money could buy. "Now, Daddy, you have to promise Mr. Dellingham won't be allowed to leave before he and I have talked in private. We get so few visitors." She turned to Del to explain. "Daddy keeps me prisoner whenever I am home from school. The Colonel wants me all to himself. Isn't that just horrible? I had to sneak out last night, and now he's locked my Benz away."

"I think we are almost done here," Del said, and half rose, but the Colonel gestured palm down for him to stay a bit longer.

"I'll be waiting." Cherry abruptly stood, bent to take Del's glass, and gave him the same full view into her halter her father had enjoyed moments earlier. She smelled of apples and cinnamon, like Calvados. "And you *will* stay for lunch. Let me tell Cook. A treat, perhaps? Something covered with mounds of whipped cream? I so like whipped cream and chocolate sauce."

The metal gate clanged shut behind her, loud as when she'd arrived.

"That would be your companion clone?" Del was in the grip of vertigo.

"Mr. Dellingham, you are a scientist. Petty bourgeois moral concerns should not inhibit you from progress. Cherry takes after her mother, and I miss the dead old witch. Nothing more." The Colonel cleared his throat.

"Then why not clone her? There must be some DNA around."

"Dellingham, you are becoming impertinent. See here, I've made you a handsome offer. Name your price."

Petty bourgeois moral concerns had sources in species survival. Inbreeding risked recessive genes finding each other. Taboos were taboos for a reason. If there was a definition of *perversion*, this was it. Incest. Del's stomach flipped cartwheels. His ever-present heartburn would soon be active as Vesuvius. "I'll think it over, Colonel," he said and stood, wiping his damp palms on his pants.

"Don't take too long, Mr. Dellingham. I'm an impatient man and far more is at stake than you can imagine." The Colonel lifted what was left of his brandy. The waxen skin on his shaking hand was loose and translucent. "You've heard about Arnie Appleton's misfortune?"

the Colonel called to Del's back.

"Heard what?"

"You had to have passed the wreck on your way here. Cherry has not heard, yet. Don't tell her. She will be devastated. It's a father's role to protect his child, you know. I will break the news in good time." His eyes briefly ignited with the light of a far younger man who felt victory. "Appleton's bad luck may be my good luck."

The world reeled in new ways. The old man was glad a rival was dead. Arnie gone? *Kyuk, kyuk, k-last fucking-yuk.* So much for Madge's notions of a Dreamer.

"My daughter's preoccupation with young Appleton was unseemly. She was unaware, but they were distantly related." When Del did not take the Colonel's proffered hand, the old man collapsed back onto his chair where Del left him.

In front of the mansion, Cherry DuBois sat in the driver's seat of the Austin-Healy, her face soaking up the winter sun. She had the look of a young woman who disliked waiting, but who endured other people's petty delays before they could move on to the more important business that was Cherry DuBois. Nothing ever came soon enough. Cherry's long left leg draped over the sports car door, her right languished in the well of the passenger seat, the transmission shift, a stubby sentinel, stood close guard at her crotch.

"Donut?" she said. She slowly tongued powdered sugar from each of her fingertips, residue from the cellophane bag of mini-donuts in her lap. Her head lolled back on the Healy's soft brown leather seat, her red hair splayed about her throat and face like a mermaid's. Cherry had shed her tennis shoes and socks; her toenails were perfectly lacquered bright red. She sucked the tip of her right thumb.

"Donuts aren't much of a lunch." Del leaned his hip against the car door. "I was promised lunch. Is it Cook's day off?" With Cherry in the low Healy, it was no trick for Del to stare down the tennis halter. Despite the cool air, a rivulet of perspiration snaked across the depression at the center of her throat, a valley beneath the coral necklace, and from that the valley trickled down between her breasts.

"Lunch can still be arranged, though Cook seems to have taken several weeks off."

"So no whipped cream?"

"I'd have to prepare it myself. Will you be wanting a cherry on top?" She giggled, then suddenly as if the game had grown dull, grew serious. Her mood swing was swift as a cloud crossing the sun.

"Several weeks off? That's a generous vacation."

"Six weeks, Mr. Dellingham, and there is no prospect of his return. My father would be disturbed to learn that the house's payroll is diminishing. I've been in charge of accounts for some time. You are, at the moment, addressing Cook. I'm also my own tennis trainer.

They've all gone except for Jeeves, and Jeeves is hanging on only because I told him he stands to inherit money if he does."

"Will he?"

"Of course not. Jeeves isn't even his real name."

"What is it?"

"Who cares? If you'd stopped on the drive on your way in, I could have warned you."

"Of what?"

"Daddy is determined and delusional. The DuBois fortune is in *rigor mortis*, as rigid as those statues of me over there. Tell me, did he offer you a fabulous award?"

"We did not get that far. I turned down the job."

"Oh? He won't like that. Daddy still has resources. Be careful, Mr. Dellingham. My father can be an unpleasant enemy, even if he is going broke. What exactly did he propose?"

"So the money is all gone? The place looks tattered at the edges."

"The money is there, somewhere. It's illiquid, so I just can't get my hands on it; Red thinks I am not to be trusted. He's spending my inheritance as fast as he can trying not to die."

"But you run the accounts. How can he spend it all?"

"I control an allowance. For me and the house. I can spend it on me or a paint job. Guess my preference." She gnawed at her thumb and batted her eyelashes until her eyes ignited with new understanding. "You aren't going to tell me, are you?"

"What?"

"What he wanted."

"No. I'm not. I may not have taken the job, but I have my principles."

"Poo. Principles. Principles are for other people."

Cherry had been spinning on her father's lap like a corkscrew; now she sat motionless with one leg in Vermont, the other in Maine, and all of the beautiful White Mountains of New Hampshire in between. Her gimlet eyes stared up at him, two pools of infinite depth. He felt like diving in. "Did you know, Delbart, I can tie a cherry stem in a knot."

"There's no trick to that."

"In my mouth. No hands. Tongue only. I have a supple tongue. You'd like my tongue." She was a girl who liked having men lose track of time. "You have wooden blocks lashed to the brake, accelerator and clutch, and you sit on phonebooks," she said, stating the obvious.

"I was wondering what that stuff was."

"No offense, Delbart. I am just noting how resourceful you are," she said. She'd dropped the phone books behind the seat. "Do you over-achieve because you are so short?" she asked, and before he could speak, blinked and added, "Does that question offend you, Delbart?"

Her thumb-tip was back in her mouth.

"Del," he said. "No. A fact is a fact. It just is what it is. I'm five-two. The question is not offensive," he lied.

"You are devoted to facts."

"Always."

Her red hair wafted from her shoulders in the light wind. She pulled his tartan cap onto her head, sat up, circled her arms around his neck, and then kissed him, hard, all tongue. When she broke the kiss, she sat back and chewed a knot of her own hair, slid a length of his woolen muffler through her fingers. "That was interesting," she said. "Do you find me attractive, Delbart Dellingham?"

"You don't need me to tell you that."

"A girl likes to hear it, even if she already knows. I like facts, too. If you and I are going to be friends, you'll need to loosen up. We *are* going to be friends, Delbart. You could uncross your arms, for one thing. How was the kiss?"

"Why would we be friends?"

"You can't have too many friends," she said, and then without pausing for breath she hurriedly added, "Look, Red doesn't know the whole story. So whatever he told you, just forget it. I am glad you did not take the job, but I would not want his version of my life spreading around town."

Delbart's arms dropped to his sides. He tried not to think of how easily her tongue had explored his mouth and how good that felt behind his teeth. What was she talking about? "The whole story?"

"What did he tell you?"

"You and your father seem to get along. Why don't you ask him if you want to know that?"

"We do more than get along." She pouted and did the thing that curled her lower lip with her thumb. "Well, he does *not* know the whole story. He thinks he does, but the truth was that the boys in the dorm said it was an art project. They promised they'd never show the movie to anyone. My teacher had nothing to do with it. But not even a genius can erase all the pictures from the Internet. Isn't that right? Not even a genius can erase the Internet."

"If you don't want it on the Jumbotron at Fenway, don't make it digital."

"Wouldn't that be glorious? Me on the Jumbotron!" Her green eyes sparkled. "I told Daddy! I told him. Those three minutes and twelve seconds will live forever, longer than his precious statues, and no matter how old I get, somewhere, someone will see how I am now, but forever. All four of us look lovely. The boys row crew. I am not ashamed. The boys are lovely and I am lovely. I love the Colonel. I do. Red is far more to me than a father. I truly adore him. But the Colonel is old-fashioned and suspicious, and unlike Siamese Fighting Fish, a girl needs space and air and light." She languidly stretched her arms over her head and sighed. "Do you have a life, Delbart? A real life? Is there a girl?"

"I haven't found one yet," he said, though for a moment he wanted to say *Madge*.

Cherry perked up. She dropped the empty crumpled cellophane donut bag onto the grass beside her tennis shoes where the light breeze picked it up and carried it away. Her bare toes wiggled. It was at least 65 degrees, a heck of a day for December. Maybe the rich *could* buy better weather.

"I told you we could be friends! Why don't you and I go for a ride in this adorable car of yours? You have to. You simply have to. The Colonel has locked away the keys to my Benz, otherwise I'd go for a drive all by myself." Her finger entwined a curl of her hair and she leaned toward him again, all promise and heat.

"Maybe the Colonel took your keys for a reason." If the old man had not told her about Arnie's death, Del would not do so.

She sniffed contempt. "The tennis coach at school told me to stay at the baseline and hit ground strokes, but I prefer the power game, Delbart. Serve, volley and charge. Force the point. Some people play not to lose; I play to win." Cherry abruptly snapped open the car door and stood close to Del. Her chest was inches before his eyes, and then she spun about, bent from the waist, and replaced his phonebooks.

Del vaulted into the driver's seat. Standing beside the Austin, Cherry set the tartan cap his head, giggling as she pulled it tight over his eyes. He adjusted it, and she giggled again. When she reached across him to drop his limp scarf onto the passenger seat, her hair cascaded over him like copper-colored vines redolent of apples and cinnamon and something else, something unashamedly delicate, something insistent and carnal.

"You'll have to return when Daddy starts the summer fountain. The estate can be dramatic. We'll feast on whipped cream."

Del depressed the clutch and touched the ignition button. The Healy stirred.

"Tell me, Delbart," she said, her elbows onto the car door, her hands cupping her pointed chin, her full lips a coral line inches from his ear. "You have not found a girl yet, but if you did, what would she be like? What is the perfect girl for a genius?"

He pulled out the choke; the Healy awakened with a throaty roar; he depressed the clutch. "She'd read Shakespeare, know pi to eight decimals, and be able to suck the chrome off a bumper hitch."

Cherry DuBois fluttered her eyes and drew back. Her hair floated about her shoulders as she sighed. "I suppose no girl is perfect. Two out of three is not bad. Shakespeare is *such* a challenge."

Del lifted his foot from the clutch, the rear wheel kicked gravel, and as he headed away he heard Cherry DuBois's laughter. She shouted, "Three point one four one five nine two…" The Healy lurched on the dirt circling the pink fountain; the tires scraping for traction on the long gravel driveway.

Del looked a final time into his rearview to see Cherry DuBois waving to him. He was smart, as smart as they get, but he'd never understand why a guy whose IQ was the same as the boiling point of water had to be a perpetual virgin. Why hadn't he entertained her for the day? How would it disturb the universe if he were to get laid? But his thoughts about his own, sorry-ass history and blank future vanished when he saw what Cherry DuBois could not.

Crouched beyond an untrimmed hedge behind his daughter, watching them both, was Colonel "Red" DuBois, peering at them like a feral cat. His expression seemed suspicious and mean, but what, after all, could the old man do?

Actually. Quite a bit. Del almost made it as far as the railroad bridge.

Maybe it was the Shadow. Maybe it was something else.

Del was done.

Came another bleak December day no different from before, certain no different from the days to come, with Riverton's schools closed for winter recess and nothing but endless, empty mind-numbing hours before her, Madge struggled with the stubborn slider door at the rear of the Klink home. It opened suddenly. She was encased in a puff of frigid air as she emerged onto the rickety back porch to kick at the patina of ice.

Unlike Big Juice, Arnie had not been reborn, but the sun over Riverton had stopped shining. More snow fell each day; never a first class blizzard, but filthy flurries that eddied over the frozen ground and would not melt.

Madge lighted a cigarette to force her pulse higher. She needed to think, but with her mother in the kitchen, coffee was not possible for her. Her mother would join her. There would be questions about proms and boys and all manner of stupidity. She needed to be sharp, but the price of a cup of coffee was far too high.

What remained in Riverton for her?

She had been wrong about everything. She was probably insane, possibly a homicidal maniac, but certainly delusional. Dreamers? Caterpillars? Cannibals? Resurrections? Juice walked the earth, and Arnie was surely dead. Her heart and mind told her otherwise, but that only proved she was profoundly ill, a troubled girl who thought too much.

Arnie's death had spun Riverton into mourning. They shuttered Riverton High the day after the memorial service, more than a week before the scheduled winter recess. Knots of kids had clustered in the high school's halls to speak softly of how much they missed good old Arnie Appleton. The building was draped in purple crepe. There was talk of renaming the high school Appleton Central. So many people wanted to attend the service in the school's auditorium that they moved it to the basketball gym. The service ended with a homily delivered by the Riverton Chief of Police. "Kids, listen to me," Chief Schmidt said, "Kids, drive carefully." The gathered mourners exhaled a collective sigh. Here was one of life's great lessons. *Drive carefully.*

Yes, they would drive carefully. Arnie had not died in vain. Arnie's sacrifice for them would be everlasting. They would think of him every time they turned a key in the ignition, at every turn and on every straightaway. Because of Arnie, they would be safer.

Mickey attended Arnie's service. He'd sat beside 'Toria in a front row seat, wearing a black serge overcoat with a black fur collar, black leather kid gloves, and a black felt fedora hat. 'Toria wore the best widow weeds money could buy. She seemed to be another accessory for Mickey. She wept and wept, hanging on Mickey's arm the whole time. He got to appear strong. By noon, when the town's church bells tolled, she'd whispered to Madge she had had memorialized Arnie with a tattoo of his smiling profile on her ass. She's be sitting on his face for all of her life. Madge thought that was wholly appropriate.

No one could locate Bughouse or Mary. They were truly gone, and hardly missed.

After the service, long lines of automobiles snaked their way to Daddy's Kane's All-American Bar & Grille where Daddy offered twofers on strawberry daiquiris. The following day, the The All-American Bar & Grille was shuttered. A brown bit of cardboard scrawled with black crayon was taped inside the glass door. *Florida.*

There was no casket, no burial, no grave, and for all Madge knew, no corpse. If he had had one, it would be just like the carrot-topped douche bag to rise from the grave in the middle of the service. He'd do it just for shits and giggles. Arnie Appleton was quite capable of coming back from the dead just to piss her off. *Kyuk-kyuk-kyuk.*

The Subaru still had a shattered headlamp. No one knew Madge had chased the red-headed prick.

She was not crazy enough to let that out. *Stupid* and *crazy* were not the same.

So Madge cultivated her newest private secret. She was probably just delusional and totally crazy, but if there was no Shadow and her ongoing hysteria about a Dreamer was just that—hysteria—what good would it do to cop to having pursued Appleton to his death?

Madge's black leather gloved hands rested on the creaky balustrade. She was careful not to lean her weight on the rotting, unpainted wood. Her too-busy father never got around to repairs; what a moron could have fixed with a few nails and a hammer was the Klink family's backdoor deathtrap. Madge hunched her shoulders against the cold, tugged her black sweatshirt hood over her head, thrust her hands into her pockets, the burning cigarette hanging from her full lips. Smoking with no hands: quite the skill, she thought. Perhaps she'd join the circus.

Her mother's four televisions murmured behind her, the sound leaking from the house through the glass slider she'd left open a crack. Long ago, someone, maybe Madge herself, had kicked a spider's web of fractures in the glass. Her father's ragged piece of metallic gray duct tape had been there since before forever. Mr. Klink was the King of Duct Tape. With four rolls and ten minutes, he'd have had Humpty Dumpty back together again.

Up the stark hill behind the field, the limbs of the dead tree-house oak bent under the accumulated ice's weight. She had no notion of why she thought of it as the *tree-house oak*. Wisps of rope like an old man's beard had waved in the breeze there a long time, desultory and limp in summer, stiff in winter. For what children and when had a tree fort been built? There must have been planks of pine in the branches, but they'd long ago rotted and collapsed onto the ground. Madge could remember too little of her past—a function of her mental illness, she was sure.

She did not want to be sick. If the memories of that kind of happy childhood had ever been meant to be hers, the sick fantasy of her disease screwed her up. Sickness or Shadow, it amounted to the same thing.

Beyond the oak tree and the tree house was an abandoned cinderblock garage, its red shingle roof collapsed years ago. The bared wooden beams were gray with rot. The single window had long since been nailed shut with plywood by the Dellingham's, the very nice, usually cheerful, but slightly dotty childless couple that lived beside the Klinks.

Madge was lonely and bored. She missed school and the school library. The Internet hookup in her room had gone inexplicably dark. Her remaining school chums would never share her nervous urgency. When they heard her rambling about caterpillars and cannibals, their eyes went from initial interest to amusement, but finally to pity.

Her choice was becoming easy.

The gaps and wrinkles in her memory had not changed. Chukker Jones's suicide, like Arnie's death, seemed irrevocable, but who could be sure? Spring would come, Daddy Kane might return, and maybe Arnie would rise with the new corn.

Just thinking about that possibility made her want to shower with her best friend, Ex-acto. If she climbed into the shower, she would carve her abdomen and thighs into half-inch wide strips the length and texture of beef jerky. She'd either emerge looking like uncooked rump roast, or she'd cut her throat and be done with it all.

Madge, however, wanted to live.

Tobacco smoke dissipated in the winter wind. Could she vanish as easily as smoke?

Nothing was left in Riverton for Madge. Why stay?

Mickey had grown rich, but distant. At least he'd once listened. Madge missed getting laid. She supposed she could have taken up with any number of the faceless no-name boys at Riverton High, but she saw no point to physical intimacy without at least a pretense of something more.

'Toria, once her best female friend, had developed a singular other interest, the same that was corrupting youth all over America. The single mindedness of her conversation left Madge in a stupor. 'Toria's life was about the junk Mickey plied; worse was that she was unable to enjoy her chemicals without pushing them at Madge.

Was 'Toria's proselytizing at Mickey's instruction? Could it have been his way to bring Madge around? Mickey was all about power. But Madge kept Aunt Sosha's warning squarely at the center of her mind's eye; she never touched the pills.

As for the rest, there was little to say. Big Juice, her alleged boyfriend, had come back from the dead to have less charm than a block of granite.

She'd have liked to have seen Bughouse, but lucky Bughouse must have gone to the greater world. She hoped it had come out well for him. One day, Grimley called class roll and skipped right over the name of Reynard Danton Bughouse Smith. He'd evaporated, spit on a hot rock.

Mary Swenson, too, had evaporated. Grimley persisted calling her name just as she had called Bughouse, dutifully marked Mary absent, and then went on to discuss the causes of World War I until one day she did not call Mary Swenson, either. What adventures did Mary enjoy?

Madge sucked in a last drag and flipped the cigarette onto the field of dirty ice, glancing one last time at the collapsed garage filling with snow and dead leaves. Madge would be a cannibal. Cannibals, Christians and Scientists. How had she come up with that? Had she read it somewhere?

There was nothing in Riverton for her, never had been, never would be.

Riverton and Madge Klink were quits.

Madge packed her treasures into a single, huge black valise she found in the double-door closet behind her parents' bedroom television. Three Russian novels, three Oxford white shirts, three pairs of white sweatsocks, three pairs of panties, two bras, her red and blue thongs, a spare pair of black jeans, and a pair of battered penny loafers. Madge debated her Riverton High sweatshirt, but left it as a puddle of cloth on the gray carpet floor in her closet. She wore her black hoodie and a pair of black chucker boots. Her black and white team jacket hung on a peg at the door. She'd eventually ditch the shoes and buy Doc Martens.

Madge wrestled the wheeled valise down the stairs, remembering the thrill of navigating those same stairs late at night, sneaking out to the No-Tel Motel. She made plenty of noise, now. Stealth made no difference. Who gave a fuck?

Her mother sat perched on a high white stool intently watching the portable television on the kitchen's granite counter.

"I'm leaving," Madge said to her mother.

Mrs. Klink waved her hand at her without removing her eyes from the screen.

"What are you watching?" Madge asked.

Mrs. Klink looked up, her brow knot with puzzlement. "Television. I'm watching television." Mrs. Klink's eyes brightened. "It's marvelous. Would you like to watch with me? I just made tea."

Madge stepped over her valise. She took a small white cup and saucer from a glass cupboard and made tea. Then she sat atop the stool beside her mother.

"This is lovely," Mrs. Klink said. "Girl-talk with my very own baby girl." Her hand patted Madge's wrist.

They watched together. The reception was perfect. Three well-dressed women talked in a studio filled with dozens of other women who wore either sweatpants or velour exercise suits. The television conversation was difficult to follow. Autistic children suffered from bad diet and inoculations, but somehow this also had to do with whether autistic children should have pets. Turtles were good, being nearly indestructible. Everyone bobbed their heads in sage agreement. Turtles were a fine plan.

After a set of commercials, everything that could be said about autism having been said, a young actor was introduced. Madge could not name him. The audience shrieked with excitement.

"Isn't he marvelous?" Madge's mother said.

Madge wondered if any of the audience women had ever had serious, heart-pounding, life-changing sex. Why should Madge feel they were more real than she? What would they do with a hard, substantial dick? Maybe the one attached to the celebrity actor. He looked handsome. Was that why they were shrieking?

She disgusted herself. What Madge knew of life was what she read in books or what she imagined after sordid encounters sweating in a motel room on boiled sheets with a boy she did not love. Rutting was her claim to worldliness. Cannibals? Christians? She'd been kidding herself.

The idiots screeching their joy on the screen were better than she. Madge was the fraud.

Her drained cup and saucer clattered when she placed them into the stainless steel sink. "I'm going now, Mother," Madge said.

"Have fun, dear. I am so glad we had this time together. Do drive carefully. You remember what happened to the poor Appleton boy."

Madge awkwardly hugged her mother from the side. Her mother's eyes never left the screen.

Madge drove south on the interstate, but fifteen minutes from Riverton, as she passed an ambulance, she thought of the Doc Martens she wanted, and that made her think to check her wallet. She idled in a rest area The Subaru had a half tank of gas and she had $16.23. Madge was pretty sure the mechanism that replenished her wallet would quit once she left Riverton. And she was probably not immortal, either.

She took stock.

What were her assets? Whom did she know? Not Aunt Sosha—the woman did not become who she was by distributing gifts, and if she went to her there was that man, Ari. His lashless blue eyes and thin lips made her shudder.

What could a woman with a great ass, two fabulous tits, and limitless heart do?

She eased up on the accelerator as she pulled off the highway into Haverhill. The Subaru took her through the winding streets as if it were on autopilot. Madge parked the car. She looked up and down the familiar Haverhill street and drew up her jacket collar before she walked a half block with her head lowered into the winter wind.

When she pushed open the glass door to Ryan's Clip Joint, the sleigh bells jangled cheer. She stamped her feet, swept the black sweatshirt hood from over her face, and shook her black hair loose. Ryan, who'd never seen her, presumed he had won some cosmic lottery, but Danny Donnelly knew what Fate had delivered to him.

He leaned back in his chair, thumbed back the brim of his black leather porkpie hat, and with a crooked Irish grin said, "As I live and breathe, if it is not our good friend Madge, and Christmas just three days away."

Del awakened in the place forgotten dreams go. You know the place. Startled out of REM sleep, you sit up in the grip of an amazing idea; it's no dream—it's a complete goddam vision, brilliant as Biblical revelation. This is how Handel wrote the Hallelujah Chorus. You hug yourself. No one could forget anything this clear, elegant, and self-evident. You roll over to sleep in the embrace of Grace and all nine of the Muses, but the flush of morning bleaches everything pale. You pound your own temples. Where did it go? Where did it go?

One minute he was nearing the railroad bridge where Arnie flipped and burned. Then he was nowhere.

That was where Del awakened. Nowhere. The land of forgotten dreams.

Place would be misleading; the word implies dimension. Such linguistic imprecision will have to suffice. There just is no vocabulary available. Useful concepts frequently have no linguistic equivalency; this makes them no less useful. What is the square root of negative one? Where is Paradise? What is it like to ride an electron inside an atom?

Awaken is equally inadequate; Del did not so much as open his eyes as he became aware. If by *eyes* we mean a photosensitive organ that with the assistance of the nervous system organizes perception into coherence, then Del had no eyes. The eyes of an octopus are remarkably different from yours or mine. The eyes of an insect are remarkably different from yours or an octopus. But all three kinds of eyes are closer to each other than to what Del experienced.

Mystics are on notice: spare us. We are not talking about some Rosicrucian higher plane of existence; those mysteries are for the Madges of our world to ponder. To explain away Del's fate with some fairytale of some higher order of spiritual existence would be about as grossly misleading as suggesting that Anna Karenina and Huck Finn were angels. If anything, Del's existence was degraded from what he'd known. Del had been forgotten even by those who loved him, and there had been a few. Riverton went *tabula rasa* on his ass. Anna and Huck — and Del for that matter — like Schrodinger's cat, exist in simultaneous, contradictory states. They are and they are not. Meat-space reality requires duration and spatial dimension, but the imagination does not.

This makes imagination no less real.

Leave it at this: Del was more self-aware than your computer, but he had far less certainty of being alive than the stupidest hummingbird. Don't even consider dreaming caterpillars. Just leave those goddam metamorphosing hairy, fucking blind worms out of this.

How long Del experienced non-sentience followed by this altered grayish awareness— there is no way to guess. The favorite cliché of over-educated seventh graders turned out for Del to be wholly accurate: *time* is meaningless. Look up at the night sky; the light of stars was shed a billion years before the oceans rolled. Perhaps the stars have been extinguished, but their light will be in our sky until the seas run dry. *Always* and *never, now* and *then,* are meaningless. *When* and *where* are the same concepts.

So Del was and was not afloat in this dimension-free non-place, a glowering spark of a dying idea encased within a pearl within an oyster covered by silt at the edge of a tidal pool on a small island newly emerged into a warm ocean that might be on this planet, but need not be.

GIGO floated close by.

Del, Del, Del. Why couldn't you leave well enough alone?

Dellingham knew what sound was; this was not sound. The fact that the source was a black goldfish that usually hung unmoving in a glass beaker and ate crumbs of rye toast did not trouble him. This was a parthenogenetically reproduced fish he had zapped into tomorrow and brought back to today. It should have been female; it assuredly was not.

"That's you, Colonel?"

GIGO did a back flip. *Yes and no. Right now, I am GIGO. I may choose to be a Bird of Paradise tomorrow. Or a Siamese Fighting Fish. Today, I choose to be your black goldfish. Does this make this interview any easier for you?*

"Interview?"

I was thinking of bringing you back. New and improved. I write a comic book, you know. The Riverton Gang. How would you like to be…five feet six inches?

"You are Riverton's Dreamer."

Oh dear, no. It's creative recall. There was such a place; I was born there. I hated the place. Now I am old. It's my privilege to remember what I wish. Chatting with you, I chat with myself. It's all one and the same. I am you and you are me and we are all together. John Lennon floated past with a Rickenbacker 325, his guitar from the years in Germany. *I am the motherfucking walrus.*

"And you are Arnie, too."

GIGO swam closer, fins slowly circling in the non-water. *Pay attention, Del. For a smart guy, you can be a pain in the ass. I am the Colonel and Cherry. And Daddy and 'Toria. And Mary. I like being Mary. Delbart, don't be an ass. Consciousness is overrated. Reality is filled with fear and doubt. But in my comics, we champion American, Christian values!* GIGO's grin flashed more teeth than a shark's.

"Riverton is insipid and stupid. It's Hell."

What is your point, Dellingham? I said American and Christian. Eleven-year-olds adore it. America adores me. I adore it.

"You're a predatory, incestuous pederast."

What could be more American? I am partial to redheads, and Arnie was supposed to be my hero, I admit, a projection of my personality, my doppelganger, but he was turning into an embarrassment. How could I let Cherry be with him? No sirree-bob-a-roonie!

"Madge was right."

But I am also Madge. Try listening to me, you fucking little egghead. And I am you. You are wasting my time, not that there is time here, but you've already been forgotten and all that is at issue is whether I want to remember you again. Dellingham, I can re-imagine whatever I need to, and frankly you are too good a creation to just forget. I'd be reluctant. A genius who is so short he cannot reach the pedals of his car?! Giant mind, tiny body. The possibilities are endless. The only reason I gave you a dick is so you'd be miserable all the time—like I used to be. It just breaks me up. Why should I make you up all over again? I screwed up, I admit.

Causality in Riverton had gotten away from me. I can't be expected to keep track of every little thing. Mickey Black goes to Haverhill, Madge is staring at computers, I look the other way, and the next thing I know, Riverton is spinning out of control. I am not God. It's my dream, but my sense of certainty is vanishing. What kind of shitty dream has doubt? I ask you.

"So there is a God?"

How in fuck would I know? I made up Riverton to get even. I was so average. Smart enough, but not that smart. Handsome enough, but not terribly so. Talented, but not so any-one might notice. Athletic, but never the star. Average. Completely unremarkable. Mind you, that did not prevent the usual do-gooders from telling me I was special. Like a jerk I believed them. But by the time I was sixteen, I knew they were full of shit. They'd say, "A determined boy can do whatever he sets his mind to." Is that a bag of shit, or what? I'd try; I'd fail. I stopped trying. But with a little creative recall, I summoned up Riverton. Not the original Riverton. My Riverton. Anyone can do it. In my Riverton, I come up winners. Lovely, lovely Riverton, where redheads always triumph.

"There was a Del Dellingham?"

GIGO circled around him. Del never lost sight. He must have had eyes in back of his head, but they were not eyes.

His name was not Dellingham; he was not as smart as you. No one could be. He was an arrogant asshole of a genius who always was the teachers' pet. I hated the little prick. I made you up to solve problems—you never fail, you know—but I also needed you to look stupid. Tell me, Dellingham, do you like being puny? Tell you what. Agree to come back on my terms; your dick will be three inches longer. I might even let you get laid.

"You are a sadistic psychotic."

GIGO smiled. Don't ask how a black goldfish can smile. Just roll with it. *Name-calling isn't going to get you anywhere. But, yes, that is part of the diagnosis where they keep me. You left out anal retentive. I also have a touch of OCD. Makes me nervous to miss a detail, and here is my Riverton spinning out of control. My creation. You cannot imagine what that feels like. What's the old expression: Neurotics build sandcastles in the air but psychotics live in them? Here we are Del. Welcome to my sandcastle. How does it feel? My original Riverton was long, long ago. I can't remember every detail, but I will always remember how impotent and humiliated I felt. It lingers like vomit on the rear of your tongue. I am old now. I grow old. I wear my trousers rolled. But I don't have to remember the way we were; I can remember the way it should have been.*

Barbra Streisand hurried by, arm in arm with T.S. Eliot. The poet had his hand up her dress. They waved to GIGO.

"That's ridiculous."

Screw you. It's my dream, genius-boy. But there you were, ready to rip the lid off. I had no choice, Del. I had to forget you. You were closing in. So I made sure everyone forgot you. Does that trouble you? It's only what you deserve. I'd forget Madge, too, but I cannot find her. She seems to have run off. Besides, I just adore that girl. Twice the balls of any boy in town, and tits to die for. Look, Riverton is no dream; it is my art. I am the Michelangelo of creative recall. Tell me, what was Madge like in Haverhill? Did you get her in the sack?

"You don't know?"

I wish I did. Haverhill is out of range. You went to Haverhill.

"Then you are no Master Dreamer."

Get over that, Del. Do you know anyone who controls every detail in their dreams? I think she was doing Mickey. No one you know dreams. Dreams don't dream. Take my word for it, dreaming a universe is not light work, and hardly in my complete control. I had to forget you. You were more becoming a nightmare. What if Riverton found out about me and Cherry?

"Pervert."

Oh no no no no no no. Cherry is real and I have never touched her. She goes back and forth between my worlds. I can't allow the poor girl to know I am going broke and I am dying. What would the poor girl do? You have no idea what it is to be a father. In the not-Riverton where I dream from, I just like to remember when I was young. It's no capital crime. It's hardly a sin. You were supposed to make it possible that my darling Cherry would never know. All I asked for was a simple clone and an implanted memory. What was so fucking HARD?

GIGO swelled to the size of a killer whale, then immediately shrank.

But you had to have this stick up your ass. Save me from petty bourgeois values. Arnie was supposed to be the hero, but he became a total idiot. He spent all his time jerking off when he could have gone out and gotten laid. And my Cherry was falling for this masturbating monkey. I'd lost control of Arnie, the champion dorkwad of Riverton who was me! Imagine— I was jealous of a projection of myself. Talk about psychosis. Talk about weak self-image. Maybe I'd have gotten over it in time, re-imagined everything just right, but Madge and you just could not leave well enough alone. Off to Haverhill. Bughouse disappeared. What in fuck happened to that boy? Mary, too. And the very first time I ask you for a tiny favor, the littlest thing, what do I get for my troubles? All I needed was a time machine or a cloning job with a memory implant. I can imagine it, so why can't you do it? Instead, you go all judgmental and in my own patio drinking my lemonade you look at me like something you found under a rock. It's just not right, Dellingham, It's not right. I am fond of my daughter, and you make it sordid.

"She knows you are going broke."

Really? Well fuck me. If a goldfish can be said to look pissed off, GIGO looked pissed off.

"Who dreamed you?"

Oh, come on! I imagined you smarter than that, Dellingham. We are not going to get caught up in infinite regressions. There is some jerk typing this who thinks I am his creature, I suppose, but he knows he has far less control than people think he does. Some entity created him, of course. It goes back to the Cause that has no Cause. That's Saint Anselm. You can look it up. The schoolyard wiseacre's proof of God.

"God. You are God."

Aaaach. Horse manure. What do I have to do to get through to you? Why do I bother? GIGO gave a flip to her tail. *You were imagined smarter than that. There must have been a Cause that had no Cause, but that does not suggest that such a cause is still with us, nor does that suggest that the Cause without Cause controlled all that followed. Saint Anselm was a simpleminded monk with an argument middle school kids can grasp.*

"What's it all for?"

Ask the Typist. He doesn't talk to me, much. Fame? Revenge? Fortune? I don't believe the Typist even likes me. I may be a goddam plot device and Mary or Grimley is the protagonist. You may as well ask the Typist why he types. Ask the owl why he hoots. See if that gets you anywhere, Mr. Genius-Boy. Those questions only make people nervous and morose. There aren't any answers. Poor, poor Madge, she's not even asking the right questions.

"You're crazy."

Well, there's news! I am told 'paranoid schizophrenic with sadistic and narcissistic tendencies that manifest in violent incest fantasies.' I am not in a rubber room quite yet. No one can take Riverton from me. They don't know about Riverton, and sure as shit I am not telling them. I just take my meds—some of them. I close my eyes and I am in Riverton where everything goes my way. There were my three girls—one blonde, one brunette, one redhead. That was it, except for male losers, Siamese fighting fish with no tails. It was rigged. Sure, Arnie always won. He has red hair. He has to win.

Frank Sinatra entered the non-space. I did it myyyyyy waaaaaaaay. Frank bowed to a crescendo of applause, and then vanished.

But then with your cellphones and your Internet and whatnot, I could not keep up. Who in fuck can? It's all getting faster and faster. I am in a leaky rowboat with nothing but a spoon to bail out the tidal wave. The future is flowing over the gunwales. I cannot get some whale to float me to safety—so I retreat to my Riverton. GIGO did a complete back flip, one that Baron von Richthofen would have recognized as an Immalmann Turn. *Come on, Del, amuse me. I bore easily. We can keep this going for eternity if you tell me. Did you ever fuck Madge? I want details. Will you arrange it so I can do Cherry? Just in my Riverton, I swear. I don't want to get too distasteful.*

"You're disgusting."

I hope you did her. Someone needs to get a firm grip on those knockers. Big Juice certainly wouldn't. I would never have imagined the Juice that way. The poor boy has the imagination of a brick, but, oh, how he runs off tackle! Madge would be the best ride since the mechanical bull came to the rodeo. GIGO floated low and then abruptly rose to be square in the center of what passed for Del's vision. *Geez, do you think Mickey did her? In those moments I don't control, I mean. Or in Haverhill? Come on. You can tell me. Did you do her?*

"Why Cherry? Why not Madge?"

Or Mary? Now there is a dream worth having. Have you ever been close to Mary? She smells like clean laundry after a day in the sun. And the brunette—I'd do her just to get even with her old man Cabot. Have pity, Dellingham. I'm just a twisted old man. I admit that. I have unhealthy obsessions. But creative recall is my art. Or the Typist's.

"I am not helping you."

When GIGO sighed, small bubble of air escaped her lips, though they were not under-water.

There was a town. I was there. I was ordinary. But in Riverton, either I win or it stops. When I die, it stops. I will be taking my ball and going home. My own imagination bores me. The place is tedious. Fuck you, Dellingham, you self-righteousness prude. Fuck you up the ass where you breathe. You are not my conscience; you are not my judge. What the fuck was I thinking when I made you up? I should have made you a dwarf. Not one of the charming little people, but an alcoholic little man with no talent. You are my goddam entertainment, but you have the nerve to be no longer amusing.

GIGO blinked.

And Del was gone.

By March, Danny talked about little except the Red Sox opener against Kansas City, or maybe it was Anaheim. Who could keep such insignificant bullshit straight? The Sox were playing in Florida; Madge understood that much, and shortly they'd return to Fenway Park in Boston. Danny would attend.

Danny talked baseball with words like *we* and *us*. What was that about? They played, he watched, and it was not as though the players were local New England boys mustered for the purpose of civic spirit. Even in Riverton they were smarter than that. The players that were not Dominicans were Japs, and, worse, the team's personnel varied year to year. Only the uniforms stayed the same. *We* were annually a different bunch of mercenaries with bats and balls who played a boy's game for the highest bidder. Why did any team command loyalty?

Like any Riverton girl who might awaken to find herself decorating the background in a cheerleader's outfit, Madge knew the rules of baseball, but the elaborate lore in which Danny immersed himself was freakishly alien. Who was Johnny Pesky and why did his pole matter? Ted Williams? No, such devotion could only be ancestral worship. As with sex, if Madge made the right noises at the right times, Danny thought she was an enthralled participant.

"It's really about them Yanks," Danny might say. "Winning is glorious, nothing finer, but I'd accept a losing season if it included beating the Yanks every time out. By God, I would. That's the real show. The rest is entertainment for your suburban types who drive in from Newton to drop a couple of yards on parking and dinner."

Madge said, "You bet." She broke off a piece of cheese danish, her pastry of choice. In Riverton, danish came in cellophane packages and tasted like glazed sponge rubber; in Haverhill, genuine bakeries made the buttery cakes. Madge put on weight.

Danish might come to her at any time, most often in the small hours. Working late, Danny took no chances on waking Baby Charity at home. The tiny house he'd equipped for Madge suited her all up and down. When Danny spent the night, in the morning over his orange juice, wheat toast, and the three scrambled eggs he prepared with a whisk and four drops of Tabasco, he sat at the table and rattled a copy of the Herald. He'd mutter about the signs and evil portents being cast by the team's play in the Grapefruit League, whatever that was. One day it seemed signs augured well for a winning year; other days the news was grim. Tendonitis stalked professional pitchers like the Red Death cut down the population of medieval Florence.

The only Florence Danny knew was a manicurist who owed Aunt Sosha three hundred dollars she'd borrowed to keep her husband from killing her when she lost that sum on a sure thing football game that turned out to be not so sure. She paid twenty dollars each week, and had been doing so for six months, meaning that on a three hundred dollar loan she had so far paid four hundred and eighty dollars and so far had not put a dent in the initial principal. Ah, those Yids and their interest! It was a thing of beauty, and the two weeks Flo had not had her twenty for Danny he'd kindly allowed her to take it out in trade, though not a manicure.

Danny had simple needs. To Madge's surprise, considering he'd once tried to tear her tits off while threatening to bugger her on the front porch of Aunt Sosha's house, Danny Donnelly was astonishingly gentle. His big hands could deliver a caress over the curve of her bare hip tender as a tongue tip probing her ear, and while Madge would never come to feel great devotion for the freckled Irishman, her terror and hatred bled away. She'd fake a shiver here and there to encourage him. Danny equated her tolerance with affection and enthusiasm; being with a stupid man had its advantages.

He kept her in a single story house at the base of a hill close by the river on the Bradford side of the Merrimack. Identical houses stood to the left and right. It was snug. The Three Little Pigs would have felt safe at home, the more so because the fireplace had been bricked solid. Lacking a state driver's license, Madge mostly left the Subaru standing in the driveway on the left. Beyond Riverton, her driving habits would not do. There were not a lot of places she wished to go. Why invite trouble for a minor inconvenience? She'd surely need the car someday, and when the time came no mere law was going to keep her from making her get-away. Madge was not averse to risk, but she knew the difference between judicious chances and stupidity. A disaster at the wheel would not have to be her fault; some asshole might crash into her while she sat quietly buffing her nails at a traffic light, and then where would she be? Never mind life and limb, she could get shipped back to Riverton.

Madge had driven as if she was invulnerable, but once she saw and smelled Arnie Appleton burning, fear of mortality settled on her like a beaded cloak. If Madge needed to trot down to the local market for a quart of milk, her two good strong legs would do. Besides, she craved the exercise, and now that the snow fell less frequently, the touch of sun on her face did much to confirm that she was alive and in the world.

The house was white with black shutters on each of the six windows. Someone owed Aunt Sosha money; since Danny collected for his good Aunt, in this case he accepted rent in lieu of dollars. Madge knew this arrangement could not be on the up and up, but she wisely kept her mouth shut, wondering how willing to deceive Aunt Sosha Danny might be. Perhaps the amounts involved were trivial. For now, fucking with any arrangement that kept food in her belly, clothes on her back, and cigarette money in her purse seemed the depths of stupidity.

It did not, however, relieve her of the certain knowledge that she required an income of her own.

The four-room house had uneven honey-colored hardwood floors that needed repair, a chilly dirt-floor cellar, and had come with some beat, worn furniture that suited Madge perfectly. She'd curl up beneath a crocheted comforter and read as light streamed in a window over her right shoulder. There was a bed, a kitchen table, two chairs—what else did anyone need? Madge drew the shades both day and night. Danny, for his part, wanted nothing more than a place that offered peace and pussy, neither of which were available to him at home, both of which were in abundance in the little bungalow.

Wooden bookshelves had been built into the thick plaster walls of the living room. Madge stacked the shelves with the books she carted back from her weekly trip to the mall bookstore, a drive she deemed worth any risk. The shelves also held knickknacks, small gifts from Danny. It pleased him when she put them out for display, though no one ever saw them except Ryan, their only visitor. Danny was fond of ceramic unicorns and snow globes, and Madge pretended that she adored the little dust collectors, though the only one that held her interest was a snow globe of New York City, not because of any fascination with the Statue of Liberty, but because of the painted backdrop depicting the World Trade Center, two buildings immolated by mad men long, long ago.

Madge resolved to go to New York. In New York City, everyone was a cannibal.

Each day brought new lessons.

Lesson number one: men are easy. She did not require vast experience to know it was so. What they did and how they did it had far less to do with their feelings for her, but everything to do with how they felt about themselves. The girl who hoped for more was a fool; the girl who did not use the fact was a bigger fool. Smile and grunt at the right times, spread your legs as little as possible, and you owned them. It was an old story. Sweep out the cave, spread your legs on demand, and with luck you'd nail a hunter who scored protein.

Lesson number two: men never were aware of the pathetic patterns they followed in their lives. Danny Donnelly wanted to believe he was an invulnerable desperado, so favored by God he could take any risk at any level of peril and never fail. Danny noted her growing stacks of books, fanned the pages of one or two, but had no interest in reading any of them for fear of learning something new. They seldom went anywhere together except a movie. Danny's taste in films was limited to fantasy epics, superheroes, or disasters in which buildings exploded as the heroes wisecracked under a shower of debris. She pretended to enjoy these movies. On nights when Danny had the forethought to plan to be with her until morning, they'd leave the theater and stop first for a pint of Haagen-Dazs Vanilla. She wanted the ice cream for after sex. It killed the taste of semen.

He kept Madge sequestered, but his sexual adventures became redundant. Hours after Danny might leave her, an unbidden wave of pleasure could ripple through her flesh like the aftershock of a temblor a continent away. She did not give a crap about Danny, so what was that about? Sex with Danny was different in ways she did not care to understand. Men needed to imagine they risked everything, but all they ever did was endlessly recreate the life they already had. Pussy reinforced an illusion of immortality and change.

Patterns kept him happy. There might be differences between Madge and Danny's wife: Margaret Mary might prefer chocolate ice cream.

No wonder Danny was awestruck at what he thought had been the gift of her virginity. *Honored* was the word the asshole had used. Imagine that. *Honored!*

Way back last December Danny had gone wide-eyed when he concluded he had taken her virginity, taking her with an initial thrust of such power that when she'd felt herself tear, there was no question that time it was permanent.

"If I'd known, Madge…" he'd said breathless, lying exhausted on her hip. "If I had known."

Her fingers curled a lock of his damp hair at the back of his neck and she let herself lightly kiss his hairy chest. He'd already moved her into the tiny house with the hissing steam radiator in the bedroom. The windows were etched by a patina of ice, the light through the frost diffuse, and beneath a white goose-down comforter they had been a tangle of hot, sweaty, eager limbs. As Danny drifted in and out of sexual torpor, Madge acknowledged that in Haverhill a girl could become pregnant.

Lesson number three: caution. Risk carried genuine consequences. She was no longer in Riverton.

The pimple-faced clerk who sold her condoms hardly glanced at Madge before returning his attention to the Sporting News. Teenage girls in Haverhill must have bought Trojans by the crate; the same clerk denied her cigarettes until Madge gave him an extra dollar that disappeared into his shirt pocket. The town's relative values were plain.

Madge stowed the condoms in the nightstand. Danny did not question her when next she offered him one. She liked him for that. His wife evidently seemed not to know their use, and Danny said he was glad Madge took what he called *precautions*.

That same week, she'd been reading *Pere Goriot* when she had absent-mindedly chewed too hard on a cuticle. She licked clean the bead of blood that welled on her nail, and she thought nothing of it until days later her finger swelled and became inflamed, painful to touch.

The notion that she could be damaged was unsettling.

One night, she'd taken the time to shave her legs and crotch. Her being hairless seemed to excite Danny, though why a man would want a woman with the appearance of a baby when he could have her looking like a woman puzzled her. Drawing the pink razor up her calf, she was reminded of the exquisite pain she'd regularly inflicted on her belly, thighs or arms with an Exacto knife, the blistering hot shower in her parents' home, how she had swooned against the cooler blue tile wall while blood in streamers flowed down her leg, over her foot to swirl down the drain.

The unbidden memory seemed someone else's dream of someone else's blood and someone else's pain.

Madge stood naked in front of the fogged bathroom mirror. She raised her arms over her head. The whiter, softer flesh was unmarred, but she'd never again need an Exacto to feel real. Time would make her feel real enough. She peered at her breasts, her dark, quarter-size nipples, her chest high and firm, and then she turned to look over her shoulder at the tight sheath of her olive skin over her hips, thighs, and ass. She would never look better than she did this day. Gravity would do its work. Gravity never rested. Every part of her would sag; perhaps she'd grow fat. If she lived long enough, she'd wither.

Madness behind her, Madge's mortal life was at last her own. She had escaped Riverton, but her body no longer had a Reset button.

Though Aunt Sosha surely had insights to share, Madge would never know them. Danny was firm on this point; no one could know Madge was in Haverhill. "My good Aunt does not care if I sleep with Patty's pig, but she'll have definite, strong feelings about my accepting your rent in lieu of cash. Jews and their money are a fearsome thing, Madge. She cannot know. She cannot. God keep me from so black a day," and he kissed his thumbnail before crossing himself three times.

He was sure the risks he took for Madge demonstrated his devotion; Madge saw the possibility of her eventual escape.

She missed having an Internet connection, but Danny said, "They can trace the Internet, my darling Madge. No. No. We can't allow that," he said and patted her head. It was the same gesture Mickey had used with her. What the fuck was it with men? Did they confuse women with poodles?

So Madge discovered the Haverhill Library and its banks of Internet connected computers. Halfway up a hill after a short walk across the bridge that spanned the Merrimack in the heart of town, the library's clock tower stood across the road from the statue of Hannah Duston, the pioneer woman's axe aloft. Madge read the statue's plaque and took some time in the library to read Duston's official history. She noted the woman's courage, but found the story of her sister, Elizabeth Emerson, far more engrossing.

The hushed forests of North America encased colonial women in brooding isolation. These were not the Pilgrims of the annual Riverton High pageant gorging themselves on turkey and sweet potato pie with crusty marshmallows.

In 1691, after keeping a pregnancy hidden, Elizabeth Emerson birthed illegitimate twin girls. Within hours, she sewed the two infants into a cotton sack that she then buried in a shallow grave. Madge imagined Bess by moonlight, kneeling on brown dirt, frantically scraping the rocky soil with her broken fingernails. Shortly after that horror, the corpses were uncovered by a feral hog. One of the babies had its umbilical cord wrapped around its neck.

Mother Duston's Good Sister Bess was tried by the Puritans of Haverhill for murder and fornication. She claimed the infants were stillborn, a fact that seemed more than plausible to Madge. Who could hide a full-term pregnancy of twins? Bess likely went into labor prematurely, and in those days, a premature birth was an infant's death sentence. But no matter; fucking was the more serious charge, the dead children, dead or alive, merely evidence that Elizabeth had engaged in sin. Worse, she seemed to enjoy fucking, having given birth to a first bastard daughter, Dorothy, five years earlier.

Sin and private debauchery? The Shadow would have found Elizabeth Emerson a hard case.

Quite a life Bad Bess knew. When she was eleven, her father had kicked the living shit out of her, so severely that in an age where children were ordinarily disciplined with strap and hand, when no child was ever spared the rod, Father Emerson was nevertheless called to account. Had Dad had been irked by a daughter who refused to put out for kin? Had he been carried away while violently doing his daughter?

Bess gave birth to her first bastard when she was twenty-three, refused to reveal the father's identity, probably a rich man, and she delivered herself of the stillborn twins when she was twenty-eight. Madge imagined the desperate Elizabeth, already stigmatized with one kid, doing all she was able to do to avoid being discovered for her sin, not to mention never revealing the identities of her children's fathers. How many sexual partners could Beth have had? One? Two? Ten? Maybe she was the village slut.

Whatever Bad Bess did, it came out wrong. Madge knew what that was like.

Elizabeth Emerson's life ended after two years of jailhouse ministry delivered by some dildo named Cotton Mather. She was hanged by the neck in a public ceremony in Boston. Prior to her execution, she attended a sermon by this Mather who'd preached that those who are unclean would die in youth. Already condemned, Elizabeth sat shackled in the front pew, a visual aid for the congregation on the wages of sin. After two years of Mather's personal ministry, Elizabeth probably raced the hangman up the gallows steps.

Haverhill's brooding past fascinated Madge. Never mind heroic, homicidal Hannah; if Madge had no ancestors, she was free to choose her own.

She saw her forebears in Elizabeth.

In February, she cozied up to a library desk to read Kafka when a burly black woman in what looked like a gray uniform settled back in a wooden chair across a table from her. Madge nodded hello, which the woman seemed to think was an invitation to chat.

"Book report?"

Madge said no, she was just reading.

"Any good?"

The hallucinatory world of Franz Kafka spoke to Madge like no other. Cause and effect—who could say for sure? Guilt and punishment—unconnected. Madge was cranking her way through the collected works. She'd read the story of Gregor Samsa, a bank teller who'd awakened from uneasy sleep to discover he was an enormous bug. She read the story twice. Suppose Gregor had been a butterfly dreaming it was a man? Suppose being a bank teller and an insect were the same thing? What good was awakening if all we did was move among nightmares? Hadn't that been Riverton?

In *The Trial*, K was on trial for his life. He'd committed no crime. No one was able to tell him the charges. His distilled desperation had no origin.

Kafka, K, and Klink. Madge saw connections. Prague could be Riverton without the flower beds.

"The book is pretty good," she answered the black woman.

But the woman across the library's maple table had no interest in Kafka. She said, "Shouldn't you be in school at this hour?" It was 10:30. "The librarians called me. They say you are here a lot in the mornings. Shouldn't you be in school?" The woman unsnapped her purse and withdrew a fat, black wallet. The wallet's plastic window held a card with her photo. The card read *Lakisha Johnson, Assistant Supervisor of Attendance. Haverhill Public Schools.*

Madge put her book face down. "I'm not from around here," she said. Madge saw in the woman's eyes that this was the wrong answer.

"Where are you from, dear? Missing school is a serious matter."

"Dusseldorf. I am visiting my family. I am from Dusseldorf."

"I don't know any Dusseldorf. Where is that?"

"Florida," Madge tried.

"Is that right? And how old are you, sweetheart?"

Madge was clueless as to how old she was, but this was no time to think about the yawning gaps in her psyche. Sixteen seemed about right, so she said, "I am twenty," and immediately disbelief flooded the woman's brown eyes.

No good could come of this, Madge was sure. She hung her head like some goon-ass kid who had been found out and felt guilty about being bad, but as she shrugged into her team jacket she saw her best chance.

Madge bolted from the library like her hair was on fire.

The truant officer shouted, "Hey!" but she was too large to follow Madge with any hope of catching her. Madge toppled three chairs behind her as she sprinted to the automatic double glass doors. In the street, she went at a dead run through the macadam parking lot, vaulted over a low fence, and never paused to look back. Madge ran three blocks until, breathless, she stopped to lean her back against a street lamp while her heart calmed.

She lighted a cigarette. No lard-ass truant officer or police car followed her. How could a kid reading Kafka pose a threat to the cause of public education?

She looked up. She had found safety on Emerson Street. The ghost of Bad Bess Emerson protected her.

Days later, Madge screwed up her courage and returned to the library, but after two o'clock. The Hillie kids were dismissed by then, and the few that congregated in the library's computer section offered Madge camouflage. Cripes, they looked dorky in their big puffy jackets. The mascara on the girls' eyes had them looking like horny raccoons with matted, filthy hair. All they did was exchange meaningful glances, look exasperated and impatient at a world that had yet to discover their exceptional talents, and then burst into gales of mean laughter over nothing. The boys sat stolid and mute, planning on going home to masturbate themselves comatose, nursing cases of terminal acne, their pants with crotches so loose they hung to their knees.

Madge made no friends. The odds of finding someone in that insipid crowd who read Kafka were slim and none, but even if she found someone, what could she say? *Yes, I have no past, but there's a guy who keeps me in a place so we can fuck. Well, he fucks me and I do my best to fuck him back. Do you want to come over? We'll do our nails.*

Come to think of it, teenage life in Haverhill was the same as teenage life in Riverton.

Madge accepted the cell phone Danny gave her. Danny texted her at odd times: *How's my Madge?* She'd respond *I m OK. U?* Never mind that he was married to Margaret Mary and was fucking Madge, he was haunted by a specter of Madge's inconstancy. He checked on her whereabouts.

But the phone depressed her. Danny was the phone's sole contact, Memory #1. There was no one else to call. She was alone and no one cared.

Had she been dosed with heroin, chained to the basement pipes, and rented out to a cult of sex-crazed flagellants, as long as she did not have rich parents looking for her, it would have made no difference. She could smoke crack and for five dollars blow derelicts under the train trestle, but as long as she kept underneath any official radar, no one gave a crap.

The realization was liberating. It put her choices in relief.

She could choose to be a victim, or she could maneuver among people unseen, a ghost in a world of opportunities.

By spring, with the Red Sox opener just days away, Madge was groping her way to her next step.

Danny Donnelly laid splayed nude on Madge's narrow bed, her bone white comforter crumpled beneath him. His thick fingers unlaced from behind his neck long enough to scratch his balls where the juices of sex had caked. The bed springs softly squeaked where minutes ago the headboard had hit the wall like a jackhammer.

Danny contemplated his luck.

The sound of Madge's shower bath filled the cheery bedroom; a short-lived cloud of steam billowed across the textured white ceiling. The girl knew nothing about shame or propriety, God bless her ever-eager heart; she kept the bathroom door open, and beyond the translucent, colorless shower curtain that circled the old-fashioned, four-legged tub, Danny watched her indefinite shape bend and stretch. An hour ago, his virgin teenage lover had surprised him with red cloth wrist ties. She'd fastened him to the maple headboard and then with tongue, teeth, and fingernails had her way with him until the wood rattled so hard against the wall that the mice must have left town. Mother of God, they grew them strange in Riverton.

The bedroom walls were painted a flat pale blue, the trim egg-shell white, the floor nothing better than stained laminate crap that looked expensive but was not. The floor needed polishing, no question; the surface was scuffed raw by years of use and ill care. Negligence was the common habit of most, Danny reflected, and was surely the habit of those who'd lived here before. Those that paid attention to detail, as he did, thrived. He'd have to attend to the polishing—but not just yet.

The empty bungalow had come his way as a temporary accommodation from one John Scapelli, the proud founder of Scapelli's Realty. Scapelli found himself embarrassed by bad times and a run of ill fortune brought on by persistent misplaced faith in Catholic college football teams. God might favor Boston College and Notre Dame, and they often played as if the Christ Himself was in the backfield, but in Heaven there were no point spreads. While God's teams won more than they lost, Scapelli's wagers doubled and then doubled again in a vain effort to recoup what had been lost for lack of defensive play. The bookmaker, one Goldberg, had sold his notes to Aunt Sosha for twenty-five cents on the dollar; Aunt Sosha in turn instructed Danny to collect five points each week at double the original debt. Faced with serious problems, Scapelli converted the bungalow, a non-performing asset, to the equivalent of legal tender, an arrangement Ryan had suggested to Danny as a compromise. "Think of it as a happy coincidence of interests," Ryan had said. Danny concurred with Ryan that what Aunt Sosha did not know could not hurt them. Danny brought her money, and she trusted him when he said that was all that could be managed that week.

Madge would emerge from her ablutions in minutes, skin aglow from hot water and the vigorous ministrations of her loofa glove; she'd smell of rose soap. Margaret Mary, his beloved wife, most often smelled of A & D Ointment, an aroma that did little to arouse Danny. Danny just might want to have at Madge yet again before he departed for the comforts of home. Wouldn't that be lovely? The girl from Riverton could inspire Danny to pinnacles of stamina he'd thought were lost at nineteen. With the spirit, imagination, and will of a woman three times her age, but with skin lacking even a single wrinkle, never mind stretch marks, even Madge's feet were smooth as a baby's bottom. Your loofa gloves could work wonders.

Lazy as a lion after feed, Danny stretched again. The knowledge that he might just as easily choose to kiss Madge's forehead and be on his way was the very pith of his luck. Madge made no demands on him, and so their little arrangement in Scapelli's riverside bungalow might last far longer than Danny had first believed was possible.

Moscowitz could wait. That would be a sad end for Madge, who surely deserved better, but it was an end that was for the girls like her inevitable, and Danny Donnelly was not one to try to change the ways of the world.

It need not be all that bad. Madge might enjoy a few good years with Moscowitz, the best in the industry sometimes did, but the life took its toll on the girls. No matter how fresh, they began to appear used up, and despite the periodic cable television documentary that showed a happy and prosperous bit of trailer trash who'd made a career swallowing cum, the fact remained that most came to bad ends. The money was in youth, so *star quality* meant little more than a moment in the sun. Eventually, Moscowitz would accept an offer for one of his made-to-order snuff films with limited circulation among a very wealthy clientele, and that would be the end of that. Ryan postulated the type that most often wanted to view the extended suffering and end of a young girl were the kind that wore turbans and had their wealth flowing from the ground as oil, but Danny had no first-hand knowledge of such things. While he liked Ryan right enough, Ryan had his eccentricities; the man put on airs and claimed expertise in realms where he in fact knew nothing.

Poor Moscowitz had put up good money for Bughouse, but the Jew had howled worse than Death deprived of souls when the lad vanished. He faulted Aunt Sosha and claimed she'd delivered damaged goods. But Danny's good aunt shrugged and did not return a dime of her finder's fee. *Meshuggah,* the old woman said over a *shabbos* dinner, *People don't disappear from an airplane in the middle of the air. Kish mir in tuchis.*

In their bungalow, Madge wanted white, and white was what she had. Asked to keep his eyes peeled, Ryan the barber did better than that: he put out the word. Some of the up-and-coming future smash-and-grabber boys from the streets of Haverhill, Lawrence, and Lowell must have thought he'd gone mad. Ordinarily, to have high cash value, goods liberated from citizens had to be small. You could put ten iPhones in your pocket and run like the wind, making delivery on a bicycle, if needs be, but carrying off your General Electric refrigerator without notice took a bit more doing.

Ryan, who specialized in alcohol, power tools, and electronics, indicated he was in the market for housewares, your Mix-Masters with matching bowls or plush cotton towels made of bamboo fabric. This was kid-stuff to obtain, to be sure, but didn't kids need to make a living, too? Ryan deemed what he did a public service, a gesture to encourage youth and advance their educations. Against retail value, Ryan offered only pennies, but his cash was green, pennies had a way of becoming nickels, nickels matured into dimes, and dimes birthed dollars. A boy lacking the skills and courage to hotwire a car or could never hope to work freight at Logan Airport saw his first chances in shoplifting.

As Ryan's money moved into the youth economy of Haverhill, social life soared along with marijuana consumption, movie attendance, and the sales of burgers and shakes at McDonald's. Ryan did not ask Danny for compensation. "Gifts," he said, taking comfort by imagining elaborate scenarios populated by fourteen-year-old girls who out of a sense of obligation and gratitude popped free the rubber-bands on their braces before bending to polish their boyfriend's knob. Indeed, Ryan's private collection of videos made by boys with hidden cameras swelled, those same boys being the ones who'd practiced five-finger discounts at Ryan's request; Ryan paid top dollar for cups, saucers, towels, sheets, but he paid much more for grainy cellphone videos of your Betty-Lou, Sally or Deanna doing the deed.

In the end, it was all commerce, capitalism at its finest. Long ago, Grandfather Timothy had filled Danny's head with tales of the Kennedy fortune built on the backs of rum-runners from Canada. "And didn't that put the old man in the Court of ™ James?" he said. "When demand meets supply, everyone is happy." Grandfather Tim was a sage. The requested goods flowed up the very pipeline that had carried the word downward.

Madge emerged from the tub and out from behind the shower curtain. She bent forward to wrap her hair in a large white towel. The shower still ran while she sat bare-ass on the toilet top. She smoothed Barbasol the length of her legs.

"What are you looking at, big guy?" Madge said, smiled, and half-closed the bathroom door, not so much to maintain her privacy but to use the full-length mirror fixed to the back of the door.

Danny shifted slightly to watch Madge through the half open door, a pinkish vision in mist and steam. Water droplets formed at her throat and trickled through the deep valley between her breasts and clung trembling to her nipples. Madge drew her razor up under her calf. Might she be shaving her pussy that day?

Margaret Mary, God bless her, had the crotch of a gorilla. No decent woman did such a thing as shave herself to look like a newborn, the wife was sure. Margaret Mary attended mass at Sacred Hearts Church each Sunday, and she attended confession every Wednesday. What the woman might be confessing was between her and God, but if it was not avarice, it could surely not be lust.

Danny was being worked to death by his wife, and yet there on the other side of the bathroom door was a woman—girl with lips like cashmere, limbs that bent at any angle, breasts that could have been national monuments, an ass that was perfect, an imagination to shame Jezebel, and who made no demands beyond food, clothing, and shelter—and none of that too fancy.

Danny knew that the right, responsible, smart thing to do would be to turn away, deposit the final dollar obtainable from Moscowitz into the girls' college funds, devote himself to raising Faith, Hope and Charity, and pray that Margaret Mary might come back to considering sex a part of her wifely duties beyond the three cursed days circled in green crayon on her magnetized refrigerator calendar.

Danny rolled to his hip and pulled the comforter around his shoulders.

He drifted into sleep like an unmoored skiff adrift on a fog-bound lake, but he abruptly awakened when Madge sat at the bed's edge. Her hip against his leg was still warm from the shower. The room was suffused with the aromas of her bath, soap, hot water, and the scent of rose. Her hand idly plucked at the fine hairs on the back of his knee. Her fingertips whorled in small circles. No green girl should have the skills of a courtesan and be able to work such magic on any man, yet here was Danny's Madge, a man's dream of what a woman could be, young, supple, willing, innocent, yet knowing.

"I was thinking," Madge said. "We should have a little more for us. A plan."

Madge had to bend close over him to retrieve an emery board from the nightstand. Her nipples brushed his bare back before she sat up again. She did what women do with her nails while she spoke.

"Okay, so I think I understand what you do," Madge said. "It is Aunt Sosha's money, not yours. I get all that. How is Aunt Sosha doing, by the way? I like her, you know."

"She'll live forever," Danny said, "Or at least until the day she dies."

"What I don't understand is why anyone would borrow from you. Or her. Whichever."

Danny sighed. Margaret Mary's sole interest in her loving husband's business was her daily admonition, *Don't fuck up*, but Danny's Madge was a different sort. Margaret Mary needed to know nothing; Madge from Riverton needed to know everything. Margaret Mary cared only that she and her babies' needs were fulfilled; Danny's Madge would turn a fact over and inside out before letting it go, and then it could never wander far before Madge seized it to examine it again.

Facedown, Danny rested his folded hands on a pillow and his forehead on his hands. He listened to the slow scrape of Madge's emery board. "They don't borrow from me," he corrected her. "I just collect Aunt Sosha's interest."

"But why? I mean, why do they borrow at all?"

Madge blew nail dust from her fingers. The bedspring squealed as she shifted her weight, drawing her legs under her, sitting Indian style.

"All sorts of reasons. There are your degenerate gamblers who are men of means. They'll gamble it all away until none is left. Then there is those for whom we do civic service. Aunt Sosha supplies cash flow to those who cannot get a loan elsewhere. To a businessman, cash is blood. You'd think they'd go to banks, but your banks have a rule: they lend only to those who do not need it. If you need no money, your bankers will trip over themselves offering it at low terms. They will come to your door, call on the phone, send you unsigned checks in the mail. But should you actually be in need of capital, then your bank tightens like the virgin's asshole—very little in or out."

"I get the gambler. But why would anyone else want a loan?"

It did his ego good to know the things Madge wanted to know. "Say a man has a store and does well; if he is ambitious, he might want to open another store."

"Maybe we could have a store, someday."

Danny envisioned a future sitting at a counter awaiting customers; he'd prefer a season in Hell as the Devil's sissy-boy. "Of course, your new store will require a cash outlay before it becomes self-sufficient. There's rent and inventory and fixtures and all manner of whatnot that needs purchasing. An ambitious merchant will go to the bank and ask for what he needs, but the first question your banker will ask is whether he will pay it back, and the proof of that is what your banker calls his 'collateral.' This means nothing less than the merchant must demonstrate he has no need of the money."

"Then why doesn't the store owner just finance himself?"

"You're the quick one, aren't you?" And there it was. Margaret Mary not only could not have cared less, but it would have taken her until newborn Charity's first communion to grasp what Madge saw in a heartbeat.

"Cash flow, Madge. Cash flow. The more dollars that are sloshing about, the easier business can be. Owning a store might make a man rich but he cannot pay the gas bill without cash."

Madge lifted her foot and took a final pass of the emery board over a toe nail. Danny's eyelids grew heavy as she kneaded the muscle in his left calf like bread dough, and then moved her hands to the right. "Why doesn't Aunt Sosha ask for collateral to be sure someone will pay?"

"No need. She has me." Danny rolled to his back and Madge's fingers ruffled the hair on his chest. Danny's dick was semi-erect. "It's five to ten points each week promptly by Friday, paid in full with no negotiation, or else there is Danny Donnelly like the wrath of God on your doorstep."

"Points?"

His big hands traced a loop on the paler flesh of her smooth thigh. She undid her towel turban and her hair fell free.

"Percentage."

"Oh, I see. In ten weeks it's all finished. Ten weeks would be one hundred percent." She reached across Danny again to place the emery board back on the nightstand and took the plastic bottle of baby oil. Then she squeezed a palm full of oil into her hands and smoothed the oil over her extended leg.

Danny laughed. "No Madge, no. That's just the beginning. Aunt Sosha wants her cash flow, too. A borrower that pays in full is silver, but a borrower who never pays in full, but pays your carrying charges regularly is gold. Say you borrow ten thousand from our good Aunt. That's not unusual. Our Aunt prefers the larger loans—fewer headaches, more money, and frankly a better class of people, those who are motivated to pay because they have more to lose. Ten K at ten points is one large each week that's owed, and no negotiation. After ten weeks, that's ten thousand earned but ten thousand still due. That new money goes out again, and so what you get is your compounding. Money earns money, to be sure. The wonder of it is a thing of beauty."

"But suppose one week they cannot pay?"

"Aunt Sosha is a reasonable woman. While a good customer pays every week, even the best laid plans can go astray. What to do, is the issue. One solution would be to add double the overdue payment into the capital loan. Miss a thousand on ten and we can see our way to making the payments for the following weeks twelve hundred, as twelve thousand is now owed. Should the client meet that mark, all is well, but should someone be chronically late, well, then measures must be taken and talk and excuses are at an end. Our Aunt leaves such determinations to me. Such deadbeats had no business borrowing in the first place."

Madge blew into her hands, warming fragrant oil before she knelt on the bed to spread the oil thickly onto his lower abdomen. She rubbed it into his skin with two hands. His eyes closed as with one hand she cupped his testicles and with the other she ringed the shaft of his erection. "It's ambition and stupidity that bring a man to grief," Danny said, expecting things to proceed apace, happy his business lesson was over.

But Madge abruptly stopped the hand job. She sat back. Danny's eyes opened. Above him knelt a girl like an erotic Hindu carving with quivering full breasts, thighs of iron, a waist he could circle with his two hands. Her arms and belly were slick. His cock was at full attention.

"If you make those determinations, you could accelerate payments, couldn't you?" she said.

"Accelerate?"

She'd seen the word on an investment site; Madge Klink not only managed a skilled hand-job, but she did her research. With Danny's balls lightly cupped in one hand, she explained her scheme.

Danny could certainly offer his people yet more money, but for fewer points. He might ask for some extra cash up front, right then and there, like refinancing a mortgage. People go for that all the time. Who wouldn't take more money and lower payments? "It's an inducement to refinance," she said, proud of the word she'd learned at the Haverhill Library.

"And where is this money coming from?" Danny asked.

Madge knew the answer to that, too. Danny could take the receipts from old clients and give it to new clients. That would keep Aunt Sosha ignorant of the whole scheme. He could deliver Aunt Sosha her regular Friday receipts, hold back the accelerated payments, but when all of Aunt Sosha's clients thought they had paid off and were free and clear with no more money to pay, by the time everyone figured out what was going on, Danny and Madge would be gone. "Maybe to Florida," Madge said.

"Don't say such things." Danny sat up thinking to give her the back of his hand, but Madge nimbly stood out of reach beside the bed.

Naked as Adam and Even in the Garden, she led him to the living room to show him where she'd pried loose the bottom shelf of one of the bookcases. It could be slid away to reveal a shelf formed by a wood beam within the plaster wall, a hiding place. She showed him the putty brown lockbox she'd bought.

"It's safer than anything. We'll put the money in here. Have something for ourselves. If not Florida, maybe California. Or Bermuda. I want to live near a beach," she said. "Near a beach with you, baby."

Danny was emphatic. "It's crazy," he said. "You can't make more money out of less."

"We'd only do it for a while. When we had enough, we'd leave. No one would know until we were gone, and by then it would be too late."

He stared at Madge in horror. "Do you recall Ari?" he asked.

"You're not afraid of him, are you?"

Danny was terrified. He said, "Of course not."

Madge pouted, and then sighed. "It was just an idea," she said and replaced the bookcase shelf. "Promise me you'll think about it."

Then she pushed him into the big Queen Anne chair and dropped a cushion on the floor before it to kneel in front of him. When she embraced him with her oiled chest, he closed his eyes and did not think about much at all.

That night, near four in the morning, Margaret Mary violently shook his shoulder to wake him from deep sleep. She informed her husband, the lazy oaf, that he could hear his own baby girl Charity was crying out for him if he was not deaf, and it was his turn to walk the floor with the infant until the colic abated, so he damn well better get his hairy Irish ass moving before Charity waked Faith and Hope, for should that happen, the day to come would be a vale of tears.

The specter of Madge's plan grew in his mind. Gorgeous, with all the sexual restraint of an otter in heat, Holy Jesus, she was smart, too. The woman knew no limits.

His first opportunity came when the Greek pizza guy asked him if Danny could accept just a few hundred little less that week, things were slow, his daughter needing the operation and all. Hearing his good wife's admonition, *Do not fuck up*, Danny nevertheless cut the Greek a hell of a deal, telling the poor bastard he could add five points to his principle, five points about which Aunt Sosha would never know but that he, Danny, might collect forever on a personal investment of zero. The dumb Greek was grateful, having expected Danny to explain the terms of his loan with a ball-peen hammer, an experience he thought was worth enduring to correct his little girls' crossed eyes. Over chicken roasted with rosemary and garlic potatoes, when Aunt Sosha pinched his cheek called him her *boychik*, instead of guilt he thought of Madge's thighs. He noted how the Jews trusted him because they believed he was just a big, dumb Mick, and he chose to be insulted by that.

More chances came his way. It was a Ponzi scheme based on theft, pure and simple. Aunt Sosha had her money on the street, but so did Danny, the sole difference being that Danny's money had never existed and had its origins with loans Aunt Sosha did not know she was making. This was no different from international banking and the carryings on that was bankrupting the world. Dumb Mick? Everyone knew Ponzi schemes were the miracle of the age, invented in Boston, a grand way to make vast sums as long as greed lived in the hearts of men. The schemes always collapsed, of course, but if those at the pyramid's pinnacle exited nimbly enough, they did quite well. As with most things, the trick was in the timing. Winners made it through the doors before the elephant stampede brought down the entire house.

Danny studied travel brochures. He was partial to islands with coral reefs and white sand beaches with palm trees, the kind where white-jacketed locals carried trays of drinks dressed with a pineapple spear and paper umbrellas.

And who was to say Madge's plan precluded an arrangement with Moscowitz at the bitter end? Wasn't Los Angeles a stopping point on the journey to Tahiti, and hadn't Grandfather Tim spoken of Santa Anita and Del Mar as if they were a sun-soaked paradise of horse racing? A trip west would be just the ticket for an enterprising Irishman needing to cut his connection to Madge Klink, the girl he'd leave holding the bag for having robbed Aunt Sosha.

With the All-Star break days away, Danny's excitement and pitch was beyond anything Madge had ever seen, higher than even the Riverton Spirit Squad the day before the annual Thanksgiving Riverton-Haverhill game. "Whoever leads at the break will take the pennant,"

Danny repeated again and again to no one in particular.

After a spring that saw the Sox playing 500 balls, they put together a streak of wins just as the Yankee pitching staff caught an epidemic case of rag arm. Relief pitchers in pinstripes either hurled baseballs at 94 miles per hour directly into the dirt five yards before the plate, or, with men on base, far over the heads of catchers. In the blink of an eye, the Sox lurked a mere single game behind the cursed New Yorkers and were coming on like sharks with the scent of blood in the water.

When Danny was not sullen, he spoke too loud; when he was not muttering to himself, he pretended to be having too grand a time. Madge was sure something more than Danny's dick was up. The signs were everywhere. Something was about to change, and it was more than the standings in the American League East.

All June, they'd made love with the usual vigor, coming to conclusions that left them spent and sweating despite the new air conditioner that hummed day and night in the bedroom window, a gift of one of Ryan's gang of middle school heist men. But as the days grew longer, her lover came to her with less frequency, and when he was with her, her arms encircling his chest, her legs his hips, Madge felt the sea change deep within him. It was palpable. He was either losing interest in her or having second thoughts about whether they could safely be off with the stash of money in the bookcase. In either case, the results amounted to the same thing.

It was time. She had to make her move before he did.

The day before the All-Star game, Madge slid the loose shelf from the white wall bookcase. It slid easily, having been worked back and forth near daily for three months. How long had she been in Haverhill? Half a year? She had no regrets; not once had the Shadow visited to wrest her mind from her. Perhaps she was well. Her madness might be gone.

The cold cuts, potato salad and beer were already stocked in the refrigerator, but when Ryan and Danny came to watch the All-Star Game on the big 50 inch TV, they would have to serve themselves.

Madge lifted the putty-colored lockbox from its hiding place and sat like a Red Indian at the center of the circular cotton braided rug. She counted twice. Forty-one thousand, six hundred and fifty dollars accumulated for four months from Haverhill, Lawrence, and as far off as Lowell. She thought for a very brief moment that she should wait for the round figure of fifty thousand, but she knew such an impulse transformed winners into losers.

Suckers played beyond a hot streak. Madge was a winner.

It was past time.

She made neat stacks of bills, curled the stacks to tight rolls, and snapped a thick red rubber band around each roll, just as she recalled Mickey Black had done. With twenty bills to the roll, she had twenty rolls of hundreds and then some left over. Not bad for a girl who'd come to Haverhill with less than twenty dollars in her pocket.

She lined the bottom of her backpack with the tightly rolled money, all except three hundred in twenties she held out for travelling expenses. She rolled three black T-shirts and a clean pair of blue jeans. She'd wear cut-offs in the July heat, but to save on space she decided go commando until she settled somewhere. Laughing to herself, she put two thongs—one electric blue, the other bright red—into the lockbox where Danny would be sure to find them. She replaced the lockbox onto its hidden shelf in the wall, turned the key, and slid the bookcase into place over it.

Danny never appeared at the bungalow in mid-afternoons, so Madge was confident she had some time to make her exit good. The dumb Mick did not roll out of bed until near noon, and he had to make his rounds some time—that was always midday. Madge took a fast shower, and then did her face to appear older. She lined her eyes and omitted the blush. Danny liked her to look young, but in the real world, she'd need to appear at least twenty-five. She'd have to buy a serious wardrobe; jeans and cut-offs were kid stuff. Pretty woman could be taken seriously, but not if they had the kind of boobs Madge did. She'd bind her breasts. She had not cut her hair since she'd left Riverton, and in Haverhill it grew like tropical forest. In her mirror, she eyed the girl she was, but she also saw the woman she planned to be, severe, unsmiling, a woman to be reckoned with.

Fuck pep.

How old was she, anyway? She had no idea, which she realized did not need to be an annoying liability. She could be whomever she wished. She decided she'd be a youthful-looking twenty-five, a woman who could pass for eighteen, born this very day, July 7. The seventh day of the seventh month. It might be lucky.

The summer sun was hot and high when she tossed the backpack onto the brown Subaru's passenger seat. Haverhill lay comatose beneath a humid haze. Her hot black vinyl seats stuck to her bare arms and thighs. Madge returned to the love shack door one last time to peer around.

She half expected to find Danny. Her heart pounded. She never before had felt so vulnerable. This was risk. This was suffering. This was real fear. To feel alive, you had to be terrified of death.

If Danny were to appear at this moment and somehow discover the money was gone, he would put his big hands on her throat and squeeze the life from her. The irony of that did not make her smile. She was seizing her life, and it would be terrible if at that moment she were to lose it. She knew the terror Elizabeth Emerson felt on the gallows, hands tied at her back, head in a black cloth sack, rope at her neck. The trap would drop, and Madge would fall through into oblivion.

But the little house was empty. Danny was a creature of habits.

Before she slammed the front door for the last time, she impulsively seized the snow globe of New York City and balanced it on the dashboard. Lady Liberty was her guide.

Madge steered the Subaru to the interstate and headed north toward Riverton. She had with some vague sense of sentimental duty, maybe bid farewell to the old town, spit on the statue of The Thinker outside Riverton High, maybe break the plate glass at Daddy Kane's, maybe stop by her mother' house and change the channel, maybe kick Mickey Black in the nuts before squatting to piss on his shoes, but two miles before the town limit the familiar ice cream headache formed between her eyes. The pain spread like a spider's legs.

Madge was no goddam butterfly awakening to wonder if it was a woman dreaming it had been a butterfly, or a butterfly dreaming it had been woman. Fuck that. Fuck that. Just fuck that. She was too goddam close to lose it now.

Blind with aggregating pain, she twisted the wheel, turning hand over hand, cutting sharply across three lanes of high speed traffic. Two diesel trucks with horns bellowing swerved to avoid running over the Subaru, and one near jackknifed as it left tire tread for two hundred yards. The Subaru bumped wildly across the grass center divider, flattening shrubs and churning up dark soil and pale dust, but the all-wheel drive grabbed the pavement of the southbound highway, lurched onto the pavement, and Madge stomped the accelerator to the floor. Madge's teeth snapped shut as she fishtailed wildly, fighting the wheel to prevent a donut and taking a header into oncoming traffic. She'd have pushed the accelerator into the ground beneath the car if she could have. What had she been thinking? Madge no longer needed answers. Madge did not care about her questions. She wanted distance, and nothing more. Distance.

South, south, she muttered. More than the July humidity left her armpits swampy with sweat. She drove blind until the headache dissipated, lingering like an afterimage in her eyes. Her nose ran with tears of pain. She'd bitten her tongue and tasted blood.

The cellphone Danny had given her buzzed as if it was filled with bees.

Three text messages glowed on the screen.

Where r u?

Where the fuk r u?

Madge, I <3 u.

Why had it not dawned on her she could be pursued? She was going simple. Dear God, was she an idiot? To quell her rising sense of panic, the girl who was the best lick in town, the girl who had defeated the Shadow, the girl who had emptied a .38 into Arnie Appleton's burning Ford, the girl who was running for her life, thumbed the only telephone number she knew other than Danny's, that very special number Aunt Sosha had whispered to her that Madge never forgot.

Good Aunt Sosha did not answer, but who would be surprised by that? The voice that greeted her was mechanical. Aunt Sosha was a lot of things, but none of them was simple. The world had ears, and if the world was listening, for the same reasons she had ignored Mickey, she'd need to deny knowledge of any call from Madge or anyone else. Madge waited for the beep.

Aunt Sosha I miss you but I am having a wonderful time. Danny and I are headed for Dusseldorf and then Paris to live on Vronsky Boulevard. Danny will be joining me soon, once he finishes with the business he used to do. He is making soooo much money. I am sure we'll be very happy as soon as he joins me.

When the Subaru crept through the toll on the Mass Pike west of Sturbridge, the phone buzzed again. Madge hurled it out the window of the moving car. For half a second, in her rearview mirror, she saw the plastic shatter into a thousand skittering pieces that rolled after her, and then it was lost to her sight.

Madge steered to New York City.

DAYS AFTER THE SPLINTERS OF MADGE'S CELLPHONE BOOGIED DOWN INterstate 84, an indeterminate amount of time before or after Del and GIGO floated in the abyss to exchange views on the nature of the Divine, the Dreamer, the Typist, freewill, and Saint Anselm, a bit after the All-Star break, but before the end-of-season-fade that would confirm for Boston fans their special status as being so loved by God that they were annually martyred, a status that fit the Catholic population better than the miter on the Pope, about six hours after Margaret Mary took the black leather porkpie hat from the hall closet, pecked her husband's cheek, and whispered "Bring home a gallon of milk and whatever you do, don't fuck up," Danny Donnelly sat at Aunt Sosha's *shabbos* dinner table.

Summers, *shabbos* dinner was served late, as the old Jew waited for the third star to appear in the sky, a custom Danny respected. For a sensible people, your day began with dawn. So simple a deduction was far too simple for your Hebes, always your tribe in search of exceptions that made them special; they could split hairs that would fit in a gnat's ass. Contrary to all common sense, People of the Book insisted a day began at sundown. This, evidently, made for heated discussions on the definition of night, the eventual conclusion being that appearance of the third star in the firmament was the moment at which God said, *So it was evening and it was morning.* Danny had wondered to himself, but never asked his tutor, Ari: *suppose the night sky was filled with clouds?* Danny supposed overcast was as rare in the desert as it was common over Haverhill. God allowed no clouds over the Holy Land.

It hardly mattered. As with most occasions, what mattered with the Yids was the food. Aunt Sosha's table was set with far more than he, Ari, and Aunt Sosha could possibly eat. He wondered if some guests had canceled a foolish gastronomic choice. More likely, the woman had once more been carried away by her love of cooking and, for once, there were no guests from Los Angeles, the cursed Brooklyn mob was not in evidence, the mayor of Haverhill was absent, not a single selectman, not the Chief of Police, not so much a traffic court judge. The crowd that regularly gathered at Aunt Sosha's dining table was absent.

It was just close family.

"Come, *boychik. Kugel.* I made it special for you. Extra pepper, no less." Danny looked forward to taking home a care package of roast chicken. The girls adored Aunt Sosha's food, though none of them knew its origin. *Kugel* and potatoes and chicken and string beans were heaped on his plate. "Eat," she said.

Ari, who like some plants and many insects seemed to live on air and water vapor, watched him closely. Danny ate his dinner with zest, and only when the walls began to recede and spin did he suspect something was amiss. He had had no wine. The drugs, he supposed, were in the *kugel*. Danny resisted falling into a beckoning black pillowcase for as long as he could and pushed back his chair. He stood unsteadily, and then hit the ground face down like a sack of wet shit dropped from a third story window. They'd given him enough dope to make Seabiscuit comatose. From the floor, with one eye, he saw Aunt Sosha stand to dry her hands on her apron, and then he saw nothing at all.

Danny could not be more wrong. Who would ruin a good *kugel?* The drugs were in the garlic potatoes.

He awakened in the basement's sound-proofed room, Bughouse's old quarters. He was shackled to a bottomless metal chair bolted to the floor. It was chilly. Except for his leather porkpie hat, his clothes were gone. His skin had gone all gooseflesh, and his testicles swung freely below him. The lamp in the ceiling was a bare yellow bulb, dim, casting murky shadows.

Ari sat backward on a simple wooden chair, his chin cradled on the chair's backrest. His pool-chalk-blue eyes held Danny. Danny greeted this vision of Ari with less joy than he'd have had for seeing mustard gas seep beneath the door. Ari reached forward and moved Danny's hat from his eyes without taking it from the Irishman's head.

"I'll pay back every dime," Danny said, knowing full well it would not suffice. "I planned to pay it back all along. Aunt Sosha must know that. I love her like my own mother."

Ari waved his hand as if to say, *What's money between friends?* "Trust once gone is never recovered," he said, his bloodless lips barely parting. His fingers twined together.

Danny spoke quickly. "It was Madge made me do it."

"With the tits?"

"That would be her. I've never asked, Ari. Do you fancy women?"

The Israeli shrugged. "In that chair, they are all the same to me," he said, then looked up and brightened. "Oh, you mean for affection. Women are good. I was married once. Can you believe it? It is true." He rose from the chair to stand beside a low metal table on casters covered by a blue sheet, and paused as if to entertain the memory. "She was blown to bits in a café. *Mein* Anna was shopping and stopped for tea. Anna liked midday tea. *Mein* Anna was pregnant. A boy, we knew. No test, but she was sure I would have a son. She tired quickly, so she must have stopped for tea." He removed Danny's hat to place it on the table. "Hamas packs its pipe bombs with ball bearings and rat poison. Come, Danny, can you guess the purpose of the rat poison?"

"Such science is beyond me, Ari. I cannot guess."

Ari nodded. "Rat poison makes blood thin. Rats die from internal bleeding. Humans are no different than rats. A wound infested with rat poison will not heal. The blood cannot clot. A hundred ball bearings in a café like a hundred bullets, even a slight wound can be fatal."

With a grand flourish of the blue sheet, like a magician at the end of a trick, Ari unveiled his table of instruments. "This, here, Danny, these are my tools. Soon my tools will be dirty. But Sosha needs to know," Ari said and shrugged. "I can clean them afterwards."

"By my children's eyes, tell me what she needs to know and I will tell you all."

Ari neatly folded the sheet to a perfect square. "Danny, Danny, Danny. I misstated. Your English still confuses me. I apologize. She needs to be sure she knows all there is to know. Sosha asks that I make certain that you omit nothing. The details are important. Reassurances will not reassure her." Ari plugged in the waffle iron, tested the heft of the garlic press, ran his thumb along the shining edge of a bone knife, adjusted the pliers, and bent double to peer where Danny's balls dangled free below Danny's seat. He hummed.

Oh Danny-boy. The pipes, the pipes are calling thee.

"Interrogation is a fine art. There is no point in brutality for its own sake. In some circles, this is not appreciated. Your CIA, for example, always crude." He spit. "But consider my art. The interrogator requires the subject to be motivated to speak; on the other hand, he has to be kept in a condition to speak. The motivation cannot overwhelm the man. It's a very, very fine line to which I bring a man close, but not across. This delicate balance is rarely appreciated. Balance at extremes. This is essential to all art. Ballet, for example. You like ballet, Danny?" Ari stepped into a shadow and returned pushing a carpeted wheeled pine dolly on which a car battery and several copper leads were balanced.

From glen to glen, and down the mountainside.

Ari clicked a remote and the flat screen television they'd installed for Bughouse ignited. It was tuned to CNN. "Television will help to pass the time," Ari said, and turned up the volume. "It's important to keep up with world affairs."

Danny repeated Hail Marys as the waffle iron went from iron gray to cherry red and two commentators agreed that the situation in sub-Sahara Africa was grave. Danny recited the *Pater Noster* in Latin when sparks flew from the positive to the negative leads of the alligator clips of the jumper cable while a Senator stressed the unreasonable nature of the opposition, reassuring CNN's listeners that the American people would no longer be fooled. Danny squeezed his eyes shut for the sports report. The Sox had dropped three games in a row by a total of four runs. Tragedy gripped New England. Manchester United was winning.

The summer's gone, and all the flowers are dying
'Tis you, 'tis you must go and I must bide.

Ari considered slicing away Danny's eyelids to be sure he would not be able to turn away should they need to show him photographs of Faith, his eldest daughter, but there was no need for that yet, and the girl was safe at home with her mother. They could always retrieve the child if needed.

"For the love of God," Danny gasped, "there's no need for this."

"'For the love of God.' This is an odd phrase. In a country where God is sold like soap on the radio, often I have wondered, 'What can this mean?' Meaningless, meaningless" Ari sighed. "I am not unsentimental. Here, for old time's sake," Ari said, "a gift." With the tip of the bone knife, Ari lifted Danny's shirt from the floor and sliced a two-inch wide strip of cloth. He shoved it into Danny's mouth. "Irish, bite on this, maybe you won't bite through your tongue. A man who bites his tongue chokes on his own blood. You understand what I am telling you?"

'Tis I'll be here in sunshine or in shadow
Oh Danny boy, oh Danny boy, I love you so!

Five hours after the application of the waffle iron to the side of Danny's face, his buttocks, and the soles of his feet, Ari, an expert, ascertained that Danny in fact knew nothing more than what he said in the first twenty minutes of his ordeal. Swathes of skin had first blistered, then smoked, and then burned crusty black. The pliers had been applied to each of Danny's toes as CNN commentators discussed the financial importance of tourism in summer. Ari was soon certain no organization included Danny in a plot against Aunt Sosha. No imminent takedown had encouraged Danny to steal. The feebs were not massing for a strike. It was equally certain that the stupid Mick had no associates, other than this girl, Madge. Ari also was sure the CNN expert was right; he made a mental note to call his broker to buy stock in Carnival Cruise Lines or Royal Caribbean, as it was exactly the kind of stupid vacations aging Americans with too much money might buy in growing numbers. Maybe best would be to buy a little of each. Play it safe.

Ari himself had once spent two weeks on the Canary Islands on his way from Israel to America. This was before he came to America. The wine was too sweet and the sun too strong; a miserable place. Danny's agony made it impossible to think Danny kept anything hidden. As a carpenter trusted a hammer, Ari had faith in his craft. He incidentally learned that Madge had been a virgin, but this did not interest Ari even slightly. He learned also that

Danny's wife detested anal intercourse, a matter of even less interest. On CNN, they were warning about rising waters along the Mississippi, storms approached the Gulf Coast, and there were firestorms threatening the canyons of California.

He knew what he had always known. Danny was a blockhead Irishman who followed wherever his dick pointed. Such men were common and had limited uses.

Danny's chest heaved with effort when Ari left him. Each breath was labor. Ari believed a little rest could do no harm; it could fortify a subject and, at the same time, deceive the subject into believing his pain was finished. The resumption of pain would therefore be that much more distressing. This was the secret of his art: any schmuck could induce pain, but inducing despair called for greater skills.

Ari climbed the creaking stairs to the house where he dutifully reported to Sosha all Danny Donnelly had told him, even the part about Madge Klink's alleged virginity.

"Ha!" Sosha said. "Smart that girl was. Smart. I liked her. What do you think, Ari, did she kill a chicken and show him a bloody sheet in the morning?" She laughed. Ari repeated the fictions Danny had created in desperation. This, too, was not unusual. A subject with nothing left to tell would implicate people he hardly knew. Danny's most plausible tale had Ryan, the bumbling barber who was a fence, an informant. Sosha and Ari knew Ryan was a child molester who hinted at his time in prison having been the consequence of a grown man's crime, but he was no more than a common baby-fucker, no threat to any woman over the age of twelve.

Aunt Sosha spit into her stainless steel sink; everyone knew Ryan was inept, incapable of discovering his own ass in a phone booth if you gave him a map, a compass, and a flashlight, but nevertheless, to be certain, Ryan's Clip Joint the next Tuesday night developed a gas leak. On Wednesday morning, Ari sat nearby in the black Escalade. At the precise moment Ryan turned his key in the lock of the front door, Ari dialed the number of the disposable cellphone he'd left packed in wadding connected to the detonator in the gas-filled cellar. Shards of glass like flying razors stripped the nose, ears and eyes from Ryan's face, but Ryan was quickly beyond pain. Smoking chunks of Ryan landed across the street, one on the hood of the Escalade. It smelled like an underdone roast, and the vehicle stank like the filth they served at Burger King until at the carwash with soap and water the last of Ryan's charred fat swirled down a cement culvert and into the Haverhill sewers.

As for Danny Donnelly, when Ari asked what she would have him do, Sosha lighted a Kent cigarette and rolled her gray eyes to Heaven. If they had suspected there was more, Danny might have had to see his eldest daughter forced into depraved acts, but this was not necessary. Sosha hated such moments. As Timothy said too often, "Life was one damned thing after another and there was no rest for the wicked." She remembered suffocating Danny's grandfather with a gold throw pillow, a sad day as she had loved the lying bastard, and here she was again, acting the Angel of Death. She exhaled, and thinking of Ari's loyal service and his morale, said, "Feh. He is nothing to me."

And so Ari returned to the basement where the fingerless and toeless hulk of what had been Danny was still shackled to the metal chair. His swollen testicles were the size of grapefruits. Blood and drool flowed over the splinters of the teeth in the hole in his face that had been his mouth. Fluids pooled on his singed chest and then overflowed to run in rivulets down his legs to the floor.

Installing that floor drain was a stroke of genius. Clean-up would be quick with a hose.

Ari turned off the television. The chatter was distracting and it was time to concentrate. Such opportunities were rare. With nothing to learn, all that remained was refinement of his art. It was an opportunity for purity. True art required purity. How much could Danny Donnelly endure?

Twenty-eight hours later, Ari had his answer. With a final jolt of electrical current, the mound of muscle, skin and bone that had been Danny Donnelly arced in the chair so hard that two of the steel bolts holding the chair to the floor bent easily as rubber. Danny's bowels and bladder opened and he sighed his last. It was the second longest anyone had ever endured, and Ari was surprised that Danny had come so close to matching the last hours of the man he'd caught in the Canaries less than a year after he'd set the pipe bomb that had killed his Anna.

There was art for you.

The plastic wall map in the Connecticut rest-stop looked like a tangle of spaghetti. At Madge's back, the place seethed with travelers, all of whom seemed to know where they were going. Having a destination was different from getting away. Madge bought a pair of dark Chanel sunglasses in hopes they made her look older. The rhinestones at the temples attracted her. Why not look stylish? She was pretty; she was young; she was rich.

She also bought a road map and a cup of coffee before she sat at a booth. They served acidic, bitter coffee in scalding hot cardboard cups, not at all like the porcelain crockery at Daddy Kane's or at Denny's, but Madge accepted that she was in the fast-paced world now and this was how it was going to be. Madge fully unfolded the map to study her choices.

Descent into New York City presented a thousand options. The highways that went north to south through Westchester crossed over and under each other in a tangled mess. With no destination, all roads look the same. The closer she drew to New York City, the more dense the traffic became. Madge was fearless, but even a minor accident could pitch her right back to Riverton, a runaway with no license or registration. Madge had lived forever, but had no past and no way to explain why or how she had come to be what she was. She was building her life, and it needed to be done with care.

At the map's bottom was a small black dot in the vast blue expanse below Manhattan. It was Liberty Island, doubtless where the Statue of Liberty stood. Why was the dot so small? Madge gnawed the frames of her sunglasses and finished her bitter coffee. No one had told her she could add her own cream or sugar. If she came at the Statue of Liberty from the west, she'd avoid the complicated roads into the city itself. She could descend south on the Hudson River's western shore, and once she had viewed Lady Liberty from the New Jersey side she could decide what was next. Surely she'd be able to see it. In her snow globe, the statue was larger than everything else on the painted skyline, taller than the tallest buildings.

Her finger traced a route. Tappan Zee Bridge, Palisades Parkway, New Jersey Turnpike, and then drop like a plumb line into Jersey City and Bayonne. The Yankees lived in the Bronx, but that seemed too far out of her way. She'd have liked to stop by long enough to thank them for making Danny Donnelly's life miserable. Poor Danny. She hoped Danny's good Aunt would not deal with him too harshly. Some delay while she made her escape was all she needed.

The Tappan Zee Bridge was a long, low roadway skimming the river's smooth surface, except where it arched like a cat's back to allow boats to pass unimpeded beneath. The Hudson was nothing like the Merrimack River she knew. If the Merrimack was a capillary, the Hudson was an artery. Lord, what could the Mississippi be like? What worlds were hers to explore?

The windless July day was hot; Madge rode with the Subaru's window open wide. Air flowing over her bare arms and thighs stirred the threads of her jeans cut-offs. She found the Palisades Parkway easily enough. No trucks. Madge felt reassured. It was nice to make a plan and have it work. There was no forgetting; there were no surprises; the world did not change at some Dreamer's whim. Maps and their permanence comforted her.

Madge maintained the speed limit and obeyed every law, keeping to the right and passing only when someone drove so slowly it put her on edge. She happily smoked, leaving her radio off, preferring the voice of her own thoughts to distracting music or the voices of idiots arguing issues about which Madge knew nothing. Maybe she'd go to college. How did people manage that with no high school? What did they do? Did they just show up?

The two-lane parkway gently curved among trees until it opened to a sudden clearing. On her left were the steel-blue lattice towers of the George Washington Bridge; beyond them stood the brown and gray city itself. She was farther from Riverton than anyone she'd ever known had gone. Madge's heart quickened.

When she glanced at the Subaru's dashboard to check her speed, she saw her hands had become translucent.

It was eerie to see through herself, past her veins and ligaments. She thought it might be some trick of the Chanel glasses, so she placed them on the seat beside her.

Without the dark glasses, her arms and hands looked even more faint. The Subaru, too, she realized was fading. Looking down through her legs and the floorboard, she saw the speeding concrete below the car. She lifted her chin to avoid vertigo.

There was no escape from a dream that was not hers.

Madge was no Dreamer; she was no cannibal. Madge was the afterimage of a forgotten memory of a bright day gone dark.

Who, really, is more?

Madge thought to return to Riverton, but fuck it. She'd try for the Statue of Liberty.

Slowly, and then with greater speed, the snow globe on her dashboard sank through the evanescent car until it fell unimpeded to smash onto the speeding concrete. Free of her satchel and their rubber bands, hundred dollar bills fluttered in the wind like autumn leaves in the fading Subaru's wake. Madge glanced quickly into the passenger seat—her sunglasses were gone.

She gritted her teeth. You cannot lose what you never had. She accelerated, passing easily beside and through cars. No one could see the girl who'd never been more than someone else's dream.

With every yard farther from Riverton, Madge's body dispersed like a fist of sand hurled into a high speed fan.

Her unfeeling fingers tightened on what remained of the wheel. Her vision darkening, she drew herself up to stand on the accelerator. The Subaru surged forward in utter silence. Madge's consciousness was all that remained of her until the instant the torch atop the Statue of Liberty became visible, when like the dream of the butterfly that awakened to learn it was a man, faster than any mere Typist might record her final thought, Madge, too, vani

The End

Books from Gival Press - Fiction and Nonfiction

Boys, Lost & Found: Stories by Charles Casillo
ISBN: 978-1-928589-33-4, $20.00

Finalist for the 2007 *ForeWord Magazine*'s Book Award for
Gay / Lesbian Fiction / Runner up for the 2006 DIY Book Festival
Award for Compilations / Anthologies.
"...fascinating, often funny...a safari through the perils and joys of
gay life."
—Edward Field

The Cannibal of Guadalajara by David Winner
ISBN: 978-1-928389-50-1, $20.00

Winner of the 2009 Gival Press Novel Award / Honorable Mention
2011 Beach Book Festival Award for Fiction / Finalist National Best
Books 2010 Award for Fiction & Literature.
"...a devilishly delicious and disorienting novel. Food, sex, ghastly
travel experiences, tantrums, Cannibal has it all, along with one of
the most peculiar versions of the family triad in literary years."
—Joy Williams, a Pulitzer finalist, received the Strauss Living Award
from the American Academy of Arts and Letters

A Change of Heart by David Garrett Izzo
ISBN: 978-1-928589-18-1, $20.00

A historical novel about Aldous Huxley and his circle
"astonishingly alive and accurate."
—Roger Lathbury, George Mason University

Dead Time / Tiempo muerto by Carlos Rubio
ISBN: 979-1-928589-17-4, $21.00

Winner of the 2003 Silver Award for Translation, *ForeWord
Magazine*'s Book of the Year.
A bilingual (English / Spanish) novel that captures a tale of love and
hate, passion and revenge.

Dreams and Other Ailments / Sueños y otros achaques by Teresa Bevin
ISBN: 978-1-92-8589-13-6, $21.00

Winner of the 2001 Bronze Award for Translation, *ForeWord Magazine*'s Book of the Year.
A bilingual (English / Spanish) account of the Latino experience in the USA, filled with humor and hope.

The Gay Herman Melville Reader edited by Ken Schellenberg
ISBN: 978-1-928589-19-8, $16.00

A superb selection of Melville's homoerotic work, with short commentary.

Gone by Sundown by Peter Leach
ISBN: 978-1-928589-61-7, $20.00

Winner of the 2010 Gival Press Novel Award/ 2012 Independent Publisher Book Award—Bronze Medal for Best Regional Fiction: Mid-West.
"Almost no other novel treats the creation of sundown towns. *Gone by Sundown* thus amounts to a one-volume antidote to American amnesia. On top of that, it's a good read."
—James W. Loewen, author of *Lies My Teacher Told Me* and *Sundown Towns*

An Interdisciplinary Introduction to Women's Studies edited by Brianne Friel & Robert L. Giron
ISBN: 978-1-928589-29-7, $25.00

Winner of the 2005 DIY Book Festival Award for Compilations / Anthologies.
A succinct collection of articles for the college student on a variety of topics.

The Last Day of Paradise by Kiki Denis
ISBN: 978-1-928589-32-7, $20.00

Winner of the 2005 Gival Press Novel Award / Honorable Mention 2007 Hollywood Book Festival.
This debut novel "...is a slippery in-your-face accelerated rush of sex, hokum, and Greek family life."
—Richard Peabody, editor of *Mondo Barbie*

Literatures of the African Diaspora by Yemi D. Ogunyemi
ISBN: 978-1-928589-22-8, $20.00

An important study of the influences in literatures of the world.

Lockjaw: Collected Appalachian Stories by Holly Farris
ISBN: 978-1-928589-38-9, $20.00

Winner of the 2008 Appalachian Writers Association Book of the Year Award for Fiction / Finalist for the 2008 Golden Crown Literary Society Lesbian Short Story / Essay Collections Category / Finalist for the 2008 Eric Hoffler Award for Culture / Finalist for the 2007 Lambda Literary Award for Lesbian Debut Fiction.
"*Lockjaw* sings with all the power of Appalachian storytelling—inventive language, unforgettable voices, narratives that take surprise hairpin turns—without ever romanticizing the region or leaning on stereotypes. Refreshing and passionate, these are stories of unexpected gestures, some brutal, some full of grace, and almost all acts of secret love. A strong and moving collection!"
—Ann Pancake, author of *Given Ground*

Maximus in Catland by David Garrett Izzo
ISBN: 978-1-92-8589-34-1, $20.00

"...*Maximus in Catland* has all the necessary ingredients for a successful fairy tale: good and evil, unrequited love and loving loyalty, heroism and ancient wisdom...."
—Jenny Ivor, author of *Rambles*

Middlebrow Annoyances: American Drama in the 21st Century by Myles Weber
ISBN: 978-1-928589-20-4, $20.00

Current essays on the American theatre scene.

The Pleasuring of Men by Clifford H. Browder
ISBN: 978-1-928589-59-4, $20.00

"...deftly drawn with rich descriptions, a rhythmic balance of action, dialogue, and exposition, and a nicely understated plot. *The Pleasuring of Men* is both engaging and provocative." —Sean Moran

Riverton Noir by Perry Glasser
ISBN: 978-1-928589-75-4, $20.00

"...Big, vibrant, laugh-out-loud funny, it is also fearless about sex and violence, which in Riverton can seem like the same thing. Don't worry—the novel's structure and theme are carefully controlled by 'the Dreamer,' not to mention the laws of modern physics, and Glasser's sentences, among such seeming chaos, are marvels of clarity. This should be the author's break-out book."
—Kelly Cherry

Second Acts by Tim W. Brown
ISBN: 978-1-928589-51-8, $20.00

2011 Runner Up for the New York Book Festival Award for Science Fiction /
2011 Winner of the London Book Festival Award for General Fiction. "Really clicking, *Second Acts* is a picaresque, sci-fi / western, such as Verne or Welles might have penned it, but with tongue planted firmly in cheek. Tim W. Brown's tale of a husband's search for his fugitive wife takes readers on a whirlwind tour of America, circa 1830. In subverting history Brown's tale celebrates it, with a scholar's eye for authentic details and at a pacing so swift the pages give off a nice breeze."
—Peter Selgin, author of *Life Goes to the Movies*

Secret Memories / Recuerdos secretos by Carlos Rubio
ISBN: 978-1-928589-27-3, $21.00

Finalist for the 2005 *ForeWord Magazine*'s Book of the Year Award for Translations. This bilingual (English / Spanish) novel adeptly pulls the reader into the world of the narrator who is vulnerable.

Show Up, Look Good by Mark Wisniewski
ISBN: 978-1-928589-60-0, $20.00

Finalist for the 2009 Gival Press Novel Award.
"..a rollicking, laugh-out-loud romp of a novel, a picaresque spin through fin-de-siècle New York as seen through the eyes of its intrepid, Midwestern-born heroine...."—Ben Fountain, author of *Brief Encounters with Che Guevara*
"Wisniewski: a riotously original voice."—Jonathan Lethem

The Smoke Week: Sept. 11-21, 2001 by Ellis Avery
ISBN: 978-1-928589-24-2, $15.00

2004 *Writer's Notes Magazine* Book Award—Notable for
Culture / Winner of the Ohionana Library Walter Rumsey Marvin
Award. "Here is Witness. Here is Testimony."
—Maxine Hong Kingston, author of *The Fifth Book of Peace*

The Spanish Teacher by Barbara de la Cuesta
ISBN: 978-1-928589-37-2, $20.00

Winner of the 2006 Gival Press Novel Award / Finalist for the
2007 *ForeWord Magazine*'s Book of the Year / Award for Fiction-
General / Honorable Mention for the 2007 London Book Festival.
"...De la Cuesta's novel maintains an accumulating power which
holds onto a reader's attention not only through the forceful figure
of Ordóñez, but by demonstrating acutely how ordinary lives are im-
pacted by the underlying social and political landscape. Compelling
reading."—Tom Tolnay, author of *Selling America* and *This is the
Forest Primeval*

That Demon Life by Lowell Mick White
ISBN: 978-1-928589-47-1, $21.00

Winner of the 2008 Gival Press Novel Award / Finalist for the 2010
Texas Book Award for Fiction / Finalist for the 2009 National / Best
Book Award for Fiction.
"*That Demon Life* is a hoot, a virtuoso tale by a master story teller."
—Larry Heinermann, author of *Paco's Story*, winner of the National
Book Award

Tina Springs into Summer / Tina se lanza al verano by Teresa Bevin
ISBN: 978-1-928589-28-0, $21.00

2006 *Writer's Notes Magazine* Book Award—Notable for
Young Adult Literature. A bilingual (English / Spanish) compelling story of a youngster from a multi-cultural urban setting and her
urgency to fit in.

A Tomb on the Periphery by John Domini

ISBN: 978-1-928589-40-2, $20.00

Honorable Mention for the 2009 London Book Festival Award for Fiction / Finalist for the 2005 Gival Press Novel Award.
"Stolen antiquities, small-time thugs, a sultry femme fatale.... a book that takes the trappings of noir then transcends the genre...." *Bookslut*

Twelve Rivers of the Body by Elizabeth Oness

ISBN: 978-1-928589-44-0, $20.00

Winner of the 2007 Gival Press Novel Award
"*Twelve Rivers of the Body* lyrically evokes downtown Washington, DC in the 1980s, before the real estate boom, before gentrification, as the city limped from one crisis to another—crack addiction, AIDS, a crumbling infrastructure. This beautifully evoked novel traces Elena's imperfect struggle, like her adopted city's, to find wholeness and healing."
—Kim Roberts, author of *The Kimnama*

For a complete list of titles, visit: *www.givalpress.com*.

Books available via Ingram, the Internet, and other outlets.
Or Write:
Gival Press, LLC
PO Box 3812
Arlington, VA 22203
703.351.0079